THE TIME TREASURE

INSIDIOUS

INHERITANCE

Mark Fulcher

and

Annet Libeau

For more information and other books published by
the authors, visit our website:

http://timetreasure.net

ISBN 978-0-9852095-0-6
Published by Sun Day Consulting, Inc.

This is a story of enduring love, courage, selfishness, greed, and corruption in an advanced civilization that once flourished on Earth, Mars, and the fifth planet, Shaytan, now known as the asteroid belt.

When a rockfall unexpectedly reveals relics left by an older civilization, a greedy observer ignores the dire warnings to leave the find undisturbed and tries to exploit the opportunity by selling information about the location. An organization of powerful individuals spanning all three planets takes an active interest, jeopardizing the fragile accord between the planets to lay their hands on the discovery.

It's up to a single Earth-based organization and a few intrepid individuals to risk their lives to identify and stop these unscrupulous masterminds.

Terminology

The term "Priest" was an everyday term used to denote someone of high learning or authority. There were Medical Priests, or medics; Scientific Priests; Temple Priests; and Ruling or Guiding Priests (politicians).

The Fighting Priests was an independent, Earth-based organization controlled by a council, but accountable to a triplanetary court of law. It was feared by wrongdoers and fugitives from justice, but highly respected on all three planets for meting out justice impartially and for its meticulous investigations.

The authors thought it appropriate to use present-day terms for distance and timekeeping, as well as for the names of the planets.

1

As she woke up early in the morning, Kinta's naturally strong intuition started to scream that she was in danger and that she must take off right now, this very morning. But she had nowhere to run to and no money secretly hoarded to even try to disappear. She was in a quandary; she couldn't refuse to go ahead with the mission without concrete evidence to support this strong feeling.

She nervously pushed her long, chocolate-brown hair out of her face, revealing her exquisite and delicate facial features. Her high cheekbones were smaller when seen from the front and regressed backward when seen from the side. She had fine nasal bones; a firm mouth with finely formed lips; a strong, though slightly pointed, chin; large, intense blue eyes with really long eyelashes; and thin, dark-brown eyebrows. Kinta was genetically blessed, but also had a unique, startling sort of personal chemistry about her.

Kinta sighed hopelessly. Operations controlled you for your entire life. You had no choice in the matter—you belonged to it body and soul, and only death released you. Agents knew too much about the doings and whereabouts of fellow agents and, even more damning, the inner workings of Operations and a few nameless faces of directors. That information was valuable to enemies, so no agent had ever been allowed to retire, since they might be bribed or captured and tortured for scraps of information.

The only ways to retire were to depart this life, hide, or run—and to keep running until you were killed, for every available agent would be on your trail. That was what you were told every now and then when a fellow agent was absent for a time. Usually, rumors would spread that he or she had tried to find sanctuary elsewhere. Kinta sometimes doubted the rumors but couldn't prove otherwise.

Failure to carry out a mission to its end without a verifiable, valid reason also carried a mandatory death sentence, for it was assumed that your nerve was gone or that you'd been reached by an enemy. So she had to finish this assassination, even though her every instinct shrieked a dire warning that this mission smelled to high heaven. Or perhaps, she thought, her nerve was suddenly gone, and her subconscious was offering a plausible excuse.

About the only thing she could do now was deviate from the pattern she had so carefully and instinctively established over the past year. There were still a few hours before the deadline, and even though she strongly suspected that this was a setup, she had no choice but to follow through. The only way she could prove to herself that the feeling wasn't just her nerves was to do a wary, early checkup, because she had never before made a final reconnaissance on the appointed day. She needed to be more careful and alert than she had ever been in her life, and to be calm, not jittery, as she felt at this moment.

She had been operational for just over a year and was very young for such a successful agent. To her knowledge, she was not yet nineteen years old, but her continuous success had brought unwanted notoriety, normally only attained after a number of years. Operations was ecstatic, of course, but her inner nature rebelled against the killings she was forced to perform. Although she had never had a choice in the matter, killing made her feel dirty.

A little over a month ago, she had become aware that her controller, Morcun, was behaving out of character. He dressed more expensively, but not strikingly so, and not very tastefully either. She noticed he had been neglecting his previously meticulously maintained fitness program, but no one seemed concerned about it. His body was beginning to look flabby, and she suspected that he secretly drank more than the rules allowed. To her, these were obvious warning signs, but everyone else seemed to be blind and indifferent.

At first she was not alarmed, for everyone was under stress just about all the time; but her finely trained mind noticed other little telltale signs until she became concerned that his physical carelessness might become a mental sloppiness that could endanger her and other agents under his control. It was curious that, when they accidentally met face-to-face on occasion, Morcun tried hard to not look guilty and, to cover up, he put on a false-ringing jovial air that finally set the warning bells clanging in her mind. It was out of character for the

2

dedicated, serious Morcun she had come to know over more than ten years. She finally but reluctantly came to the conclusion that he was cooking up something detrimental to her or someone else's health. But any kind of valid reason for her conviction eluded her.

Kinta had been secretly following Morcun for only two days when this mission came up out of the blue. They called them "missions" instead of plain murders, which she and her fellow agents were required to commit. She had to put her suspicions on hold to give her undivided attention to the mental and physical preparation for her role in the forthcoming mission. The fortnight of intense training and practice had taken her mind off her mistrust until ten days ago, when they had arrived, as usual, on separate commercial air transportation here in Bojon.

On the morning after their arrival, she had left her room early, disguised as a boy with light-brown eyes and clad in a used, loosely fitting messenger's uniform, to meet the boy whose place she was to take for a fortnight, as arranged by a resident agent. As usual she had to become part of the almost invisible everyday life, and as a humble messenger boy, she could come and go almost unnoticed once she was established on the daily route.

She accompanied the loquacious messenger boy on his usual rounds to learn the route, as well as delivery and collection points. She tried not to feel sorry for him, that on his return he might have to answer a lot of difficult questions he wouldn't know the answers to.

That first day, after official working hours, she had an early supper and on impulse went back to the hotel instead of wandering around to memorize possible escape routes, as the rules required. As usual, the first thing she did was check the secret compartment in the specially designed travel case in the event that her luggage had been searched during her absence. The complicated lock, which required specialized training to unlock safely, did not show any evidence of being opened or tampered with, but her intuition prompted her to open it right away.

She always cleaned and then wiped fingerprints from her weapons before she retired every night. She had been taught that her life might be forfeited if the weapons were not always in perfect functioning condition. So, when she carefully unlocked the secret compartment, she immediately saw that her familiar, well-cared-for plop gun had been substituted with another one of the same caliber and make; it was even worn a bit. But she instinctively knew it was not the same one she'd been issued two years ago. In shock, she checked the memorized serial number to make sure, but she already knew it was not her own weapon.

The sickening realization that only someone trained at Ops Base could bypass the explosive traps in the locking system made her feel green around the gills. Who else knew that she was here but her controller? The resident agent would not know they had arrived until the mission was concluded. And why would Morcun want her personal gun? It smelled of dirty, underhanded treachery.

The culprit could only be Morcun. He obviously wanted to make her the fall guy for something he had concocted in that brilliant, devious mind of his. It could not be an officially sanctioned slaying to get rid of her in this roundabout way. Operations was practical and would have had her killed without any warning whatsoever back at base. She also knew she hadn't done anything that warranted her execution.

She wasn't worried about fingerprints on the missing weapon, but what was the idea behind this substitution? Morcun wouldn't know that she always wiped her weapons clean after handling, so he could have exchanged the weapon in the mistaken belief that her fingerprints would be on it, which would allow him to implicate her in whatever he had in mind. Or was it the serial number that mattered?

She had another thought. Was this substitute a dummy? It seemed genuine on the surface—the weight was the same as her own gun, and it felt well balanced—but later that night she fired it anyway, in the huge, icy-cold, deserted public park, hitting a target tree in the shadows away from the electric light every time. There was no one in the park, and the quiet coughs emitted by the weapon would not have disturbed anyone who might have been silly enough to brave the icy winter night. She fired a whole clip just to make sure the substitute had not been tampered with.

The only conclusion she could arrive at was that Morcun

had taken her gun to leave it where it would implicate her in an unsanctioned crime. Her instinct told her that if she was right and it was Morcun, it was a sure thing that it would be the scene of the planned execution.

She didn't see Morcun at breakfast or supper at any time, although she waited around every day for as long as she could without arousing suspicion. This was very unusual because he had to be available for emergency consultation; she concluded that he was deliberately avoiding the hotel's restaurant and pub during the times she might be there. His absence from the hotel, especially from the pub, spelled guilt, and it angered her to think that her controller had the audacity to throw her to the wolves for his own selfish interests. All the years of intense training and her successes meant nothing to him. He had probably sold her out for blood money to live like royalty while avoiding retribution from Operations.

2

A fortnight ago Kinta had been told that the execution of the enemy-agent paymaster Hezmet must take place at exactly noon today. The constant worry about being made vulnerable by Morcun's suspected treachery made her too restless to sit still and compose herself until the time arrived for her to do what she was ordered to do—and thus walk into a trap.

Thinking about the mysterious gift and note she had received from an unknown source two days ago, which had warned her and really brought home the fact that her life was in danger, added to her uncommon sensation of restlessness before what was supposed to be a perfectly normal execution. She needed to be calm as always, to be absolutely focused. Otherwise she might make an involuntary, fatal mistake.

She knew that a calming walk in the park, which she loved to do whenever she had the time or opportunity, or just some idle window shopping would bring clearness of thought and focus her mind anew. *I will act out of character today and do the usual morning collection rounds*, she decided. *I must check if anything is amiss and if anyone does not act normally.*

With noon still four hours away, she prepared her disguise. She arranged her hair expertly on top of her head and then pulled the tight blond wig over it, down to her ears and the back of her neck. Next, she carefully applied the thin, clinging film of padded artificial skin that covered her face and neck. It transformed her remarkable features into those of a mischievous-looking youth with unusually well-formed eyebrows and girlish eyelashes, though the now-somewhat-prominent ears drew attention away from her eyes. The thermal underwear and loosely fitting uniform covered her from the neck downward, and her breasts were uncomfortably flattened by a tightly wound bandage. The brown contact lenses and well-used cap completed the somewhat extraordinary transformation.

In special nondetection cloth, she wrapped two very special instruments she had wangled out of the nice, old depot keeper she had become friends with, as well as with her weapons—the plop gun and a short, broad-bladed dagger—and placed them on the bottom of the empty but almost awkwardly big delivery rucksack. The other weapon—five marble-sized paralysis bombs—she put in an outer pocket of the tunic. These were the only weapons that could stop angry crowds in their tracks without permanent damage to anyone's health.

What little money she possessed she put in a trouser pocket, since she had an uneasy premonition that she would not be able to return to this room. On top of the weapons, she placed her well-used running shoes; a new, plain, gray tracksuit; and feminine things she might need. As a disguise, the tracksuit would not attract too much attention because a lot of fitness-conscious people jogged every day during lunch hour. If anything went awry in the vicinity of the target, and she had a chance to slip away, she would don the tracksuit and try to jog out of the danger zone. She kept very fit, and as a distraction, her jogging would be convincing to observant bystanders.

As a matter of principle, she made sure that the valuable gift from the mysterious friend, a mini stun gun that not even Operations was aware existed, was in the holster strapped on the inside of her left wrist. She smiled as she thought of the note, in the same neat handwriting as the warning on the envelope, which had been left with the stun gun in her room two days ago. The envelope was addressed to her by the name she had registered under and urged her to read the note inside as soon as possible. It warned that the note was self-destructing, that it was vital she read it quickly and before four minutes elapsed after it was opened.

She had studied the envelope carefully and only after making sure it wasn't explosive, opened it cautiously and quickly read the note:

Reminder: read quickly and drop this note in the washbasin as it will flash-destroy less than four minutes from now. Thon burn the envelope and flush the ash.

Please accept this gift from a sincere friend, as you may need it in the very near future. Your life is in more danger than you realize. The existence of this mini stun gun is known only to a very few selected persons. It is not detectable by commercial scanners. Please guard it well and keep it secret for your own safety. Although the clip holds only ten blasts, it is more vicious

7

than a regular stun gun, and it can kill when aimed at the heart on narrow beam (twist barrel clockwise). Aimed at the head it produces 1 to 8 hours of unconsciousness, and the recipient will have an exquisitely vicious headache lasting from 1 to 3 days, depending on the upward setting (push the lever above the thumb position up).

The neck is the usual target to produce unconsciousness. I recommend that you target the head at maximum (up position) only if you have a grudge against the person. The holster is designed for the inside of the left wrist where it is easily accessible to the right hand for a fast draw. Jerk your left hand up at the wrist to make the gun jump into the opened right hand. Maximum distance is ten meters. Practice the draw, but don't experiment on targets. Keep it strapped to your arm at all times, even when you sleep, as it is the only safe place. I will contact you when I can.

She had opened the envelope above the basin in the bathroom. As she read it a second time, the note crumbled and flash-burned briefly, and she quickly let it drop. It wasn't strange that it was unsigned. Even as she wondered about the reason for this invaluable gift out of the blue, she knew the reason there was no name. She liked the way the message came across and wished that this self-assigned friend had arranged some sign or signal so she could recognize him or her. She acknowledged only one friend: the old man in the weapons shop. All others were only acquaintances or colleagues. Then it finally clicked: this self-appointed friend knew her, and the gun itself would be the recognition sign.

Highly trained on every type of weapon and close combat, she could appreciate the value of this weapon for any man or woman who needed to constantly live on the edge of danger.

When she was dressed in the messenger disguise, Kinta left the hotel as usual through the unwatched back entrance. She carefully checked the alley before closing the door against the force of the subzero wind. With the thermal underwear and gloves, she could endure the iciness that chilled her false face and ears. It would become somewhat warmer later in the day, but spring was still two months away, and although snow wasn't likely to fall this far south, the bite in the air could be ferocious, especially this early in the morning.

8

She wouldn't have told Morcun of her change of plans, and she did not have to tell him anyway. During assignments, interaction between controller and executive was minimal.

Her missions so far had always been planned to be executed at a certain time in a certain way for maximum effect, and she did her killings right on the minute as ordered. Her instincts—or perhaps it was precognition—had prompted her to build a reputation for being fearless, ruthless, and incredibly punctual, and she had rigidly stuck to this image during the past year on every assignment.

She had been well trained in every known form of combat since she was eight years old, and she stayed superbly fit. Privately, she reveled in the very unusual strength that nature had bestowed on her, and she instinctively controlled it in hand-to-hand practice fights. The instructors thought only that her reflexes were fast; somehow she knew she needed to keep them unaware of the full power she could unleash if the situation called for drastic measures. She understood very well that practice sessions were not for killing her training partner anyway, but for both to learn from each other with supervision under controlled conditions.

As an orphan she'd had no choice or a say in what others thought she must be taught or trained to do. The teachers in the orphanage tested their charges aptitude and then sent them to the appropriate institution. Kinta detested these executions she was forced to do and had vowed she would quickly and quietly disappear the minute she could acquire the means and safely do so. Until then she would do just about anything to stay alive. She would plan more meticulously than Morcun ever had, if she was still alive and well after today.

She had plenty of time left to check possible problem areas that might jeopardize this execution and prevent her escape, but she just couldn't shake off the conviction that the mission itself was all wrong. She couldn't ignore the urge to get away as far as possible, right now, and the urge became stronger and more insistent the farther away from the hotel she walked.

Her iron discipline and the fact that she had nowhere to go or the means to go anywhere forced her to resist and repress the desire to abort and run. She didn't have a valid reason to drop the mission, but she needn't rush in blindly to do what she was ordered to do right on the minute. What difference would it make if she did it an hour earlier than instructed? Was it really that important, and who would care or do anything about it when it was an already accomplished fact? She could always find a plausible explanation for the earlier execution. Or should she just call it plain murder? For she had to accept that that was what it really was. To continue to call it an execution, as the instructors insisted, was just trying to blind herself to the truth.

In this deeply disturbed state, she was not as vigilant as she thought. She didn't sense that she had acquired two shadows: one in animal form and one human.

Her shadows would have been very embarrassed indeed if she had become aware of them, for they too had been finely trained in the art of observation and stealth tactics and had followed her the previous day without making her aware of their presence. The human followed at a distance, usually just too far back to be noticed, but the animal—a huge cat—stayed near and examined Kinta's thoughts and the intentions of any other humans who passed near her.

At a mental command from the cat, the human stopped suddenly and faded into a doorway while Kinta paused in front of an upmarket dress shop. The cat just stepped casually behind the nearest pillar to become invisible. These huge, red-brown cats, with their tufted, pointed black ears, originally came from far south and were such a common sight in temples of religious instruction that they normally came and went unnoticed in public.

Kinta let her eyes wander idly over the display of dresses, feminine trousers, matching warm tops, and other female accessories. She saw a particularly elegant, nondescript, gray pantsuit that would not attract attention anywhere and was just her size. She checked the displayed price tag and sadly calculated that the paltry sum in her pocket was far from adequate to buy such quality.

Suddenly conscious that it was out of character for a messenger boy to show so much interest in feminine things, she set out for the nearby park. There she found that her favorite seat was much too cold for comfort, so she wandered around with her hands in her pockets and the rucksack on her back. After checking carefully that no one else was within hearing or seeing distance, she took the plop gun out and quickly fired two shots at a tree to make sure it was still functional. Then she rewrapped the gun and returned it to the rucksack.

For the first time, she felt the sensation of being watched, but couldn't see anyone. She quickly walked away to avoid anyone who might come to investigate the suppressed coughs and maybe force her into the kind of violence that filled her whole being with abhorrence.

As she walked around in the chilly morning sunshine, housewives and nannies with prams or noisy, complaining children in tow began to frequent the footpaths, and her presence in the uniform was being commented on. Glancing at her watch, she noticed with surprise that it was already ten fifteen. The fact that a loafing delivery boy at this time of day would be remembered made her decide to go ahead with her intention to do her abhorrent job much earlier than ordered. Okay, she could be reprimanded severely later on, but her dread began to abate. She hurried out of the park as if she were late for an urgent errand.

3

A sense of imminent danger, an inner warning she never could explain, made her duck seemingly casually into the recessed entrance to a coffee shop to get off the sidewalk. She was suddenly aware that she had been so engrossed in her morbid thoughts that she was walking almost in a trance, dead to happenings and people around her. She didn't even realize where she was going. The building across the street was where the execution was to be performed a little over an hour from now. This state of inattention wouldn't do if she wanted to survive today, and she determinedly focused her attention on the street.

Even before she decided to pause, the human shadow became a doddering old man out for early shopping with a rucksack, hands clasping the straps as if they required support, head and shoulders slumped as if in dejection, eyes seemingly focused on the pavement before his almost-shuffling feet. The cat walked casually into the nearest hiding place and wasn't noticed at all.

Kinta behaved as a messenger boy would if he were about to sneak in for a cup of coffee. She needed a second or two to compare the mental image of the street and the buildings with the one she remembered from yesterday's reconnaissance. She sensed that something was out of kilter but noticed nothing out of the ordinary and no suspicious loiterers, only the feeling of impending danger, which had almost become a physical restraint. So what was different?

She had just decided that her early warning sense was wrong this time when a hover taxi arrived and grounded in front of the building that was her destination. She hadn't expected Morcun, but she wasn't surprised when he stepped nonchalantly out of the taxi as if he had arrived at home. He paused, appearing uncertain, then looked casually up and down the street as if checking the numbers. But she knew he wouldn't miss the tiniest warning sign. When the taxi was out of sight, he confidently entered the building as if he was a welcome, frequent visitor.

Kinta was so stunned she couldn't move. What was Morcun up to?

Suddenly she was sure that this execution was not set up by Operations. She would be surprised if they had any knowledge of it at all. She mentally thanked whatever gods were responsible for making her feel so uneasy that she showed up early.

As Morcun disappeared into the building, she crossed the street at a run, dodging the few slow-moving hover cars. Perhaps she could now find out why she had such doubt about this assignment, and she had to know what her controller had cooked up for her. Her intended victim's office was on the third floor, which she somehow intuited was Morcun's destination.

She knew the guards never bothered to look at who entered and left the personnel entrance, as it had become an unconscious part of their everyday lives. The electronic scanner at the door let her through the moment she put her left hand on the biometric fingerprint reader, but she was so focused on Morcun's confirmed treachery that she didn't even think of looking back when she went through the impersonal electronic security check. She was therefore unaware that her shadows entered right after her and that the scanner had let the old man through without an access card.

While donning the thin, skin-colored gloves she always wore so as to not leave fingerprints, she effortlessly flew up the stairs. She wasn't breathing much faster when she reached the third floor. She heard the elevator arrive just before she cautiously opened the fire-escape door. She hesitated a few seconds until she heard the doors shut and footsteps slowly receding. *That must be Morcun going to Hezmet's office*, she thought. *So what the hell is that supposed to mean?*

She carefully opened the door a crack and checked the corridor. Morcun was just passing the records storage room she had explored a few times during her visits, and, as she'd expected, he entered her supposed-to-be victim's office after knocking in a certain way. It was the second confirmation that Morcun was the culprit who'd switched guns.

She dashed into the storeroom and in a feverish hurry unwrapped her valuable gadgets. She clamped the earphones

13

of the listening device over her ears. Depending on the amplification, it could pick up sound up to a distance of one hundred meters in the direction the antenna was pointed. She switched it on just in time to hear the end of Morcun's hearty greeting and the guttural welcome from the paymaster.

She pushed the other apparatus—a penetrator—against the wall that separated the office from the storeroom, and then put her eyes to the elongated eyepieces. She adjusted the eyepieces to focus her sight on the next room. It took a second to see clearly, but it felt like endless minutes. She breathed deeply a few times to calm her jumpy nerves.

Morcun was saying, "You must instruct three of your guards to enter this room at precisely five minutes to noon, and they must do so quickly without even looking at you. They are to hide with drawn guns where they can't immediately be seen from the door by anyone opening it, but they must be able to see the door clearly and be able to shoot by just pulling the trigger. Our notorious murderer, Tuala, will open the door precisely at noon on the dot and shoot immediately without even saying hello or taking the time to inquire after your health." Morcun laughed loudly, like a braying donkey, at his own sick joke, but Hezmet's face didn't even twitch. Only his eyes showed aversion.

"You must instruct your guards to kill anyone who opens the door at twelve without even checking the identity of the person. Your life will depend on their split-second response, but you must also duck down to make sure you stay alive. Will you instruct them now before we discuss anything else, Hezmet?"

She felt her anger boiling up at this cold-blooded, callous sellout and began to breathe deeply and rhythmically to control her rising ire. She had to calm herself; she couldn't afford to let anger overcome her better judgment. She needed all her wits to decide what to do about Morcun's treachery. The directors of Operations wouldn't believe just her say-so that Morcun would betray them or the outfit after twenty years of excellent and dedicated service.

Hezmet favored Morcun with a disapproving look for a few seconds before he activated the comm-unit on his huge desk, asked for a specific individual at security, and distastefully repeated Morcun's orders.

He doesn't like being treated as a subordinate, she thought, *and Morcun should know better.* She fervently wished, *May he make more serious mistakes and be executed, for this is dangerous enemy territory.*

But Morcun must have realized that his terse tone had rubbed hairs the wrong way. He skillfully rectified his error: "I'm sorry if I sounded as if I'm giving orders, but you must understand that I'm almost soiling my pants with terror. I walk in dread, and I'm trying not to make it obvious. This woman is utterly remorseless and totally without any conscience. She has become so notoriously dangerous that even her handler has to walk and talk softy in her presence. She doesn't take chances, and she won't hesitate for one single second to kill me if she even thinks I might have given information about her to anyone. She would immediately come after me if your guards miss and she became aware of my involvement. You *know* that I've put myself in deadly danger and that my life, and yours, depends on the marksmanship of your chosen guards."

You lie convincingly by corrupting the truth, you low-down, shitty skunk, Kinta thought viciously. *I bet you're doing it for a lot of money so you can retire in luxury where you can't be found. No, I wouldn't kill you, even if I'm ordered to do away with you, but I'd like to expose you so you can run and live in dread of Operations for the rest of your miserable life.*

Hezmet seemed convinced, but he said with some petulance, "You haven't even given me the faintest clue as to what she looks like. I want to know before you receive payment for your vague, unconfirmed information. As it is, I will only pay you half a million credits now, and the other half you can collect after she is killed, disabled, or captured. Know that I've put a close watch on you around the clock, so you can't run with the money before delivery."

Morcun smiled and told another half-truth. "I would gladly have given you a picture of her if I could, but there are no pictures, and she always uses a disguise. A picture, if any existed, and personal information are kept top secret. Only the agents involved in the hit know what's going on and who's who. I only found out late last night that her disguise in this hit is that of a messenger boy. Please remember that she is finely trained and as strong, fast, and nimble as a mountain leopard. I must

15

stress the point that she is very, very dangerous, as you'll find out in just over an hour."

He has perfected the art of lying, Kinta thought with disgust. *I wonder how many times he lied to me with a straight face.* She noted that Hezmet didn't waste even one second on a disapproving look this time. He activated the comm-unit and asked the security guards at the entrance if the messenger boy was already in the building. He waited while they checked and then ordered them to push his alert button unnoticed when the boy arrived. They must not arouse his suspicion in any way whatsoever, or their heads would roll. They were not to detain him or even look at him closely if they valued their lives.

They won't find that difficult to do, Kinta thought, but she was grateful once again that her intuition or subconscious mind had made her so uneasy that she'd come earlier than instructed. She decided to change into her tracksuit before she left since they would not be on the lookout for a female leaving a little earlier for some lunchtime exercise. She knew the guards at the entrance had grown lax because nothing had happened in years, and they wouldn't be aware that the "messenger boy" was already in the building. She was also sure they never took notice of the regular messenger boy.

From the first day, she had taken great care to escape their observation. Her presence was not recorded unless the scanner was routinely updated or reprogrammed, which was unlikely. She had tampered with it the first day she was on her own, and the scanner wouldn't have any memory that it had ever let the new messenger boy in or out of the building. She never left any trace of her presence behind during or after an assignment. It was not part of her training but rather a healthy mistrust—or perhaps it was natural instinct that had made her secretly acquire the knowledge to fiddle with access computers some years ago. Now she thanked the nameless gods who so looked after her welfare that not even Morcun was aware of her knowledge in this area. Come to think of it, even though she obeyed his every order, she'd instinctively mistrusted the loathsome betrayer for some time.

4

The mention of the blood money reminded Kinta of her wish to get out of this murdering career. The only winners were the hefty directors at Operations who lived in luxury on their ill-gotten proceeds. She was nauseated by this sick profession she'd been forced into at such a young age.

She resolved to take the money away from Morcun, if only to make him pay for this despicable sellout, as if her life were his to do with as he pleased. She often wondered what it would feel like to live a normal life in the real world. Perhaps she would get a chance to find out, for a short while at least. It wasn't much money, but it would allow her to make a run for it, even if she hadn't the faintest idea of where to head—as long as it was away from this dangerous, deceitful life in the shadows. She might pay with her life, but she was prepared.

Even before she was sent on her first mission, she had come to the conclusion that she was in a no-win situation with no way out except an early death. Although half a million credits was nowhere near a princely sum, it was enough to start a new life with a new identity somewhere as far away as possible, preferably in a country not as cold as the one in which she was born. She would make the money last until she had retrained herself for a useful, less violent occupation.

This mini stun gun, which she still hadn't tested, would come in handy, for she felt a reluctance to kill the traitor, even though her common sense told her it would be in her best interest to do him in permanently and that he deserved an ignominious fate. She knew that left alive, he would hunt her implacably, even though every available agent would be sent to make an example of her within hours after she was reported missing. She was now certain that Operations had not ordered the killing of Hezmet. Morcun might be delayed by the interrogation that would follow, but he'd fib his way out adroitly by making her the culprit he was trying to stop. She didn't think Hezmet would let him off easily, either. He'd be lucky to escape with his life, since he wouldn't have the means to take off and

17

might not be left alive for long, just on principle. She didn't question her reluctance to put an end to Morcun's ignoble career, but she sincerely wanted him to experience the terrific headache the note promised.

Even while these thoughts flashed through her mind, her attention stayed fixed in the other room. Hezmet was obviously certain he was in control because he turned his back on Morcun to open a huge safe, shielding the combination lock from his view. She wondered why Hezmet used such an antiquated museum piece, since intelligent safes that recognized palm, finger, and eye prints had been in use for more than thirty years.

Morcun stayed seated but casually watched Hezmet. As the latter turned his back, Morcun quietly took a pair of thin, skin-colored gloves from an inner pocket of his expensive suit and slipped them on noiselessly. Then he calmly took a gun from another pocket. She wasn't surprised to recognize her missing plop gun.

Kinta felt no surprise when she realized that Morcun had planned to murder Hezmet all along, for that explained the reason for swapping guns. If things had gone according to his plan, she would have walked into concentrated gunfire at noon, and even if she survived, she would take the rap for Hezmet's death. But there must be more to it than met the eye, she thought, for Morcun wasn't a loner.

When the door of the safe swung open, an astonishing amount of money and jewels was revealed on overloaded shelves. Morcun turned slightly in his seat and calmly shot Hezmet in the spine, where his neck met his shoulders. It was a slowly killing, paralyzing shot, and she knew from experience that the quiet cough would not be heard beyond the closed door.

Hezmet sagged like a deflated bag. He grunted in disbelief and tried to turn his head. Morcun got up from the chair, put the gun on the desk, and calmly pulled Hezmet up by the shoulders. Morcun might be turning into a flab-belly, but he was still very strong, she realized. He arranged the paralyzed Hezmet in his chair so he wouldn't fall off.

Then he stood back, as if admiring his handiwork. He looked into Hezmet's uncomprehending eyes and said with obvious satisfaction, "That's what you get for being dishonest, you scrimpy old crook. Next time you'll know better, eh? I was warned of your foul habit to renege on your promises by your so-called guards and their coconspirators, who each wanted a hundred thousand to side with me," he explained. "So, you do understand, don't you, that I need much, much more than a measly half million.

"Apart from that, beautiful Tuala's life is worth much, much more than a mere million credits or even ten times that amount. Perhaps I should stop her from blindly walking into her death." He sighed heavily. "It's such a pity she never wanted anything to do with me, as I had planned from the day I kidnapped her, so to hell with her anyway. Now I can buy any beautiful girl, as many as I want and when I want. While I enjoy my life, you can rot in hell, you miserable misfit!"

Then he calmly picked up the gun and shot the dying man in the forehead. He put the gun back on the corner of the desk so it would look as if it had been forgotten in the rush to get out of the room. How anyone would explain the bullet wound in the spine at the back of his neck she couldn't begin to guess. It confirmed her earlier surmise that Morcun had made arrangements within arrangements, for, if she had turned up at the appointed minute of the hour as usual, how would any sane person explain two guns? Morcun was an old hand in the game of bribery and corruption, and Hezmet had been taken for a ride by his own employees.

Morcun always planned carefully, but he'd slipped this once, Kinta thought, through no fault of his own. As she watched him, he took a couple of money sacks from the bottom shelf, then filled one to capacity with money and the other with an assortment of valuable, rare jewels. He seemed to consider an idea for a brief moment, then shrugged his shoulders, as if to say "might as well." Then he took more sacks and filled them with money and even stuffed a few thick bundles into his pockets.

Morcun really wants to be filthy rich, she thought with a grimace of distaste. He was taking as much as he could carry away while he had the chance. She watched him empty Hezmet's uncommonly huge briefcase on the floor and fill it with the stuffed sacks. The briefcase would not cause comment unless someone recognized it as Hezmet's, and even then Morcun could easily explain it away. He planned it well, as

19

usual, she thought, but he's in for a huge surprise. She almost chuckled at the thought.

While Morcun calmly rummaged the shelves for more jewels, Kinta quickly deactivated the two instruments with practiced ease and put them back in the rucksack, then slid the plop gun into a side pocket. Within seconds she glided to the door, listened for a brief moment, then quickly opened it, slipped out, and closed it while she drew the mini stun gun, which was already adjusted for maximum effect. With noiseless gliding strides, she ran to Hezmet's office and opened the door equally soundlessly. Morcun was still bent over in front of the safe with his back to the door while he dropped more jewels into the overstuffed briefcase.

So who is he to talk about greediness? she thought, and shot him in the back of the head without compunction. He collapsed onto his face into the safe like a brain-shot pig. *Ah,* she said to herself with a satisfied smile, *this gift is a real beauty, and it works like a charm. I sincerely wish this overnourished pig the granddaddy of the most awful headache in history when he wakes up.*

She hurriedly shut the door behind her, then took the substitute plop gun from her pocket and closed Morcun's still-gloved right hand around it with his index finger on the trigger. There were no prints on the gun anyway. As she picked up her own plop gun, she thought she heard a faint scratchy noise, as if a door was being cautiously opened. She went cold with guilty shock, and her mind blanked with unaccustomed panic.

Thought and reason left her, and caution took a backseat as she realized in a confused sort of way that it would be disastrous to be caught at the scene of this incriminating situation; there was no way to explain her presence. She jumped around like a wild animal, her teeth bared without realizing it, and faced the door with the gun ready to fire. Although it was not a conscious decision, she was ready to defend herself and this opportune windfall to escape Operations and all it stood for with every means available to her.

Vaguely realizing that this particular door was not opening, she feverishly closed and grabbed the stuffed briefcase, but retained the presence of mind to listen for footsteps in the passage before she silently fled the office. Back in the storeroom

20

she hurriedly glanced at her watch. It was almost half past eleven. She realized with a shock that time was running out fast, which made her throw what little caution she still possessed to the wind. Her brain seemed to stop functioning, and she almost went into an uncontrolled panic, despite her iron discipline. Her heart hammered in her throat, and she didn't realize she was acting like an untrained novice, breathing loudly and hurriedly through an open mouth, like a hunted animal. She only wanted to be out of the building with her loot without delays of any kind.

After emptying the pockets, she almost tore the uniform from her body without loosening the buttons and threw it and the boots over and behind a stack of boxes against the back wall with a dull thud. In a feverish hurry, she pushed the bandage that flattened her proud breasts down over her stomach so she would look like the female she was. She instinctively knew that the guards would appreciate the distraction of an obviously well-built female going out early for a run and that they wouldn't connect her with the delivery boy. That thought reminded her to pull the boy disguise from her face and stuff it into the rucksack.

As she donned the tracksuit and running shoes, she dimly realized that any briefcase, especially Hezmet's, was conspicuous and out of place with a tracksuit and would draw eyes as if she were waving a flag for attention. Her hands shook in her feverish haste to transfer the bags to the rucksack, but there wasn't enough space left for one bag of jewels, so she emptied it into the rucksack and spread the empty sack on top of the rest. The abandoned briefcase would raise a lot of curious questions, but without evidence it would remain just speculation.

The rucksack looked very bulky, but it would not be out of character on her back, since it was common practice to carry a little bit of weight for more intensive exercise. It appeared heavier than it actually was.

Although the rational part of her brain tried to tell her that it was stupid and unfounded, she felt and behaved like a hunted animal with vicious dogs snapping at its heels. She felt guilty and expected discovery at any moment, but she controlled her mindless panic long enough to quietly close the storeroom door and tiptoe to the stairway. She took the stairs two at a time, and although she had to fiercely suppress the urge to run, it was second nature to be silent and cautious.

When she belatedly discovered that she was breathing heavily, like a panicked thief, and that her throat was parched, she tried to control her nearly out-of-hand panic. She forced herself to slow down and walk down the remaining stairs so she would have time to compose herself and control her breathing before she reached the exit, where the guards would be more on the ball than usual.

By the time she reached the ground floor, she had only partially succeeded, but there was a ladies' restroom near the exit. She nearly bypassed it because she was still mentally impersonating the messenger boy. She controlled her panicky hurry, entered, and drank some water from the tap, which relieved her dry throat somewhat. The cold water fractionally calmed her nerves, and a glance in the mirror showed her eyes wide open with panic. She washed her face deliberately to remove all makeup and rubbed her face and eyes to get rid of the panicky stiffness.

She forced herself to calm down by taking deep breaths and holding them in until she had to breathe out, and even then she let the breath out slowly. This calmed her quickly, but she stayed in the restroom until she was sure her breathing and panic were under control. When she left, she hooked her thumbs into the straps of the rucksack as if to hold the bag so it wouldn't bounce when she started jogging.

As she approached the exit, the now-alert guards heard her and turned in her direction. The ugly one disfigured his face further by contorting his lips into a silly grin. He nudged his colleague with an elbow, forgetting or ignoring the fact that the colleague was already looking. The ugly one, as Kinta had thought of him since she'd first seen him, seemed to imagine that his uniform and smile made him irresistible. He was obviously not very intelligent and still new to the job.

5

"Hi beautiful," he croaked hoarsely. "Where have you been hiding those lovely curves and the serious brown eyes?"

Perhaps he thinks he is being cute, she thought, but even his voice is repellant. Maybe it was the coy nudge that aroused her ire, but it came across as a coarse advance and made her reply testily, "You can't see me when you come here to sleep with your eyes open, handsome. You've never been awake before, so what made you wake up today? Go back to sleep, Pretty Boy! I was under the impression that that's what you're being paid for."

The dangerous calm she felt arose from her annoyance at being detained by an inquisitive, bored guard with a grating voice who had nothing better to do. She knew she could easily handle both of them at the same time, which made her saucy. It also aggravated her that she would now have to get rid of the brown contact lenses, which were a valuable disguise. Maybe she shouldn't just throw them into the nearest bush, though; they might come in handy again.

Both guards blushed. The ugly one obviously thought he could teach her a lesson by using his authority to bully her and build up his damaged ego at the same time. He came out from behind the counter and advanced menacingly toward her, demanding harshly, "Let's see what you are trying to smuggle out in that heavy bag." A smug expression replaced the flush on his face.

Kinta didn't want to kill them, but she was ready to if "handsome" tried to enforce this lowdown trick to embarrass and delay her. It would take less than two seconds to knock them out, for she knew that ordinary access guards like these usually didn't even suspect the existence of the deadly combat tactics she was well versed in. No one was around to raise the alarm, and her daring spirit made her reply with most of the truth, but in a warning tone of voice.

"Make me! Do you expect goldbricks, jewels, money—or are you hoping to find feminine things in here? You can satisfy your morbid curiosity when I get back if you're still awake an hour from now. If you ever had any fitness training in your life, you would know that you carry a bit of weight if you're serious about keeping fit and haven't much time. Now please stop harassing me! You're wasting my time, and I'll report you."

"Oh come on, Flelik, you've asked for it," said the other guard. "Let the chick have her fun run. The boss will kick us out on our noses if that messenger boy slips past us while you're trying to take your spite out on this lovely lady. Where would we get another job if she reports us? On your way, girl, and enjoy the run. Please forgive my coworker for his unwarranted advances."

Kinta nodded her thanks, but some devilish impulse made her reward him with a heart-melting smile while she pushed a programmed card, which resembled a regular access card, into the exit-card slot. If one knew how, it was very easy to reprogram an unsophisticated entry-control system such as this one by presenting this special preprogrammable card in place of the regular access card. Now there wouldn't be any record of the relief messenger boy in its memory bank, and the tampering with the system couldn't be detected by a sophisticated program or any other means.

She waited for the card to be returned, because it would self-destruct if it wasn't returned within three minutes to her hand for a thumbprint. If there was a delay, the card would ignite, and if the area where the card was being scanned caught fire, chaos might follow.

Perhaps envy over the luscious smile his fellow guard had received from this beautiful girl without any effort at all or maybe the imagined insult to his immature ego overcame Flelik's better judgment. As she secured the returned card in the correct way, he angrily tried to grab her rucksack, but she sensed the silent rush and quickly dropped to one knee and turned around to face her attacker. It was so fast and unexpected that Flelik grabbed empty air and almost fell over her as the gate clicked open to let her out. Kinta heard the click and pushed a foot behind her to prevent it from locking again.

Flelik tried to recover his balance by hurriedly raising his arms to grab for the gate's framework, but he lost his balance anyway and hit the grillwork as he diverted both hands to clutch his suddenly complaining testicles. He had yelled in exquisite agony when Kinta delivered the lightning-fast punch upward into his unprotected groin while she was still turning around. He slid down the grille and curled up into a fetal position on the floor, groaning in agony.

Kinta easily pulled him to his feet by his hair with one hand. She grated the words into his ear, "Listen carefully, Flelik, and remember…if you want to get anywhere with a girl, show her respect and don't try to force yourself on her by being coarse. She might be better trained than you can imagine and might not restrain herself as I just did. Do…you…hear…me, Flelik?"

As she hissed the last words into his ear to make sure he understood once and for all and to imply that she would come back to haunt him, she put her other hand under his chin and twisted his head, threatening to break his neck.

Flelik tried to nod, but she wasn't satisfied. "What did you say?" she yelled into his ear. She wanted to intimidate him in case he had the courage to overcome his pain and follow her outside. While she was at it, she might as well teach him some manners. He would walk with a mincing gait for the rest of the day, if he was able to walk at all, and would leave girls alone for quite a while, she thought. This was a lesson he would remember for the rest of his life, and it made her grin nastily into his pain-contorted face.

Flelik was completely intimidated. "I heard, I'll remember, I'm sorry!" he sob-groaned between clenched teeth. The agony in his crotch and the lameness in his legs made him retch. When Kinta let go of his hair, he dropped limply to his knees in a worshipping posture with his face sideways on the cold floor, preventing the gate from closing.

His fellow guard just stood with mouth agape, giving the impression that he was extremely glad he wasn't in Flelik's shoes.

The encounter had calmed Kinta's nerves completely, and she winked wickedly at the standing guard, then mock-saluted him. He showed her a thumb in approval, grinned his best grin, and waved her away. His attention was on the shapely girl's posterior, and he didn't notice the cat waiting impatiently for him to turn his back so it could squeeze through the bars to follow the girl.

The pack wasn't very heavy, and Kinta jogged easily toward the park. She realized it was too risky to return to the hotel, where she might be exposed to the agents Morcun had bribed, none of whom she had noticed and whom she now knew to be his fellow conspirators. Her instinct told her to go to the park, where she could be alone to think and see anyone approaching. The quiet of nature, albeit the cultivated nature of a park and even at this temperature, always soothed her mind and calmed any latent nervousness so she could think clearly. She knew she had to look for alternate accommodation while she decided what to do, but that wasn't her top priority.

Morcun's mention of undercover agents and paying them off implied that she was known to them. She knew he always planned meticulously. In the unlikely event of her eluding the noon trap, he would have made sure she could be identified and killed while he prepared to decamp, and her demise would be a ruse to take the pressure off him while he escaped safely and in comfort. It was important that she acquire the means to alter her appearance as soon as possible.

She had a fortune in the rucksack and could indulge her every whim if she were so inclined, but first she must find a way to survive today. As she passed the dress shop, she stopped with the idea that she could buy here what she required to alter her appearance, but the gray, nondescript pantsuit she desired was no longer in the window.

She entered the shop anyway; there probably would be more of them in stock. Her rough, well-used, old rucksack was out of place in an upscale shop like this, and an assistant quickly approached with the obvious intention of politely hustling her out before a well-to-do client would arrive.

Kinta quickly smiled disarmingly and explained, "I'm on an early lunchtime training run, and I have this extra weight to make me sweat, or so my boss thinks. I saw a gray trouser suit in the window this morning and thought I might come by and ask about it during my lunch hour, but it seems I'm too late. Do you have another like it or perhaps something similar?"

The girl smiled with a sigh of relief and replied, "Yes, I remember that one. An old man bought the suit about an hour ago. He said that it's his daughter's birthday and he wanted to surprise her as he knew that she was interested in that particular suit and it was her size. Quite a nice old man, too. He made me wish that I was his daughter. We have more of the same style, but not the same color, as they are supposed to be exclusive—you know, one of a kind only. Let me show you. I have just the one to emphasize your lovely eyes."

With a shock Kinta realized she still hadn't removed the contact lenses. Maybe it was just as well, but she must remember to do it before she approached any hotel for accommodation.

She tried two trouser suits on, one a dark brown and the other a mottled green. While she was in the fitting room, she made sure she transferred more than enough money, but not extravagantly so, to the wallet that contained her own measly travel allowance. Then she opened the door and informed the smiling assistant that she would take both. She also chose a dark-gray, nondescript handbag and makeup to go with the color of the suits. With a smile, she asked the assistant where she could get a better-looking rucksack than the one she had, for she was tired of it and couldn't carry her purchases back to the office in a shopping bag or her boss would become suspicious of her training runs.

The now broadly smiling assistant said she personally knew the manager of a shop nearby that specialized in all types of camping equipment. He would send one over immediately if she asked. Kinta said she would like a dark-green one, if they had any in that color.

The canvas bag arrived within ten minutes. In the meantime, Kinta was glad that the shop assistant thought it was her clever sales talk that had made a seemingly reluctant client spent additional money on more personal things and makeup. She'd had to leave most of her personal items at the hotel to give the impression that she would return to collect them, as any normal woman would do. She was trained to resist the impulse to carry valuable or sentimental things with her, since she might have to abandon everything at her hotel after a mission, but she didn't have such things anyway.

As she paid, she was shocked to realize how much time she'd spent in the shop. It was almost twenty minutes past twelve. The hunt would already be on. She felt a renewed urge to run, but nevertheless calmly thanked the assistant and said she now really had to run, for she'd already spent too much time away from the office and would be late. She picked up both bags easily and, after surreptitiously making sure that no innocent-looking characters lazed around outside, hurried out of the shop. Away from the shop, she stepped behind a tree to take the lenses out of her eyes and wrap them in a tissue before she put them into a pocket of the new rucksack. She now sported her natural blue eyes, which were a bit red from the constant use of the colored lenses.

As she left the shop, Kinta hadn't noticed the big red-brown cat in the shadows across the street that had been waiting impatiently for her to finish her shopping. These huge cats were such an everyday sight that people tended to overlook their presence, and this particular cat knew how not to attract unnecessary attention. She was carrying some kind of purse in her mouth, and if anyone took notice of her, she would soon be forgotten. Priests sometimes asked cats to deliver confidential messages outside the temple in the sure knowledge that the cat would protect it with its life, but very few knew that these cats were highly intelligent.

6

As Kinta walked warily along the street, the huge cat slinked after her on the other side of the street without looking directly at her, and she still hadn't become aware of her shadow when they entered the park almost side by side.

The cat stopped for a moment to lift her head as if to sniff the faint breeze, then deftly vanished into the shrubbery and undergrowth to be out of sight. She had sensed enemies of the human female in the vicinity and had to protect or warn her—or both. Although she knew where Kinta's favorite spot was, she kept pace just out of sight while her senses scanned the immediate area so that enemies could not approach the girl without her awareness. The cat sarcastically thought about how she was diverted from a more important mission, and politely requested, mind you, to make sure that this noisy-footed, blundering human female stayed healthy if she was attacked, because she was panicky and didn't think clearly. As if *that* had stopped her from buying out a shop at the first opportunity!

This particular cat had been the companion—or rather the guardian angel—of a very unusual male human child for most of her long life, but she still couldn't understand why the finer senses of humans, without exception, stayed so dull unless they were trained from a very young age. She was proud of her young ward and believed that no other human would fit into even the rottenest-smelling pair of his running shoes.

Kinta went directly to the secluded spot she preferred and dropped both rucksacks on the middle of the bench before she sat down next to them. But before she could even think of transferring the contents of the old bag to the new one, a huge, powerful, red-brown cat leaped onto the bench on the other side, and she jumped with fright and shrieked. The first things she noticed were the sharply pointed black ears adorned with tufts of hair on the apex, traces of graying hair on its finely shaped head, and the calm, intelligent eyes staring straight and intently into hers.

She almost fainted when a calm, female voice spoke

soothingly in her mind. *Stay calm, Cookie. I'm here to look after your welfare and help you stay alive in spite of your efforts to the contrary. I must warn you that enemies are on their way right now, and a few are combing this park without any intention of cuddling you. Here, take the tube that's inside this purse and apply the gooey contents to your face, neck, ears, and the back of your hands. It'll dry within a few minutes to make you look older. It will wash off easily if you apply a special soap when you no longer need the disguise. Uh oh! One clever searcher is almost upon us. Trust me and stay calm, Cookie. Listen to me, for I'll be nearby and I'll tell you what to do and when to do it. I'll be ready to kill him if he tries to harm you in any way, but be quick now. Hide your face in your hands, bend over, and shake as if you are crying or laughing.*

It was a command, not a request, and Kinta did as ordered since she also heard the rapidly approaching footsteps. The cat jumped lithely over the back of the bench and seemed to become one with the shrubbery; not a single leaf stirred to mark her swift passage. All too suddenly the imminence and extent of the danger Kinta had invited hit home, but it was too late to regret the wasted time of her impulsive shopping spree.

The footsteps stopped abruptly right in front of her and a man's satisfied voice rattled in her ears. "I just *knew* you would be here! We've seen that dirty canvas delivery sack often enough, and it is a dead giveaway. When you didn't come back to the hotel, we thought that you might have come here to enjoy the scenery as usual. What took you so long? Did you stop for the last lunch in your murderous life?"

Her sudden realization that she had been acting like a novice indulging in unnecessary, time-wasting shopping, without a single thought given to her immediate or future safety, sent an icy chill through her veins. Now that it was far too late, she realized Morcun would have told his accomplices of her habits. He never left anything to chance. She sighed heavily and slowly lifted her head from her cupped hands to look at her would-be executioner. Like a professional, he had stopped just out of reach and was smiling happily at figuring out where she would be found. The man aimed an older, noisy type of percussion gun at her forehead, and she prepared to at least try to fight him; she had completely forgotten the mini stun gun strapped to her forearm.

Wait, Cookie! He just wants to make you cringe, for he is a coward at heart and wants to brag about how clever he is before he kills you from a safe distance. I'll get behind him, and as soon as I jump onto his back and dig my sharp claws into his eyes, he will forget everything else, believe me! He'll instinctively take that noisy cannon out of your face to grab my claws. When you see that happen, act immediately and kill him without spilling any blood. There must not be a single drop of blood on the path or on the bench to indicate the presence of his cadaver. You have blundered enough for one day, so don't hesitate, or we might both end up dead. Watch his eyes for telltale signs, and do not look for me. Keep him talking if he stops before I'm in a position to attack.

The thoughts came calmly into her mind, driving out the despair and calming her screaming nerves. She had listened to tales of the intelligence and bravery of temple cats, but had dismissed them as imaginative storytelling. Now she found herself obeying a cat's orders without question. But the guy was talking, and she had to pretend interest.

"When Morcun didn't come back to the hotel by noon as we had agreed upon, we called our ally at the security desk to check if he had left the building, for he isn't one to inspire trust. Our contact had been kicked in the crotch by a female who answered to your description and who had left just after half past eleven, even if she had brown eyes as he believed. Morcun had not come out of the paymaster's office before or since then…"

Kinta quietly prepared to dodge, jump, and kill. She was well trained in the art of barehanded killing and had done it before. She didn't have to move her legs, but she slowly straightened up and then bent forward a little without alarming him. Her demeanor conveyed the impression that she was intensely interested in what he was saying. She didn't know how she could let the cat know she was ready, but the cat already knew from the impressions she received from Kinta's mind and told her so. She was crossing the path at a hard gallop some distance away.

"…but we put two and two together and came up with the fact that you must have known what Morcun was up to and outwitted him. Did you kill him and our dishonest paymaster?"

31

The abrupt question almost caught her off guard, but she shook her head and lied by telling a half-truth, as Morcun had. "No, they are not dead as far as I know. I became suspicious when Morcun avoided me a bit too deliberately this entire week. It was out of character, so this morning I followed him to the paymaster's office and overheard them talking about setting me up for a kill or capture at noon, when I was supposed to arrive. I was so dazed and shocked that Morcun could sell me out cold-bloodedly that I wandered around until I found myself here. I do not have much money, and I was just about to cry when you arrived. You're very clever, and I wish you were on my side." Talking about her ex-boss reminded her of the "stunner," as she now thought to name the little gun.

Then, acting on the cat's observation, she decided to stroke the man's ego to encourage him to brag some more. It was also the best way to gather knowledge and information.

"So how much was he going to pay you? You mentioned 'we.' How many of you have to share his loot—if he gets paid, that is, for I obviously did not fall into the trap? I overheard something about him being paid half a million then and the other half after I am dead. Perhaps they were still arguing about it at noon."

The man's eyes showed half belief and also bewilderment, but before he had a chance to decide either way or open his mouth, the cat jumped onto his shoulders with a terrible screech and hooked her front claws over his ears into his eyes. Her back claws dug into the back of his neck, and she pulled his head back as if she intended to break his neck. The sudden, unbearable agony in his eyes made him yell hysterically, and his gun flew over the bench when both his hands flashed up in reflex to rip the tormentor's sharp claws from his tortured eyes.

The drawn-back head exposed his throat, and Kinta crushed his windpipe and Adam's apple with a much practiced punch from her right hand, her fingers bent tightly at the second joints and her bent thumb supporting them. The cat jumped away with a somersault as their victim fell onto his back. The man thrashed weakly as he fought to draw in a breath of air.

Even as the man fell, the cat's command rang in her brain: *Hide the body in the bushes behind the bench and try not to leave drag marks. We have to leave almost right away for there are others converging on this spot. Unfortunately, you are a creature of habit, and everybody seems to know about the park and this secluded spot you prefer. Your time is running out, and you still have to disguise yourself by rubbing that aging cream onto the back of your hands and face before we leave. The Saphead is on his way at last with the rest of the things to complete your disguise, which you sorely need to stay out of trouble, but he was delayed, for he first had to clear up the mess you left behind at the office. He is making his escape from the building right now.*

Kinta was stung to the core. What mess did she make that an idiot had to clear up? She turned the dying man over onto his face and callously grabbed him by his belt and the jacket at his neck. She lifted the body effortlessly and threw it into the shrubbery, for she was sure the man couldn't feel anything by now. Then she quickly applied the cream to her face, neck, and the back of her hands. When the tube was empty, she threw it into the shrubbery without a second thought.

The cat hissed angrily. *Do you live on reflexes without ever thinking for yourself, Cookie? I'm not surprised you messed everything up. That aging cream is still so secret that even the manufacturer had never heard of it, and neither have you. You are leaving an almost empty tube of top-secret goo with your fingerprints on it near a body that will soon be discovered by a very elated finder. Don't you know that the area will be searched with a fine-toothed comb and that the tube will be found and the contents routinely analyzed? Didn't you receive any decent training at that notorious place you call Operations? You are wondering what you messed up on in the paymaster's office? Must I explain every detail?*

Firstly, you didn't pick up the shells of the two cartridges you fired here this morning. Next, you didn't pick up the spent shells Morcun fired at Hezmet. Next, you left Morcun alive so that he can talk and implicate you and then go free to come after you to retrieve his loot. How far do you think you will get with him on your tail? The way you're spending the money will leave a trail a blind man can follow. As it is, it will be very difficult to get you out of this city with the security forces in this country and almost every enemy agent out looking for you, and more being flown in as fast as they can be found. They will stop at nothing

*and spare no expense to nail your shapely rear to the nearest
wall. And what do you do? You blunder blithely about, getting
yourself suckered into unnecessary shopping instead of thinking
your way out of your predicament. Is your severely limited
intelligence sophisticated enough to understand me when I spell
it out word by word, Cookie?*

Kinta felt her self-esteem dropping through the soles of
her running shoes. The unexpected sarcasm from an animal
really hit home. She truly was a mess today, and she hadn't had
a single lucid thought since she'd zapped Morcun. Still, she
resented the blunt reproof.

"So why are you and this one you call the Saphead
helping me? What do you get out of it?" She was suddenly
suspicious of this freely offered help; no one she knew ever did
anything for nothing.

*Because we were ordered to, Cookie, and we get nothing
out of it except your time-wasting arguments and exposure to
death! Have a little patience, girl, and everything will be
explained in due course. Now get the hell going, and fast, while
you're still alive to do so, but don't go blundering to any of the
exits, because all are now guarded. Go somewhere where there
are dense shrubs or undergrowth so you can duck into it until we
can catch up. This bragger you killed has a wrist communicator,
and he used it to gloat about how clever he was just as he saw
you. His fellow conspirators are running their hindquarters off to
get here because they don't even trust their own mothers, and
they know this one likes to talk first.*

*I'll find the damn tube because I smell better than you do,
and I'll catch up with you in a few minutes. You have your
weapons, so use them if you have to, and don't forget the mini
stun gun we gave you. Your time is running out fast and the
need for caution has ended, but you don't have enough time left
to grope for your weapons right now. GO! They're coming fast!*

7

Having been reminded of her carelessness, Kinta put the cat's purse, as she thought of it, into a pocket and then shouldered both bags to have her hands free. The mention of the stunner eased her doubts. She ignored the pathways and ran with long, easy strides over the well-kept lawns to a destination she knew of but hadn't explored in detail yet. It was a few acres of dense, uncared-for natural forest that ended at the eastern boundary of the park. She hadn't received any training to survive in the wilderness, but she thought she knew enough to elude any pursuers.

Just as she wondered how the cat and the Saphead would ever find her, the cat bounded past and commanded, *Move it, Cookie! You're dawdling, and the men rapidly converging on the bench we just left will appreciate the sight of your shapely posterior if they glance this way. Fortunately, they are lagging somewhat because, like you, they aren't very fit. Remember not to call the boy a "saphead" to his face or he may dislike you violently, and we can't waste time on trivialities right now. Treat him civilly, and he'll treat you with respect. Remember that because he'll find us before too long. Now run like hell if you value your life!*

Kinta sprinted as hard as she could to keep up with the cat and found she wasn't as running fit as she'd thought she was. After three minutes she was gasping for breath like a fish out of water. The rucksacks were getting heavier by the second, but she could be stubborn and didn't slow down perceptibly until they reached the patch of natural forest. She was breathing heavily, and her throat was parched and scratchy.

When they reached denser cover, the cat said, *Good show, Cookie! Now we walk so you can catch your breath. We barely made it, and we can only hope that one of them isn't a tracker. Avoid disturbing leaves and branches unless you want to leave a signature for any half-decent tracker to follow with his eyes closed. Watch where you're going, and try not to step on* soft ground or grass. Ask the idiot-boy to teach you how to breathe properly when you run. No, I'm not angry with you. You needed to be jolted out of that panicked, empty-headed condition so you can function again. Remember that a feline will always tell you honestly what it feels or thinks. As a matter of fact, so would any animal if you could converse with them. We will not lie.

It's difficult to keep track of your enemies' progress all the time, for I have to talk to you and guide the boy so he can avoid them and find us before they do. He should be here in about five minutes, as he can run like a scared antelope with a leopard after it, and he's running fit and every other kind of fit! Please put this tube back in the purse when we stop. She held the tube in her mouth for Kinta to take.

The cat's mental speech was so sincerely honest and matter-of-fact that Kinta had to smile, and the inclination to smile lightened her somber mood. She took the tube and dropped it into the purse in her pocket. She asked, "Why do you call this boy a saphead and an idiot? I sense that you're proud of him."

Yes, I love the kindhearted idiot, but it's a long story. He's an idiotic saphead because he oftentimes acts like he's soft in the head. He's too ready to help and has put his life in danger too many times for me to remember, to rescue an idiotic person or animal that wasn't worth the effort, and that's really foolish in my opinion. There are other reasons, which you will come to know if you decide to stay with us. Yes, you may go your own way if you don't want to trust us, but we'll talk about that when you are out of immediate danger. Now stop talking and follow me. Step lightly on your whole foot and not on your heels first, as that leaves an indentation. Take short steps so you won't leave heel dents.

The cat chose a way she knew would be easier for the girl to follow, but unfortunately, a tracker could easily follow the scuff marks the girl left. The cat knew it could not be helped and sent a mind call to her longtime partner and protégé to get his lazy behind in top gear, to which she received a scathing mental retort that she should know that he was running at full speed, even with the load on his back. She directed him with a picture of the east wall, to which he replied that it would have saved a lot of time, distance, and energy if she had told him sooner, as it was easier to run on the paved streets outside the park. She wisely cut communication and mentally scanned the area for the girl's and other enemies.

They entered a clearing in the dense bush where numerous tracks and dried droppings of wild animals indicated that they sometimes gathered in this sheltered spot overnight. The icy breeze was filtered by the vegetation, and it felt warmer here. The cat told the girl that this seemed the best place to wait and that she should find a clean spot to rest. She silently approved as the girl dropped the rucksacks but didn't sit down, and then listened for footfalls or noise made by pursuers while she breathed deeply but as silently as she could.

A few minutes later, Kinta almost jumped out of her running shoes when a strongly built old man with a backpack and a tight-fitting knitted cap over his hair and ears stepped into the clearing without the slightest sound. She reflexively grabbed the stun gun out of her sleeve, but the cat sharply told her to relax; this was the boy for whom they had been waiting. Kinta couldn't shake the feeling that she had seen this old man somewhere before, but she couldn't remember where or when.

The old man wasn't breathing as if he had run a long distance at high speed. He smiled at her astonishment and quietly introduced himself in a young man's melodious voice. "Sorry to startle you, but it seemed best not to make undue noise, as our adversaries are closing in. Ah yes, look at your hands. You look as old as I do. Very convincing, isn't it? You should see your own face, old lady!" He smiled as she made the startling discovery that her hands were as wrinkled and splotched as that of a very old woman.

"I go by the name of Dai, short for Daiyus. The cat's name is Kyr, and you may address us so if you like. It saves time." He took the rucksack off his back and, to her surprise, took out the neatly wrapped gray pantsuit she had desired and a matching blouse and pair of flat shoes.

"Kyr got the shoe size from your mind. The blouse may be a bit too big as I had to guess your size, but the shop assistant said it matches the size of the suit. Please go behind that dense clump of bushes behind you and change. Then put your tracksuit on over it, as we may encounter some thorny thickets to push through before we reach the wall. Keep the running

37

shoes on until we are over the wall. Don't use the suits you bought—your enemies have their descriptions."

He laughed at her surprised look while he produced a tube from a pocket. "No, I'm not psychic. Kyr is the one who is sensitive to the surface thoughts of a specific type of person, but she is not a mind reader," he said, twisting the truth a little to put the girl at ease. "When you've changed, rub the contents of this tube thoroughly into your hair to complete the disguise." He silently asked Kyr to see that she complied. The cat, with her peculiar senses, didn't need to be told that the girl's enemies were closing in fast.

Come on, Cookie, and hurry up! Do as the boy says, for our time is running out faster than you realize.

Kinta found herself obeying. It's funny, she thought. She didn't resent the cat calling her "Cookie" and ordering her around. She usually resented being called by that common moniker and once nearly killed a man who called her that. This cat was sort of different and made her feel comfortable and…well, loved, which was a strange feeling. Kinta felt for her plop gun and put it on top of the sack after closing the flap again. The air felt cold as she quickly undressed to her thermal underwear and then stepped out of the breast-bandage she still had around her hips.

Kyr silently approved of the rippling muscles she saw under the tight-fitting, almost transparent underwear. She won't be an unfit, flabby, complaining burden to us, she thought, and she looked as if she was training hard to get rid of any development of fat. She would soon be as running fit as they were if they had to take to the wilderness to escape. Kyr got the impression that Kinta was willing to learn and didn't ask stupid, unnecessary questions.

Kinta had just shaken out the blouse to put on when she heard an unnecessarily loud, harsh voice in the clearing. Holding the blouse sideways off the ground with both hands, she bent over and looked through the dense foliage that shielded her from the men in the clearing. Her heart tried to sink through her cold, naked feet when she saw five men armed with an assortment of handguns confronting the old man. Her heart went out in sympathy, and she decided that, come what may, she must help the old man.

Dai had slumped very convincingly into the stance of an elderly man with a backpack clutched in his old, wrinkled hands just before five men stormed into the clearing. Their chests were heaving mightily, and they were blowing heavily, which told him they had reached the end of their staying power. He didn't mind unfit opponents since it made a physical fight so much easier, but these held guns and seemed willing to use them.

"Where's the girl, old man?" the leader demanded in an overly loud voice. Dai noticed he wasn't as spent as the other four and decided he would have to be the first to go, but that unnecessarily loud voice couldn't be anything else but a signal to someone not present.

Five men with firearms were just three too many to take on since he had given the stun gun to the girl. Dai sensed that these were well-trained, rough characters but bordering on the criminal or even worse; they looked nasty and ready to kill on the slightest pretext. They obviously didn't keep fit since they panted like fat, tired dogs, but he knew he had to establish the fact that he was an old man to have even a slight chance of surviving the confrontation he sensed was going to be forced on him. They clearly had no respect for age.

"As you may have noticed, young man, I haven't got a girl with me. Wish I had, though," he cackled in a practiced voice and a leering face that matched his artificial age. He must make them relax, for they were very tense and eager, like dogs being held back on leashes. In their nervousness they might just pull the triggers, since there were no witnesses around to make them cautious. "It's very cold, and if one had arrived here, I would have persuaded her to stay."

"Don't play stupid games with us, old man! We followed her trail into this clearing, and you should have seen her at the very least." He turned to face his companions. "It's a chance to try out our new lead-pellet saps, men. Let's work the old codger over until he begs to tell us where she's hiding."

Dai saw the speaker's wink and eager look of anticipation. They all put their guns away and enthusiastically produced heavy, thick leather saps about thirty centimeters long and six centimeters thick from inside pockets.

It seemed to please them immensely to see the old man suddenly slouch over, drop his rucksack beside him, and shuffle his feet as if in dejection because he knew he could do nothing about the unavoidable pain and subsequent maiming he would be subjected to. Dai sensed their eager anticipation as they surrounded him like a pack of hungry wolves circling a defenseless calf. When they didn't attack immediately, he knew they were waiting for someone or a signal, but wanted him to suffer mentally.

There was no way they could divine that they were about to receive the most unexpected surprise of their lives. It might not be their first, but it would definitely be their last surprise, for Dai couldn't afford to waste time or to show mercy when his client's life was threatened.

He didn't reveal his approval of the switch to saps; now he could do with them whatever he liked without getting seriously hurt. Armed with only clubs or those clumsy, ridiculous saps, they were no match for a fit young man relentlessly trained by the best among the best of the Fighting Priests. They would be slow and off guard because of his disguise. He shuffled to place his legs in the right position to balance his body no matter which way he had to move. He tensed his upper leg muscles and bent his knees just a little, which made the difference for perfect balance and speed. He waited, as they did, for some signal to begin the assault.

Kyr, who had known Daiyus intimately since he was born, also knew that his stance was accompanied by only a slight tensing of muscles to make ready to attack or defend. That particular posture told her to expect tricks or other stalkers, because he could go into lightning action without tensing his body muscles that much. She felt proud of her ward, for he was learning to read between the lines of an act, even though his finer senses had been suppressed for his own safety. He also seemed to sense that something wasn't quite as it should be, even if he was as dense as a blindfolded ox. But then, no human's hearing could be as acute as that of a feline.

8

To Kyr it was quite obvious that their intention was to play with the supposedly old man and traumatize him before attacking and killing him as slowly as possible to prolong his screams and their own perverted feeling of power over someone else's life. They were scared of their female quarry and were only too happy to provide a diversion, to distract her attention so the tracker could sneak up and overpower her. And of course they thoroughly enjoyed the sense of power they got from intimidating a supposedly defenseless old man before they slowly pulverized every bone in his body and left him to die slowly and painfully.

If Kyr were human, she would have smiled in anticipation of the unexpected, shocking surprise they were about to receive. Even without the physical indications, she sensed that Dai suspected there was a sixth man and that he, or one in the mob, might be a sensitive. Dai had shielded his mind and thoughts, but he would still be able to receive impressions from her.

She flashed a brief, silly, ambiguous picture into his mind that she knew he would understand: *I'll jump and screech as you play.* In a previous situation similar to this one, he had used the same picture of a small, spotted wildcat jumping comically up and down with stiff legs in a circle around a demoralized mouse, spitting and screeching its silly head off while feigning attacks on the pathetic, cringing creature, which Kyr had correctly interpreted as a request to attack to create a diversion, the same as these perverts thought they were doing now.

Dai nodded his head slightly—almost unnoticeably—to let her know he understood that he must delay attack until she jumped for the kill with a bloodcurdling scream. As she faded away underneath the leafy branches of a low bush behind the girl, she received the faint impression of approval that accompanied the infinitesimal nod.

The tracker was near, and he thought he was stealing along noiselessly upon a distracted girl, but Kyr thought he couldn't even fool a quail with a major hearing problem, not to

41

mention a cat that also used her sixth sense to check the progress of enemies.

Kinta was completely engrossed by the plight of Dai—or the old man, as she still believed him to be. She forgot she was still clad only in her tight-fitting, revealing underwear. Without thinking, she dropped the blouse (as luck would have it, on a rucksack) and leaned over to grab hold of her plop gun, intending to leap into the clearing to help an old man against what she thought were impossible odds even for her.

But Kyr sensed her intention and projected a sharp, dissuasive message. *Do you want to distract the boys from having a little perverted fun by parading around like that in front of them? Have you no sense of decency, Cookie?*

Kinta had been deeply immersed in Dai's imagined plight. Abruptly brought back to reality, she involuntarily yelped, but not loudly. She dropped the gun in reflex, clamped her knees together, half straightened, and covered her strategic places with arms and hands before so much as one lucid thought flashed through her bemused head.

When it dawned on her that she was not visible from the clearing, she started to relax, then froze as a man's voice, full of satisfied glee and thick with lust, exclaimed behind her, "Oh! Look…at…you! Are you getting ready for your new boyfriends when they are finished with your ancient old crock of a father, or is he your current boyfriend?" The man laughed coarsely. "Don't you worry…I'll be the first in line. You can bet on it."

Then he commanded harshly, "Step away from the gun and the rucksacks. NOW!" he shouted. It was the arranged signal for the men in the clearing to make the old man scream his lungs out.

Kinta didn't even think of the stun gun attached to her arm. Caught unprepared again, she spun around as quickly as a cat, but found that the man was an old pro. He was out of reach and pointing a deadly spit gun rock-steady at her chest. But his eyes widened and his neck jerked with shock at the unexpected contrast of an ancient face on such a beautifully proportioned, young-looking body.

Kinta knew she was outmaneuvered even as she wondered at the reason for the shock on the man's face, but before she could think of anything to say or do, Kyr jumped onto the man's back with a horrific war cry, dug her hind claws into his back, and clawed his eyes to shreds in one practiced movement. Dai went into action when his would-be assailants stiffened in surprise at the cat's terrifying screech and the simultaneous tortured scream of agonized shock that rent the air.

The stalker responded the same way as Kyr's previous victim had some twenty minutes earlier. He uttered a shocked, horrendous scream, dropping his forgotten gun involuntarily as his open hands flew to protect his already shredded eyes. Kyr quickly shifted her claws in one practiced movement to his neck and ripped his throat and arteries open, changing the man's terrible scream of agony into a ghastly gurgle.

Kinta, shocked to the core but more worried about the old man, who she had taken a liking to, quickly spun around to focus her attention on the clearing. She was just in time to see the supposedly old man dispatch the last of the gang with a lightning-fast, powerful half-circle kick to his chin. She heard a dull, sickening crack as the man's jaw and neck broke, and then he spun halfway around before he plopped onto his back. The other would-be torturers were already down in varying positions, all with looks of astonished disbelief in their staring eyes. She saw the old man stoop over each body and search pockets with apparent indifference, briefly checking documents when he found them and then replacing them in the same pocket.

Like most people, she was in the habit of believing what her eyes saw, and she couldn't understand how an old man could dispatch an assailant in less than a second, even though he looked fit and powerful. How could he, at his age, slay five men with only his hands or feet in the little time she was turned away—definitely not more than ten seconds?

The boy is well-trained and doesn't dawdle when his life is at stake. Dress, Cookie, or is it a perverted habit of yours to parade in your undies in cold weather before men? Kyr's tone was scathing, and Kinta became aware that she was goose-fleshed and shivering, but not with cold. She started to dress but had a burning question, and a dozen more: "You call him a boy, but he's an old man. I don't understand."

You're not even using one percent of one percent of the brainpower you were born with, my confused Cookie! He's in disguise, the same as you are, and he told you to look at your hands. You forget very quickly, don't you? If you have a mirror, look into it before you go any further, then start thinking, for a welcome change—it would take the burden off me. Didn't you see the shock on the man's face when you turned to face him? Humans really are stupid and unthinking, even though they are born with the right equipment. They expect old-looking people to be feeble and slow-moving. That's the real value of the disguise, as you've just witnessed. Humans are an unthinking lot, despite their supposed intelligence. They even perceive other humans or animals with hearing defects as slow-witted because they cannot interpret soft, hurried, or unclear words. That's normal human perception for you! Now get dressed before you get pneumonia, or you can stay here and parade naked for the rest of the day, for all I care.

Dai was finished and walking in their direction, but paused when Kyr asked him to wait a while for the lady to make up her mind about whether she wanted to get dressed or not. Somehow Kinta was made party to the exchange of thoughts, and she blushed furiously as Dai, innocently and apparently serious, asked if the lady was a slow dresser or if she wasn't happy with the new clothes bought by a young man disguised as a stupid, old man.

The seemingly serious, casual exchange suddenly made Kinta lose her last vestiges of distrust of the odd pair, and she decided to let them guide her for the time being. For some obscure reason, the cat felt like the mother she had lost when she was five or six years old, and, well, she just couldn't imagine Daiyus as a young man in that disguise. She didn't realize that her thoughts were transparent to the cat and that the same cat was relaying them to an approving young man. She almost fainted when she saw her own face in the small hand mirror the saleslady had foisted on her.

When Dai was at last allowed through the thicket, she asked him, "Why are you helping me? It seems odd that the two of you show up out of the blue at the right moment, have money to buy the clothes I covet, and then kill men left and right to protect me. It was you who left the note and this mini stun gun, wasn't it? Please explain this timely coincidence and how you know my thoughts."

44

Dai was checking the tracker's pockets for identification and also picked up the very difficult-to-obtain spit gun. He came across two spare clips in the man's jacket, which he put in his backpack, along with the spit gun.

When he stood up to face her, Kinta could see he was serious, and she immediately liked the direct gaze and the honest, striking, dark-gray, young eyes that were incongruous with the old face. She now sensed the powerful aura of strength and honesty he emanated. It inspired trust that calmed her instantly.

"If I know Kyr, I think she already explained in a rough sort of way," he said. "I've already told you that I'm not psychic. Yes, I gave you the mini stun gun, which was my own, and I have two more clips for it at the hotel, but let's leave this place right now. We must get away from here fast, as it seems that this whole country and half the world are after you. All sorts of agents in this area are converging on this park right now to block it off, as word has gone out that you are trapped here. I'll try to tell you the why and the wherefore of our presence as we go and will explain in more detail tonight. Let me help you carry that old rucksack, but keep your gun in your pocket.

"But first, permit me to rub the temporary graying lotion into your hair, for it takes a while to dry. I hope one tube is enough, because the color of your hair must match your seemingly advanced age. Only your eyes will be a dead giveaway, as mine are, so please remember to look down if we pass or meet anyone. I'll get a pair of tinted glasses if we find any shops open. This disguise gives one an unfair advantage, as you just saw, and that's one of the reasons it was invented. But I must ask you to keep it secret, for it has saved many lives."

Dai explained a bit more as they walked toward the boundary wall. "There's no need to hide our tracks because they can't be followed on the hard pavement or streets unless special equipment is available at short notice, which I doubt. I'll explain our convenient presence in as few words as possible.

"Briefly, we were ordered by the Fighting Priesthood to persuade you to abscond. As to the why, I'll go into detail tonight. We arrived in Bojon three days ago, and I booked in at the same hotel you did, the Traveler's Rest. 'Traveler's Unrest' would be a better name, because I think every room is cluttered with listening devices. Kyr snooped around and picked up the impression from various sources that you were marked for extinction, and that is why I gave you my secret weapon. We followed you on your rounds yesterday to form an idea of what you were up to because we were not sure when to talk to you and how we could persuade you to come with us. We tagged along when you left the hotel this morning, and we were close when Morcun killed the paymaster.

"Ah, yes." He coughed, a little embarrassed. "As Kyr may have told you, I had to arrange a little accident for old Morcun. He didn't look where he was going, and in his haste, his foot slipped in the paymaster's blood. He fell and hit the corner of the desk with his temple, thus killing himself. Now he can't point a finger at you for his own misdeed. I picked up the empty shells you unwittingly left in the park earlier. I forgot about them and then happily remembered when Kyr told me you had switched guns. So I exchanged them for the ones at the crime scene because they will match the gun you left in Morcun's hand. I'd just had time to return the briefcase to Hezmet's office and drop a bundle of notes in it when I had to hide. Fortunately, it seems that Morcun had arranged for your executioners to arrive at five to twelve, and even then they were three minutes late—would you believe it?" He paused a moment to gather his thoughts.

She interrupted. "I've been trained to kill without pity, but it didn't occur to me that I must kill that despicable traitor. I didn't even consider it, and it's very strange that the thought never crossed my mind."

Dai looked at her. "I understand that Morcun had hypnotic commands implanted, over many years, that you must not kill him under any circumstances. To put your mind at rest: no, I definitely can't read thoughts. Kyr has the ability to pick up strong impressions, and that is one of the reasons she calls me an idiot and other names to that effect. Most cats are very good at divining thoughts, but only some humans can receive thoughts from, or project thoughts to, cats. We were lucky that you have that rare ability, or talent—whatever—for it comes in handy at times.

"We gathered that Morcun was persuaded to sell you out, but we don't know why. We only know that he was just an insignificant puppet for a worldwide, and perhaps even interplanetary, conspiracy we have been trying to track down to its source. We are still groping in the dark, but the evidence we have come across so far leads us to suspect that it may come to war, and we are trying to prevent that from happening. Your planned demise may be connected to it.

"The papers I found on these men show that they are from different agencies and various governments. Someone very powerful indeed is behind this, and he, or they, can pull strings all over the world. The tracker was from the local Aikon religion's priesthood, which makes me suspect that someone with influence locally wants you to be the scapegoat for a very different crime or reason than killing Hezmet. It seems to me that your death was planned to cover a trail, but we don't know the why, who, or what...yet.

"I have a nasty foreboding that even with our disguises, we may find it difficult to leave by public transport, but I'll check, starting tonight. The information we have been able to gather so far points to Morcun only as a recruited minor cog in a much bigger wheel. Perhaps he looked upon it as a heaven-sent opportunity to enrich himself for retirement at your expense. I don't know his reasons for involving you, but I can't shake the feeling that we are in it up to our eyeballs, and we may have to play a reluctant part.

"That's all I have time for because we must be on the lookout on the other side of the wall. We can't let Kyr have all the glory for saving our butts all the time, and we must do our part, even though she is the best lookout one can wish for. In the meantime, please accept the two of us on trust. As the saying goes, 'Trust, but keep your guns within easy reach.'"

Kyr spat angrily, as if offended, but didn't comment as she led them through the last of the dense thickets to the boundary. She waited for Daiyus to pick her up to look carefully over the stone wall. She could easily have jumped up, but experience had taught them that a quick, sudden movement attracted eyes more readily than cautious peeps. She didn't see anything suspicious, nor did she sense anything out of the ordinary. She told him that the road was quiet and to put her down on the wall. They scrambled over after her.

Shortly before they reached the road, Kyr commanded them to stay put until she told them that it was okay to move.

47

She melted into whatever cover was available.

Dai took a bundle out of his backpack that looked like short, thick wooden dowels. He screwed them together to form a seamless cane. He then measured the distance from the ground to Kinta's hand and took a shorter dowel out, which he returned to his backpack. He handed her the cane with an explanation. "This is a nice cane to complete your disguise as an older woman. It's made from a light metal and is quite strong, so you can use it as a weapon for close encounters. It won't bend if you hit someone over the head, but the best way to use it is to shove the point into an eye or any other vulnerable place.

"From now on, you are my mother, Fov Pabruk, and you are booked at the hotel as such. You must practice walking bent over just a little, using the cane only now and then as a support and only to keep your balance. Let me show you how to behave as my mom while we wait for Kyr to call us when she has completed her reconnaissance," he continued.

"Take that tracksuit off and put this light overcoat and the flat shoes on. It is warmer than the tracksuit, which is out of place on an old lady anyhow. Remember, for your own and my continued health, not to walk like a proud, young girl, and never forget that you're supposed to be a living fossil with hunched shoulders, although not obviously so. Stoop just a little, and bend your shoulders somewhat. Walk with your chin somewhat tucked in, and keep your knees slightly stiff."

9

Kinta tried hard and memorized every correction, so when Kyr thought-flashed them to get going, she was confident she could pose as a woman past her prime. She could even imitate a mother's disapproval. When they reached the road, she asked a question that had been bothering her. "I'm not sure whether it's polite to ask this question, but I'd like to know who's the leader—you or Kyr."

Dai laughed. "We're a team and it doesn't matter. I never take command, but I usually make the decisions in human company and she does in her environment, or, as a matter of fact, whenever she feels like it, for she is like a mother. She is more intelligent than any human I know, and I respect her more than any human, but I'm not sure she has respect for any human, including me. I suppose we also love each other, but it's a special bond I cannot describe with words. I'd feel lost without her, for she has been looking after me since I was knee high to a stork with short legs. I think that...no...*I know* that I will drop everything and follow anyone who harms her to hell and back until I catch up."

"I think I'm vaguely beginning to understand how you feel," Kinta said. "She reminds me of the mother I cannot remember." She didn't see Dai giving her an odd look because at that moment she also heard Kyr's advice to Daiyus to apply the lotion to remove his disguise because she had come across a clean brook a little way down the road.

Dai fished a tube out of a pocket and squeezed some lotion into his hand, which, after concealing the tube again, he applied to his face and hands. At the brook he washed his hands and face with a small squeeze of liquid soap from another tube and then rinsed. He removed the cap and looked up at Kinta with a mischievous smile.

"You...you...you're..." Kinta swallowed hard. "...the effeminate pretty boy with the golden-brown hair I saw chatting up the very attractive receptionist at the hotel last night! I wouldn't have believed that you could knock a fly over with your best effort!" she gasped in astonishment.

"Another valuable disguise, don't you think? She knows me as Pob," he said and laughed heartily. "We're booked in as Pob and his mom, Fov Pabruk, and we share adjoining rooms. Please memorize the names, since Pob and his mother really exist. We have to be prepared in case someone decides to check up on us. Call me 'Pob' or 'Son' from now on, even if it feels silly. You'll get used to it. In real life Pob is a famous long-distance runner and his mom is his dedicated trainer, which gives us a reason to take to the wilds if we have to. It also explains my athletic build and the reason I have to stay running fit.

"The real Pob and his mom know about me and are reported to be really amused when they receive surprise prizes, as they call them, for races he never participated in. I also pass on any medals I receive, to keep the impersonation genuine. Before you ask, there's additional payment for using his identity. It is also said that he and I could have been twin brothers, but we have never met. The Fighters take them on an all-expenses-paid, incognito holiday when I need his identity, and they tell him about his meeting someone special if I have to deal with anyone he may meet in the future.

"Pob's next race is cross-country in very rugged terrain, including mountains. When I checked in, I emphasized that my mom might join me in a day or two, as we have decided to train in the foothills of the mountains that surround Bojon, which is ideal for my next challenge. I introduced the thought so we have a legitimate reason to take to the countryside without too many questions being asked if your rescue was problematic.

"Now, Mom, may I put your old rucksack into my almost empty one to hide it? Kyr overheard your victim saying that they know it very well, and, besides, it will be all over the city by morning if Pretty Boy let his old mother carry her own bulky luggage."

"Uh, I was going to transfer the contents I took from Morcun to the new rucksack. Will that be okay?"

"Sure, just stuff the old one into the new."

After those tasks were completed, Dai shouldered both his and her bags. They walked back into the city's business area, talking quietly about Fov Pabruk's character and the severe discipline she exercised over Pob to make the most of his natural aptitude for long-distance races until the time someone better came along to beat him.

When it at last penetrated her bewildered mind that they would be returning to the hotel she dreaded to see again, she almost panicked. She geared up to hit Dai's shin with the walking stick to disable him, but he received a timely warning from Kyr. He quickly explained that the hotel would be the last place they would expect her and that they wouldn't connect an old woman with the wanted girl as long as she stayed away from her old room, which would be under surveillance and bugged with every available device. The connecting first-floor rooms were arranged so that Kyr could guard her while Dai made arrangements for their departure. Kyr would jump in through his window every night by way of the fire escape, which passed conveniently beneath his window. Otherwise, he would have lowered a special sling for her because, for their mutual safety, they never slept apart.

It was still early when they reached the business district between the park and the hotel. At an optical shop, Dai purchased a pair of tinted glasses just dark enough to hide Kinta's young eyes. As they left the vicinity of the shop, Kinta was astonished to see Dai visibly transform. His whole manner changed in an eyewink. His shoulders slumped almost imperceptibly and his balanced, easy stride changed into a cocky almost strut. When he pasted an easy grin on his face, the manly self-assuredness was replaced by a boyish cockiness.

She was amazed at the transformation and said so. With the same confident grin, he assured her that the real Pob walked and acted like this and that he must assume someone might see him and report out-of-character behavior or a different posture. One must never forget to maintain the character one is imitating, he emphasized. Kinta was astonished. Even his voice had changed.

She had decided to accept Dai's assurance that she would be safe at the hotel, but her apprehension increased as they neared their destination.

Kyr told him of Kinta's almost out-of-control panic and then went her own way. It would attract attention if the cat accompanied them, and she wanted to catch her own supper anyway. Humans tended to overcook meat, and she preferred hers in its natural state.

Dai suggested that they stop at the coffee shop across the street from the hotel. He explained that they might as well have some decent coffee to raise their caffeine levels to abnormal, which brought a smile to Kinta's old-looking face and strangely relaxed her jumpy nerves.

Distracted and relaxed by his witty, nonsensical conversation, she was back to her normal courageous self by the time they finished their second cups.

When they entered the hotel lobby, the same girl was on duty again. Her face lit up. "Oh, *hellooo*, Pobby! I was *wondering* what happened to *yeow*. Is this your dear, *dear* mother, Fov, you spoke of *sooo* lovingly?"

The insincere tone of voice and the words came across as so silly that Kinta snorted in an almost normal voice before she could stop herself. She recovered and smiled at the girl. "*Pobby?* That's a good one! I must remember it." She softened the tone of her voice: "Yes, I'm the idiot's mother, and I love him to distraction—when I think of him. Does he behave himself in your company, or should I clobber him a few times?"

The girl laughed easily, but Dai noticed an almost imperceptible hardening of her eyes. On show as "Pobby," he coughed embarrassedly. "Ahem! Mother, this is Sorcuk. If you don't mind, I'd like to take her to supper with us tonight—if you're not too tired from your journey, that is. She's going off duty at eight."

Kinta put out a hand, remembered her pasted-on age, and gave the girl a limp handshake. She immediately received the impression that the girl was hostile for some obscure reason, but she said, "It's nice of you to remember my name, Sorcuk. I'll be glad to have you, girl, but I'm tired and must rest for a while. Will you take me to my room, Son?" She fought the urge to giggle hysterically about this silly role she was forced into, but fiercely controlled her facial muscles since her life might depend on it. Still, she wondered what made this girl hostile toward an old woman she had never met. She decided not to mention this first impression, but a sixth sense warned her there was something very wrong with this girl.

"Sorry about the almost blunder with my voice," she

whispered as they climbed the stairs slowly, to suit her apparent age. "I was taken by surprise by the hussy's familiarity and false sincerity. How do you manage to slip so easily from one role to the other? I saw you change, and I still can't believe my eyes."

"Practice, Mom, practice, that's the secret, but one should always think two steps ahead and not be distracted from the disguise of the moment. It's not unusual for older women to have young-sounding voices, and I thoughtfully warned her last night that she may find your voice a bit odd. I may be wrong, but I have this odd feeling that Sorcuk is a dangerous woman to have as an enemy.

"Did you notice how many 'guests' loiter in or near the reception area? I think they are just covering all avenues to catch an innocent girl who escaped a deadly conspiracy. I should have remembered to buy you a suitcase, because an old lady with a backpack is a bit unusual. I must keep in character while I play the role of Pob Pabruk, and fortunately I told Sorcuk and everyone else who showed any kind of interest in me that we planned training runs in this ideally suited countryside.

"I'm not a sensitive, but I have an uneasy feeling that something is out of place. Maybe it's just my overactive imagination. Ah, yes, as I told you, this is a hotel where listening devices are routinely planted in the rooms of new arrivals, but I don't know why or by whom. There was one in my room last night, and I left it where it was. We should only speak of trivialities until I have checked our rooms for additional or new bugs."

In his room they made normal mother-and-son everyday conversation about supper and so on while he produced a miniature gadget from a hidden pocket and something else from another hidden pocket, quickly fitted them together, and put the earpiece into an ear. It seemed that his role as an empty-headed rich young man was already well spread because the listening device in his room was gone. He thought Sorcuk might be connected to the hotel's spy service and decided to play it safe in her company. Even last night he had noticed that too many people showed unusual respect for a mere receptionist, although they were not too obvious about it.

The two slowly moved to the connecting room and, as he dumped the rucksacks on the bed, the earpiece buzzed almost inaudibly. He followed the directional sound to an ornament on the comm-unit's table. He looked at it for only a moment before he pointed to it, then made sure the outside passage door in her room was locked and beckoned her to his room.

He switched on the radio, then opened his window, which was oiled to operate noiselessly, and motioned her out onto the fire escape. He closed the window again and told her in a low voice that the microscopic listening device he had found in her room was the very best he knew about and that it might be sensitive enough to pick up voices in his room as well.

"Last night I came to the conclusion that Sorcuk is only playing a role as a receptionist, but I have no evidence to confirm my suspicion. I suspect she is something more dangerous, and I'll be glad to shake the dust of this place off my feet. I have a sudden urge to see other places, and I think I should try to get seats on the fastest transport out of here late tonight or early tomorrow morning. I'll take the lady to the aerodrome for supper and see about getting seats on the first available aircraft out of here. Would you mind staying here this evening, with Kyr as a silent companion of course, and have a noisy supper in your room? You only have to think at her because talk is not necessary."

"I'd prefer it, to be honest, because I still feel nervous and out of my depth. I'll recover and adjust sooner if I'm on my own for a while, because I must get used to the idea that this face is not mine and that I'll not be recognized. What do you mean by 'having a noisy supper'?"

"Remember the bug? You have to play the role of Pob's mother to the limit. Complain, for instance, about an unappreciative son deserting you on your first night together in weeks. Clink the wine bottle against the glass very often, or the other way around, to give the impression that you're cork high and bottle deep. I'll flash Kyr to come and guard you as soon as it's dark, but she should be here before then."

He paused. "I know I was going to explain our presence in detail, but would a short explanation with evidence do for a while?"

10

"Good enough for the time being," Kinta replied. She, too, had felt an intensified need to depart for remote places when they'd entered the lobby, but had ascribed it to her reluctance to return to the hotel. "I don't think you have unlimited resources, so I'll give you some of the money I 'liberated' from Morcun. As we entered the lobby, I received this strange impression that we're both in danger, so get us out of here by any means you can, and don't spare the expense. It's funny, you know. I've never trusted anyone in my life, but I feel I can trust you with my life. I can't explain it, but I feel safe with you and Kyr. I know, of course, that temple cats are totally incorruptible, and Kyr acts like a mother."

"She does that. Thank you for the trust. We won't let you down, ever, because we promised your parents that we'll protect you if you really are their lost daughter—which you are, believe me. But apart from that, since you're a ward of the Fighters, we are obliged to protect you with our lives, and that you can take for granted. I want to pump Sorcuk for information tonight, but I have this strange intuition that I must be extremely cautious. It might not be wise to allow traffic in your room after I'm gone because you are supposed to be an old woman, and Kyr always leaves a bloody mess if she has to do away with anything bigger than a hare. Let's go in for a moment so I can get the evidence I promised you and also ask Sorcuk to arrange supper for you. She asked me yesterday to let her arrange anything I want because she has the contacts and the know-how, which should have warned me to be on my toes. I sometimes am a bit slow on the uptake when I'm tired."

He followed her back into the room and produced a battered-looking leather travel bag from the storage locker. From a secret compartment he extracted a glossy photo sheet and handed it to her while putting a finger to his lips to indicate silence.

While she looked at it, he activated the comm-unit and asked Sorcuk if she would arrange an ample supper and a bottle of wine for his mother at seven thirty, since she wasn't feeling her sprightly self and preferred to relax tonight to recover. He asked her a few questions about certain types of food and then deactivated the comm-unit before motioning Kinta through the window again.

He silently closed the window and told her, "Our Sorcuk seemed quite pleased that you won't accompany us tonight. She's quite knowledgeable about food, too, for she recommended a certain restaurant at the aerodrome when I asked about certain dishes I'd noticed there when we arrived that seemed quite popular. So it wasn't *my* request that we go to the aerodrome. I'll try and find a way to book seats without her knowledge, if possible."

He pointed to the picture in her hand. "That shows you with your father and mother on your fifth birthday. That was the last picture taken before you were abducted. You can see that you're almost an exact copy of the older woman, even at that age. She is, of course, now a dozen or so years older." He smiled. "But still without your current wrinkles."

Kinta again looked skeptically at the clear picture in the fading light. She shivered suddenly. "Yes, the woman looks like me, but the accident in which my parents were killed is still vividly in my mind, and I remember they didn't look like this. So tell me the real story behind this fabrication…"

Dai threw his arms up in exasperation, but he stayed calm. "I should have waited until Kyr returned, but time is something we don't have at the moment, and you'll want to hear this from me. Please listen with an open mind, and remember that you've been bombarded repeatedly with false images under deep hypnosis. Then think about what I tell you, and talk to Kyr, because she has the story directly from the mother you were very close to, and, as you should know, a cat never lies. Will you listen to me now—because it's cold, almost dark, and near seven, and we should go in soon?"

She smiled and nodded, and he continued. "We were told that your first name is Tumarok."

Kinta's senses reeled when she heard that name, and she gasped audibly. Dai grabbed her, fearing she might fall off the steps.

After a few moments she told him she was okay and he

continued. "Your father is a very wealthy and influential merchant in Dronin. He has very important contacts all over the world and buys and sells just about everything, from spices to strategic minerals. Your mother is a high official in the government of Dronin. Just after your fifth birthday, you were kidnapped on your way to a party. Another little girl was murdered, as was your family's chauffeur, and the kidnapping was made to look like an accident. The ground car was set ablaze, and the occupants were burnt beyond recognition, but your father, being the meticulous man he still is and knowing the chauffeur, had autopsies done by the very best medics and confirmed that it wasn't his daughter's remains in the car.

"Your parents expected to receive a demand for a huge ransom, but it never materialized. As time passed, they realized there were other motives for stealing their only child. She was one of those rare children born to the Palim who are physically abnormally strong and possess inborn psychic abilities that should be carefully trained from the age of seven, when children normally begin to develop.

"Your parents paid many fortunes to opportunists for what proved to be false or fabricated information, and they employed the very best detectives from different nations to try and trace your whereabouts. Your mother also used her influence in the government to make inquiries, but not the slightest trace of who took you and what happened to you was found throughout the years. They are not the type to lose hope and give up, however. They persisted.

"A few months ago, word filtered through to them that a very efficient young female assassin was being offered for hire at astronomical prices by an institution known by the name of Operations. The somewhat superabilities attributed to her made your parents think it might be their lost child. Your father started discreet inquiries as to how he could obtain the services of the special assassin, but every inquiry from him or your mother using official sources was rebuffed, which was suspicious, of course. It gave your father the incentive to persist, and he somehow recruited someone within that organization who was willing to furnish a description for a suitable bribe.

"Now, it's time for me to get dressed and for you to enjoy your supper. Most of the booze you can pour into the toilet and flush. But to finish up, your father was sure then that he had found you, and he approached the Fighting Priests for assistance to bring you out alive and unharmed using any suitable means. Two weeks ago, the highly paid contact in that notorious institution let him know that you and Morcun had left for Bojon, but he didn't know who the target was or when the hit would take place. There was no time for careful planning, but it was thought that Kyr, with her special talents, and I were the best hope for getting you out of here. We had to come from the other side of the world in a hurry, and it seems we arrived just in time. Ah, here she is. Hi, Kyr."

Kyr had arrived as silently as a ghost and was waiting for the window to be opened. She silently jumped through, telling them to follow her: *We may have foiled a very carefully planned operation today, and we don't have the resources to fight back on their terms. Get dressed and get going, stupid. Get us out of here any way you can, even if you have to steal a spaceship. We may not have much time, for we have disturbed a very, very big hornets' nest, and they are buzzing around for blood, but they don't know whose blood yet, and perhaps any blood will do.*

Daiyus whispered, "Will it be all right if I leave now? Kyr can tell you more and answer questions. I will fill in any gaps later, but I doubt there will be any."

Kinta wanted to believe what Daiyus had told her, but she felt a need for more information, and she really wanted to be called Tumarok—it strangely felt right. She had fervently wished for a way out of Operations, and now she had a golden opportunity with expert help thrown in for free. She nodded and quickly went to her room. After a few minutes, she returned with a big wad of money. She entered quickly without thinking to knock and caught Dai almost naked, since he had started to undress.

She blushed and looked away, but smiled at his discomfort and put the money down on the bed. She whispered, "Keep this. There's a lot more where that comes from. Enjoy your meal and come back soon. I'm nervous and won't be able to sleep before you're back. There is something about you and Kyr that makes me trust the pair of you without question."

He thanked her, showered quickly, dressed, and went out just as the waiter with Tumarok's (he must start calling her

Tumarok to let her remember the suppressed name and associated memories) supper on a trolley passed his door. He paused instinctively until Kyr told him, *Don't worry about us. We can easily wipe the floor with this pipsqueak. On the surface he seems to be okay. Your date is waiting impatiently, and she made sure that your "mother" will be well looked after. She alerted security, and they'll be wide awake to respond, even if, in her own words, the old lady so much as sneezes loudly. Go on and enjoy yourself for a change, Dai.*

11

As Daiyus locked his door, the waiter came out of the adjoining room with a big smile on his pinched face, admiring a too-generous tip in his hand. Dai felt that Tumarok had made a mistake and made a mental note to warn her about flashing money around. He knew he needn't worry about her safety tonight, since she was capable of looking after herself, and with Kyr, she would be unbeatable, but he wondered why he didn't feel too happy about leaving them alone. Perhaps it was his training to act responsibly. On the other hand, he had a job to do, and it could be made more pleasant by Sorcuk, as she'd already proved last night. It was just past seven thirty, and he knew that Sorcuk would have to pull a couple of strings to be able to leave so early. He hurried downstairs.

Tumarok did her best to suppress her life as Kinta and, encouraged by Kyr, played her role as the deserted mother who hadn't seen her only son for quite a while and was being deserted by him on their first night together. She found that she enjoyed the playacting as a relief from the loneliness and boredom that usually was her fate.

Kyr waited patiently until Tumarok had finished her supper and had poured most of the wine out in the bathroom. She had hunted for her own supper, which she preferred to spiced and overcooked human dishes.

Tumarok acted intoxicated when the waiter arrived to clear the dishes. He presented her with a "complimentary bottle of wine from management," he said, "to show appreciation for her and her son's valued custom." She sensed that the "compliment" was insincere, which immediately made her suspicious, and when she saw that the bottle had been opened, warning sirens went off in her mind. She told him in carefully slurred words that she would personally thank management and reached toward the comm-unit.

Hurriedly, the waiter assured her that they already had gone home, and anyway, it was quite unnecessary to thank them since nobody ever did so and it wasn't expected. That confirmed her suspicion, and she didn't even touch the bottle with a fingertip after the grinning waiter left. Kyr told her it was a wise decision because she had sensed that the waiter had treachery in mind, something to do with unconsciousness or sleep. To ease Tumarok's fear that she could read minds, she told a half-truth, saying the waiter's thoughts were so chaotic she couldn't quite sense what it was. Perhaps he thought with the bottom end of his digestion tract, she said. Then she asked the girl to check that the door was properly locked so they wouldn't be interrupted while they talked.

Tumarok was seated on the bed facing Kyr, who sat alertly on the chair in front of her. The conversation was silent and mostly one way: *Don't use your voice anymore, Cookie. Dai summed up quite briefly what we have been told. I just want to add this because I did not have the time or thought to tell Dai about it. Think at me if you have a question, okay?*

The girl nodded her head.

What I'm going to tell you first is what Morcun reflected upon this morning as he murdered the paymaster. I won't go into detail, but the directors of the place you call Operations sent him to Dronin to gather certain information when he was a young man with too much ambition and marvelous plans. He became a drinking pal of your family's driver, whom he killed when he abducted you, but he lived in dread that you would kill him if you found out that he'd abducted you for his own purposes. When you were hypnotized, which was more often than you would believe, he planted and reinforced a command for you to never kill him under any circumstances. Fortunately, he slipped up. He never thought of commanding you to not hurt him, which was a very serious mistake. He and his greedy masters really messed up your psychic potential just to forge you into an obedient killing tool for their insatiable appetite for power and luxuries. Now ask your questions.

Tumarok thought her question to Kyr. *Why do you call me Cookie? I'd resent that from anyone but you, and coming from you, I sort of like to hear it.*

It's because I'm also female, Kyr replied. *Your mother called you her sweet cookie, and your father called you Tumar. She thought, and I hoped, that your subconscious might remember that nickname and make you feel comfortable with me, which really did make our task easier. I like to use it, though, as it makes me feel motherly. Anyway, your mother and I had a long talk, and she told me many things about you.*

Your parents were told that you were kept drugged for a very long time, and then you were deeply hypnotized and given false memories over and over. I could remove the false impressions but would hesitate to do so without expert help, unless an emergency develops that makes it imperative. Your parents were also told that your hypnotic blocks are routinely reinforced—without your knowledge, of course. Those pretentious leeches may have damaged your natural talents irreparably, and for what? They just want to feed their greed and don't give a thought for those they misuse or destroy for the sake of filthy lucre to live an easy life of false grandeur and imagined respectability! I would like to feel my claws embedded in their multilayered throats!

Tumarok almost smiled when she received the violently transmitted eloquence. *What are you and Daiyus really?* she thought to Kyr. *It seems that Daiyus can defeat five trained men in about as many seconds. He must be finely trained.*

Now you are fishing in forbidden streams, Cookie. But Kyr was not annoyed, for she sensed that the girl was not digging for information to use against them. *I can tell you this, though, because he already told you that we are from the Fighters. He was trained by a very special man of the Fighting Priests, as they are called. You may have heard of Dart.* This was a test to drive a point home, and Kyr was alert.

Tumarok jumped up with a loud exclamation, as if stuck with a pin in her buttock, but before she was halfway up or could utter another sound that could alert anyone listening in on the planted bug, Kyr's superbly muscled, twenty-five kilogram body knocked her over onto her back on the bed. Before she could even think or respond automatically, she felt sharp claws prickling the skin on her neck, threatening to rip her throat open. She froze in shock. The close proximity of a viciously fanged, savage, and apparently enraged spitting cat was enough to smother any thought of resistance even before it formed. At the same time, the silent, penetrating command flashed fiercely into her stunned, bewildered brain.

Don't even move your bowels, Cookie, because I'll rip your throat out if you so much as even twitch your little toe. Think before you act, Cookie, and keep your mouth shut. That was a test to see if you're listening to what I tell you, but already you have dismissed as irrelevant what I told you a moment ago, that you were periodically implanted with false information and commands! Realize that you can overcome conditioning by thinking about it and pushing it into the background as unimportant! One of the many commands given to you is to kill Dart the moment you identify him because he is your ex-director's worst nightmare. I'm sworn to protect Dai, and I love the blundering idiot fiercely. Now think carefully: I didn't say he was Dart, and if you can't control your conditioning, I may have to enter your mind to show you how they have messed it up and try to purge some of the false commands you have been burdened with. I'm not qualified in that area, and you have to be absolutely calm because it's a dangerous thing to do alone. Now relax—and that's not a request!

Tumarok slowly calmed under the enforced inaction and the threat of the sharp claws in her neck and, even worse, the sharp white fangs and furious eyes so close to her nose, which, as intended, irresistibly held her attention. Somehow she forced her rushed breathing to slow down, and she started to think for herself. Yes, Kyr is right, she thought. She couldn't trust her reactions, but she must accept the help and advice of this remarkable cat crouched on her chest with her sharp front claws just touching the pulsing veins in her neck.

Before Tumarok was quite calm, Kyr suddenly stiffened and retracted her claws, jumped away, and commanded her in no uncertain terms not to hesitate one second but to quickly open and then close the door hard, lock it again, and then push the chair firmly under the doorknob. Tumarok was mystified but obeyed and did as ordered as fast as she could. Kyr then told her to grab her rucksack and come to Dai's room, and to slam the connecting door and lock it as well.

As the connecting door slammed closed, Kyr commanded her to block the door to this room as well. While the girl pushed a chair under the knob of the corridor door, Kyr explained: *That scrawny, rat-faced waiter you so thoughtlessly tipped beyond generosity and a crony are coming up the stairs to rob a drunk, ugly, dimwitted, rich old bitch of her money, and the night shift at*

63

reception is in on it. The two of them paused on top of the stairs to put masks on, although the other lowdown, sneaky little knave thinks that you have passed out by now because he drugged the wine the dense one presented you with. Now dial the hotel's security and tell them in a panicked voice that you just opened your door to go out and saw two masked men approaching your door, and they are now trying to break your door down. Be quick now and remember to identify yourself and give your room number.

Tumarok had been trained in the art of putting on an act, and when she had put the comm-unit down, Kyr reminded her that an old lady, as she was supposed to be, logically would not be able to defeat two young assailants, so if she did, it would be unusual enough to make even a brainless moron sit up straight and think. They must only try to delay the would-be robbers long enough for the hotel's security to wake up. If they managed to break in before then, Tumarok would have to disable the robbers with the cane that should still be somewhere in the room, and ascribe it to an act of desperation. Kyr would stay around, but she could only participate if things went seriously wrong, since she would leave too much of a mess that could not be explained away.

The comm-unit was scarcely down on its hook when there was a loud knock on the adjoining room's door. When it wasn't answered, Kyr heard a key grate in the lock and then a curse as the door would only open to a crack before it stuck. A slight pause, then a supposedly cunning subterfuge: "Hello, Mrs. Pabruk. I just want to know if you are okay."

When no answer came, he grunted in a bullying tone, "The drunken old hag had time to barricade the door before she passed out from the wine she gulped down her wrinkled old throat. The stupid old bitch must have tasted something wrong, or you were stingy with the sleeping drug, you damn idiot."

Tumarok smiled wickedly. She picked up the light metal cane, which was leaning against the wall near the connecting door, in her right hand, hefted it twice, and then leaned against the wall to relax while she waited for the door to be forced open. If security didn't arrive in time, the robbers were in for a nasty surprise and broken kneecaps when they broke this door down.

She heard thuds and grunts as they slowly shouldered the

barricade out of the way, and then loud curses as the light came on and they realized they had been outwitted. There was no attempt at silence anymore, and she overheard the waiter telling his accomplice to check if the same key would unlock the door of the adjacent room and to guard it if it didn't. He must clobber the old hag good if she tried to escape with the money she flashed around so foolishly. Then he began to kick the connecting door. It was obvious they had made sure there was no one else on this floor, and perhaps nobody directly above or below who could complain about the noise.

Tumarok suddenly grinned wickedly; she would use the mini stun gun if they gained entry and then clobber them over the heads to make it look good. It could be explained away and would be the least effort. She was fed up with greedy individuals who didn't care how they enriched themselves or who got hurt in the process, as long as it wasn't them. A terrific headache might be a grim reminder for a few days to make them think twice about robbing defenseless old ladies.

Fortunately, just as the door started to splinter, three men from the hotel's security arrived and arrested two very surprised masked men. Caught in the act of breaking in to rob a quivering old woman, they couldn't offer a protest of innocence. It was a genuinely relieved old woman who tearfully thanked the three handsome young men who had saved her from being murdered. Kyr had disappeared under the bed so she could remain unseen but still protect Tumarok if necessary.

One of the security officers offered to accompany her downstairs so she could put her valuables in a safe-deposit box. She protested that there weren't any and that she hadn't realized she had given the now unmasked waiter a big note. She hadn't even looked at it because she was upset that her only son, whom she hadn't seen for a month, had left her alone on their first evening together to take a girl out to supper. "It just shows you what happens when an ungrateful child does not respect an aging mother who gave up everything to help him," she said. Tumarok was starting to enjoy the role she was playing, and she knew that her harping would make them anxious to leave quickly.

The senior security officer smiled knowingly, but with a pained look in his eyes, and said he would see about getting her another room, to which she replied that she would rather wait for her uncaring son so that he could see what danger his thoughtlessness had gotten her into.

Kyr silently told her to lay the honey on with a trowel now because the security personnel were somewhat suspicious of her reluctance to move.

Tumarok assured them she felt safe, now that such brave, unselfish men had rushed to see to her safety and had arrested the evil robbers. It was unlikely that someone else would try to steal what little she had, with three such alert young men ready to pounce on them. The outside door locks weren't damaged anyway. She couldn't thank them enough and made them feel themselves the heroes they had come to think they were. Tearfully, Tumarok really buttered up the three "handsome" men, saying she wished they were her own sons. They blushed but lapped it up.

They eventually left, handling the dejected robbers roughly. They promised they would come in an instant if she called, and of course the old woman, convincingly leaning on her cane as if tired, thanked them profusely for being so prompt and courageous. She firmly locked her own room after them and pushed a somewhat battered chair under the knob again.

Relieved that everything had turned out better than she'd hoped, she thanked the cat by thinking at her, *I'm so glad that you and Daiyus agreed to come and rescue me. I don't think I can ever thank the two of you enough. I could have been dead thrice over today if it wasn't for you.*

She received a chuckling reply, which she interpreted as the cat's equivalent of hearty laughter. *My dear Cookie, didn't you listen to what we said? We weren't asked! The truth is that your parents asked the council of the Fighting Priests to verify that you were their daughter, then have you abducted and de-hypnotized, and then be told the truth of who you really are. We were ordered that if you had any resemblance to your mother in the picture, we were to make you defect in any way we could, or abduct you as a last resort and see to your safety. We followed you around, since we didn't know how to go about it, and are extremely grateful that it wasn't necessary to coerce you against your will.*

Tumarok started to laugh uncontrollably, almost

hysterically, and Kyr knocked her over onto Dai's bed, but gently this time. Tears were streaming down the girl's cheeks, and she impulsively hugged an uncomplaining Kyr.

Kyr usually wouldn't allow such human familiarity, but she had developed a soft spot for this unfortunate girl. She purred and comforted the girl as if she were her own kitten. When Tumarok fell asleep at last, Kyr crept out of the embrace and sat down next to her to keep watch.

12

To his dismay, Dai was still being addressed as "Pobby." Being called "Pob" would have been all right, but Sorcuk persisted in using that stupid moniker as if she owned him, and some sort of intuition warned him that he couldn't risk irking her by objecting. It was insincere and irritated him, so he showed his appreciation with an idiotic grin every time she uttered the offensive, belittling name.

The moment they alighted from the public transport system at the aerodrome, he saw that every entrance, sales counter, and check-in point was being monitored closely by an unusual number of men and women. They were careful about it, but he was a finely trained observer, and it was immediately obvious to him that they were on the alert for someone, and that someone could only be Tumarok. But why was she hunted so persistently? She wasn't that important, except perhaps to the late Hezmet's bosses and employees, and they just couldn't have any say in Bojon. It was one of those enigmas he intensely disliked, and he didn't dare start inquiries.

Even before their meal was served, it was confirmed that there was much, much more to Sorcuk's real occupation than he had been allowed to glimpse. She was extremely careful, but he was meticulously trained to interpret every nuance and expression. He noticed the almost imperceptible exchange of signals by passing men and women, and she excused herself a little too often to go to the ladies' room after they had passed by. Even to her it should have been obvious that no one could have a bladder that weak all of a sudden, but it pleased him immensely to see that she didn't have much of an opinion of the character he was playing.

He also noted that too many people were idling at strategic points, trying to act casual but not succeeding very well. Even a layman would have noticed the covert alertness, and a half-asleep person with a guilty conscience would immediately be warned. In his book they came across as amateurs because it was obvious that some of them were there to watch his every move, waiting for him to make a false move. He made a show of enjoying the meal and ate more than he normally would.

If Sorcuk was a member of this small, one-city-one-country's security, as he suspected, what made her suspicious of him? There was no accurate description of him on record anywhere—even as Dart—that he was aware of, and Dart was not a criminal. On the contrary, he was feared as the nemesis of criminals. He thought about his suspicion and then mentally kicked himself for his stupidity and lack of attention to detail. He realized that Sorcuk would have checked up on his "mother's" arrival, which he had forgotten to think about and explain, but then, how could he have guessed that a hotel's attractive receptionist was not a genuine receptionist, but someone high up—he was now sure—in Bojon security? He realized a little too late that a man can easily misjudge someone so pretty in an innocent-looking job, and perhaps she made use of that possibility. With his training and background, he should have been on guard, but it was tiresome to think of everyone he met as being suspect or a potential enemy.

He sighed heavily and started to formulate a plausible answer to a direct question to explain his "dear mother's" unrecorded arrival, but he arrived nowhere very quickly. The question remained uppermost in his mind, and he knew his subconscious mind would work on it. He could only hope that he would not be asked to explain before he was ready with a plausible answer.

After the meal, he suggested they take a stroll around the aerodrome's public area to let the heavy meal settle before they had coffee somewhere else. While they strolled, he noticed that every female arriving, regardless of age, was secretly compared to a concealed photograph in the observer's left hand. The right hand, he assumed, was being kept free to grab for a weapon, for the girl assassin known as Tuala was a dangerous kitten indeed. Those who probably had the right proportions and age were surreptitiously being isolated and herded, he guessed, to an interrogation room after they passed the check-in points. He looked at the day's electronic arrival and departure boards, hoping for some inspiration to explain his mother's arrival.

He became aware that two men and a pretty, blond,

athletic-looking girl, all in their middle to late twenties, had been following them for a while. He sensed that he was marked, but for what? He wished he had Kyr's ability to eavesdrop on people's thoughts so he could be prepared, but it seemed that the goddess of luck had deserted him tonight.

He couldn't help but notice a powerful-looking, middle-aged man, striding along as if he owned the aerodrome and perhaps even the rest of the world, approach a check-in counter. The rugged, oddly attractive man suddenly stopped when he saw Dai. He frowned as if he was trying to remember something.

If Dai had seen this man before, he would have remembered, for he had a truly remarkable, powerful-looking physique and moved lightly on his feet like a trained fighter. At last a faint memory stirred at the back of his mind, but the man suddenly snapped the fingers of his right hand and smiled broadly. He said something to the hostess at the counter and approached, with his eyes fixed on Dai's face, right hand half extended in greeting, smiling broadly all the while. He obviously was proud of his superb memory.

Dai pasted a questioning frown and half smile onto his face, narrowed his eyes as if he were beginning to recognize the man, and went to meet him—for the man's eyes were riveted on him only. This clearly was an incident of mistaken identity again, and he had to play along, whether he wanted to or not. Dai smiled genuinely when he thought that this was one of those awkward situations when one suddenly finds it convenient to remember a place where one should have been an hour ago.

To his dismay, Sorcuk suddenly clung like a leech onto his arm, which irritated him like never before, but he couldn't just shake her off. He mentally prepared to disable or kill her and anyone else if it became necessary, but first he would see what this chance meeting brought in the way of unprepared-for trouble or blessing.

As the man opened his mouth to speak, Dai beat him by a split-second: "I know that I should recognize you, sir, but it seems that you already have the advantage. I'm Pob Pabruk." He extended his right hand enthusiastically.

He didn't have a single weapon on him, but he could fight with his bare hands and feet like a cornered rat if unmasked, he thought wryly. Anything could serve as a weapon when he had none, but if it came to that, he would try to flash a warning to Kyr so that she and Tumarok could make an escape.

Then the stranger grabbed his hand and pumped it enthusiastically, trying to crush it without success. Dai tightened his grip just enough to prevent it. "I never forget a face," the stranger bragged. "I'm Bazir, as you might remember. We only met briefly about two years ago when you thrashed my younger brother Kumet in that race in the semidesert of Rashidin. I brought a load of tourists in this morning, and now I have to rush back. How did your dear mom make out? How is she?"

Dai didn't have a clue what the guy was talking about but could have hugged him. When he mentioned his name, the light finally flashed on blindingly. This man was known all over the world as the very rich and daring tour operator who rescued an expedition from the perilous jungle on Shaytan, the fifth planet, three years ago. He didn't have the faintest clue what Bazir was talking about, but he seized the opportunity with both hands:

"But of course! Now I remember! My mother is in fine fettle, although a bit tired at the moment, thank you, sir. She traveled incognito, as usual when she is alone, to escape attention. She is now resting, I fervently hope." The explanation was for Sorcuk's information but it really was true for the real Fov. He sincerely hoped that Bazir wouldn't query this uncalled-for, moronic-sounding statement, but it was the heaven-sent answer he had been praying for.

To take Bazir's mind off the subject, Dai said, "Maybe I should give you a tip you can pass on to your brother if you like. We came here to train for the race in Bireria in two months' time because the terrain is similar, but harder. I am becoming too bigheaded, and I must finish second sooner or later. Oh, pardon me"—he hoped to distract the man's attention further—"this lovely lady's name is Sorcuk. She rescued me from my mother for the evening, for which I'm grateful."

Bazir laughed heartily without batting an eyelid and shook her hand with equal enthusiasm. "Glad to meet you, Sorcuk. I'd like to stay a while and get acquainted, but I'm late and have to rush. I just wanted to say hello." He glanced at his watch a second time. "Now I have to run. Look me up when you're in town again, Pob, but try to escape from your mom. Bring her along if you can't." He laughed heartily, which seemed to be a

71

habit with him, but it was well known that Pob's mom was possessive. He pumped Dai's hand again and left with his usual confident smile.

Dai genuinely blessed the man from deep in his heart. Sorcuk, or her superiors, might accept that explanation until they'd checked everyone's whereabouts on Bazir's passenger manifest. He didn't think they would, though, since it would be an unnecessary time- and manpower-consuming task. He made a mental note to ask Kyr to report this meeting so Pob could be prepared if he met Bazir again.

He saw Sorcuk passing a signal to the girl at the desk and the observers at the check-in, and a clearly surprised-looking Bazir was let through without the usual checks. She must be a bigwig for someone so young, he thought with consternation. She fooled me, all right, and good. He wondered what would happen next, because he still wanted to book seats out of Bojon, but a sixth sense, which he always heeded, warned him not to try it right now. He couldn't shake off the conviction that he still was in danger, and he couldn't even guess what had triggered that odd feeling—or was it a premonition?

As they passed the restrooms, Sorcuk asked to be excused once again, saying she hoped this problem would clear up before long. He wryly thought that if she was referring to her bladder, it surely would, but he suppressed the impulse to say so out loud. The attractive and well-shaped blond girl who had been following them went in after Sorcuk without hesitation, as if she, too, had suddenly developed a need. Dai thought the secretiveness was stupid and juvenile.

Because the two men with the blond eyed him intently, as if willing him to do something stupid, he entered the men's restroom to see what would happen. He realized that trouble was coming his way when they entered directly after him, almost crowding him into the room. He'd had plenty of experience in this type of tactic, and he knew he had to decide quickly whether to offer effective resistance in an untutored manner or just meekly submit to their punishment, as if he were an innocent victim. It could be a test engineered by Sorcuk, so he decided to follow his instincts as the situation developed. The way they rushed him made him expect to be beaten up, but he might learn something useful.

The one with the violent looking blue eyes seemed to be the leader. He was scarcely inside when he grabbed Dai by the front of his jacket and viciously slammed his back against the nearest wall. In the same motion, he expertly fished Dai's wallet from the inside pocket. He was obviously well versed in this type of search and had watched his victim's every move during the evening.

He tossed the wallet over to his companion and ordered, "Go through it." Then he viciously slapped Dai twice in the face with a hatred that really surprised Dai. "I'll teach you what happens to those who mess around with my woman, you conceited little schmuck. You won't be a pretty boy when I'm finished with you!" He pinned Dai against the wall with his left arm, obviously expecting little or no resistance, and hit him hard in the face with his right fist, apparently thinking his victim not even worthy of the classical punch to the ribs to wind him before working him over.

Dai didn't dodge the fist too noticeably. From his earliest childhood, he had been taught how to accept pain and control damage, for his life might depend on the ability to endure pain. He did so now as a matter of habit, which seemed to infuriate and drive his assailant over the edge. This man with the wild eyes obviously wasn't too sane, and Dai somehow sensed that he would be killed or maimed if he didn't take care of himself.

But first there had to be a lot of his own blood if he was to convince anyone that this maniac was hurt by an accidental fluke. Under any other circumstances, both men would already have been put painfully to sleep, but he had to remember that he was Pob the runner, not Dart the avenger. He was aware that Pob had started wrestling lessons two months ago to improve his stamina but that he wasn't good at it yet. Dai hoped the guy would improve soon, for it would help him in situations such as this.

The second man seemed to wake up out of a bad nightmare and shouted in genuine alarm, "Stop it, Sergeant Mohaz! You're overreacting again. We were ordered to search this guy but not to harm him! Now you're trying to kill him, and you can see that he can't fight back. We'll be jailed and kicked out of the force. Stop it, please!"

"Shut up, you sissy, and mind your own business," Mohaz

grunted through his teeth. His eyes insane with bloodlust, he drew his fist back as far as he possibly could, intending to make this runt swallow his own teeth and disfigure him for the rest of his life if he survived this beating.

Dai felt the tension to gather power and knew the intention, but he also knew how to deflect the punch and make it look accidental. As Mohaz let fly with all his concentrated power behind the fist, Dai threw an arm up with a small cry of pretended fright and, as if by accident, his arm deflected Mohaz's fist just past his jaw. The fist ended up against the unyielding wall with a satisfying crunch of bones.

Mohaz's face contorted in shock, and he yelled in exquisite agony as if he were tormented past endurance by the devil. He arched his back and grabbed his injured hand with his left, while his terrible yell of utter agony seemed to make the restroom's walls vibrate in sympathy. At the same instant, he automatically stepped back half a pace and opened his legs as he began to bend over in terrible pain.

Well, such flukes could be explained away, but what happened next was pure, unconscious reflex as a result of years of grueling training. The inviting opening of the legs made Dai knee him with all the power he could muster before he could control himself. He knew the sergeant wouldn't be able to walk for at least two weeks, and then only with a peculiar shuffling gait and crutches for balance.

The door of the restroom crashed open with a bang, and Sorcuk, in the company of a more mature-looking woman, rushed in withdrawn guns as the hapless Mohaz fell stiffly onto his face, incapable of cushioning the impact. Like most bullies, he was good at inflicting pain, but couldn't take it himself. Seeing the women rush in, Dai quickly slumped head down on his heels and with a convincing groan clasped his bloody face between his hands. They mustn't see the satisfied look in his eyes.

"What the hell is going on here?" Sorcuk demanded harshly, but Dai wasn't looking at her. He knew he had to play a convincing role, so he groaned again for effect before he pointed a finger in the direction of the other man.

"They are assaulting and robbing me," he groaned in an agonized voice, as the real Pobby probably would have done, and it wasn't really an act anymore. His face was starting to throb as if in sympathy with Mohaz's self-pitying groaning. He didn't look up, so he couldn't see Sorcuk's furious face as she looked at the other man.

She gritted just one word, dripping with venom, through clenched teeth. "Explain!"

"We followed him in as ordered, Major," the man explained hurriedly in a parade-ground voice. So she's quite high up for one so young looking, Dai thought. "Sergeant Mohaz grabbed the suspect by the lapels, grabbed his wallet and threw it to me with the order to go through it. He seemed to lose control for some reason and started to hit the suspect in the face. I asked him to stop, but he told me to shut up. He then tried to deliver a killing blow, but the blow partly missed the suspect's face and ended against the wall. The suspect jerked his knee up in reflex to the painful blow. You heard the rest, Major. The content of the wallet says he is who he says he is, and there isn't a lot of money in it."

13

Through his bloody fingers, he saw Sorcuk put her gun away before she knelt in front of him. She took his hands tenderly away from his face, looked at it, then ordered the man to go fetch a first-aid kit on the double, ask the doctor to come to the small lounge, and tell someone to see to the removal of the "smelly bag of excrement" on the floor beside her.

Time to go into my act again, Dai thought. "I heard the man say that you're a major. Why did you order him to do this to me?"

"It wasn't my instructions," she said in a surprisingly gentle voice. "Someone obviously thought you were someone else and stupidly set Mohaz onto you. He has a reputation for getting out of hand. A state of emergency has been declared, and we are checking out everyone who arrived within the past few days and who leaves. You were under suspicion since we couldn't find your mother's name on any incoming flight manifest, but that was explained when you met Bazir. Unfortunately, there wasn't time to pass the information on."

She seemed to come to a decision. "Come with me, please. Let's attend to your face first, and I'll explain as much as I am officially allowed to. I'm very sorry this happened to you, but I assure you it wasn't on my say-so. The least that will happen to Mohaz is that he will be demoted to toilet cleaner, but I will do my level best to get him dishonorably dismissed, because he has a mean streak that cannot be tolerated in security matters."

Sorcuk returned his wallet, then led him to a small but luxurious lounge that obviously was for very important people only. They were met at the door by a medic, who checked Dai's face while Sorcuk cleaned it gently. The medic stitched a few deep cuts after administering a local anesthetic, then said the wounds must be sprayed with artificial skin to prevent infection and speed up healing but that there wasn't any at the aerodrome. He then left to attend to the hapless Mohaz.

While she cleaned his bloodied hands, Sorcuk said something into her wrist communicator. A few minutes later, the pretty blond girl with the athletic walk came in carrying a tray with a bottle labeled with a well-known brand of strong alcoholic drink and three glasses. She put the tray down on a chest-high table against one wall. Sorcuk introduced her to him but not the other way around.

"This is my half sister, Surra. She's a lieutenant in our local security force, and I've asked her to escort you back to the hotel. She is going off duty at midnight, and her apartment is in the city close to your hotel. In your condition I'm afraid that you might be arrested on suspicion or be assaulted to part you from your money. You really must learn to defend yourself. You have the muscles for it."

It sounded like a royal command. He assumed that Surra already knew who he was. He didn't show his surprise at the contrast between the half sisters. Sorcuk was a black-haired beauty with greenish-brown eyes, but her half sister sported honest, blue-gray eyes and honey-yellow hair, which couldn't be artificially colored because her aristocratic eyebrows were the same. Sorcuk could be called beautiful, he thought, but her half sister was absolutely stunning from close up. This was a face any man would kill for, he thought as she handed him a half-full glass. Surra's face was calm and composed as she nodded, so he just said, "Thanks," and swallowed half the drink.

"Oh, I took up wrestling some months ago," he said to Sorcuk, "but I wasn't given half a chance to defend myself. I am strong, but it would seem that I must become a better student." He acted rueful because his face was beginning to stiffen up. His lips felt pulpy, and he knew his face would be painful for the next few days. But it was a small price to pay for keeping his cover intact so they would be left in peace. He was thinking about how he should ask to be told what had really stirred up the hornets' nest, without sounding too inquisitive.

"Could you perhaps tell me what this is all about, please?" he asked with an apologetic tone in his voice.

"Well, this is a clandestine operation, and I'll be in trouble if I tell you too much right now." He sensed Sorcuk was lying, but what could she achieve by it? Was insincerity a habit?

"I don't think I'll be talking to anyone for a couple of days, including myself. My mouth is painful and will stiffen up. Whatever you are permitted to tell me, I promise not to repeat to anyone even if you tell me very little. You have my solemn word."

Sorcuk suddenly smiled. "Okay, I'll accept your word. We tend to be suspicious for no apparent reason, for we are a small, isolated nation surrounded by almost inaccessible mountains. Many of us are doubly employed—a chosen career and part-time employment in one of our security agencies, or the other way around. Anyway, late last night or early this morning, the king's governing council received information that a top-brass foreign spy paymaster would be assassinated at noon today, by either an elusive young man called Dart or a beautiful female assassin named Tuala. We have a picture of her, and she really is extraordinarily beautiful. Everyone connected with any of our security agencies was pulled in and has been given a copy of her picture. I'll give you a copy so you can report her if you 'run' across her."

She smiled, but he didn't return the smile. His voice was slurred because his mouth really felt stiff and awkward with the stitches and the local anesthetic.

"The supposedly young man called Dart is unknown. Nobody knows what he looks like, but we are told he is a master of disguise, and no one can tell whether he really is young, or old for that matter. For all we know, the girl might be him in disguise, or the other way around. Here is a copy of her picture—and she doesn't look like you, even remotely. You may keep it as a souvenir." She produced it out of an inner coat pocket and handed it over.

Dai was floored, though his face only showed it as a grim surprise. What, in all sorts of hell, was going on? It was almost, but not quite, Tumarok, though there was a remarkable resemblance. It could be a touched-up, full-length photo of her, but the color of the eyes told him it was a photo of her mother in her younger days. The late Morcun must have had a hand in this, and someone might be trying to be cute, but he couldn't even guess for what purpose. Was someone trying to get him, or both of them, killed—or what? He put the picture away in an inner pocket.

Sorcuk smiled, apparently misinterpreting the grim look on his battered face as astonishment. She took a sip of her drink and continued. "Yes, one wouldn't think that such a beautiful girl

78

became the most notorious and sought-after assassin of our age in, as reported, less than a year. We can't figure out what the connection between her and Dart is supposed to be. It doesn't fit our image, or more correctly, our knowledge of him.

"A state of emergency was declared this morning, and freedom of movement will be restricted from midnight until we find her. All exits from Bojon are closed as of this evening. Your acquaintance was the last one allowed out because we know he and his flight crew are above suspicion. Even the few snowed-in passes will be guarded by now, and every aircraft, spaceship, and hovercraft is grounded and guarded around the clock. Every avenue of escape is blocked. We'll search the city house by house if necessary." She seemed grimly satisfied.

"But"—Dai really was floored by this news—"But...but I was thinking of buying seats for me and my mother out of here because I can't train for at least a week with a face this painful." *A good thing I wasn't stupid enough to try and procure seats when we arrived*, he thought. *That would have been the final nail in our coffin for sure.*

"I'm sorry, but this restriction of movement is by royal decree."

She paused slightly, which gave Dai the impression that she was not telling him the whole truth.

"Not a single person will be allowed out of Bojon until one or both criminals are caught. That may take a week or two unless a person can get an audience with the king, which won't be easy because that person must first be thoroughly investigated. The best I can do is to try and get you permission or a travel permit allowing you to train outside the city limits or out in the country, as you intended doing anyway. Even that may prove to be difficult, as you and your mother would have to go on foot or use animals. I'll see what I can do about the permit in the morning. In the meantime, stay in or near your hotel until I let you know one way or the other. If I'm busy, I'll ask Surra or someone else to deliver the permit, but I can't promise it will be tomorrow."

Dai didn't show his dismay in any way, but he somehow felt that she was not telling the truth. It seemed the odds were overwhelmingly against them, but he was used to all kinds of setbacks, and at least he now knew what they faced. Now he could plan, and they could take to the wilds with little equipment if forced to go on the run. He had done it often in the past, and he knew what he would have to buy—or steal outright, if forced to. He shrugged his shoulders.

"I can't even give you a peck on the cheek, but I thank you from the bottom of my heart. If I must stay, I must, but I also must start training soon or I might as well stop my racing career right now instead of in a few years' time. I'll run, even if I have to carry my mother on my back every day. Please try to get us a permit for a pack animal at least so that we can camp out for a few days at a time, for I have to train in the foothills as well. We have done it before, although she complains and nags just about all the time." He tried to give the impression that he was just joking, but that he meant it seriously.

"I may see you tomorrow evening, but I can't say for sure. Surra, you two might as well get going, but we'll have another drink first. Take the bottle along because you're not in uniform. Pob may wish he was drunk by the time you reach the city center. And don't forget to visit the clinic for artificial skin as soon as you arrive in town." She paused while she turned away from them and poured fresh drinks into their glasses. "I think I can get authorization for an official hover car. Pob was attacked by a security official, after all, and he would be conspicuous on the public transport system."

It suddenly dawned on Dai that Sorcuk was an extremely cunning adversary. Any normal person would want to know the necessity for the severe restrictions. He was still being tested, and he had almost fallen for the subtle trap like an innocent amateur. He rectified his mistake by asking hesitantly, "I know I shouldn't ask, but could you at least tell me why the hubbub to catch one or two assassins for killing or trying to kill a foreign paymaster? Is the paymaster or the killer that important to cause all this inconvenience to everyone? I know my mom is going to nag the hell out me, but what am I to tell her?" He was thankful that his now painfully swollen lips made him sound so desperate.

Sorcuk smiled, but her eyes didn't reflect the smile on her mouth. He could almost sense her disappointment. What was she up to? This woman is as wily as a mad fox, he thought. Yesterday she seemed so soft and utterly feminine that he

80

would not have imagined, nor expected, this hardness, and, yes, ruthlessness. Sorcuk lifted her glass to him, forcing him to swallow some of the second drink she had pushed into his hand.

She continued, "I might as well tell you, because it will be the main topic on the early morning newscasts and during the day. Nine people were killed today. The first killing happened about noon—the paymaster, but the assassin killed himself accidentally by slipping in his victim's blood. Another man was attacked in the park by what seems to be a cat—or maybe this Tuala can transform herself into a cat. He was killed by having his Adam's apple crushed with a blunt instrument. A priest from the local Aikon temple was definitely attacked and killed by a cat or catlike creature in a wild area of the park. Five others were found dead in a clearing next to him, with expressions of disbelief on their faces, as if they had witnessed a supernatural event, perhaps a shape-changing. Tell your mom only that the reason for the restriction is that people were killed and nothing else. She can look at the telecasts on the hour from six o'clock tomorrow morning and throughout the day."

He wasn't satisfied but shrugged his shoulders as if it was hard to believe and nodded his thanks. Something didn't quite ring true, but he decided not to act too bright. He could tell she wasn't parting with the whole truth for some obscure reason. Acting on impulse, and because he suddenly felt a need for more alcohol, he poured himself a full glass of the strong drink and tossed it down in two gulps. He had been taught how to handle alcohol, although he wasn't fond of it. The headaches resulting from overindulgence were terrible, but his head was starting to throb anyway, so he might as well try to dull the pain until he could get some tablets.

Sorcuk returned after a while. "Sorry, but you two will have to use slow public transport. But a car will be waiting for you at the city terminal to take you to the clinic. That's the best I can do. I'll try to see you tomorrow, Pob, but I think I might be too busy. Good-bye now." She hugged him just a little too long, and he sensed that he was history as far as she was concerned. It didn't bother him, for she had more or less forced herself off on him the night before. They had both known it would be a temporary affair, and she wasn't that good anyway, he thought.

14

Dai was propped upright into a corner, and the lovely Surra was sitting rather close to him, as if she were concerned about his health and afraid he might fall over sideways. It was very cold in the drafty coach, and he welcomed her nearness and the accompanying warmth.

He was puzzled by his unwell feeling because he had a tough constitution, and this beating wasn't as severe as he pretended it to be. He had permitted better experts to work him over before for the sake of appearances, and he hadn't felt like this afterward. He thought about this unusual condition and decided to leave the casually proffered bottle in Surra's shoulder bag alone, as Sorcuk could not be trusted. Some drug might have been added that affected his well-being, and he didn't want to pass out or have his reaction time slowed to a crawl, if that was the intention.

While they were waiting for the train, he developed a nauseating headache, and the outdated, drafty, and sluggish train that hung from a single overhead rail made it worse as it stop-started jerkily from station to station. The too-bright glare of the overhead lamps was aggravating, and he thought closing his eyes might help. After all, the lovely Surra was there to keep watch over him. He closed his eyes, and as if she had been waiting for him to isolate himself, Kyr asked if she might talk.

What's up? The question was in his mind only.

Nothing really, I just wanted to check in with you to know if you're okay. The girl was waiting for you and went to sleep on your bed.

She then told him what had happened at the hotel after he'd left, which didn't take long with the transmitted pictures. He was just about finished telling her what had transpired at the aerodrome when Surra asked something. Perhaps she became concerned when he didn't answer immediately and tapped his hand to get his attention. The throbbing headache made him concentrate on what he was telling Kyr, and he wanted to finish it because she had to let the head of the Fighting Priests, Karna, know about meeting Bazir and his invitation to Pob. He touched his forehead and flicked his fingers to show Surra that his head was throbbing.

As Surra touched his hand again to demand attention, he absently took her hand into his own and hooked his elbow over her arm to imprison her pestering hand. Then he became aware of the familiarity, gulped inaudibly, and asked Kyr to hold on for a moment while he apologized to his escort for this inadvertent show of intimacy.

But Kyr fiercely told him to stop. *Keep a tight hold on that warm hand, stupid, and don't let go! Our lives may depend on it*, Kyr almost shouted in his throbbing head, which made him reach for his forehead with the free hand. Then she calmly told him that images were being transmitted to her via that link and that he must maintain the hold as long as she allowed him to.

Dai waited, holding the girl's warm hand, and wondered vaguely why she didn't withdraw her hand and what Kyr was reading. His head now throbbed with a vengeance, and he could scarcely think straight. He pressed his other hand onto his forehead again and kept it there.

What I get is that she was ordered to watch you closely until you parted and to report any out-of-character behavior or if you say anything suspicious. She is wondering what she must do to persuade you to make love to her, as she is physically attracted to you. She is some years older than you are, and it holds her back, as she is afraid of a rebuff. You must do something to help her along. She will be a very valuable ally, and I think we need everyone we can get, in any way possible. Our lives may depend on it.

She was mentally and physically abused as a child, and you must be totally honest in your personal dealings with her, but not about who we are, of course. She is the loyal, sincere type of woman but with a fierce pride. She will follow you to the ends of the earth to extract revenge if you play her false and discard her like a piece of dirt.

I do not get as clear a picture as I would if I could see her directly, but my impression is that this thing we are being pulled into is intricate and more serious than you were told or we thought. Someone tried to kill the king early this morning, but your escort doesn't think you are involved. She suspects it is more likely that her sister had a hand in it. When Tumarok wakes up, I'll tell her that you were in a fight and getting attention, and that you will not be back before morning.

Okay, Kyr, and thank you, Dai thought to her. *I somehow intuit that Hezmet's death was planned so that it could be linked with the king's murder and Tumarok blamed for both. I can't think clearly with this murderous headache. It's driving me nuts. Keep a trace on me, please, so I can report anything that may be important the moment I hear or find it.*

After a pause, he continued. *Ask Tumarok to spray perfume in the rooms so nobody can smell your presence, for we'll have the whole of Bojon after us the moment they see or smell you because of the tracker you killed in the park. Please tell her how possessive the real Fov is and help her practice it when you can. Ask her not to wash that aging cream off as I haven't much of it left.*

Oops! I almost forgot about that picture and Bazir, he added. *Please send a message on the relay to Karna. Ask him to warn Tumarok's family that they may be in danger and to tell Pob about this meeting and the invitation to visit Bazir when he is in town, wherever that is. It could just be that someone may be trying to implicate Tumarok's parents in the attempt on the Bojonian king's life.*

Kyr replied, *While we are on the subject of forgetting things, remember that Tumarok has been conditioned by hypnotic commands to kill you if she hears your operational name is Dart. Don't ever mention that name in her presence until I can find someone to help me de-hypnotize her.* Kyr withdrew.

Difficult as it was, he thought a while about his immediate future and actions, then stirred and opened his eyes with a deep sigh. Warning bells rang in his mind when he felt an urge to talk, but he smiled at Surra and deliberately looked at their locked hands. "Sorry, I don't know how this happened, but your hand is warm and I like to hold it. It seems to lessen this throbbing headache I have developed. Thank you for not clobbering me."

He relaxed his fingers as if he wanted to let go, but she tightened her hold and snuggled closer immediately. "I find that I like it, too, and I'd like to spend more time with you, starting right after you've been to the clinic. What do you say to that idea?"

"A perfectly brilliant idea is what I say, but I'll have to get about a hundred powerful headache capsules or tablets. I won't be able to run for a few days, and I'd like an excuse to get away from my mother, even if it is only for a few hours each evening. Mothers seem to be a necessity, and I love the old lady, but a few of us are burdened with a mom who cares too much and interferes with our lives without realizing it. There are others who may be less fortunate, I suppose."

She seemed to wince. "I wouldn't know. My mother died when I was born. My father almost immediately remarried, but Sorcuk, who is just a year younger than I am, and I walk two different paths. We won't ever be close as sisters should be. It's a long story you won't be interested in anyway. Let's forget it for the few days we might be together, starting right now.

"I wanted to tell you what Sorcuk neglected to tell you tonight, because it's relevant. Someone tried to assassinate our king early this morning. It has been kept quiet, but it will be in the news tomorrow—no today, for it is just after midnight. That is the reason why no one is allowed to leave Bojon. Fortunately, it was a botched attempt, but the masked perpetrator managed to get away after he or she dropped a metal cat's claw, which was used in an attempt to rip out the king's throat. I, for one, don't believe this Tuala had anything to do with it."

Dai stiffened, but fortunately Surra misinterpreted it. "Don't let it upset you. Unfortunately, no fingerprints were left, because the intruder used some sort of rubber or plastic gloves, which also let the murder weapon slip out of his hand when the king knocked it aside. I don't believe any professional would be that stupid or physically that weak. The cat's-claw weapon may be a trademark of the man they call Dart, who may be the same person as this Tuala, but we won't know until we catch one or the other, assuming they are here and one of them is responsible. It doesn't make sense to me that a professional would make a stupid mistake like that. I have my own suspicions, of course, but I can't prove it."

Dai wisely didn't offer an opinion because a professional runner shouldn't know anything about assassins, killers, avengers, and so on. He shrugged his shoulders resignedly and said the tight net around Bojon was explained at last, and it helped one to accept the restrictions if one understood the reason for them. Privately he thought that these people were so paranoid, they would keep personal secrets from themselves. Everyone knew that Dart was not an assassin, and it was obvious that the attempt on the king's life was a bungling amateur's work. Any professional assassin would have completed the job by using more conventional weapons or his hands, even if the requirement was that a cat's-claw weapon be used.

Silence followed. He closed his eyes again, managed to get hold of Kyr, and asked her to check with the local temple cats if the Aikon priests were involved in the attempt on the king's life. He didn't warn her to be discreet because she would only have sent a scorcher into his already-tortured brain.

15

After giving it some thought, which was something of a torture, he decided to steer Surra in the right direction. "I seem to recall something about a cat's claw being used as a murder weapon in rituals by a religious group or cult ages ago, but my head is throbbing so much I can't think clearly or remember whether I heard or read about it. I really should get some strong headache tablets if the clinic will let me have a few hundred of them."

Surra squeezed his hand and said she would make sure he got enough for weeks. They lapsed into silence, still holding hands, but when they arrived at the station and he tried to rise, he couldn't keep his balance properly without her support. "Something is wrong with me," he slurred, "but I'm not drunk from two or three small glasses of alcohol, and it can't be from the punches, and neither one could have caused this nauseous headache. I was looking forward to being with you, and I hope I don't end up alone in a bed in the clinic instead."

"You won't, I promise. I'll doctor you myself if need be. Concentrate on staying upright and keep your legs moving. Now, where is that bloody car Sorcuk promised us?" She cursed under her breath.

He concentrated on staying conscious, and suddenly he knew what kind of drug he had been given, for he recognized the symptoms. He also remembered that Sorcuk had turned her back to him when she poured the second drink. He started to breathe deeply, which was one way to defeat the effects of the Happy Drug. He knew the drug made a person so talkative and light-headed that any question would be answered truthfully without a conscious thought, but it also left a nasty after-effect, namely vertigo and nausea.

He suppressed a chuckle when he remembered taking another drink on impulse, or perhaps his subconscious mind had urged him to do it. It was not generally known that alcohol lessened the drug's effectiveness, though too much alcohol could cause unconsciousness. He was sure it was Sorcuk's idea, and Surra was the unwitting watchdog. He had to tread carefully but also keep Kyr's observation of Surra in mind.

The hover car, marked "Government Property," waited just outside the exit. The driver saw Surra as they emerged from the City Transport Center, jumped out of the grounded car, and ran over to help her with the staggering companion, who obviously couldn't control his body movements. Dai thanked him in a slurred voice, but Surra told him in a hard voice to shut up and concentrate on staying conscious. The driver switched the sirens on and called the clinic to stand by to receive a very sick patient.

Dai's brain was clear and unaffected, and he marveled at the anxious expression on Surra's lovely face. Perhaps she was a reluctant accomplice to the drugging, working under orders; she had brought in the tray and poured the first drinks. But judging by the concerned and baffled look on her face, he elected Sorcuk as the culprit. She had insisted on the second round, and he had a feeling that she was a rather ruthless character. Had she decided to use him and his "mother" for some sinister purpose, even if she had to frame them? He wished, as he had so many times before, that he could develop a cat's ability to pick up thoughts at will. It would have saved him much pain in the past.

Then the realization hit that he must check his clothes for bugs and guard his tongue until he had done so. In retrospect, that longish hug from Sorcuk was unnecessary and therefore suspicious. He concluded that either he was up against formidable agents this time, or some Bojonians were so paranoid that they suspected their own mothers of criminal intent in giving birth to them. He was grateful when they arrived at the clinic and thanked the driver for being so quick.

The young medic on duty took blood samples, which he said could only be analyzed in the morning. He checked Dai, or Pob Pabruk, as he was known, and told his patient that everything pointed to normal functioning and that he couldn't find anything wrong. The result of the test should be available by ten at the very latest, he said. Surra looked visibly relieved. The medic told her to bring the patient back if his condition didn't improve within two hours. He then told Dai to be careful about washing his face for a few days. The artificial skin would start peeling off in about eight days if the lacerations healed normally, and there should be no scars. He provided Dai with pain tablets and a prescription drug, then let them go.

At the hotel, for appearance's sake, Dai left a note for his mother at the reception desk, saying he didn't want her disturbed this early in the morning. The note was to be delivered with breakfast and only stated that he was slightly injured and might have to stay at the clinic until about nine; a friend would accompany him, for he didn't want to disturb her sleep with a triviality. Dai was sure that security would be there to scrutinize the note as soon as he was out the door.

16

At Surra's apartment he left his overcoat on a hook just inside the entrance. It was the only garment Sorcuk logically could have attached a bug to, and if so he hoped it was too far away from the bedroom to pick up intimate details to transmit to a listener. He could only check the overcoat in the morning, for he couldn't do it in Surra's presence, and he didn't dare remove any bug without advertising the fact that he knew more about listening devices than an innocent athlete had a right to.

Surra insisted that he be the first to shower to remove the smell of antiseptics and any remaining traces of blood. The hot water and steam might also remove the last vestiges of whatever was wrong with him. It had been about forty minutes since the medic gave him an injection to neutralize the effects of the Happy Drug. The slurring of his voice was almost gone, and he kept his balance without effort. He was thankful he hadn't experienced the usual nausea that accompanied withdrawal. He showered lazily, but not for long. He rubbed himself dry quickly and then wrapped a dry towel around his hips, since he felt a little bit uncomfortable parading bare in front of a woman he had known for only a few hours. As he stepped out of the shower, Surra was sitting on the only chair in the bedroom, barefoot and wrapped in her gown. He saw her eyes widen involuntarily.

She didn't expect the ropy muscles on his upper body and arms that rippled and played underneath his tight, bronzed skin with every movement. It didn't belong to her image of a long-distance runner. His stomach was hard, and there wasn't a sign of fat anywhere. His legs were strongly muscled, as she would expect a runner's to be, but he walked as balanced and lightly as a trained fighter. She guessed that he was about 1.85 meters tall in his bare feet, and would tip the scale at around a hundred kilos, which was quite heavy for a long-distance runner. He must be very strong.

"You are an unexpected surprise, Pob. You look more like a practitioner of the fighting arts than a runner. Your superbly developed upper body doesn't quite fit the image I have of the usual long-distance runner. You should take up a fighting art in your spare time, for you have the build for it. With a body like that, you must train for hours just about every day."

"Thank you, Surra." He wasn't surprised that she was impressed. Professional runners usually concentrated on developing leg muscles and stamina and got rid of any extra weight. He'd expected a question or remark about his well-trained body and was prepared to explain the hard muscles. Fortunately, it was true for the real Pob as well, although he was not as heavily muscled as Dai.

"My mom made me train my whole body when I showed a talent for running, but she didn't want my face drastically altered by rough characters. A runner's career doesn't last very long, and she made sure that I could beat the best. She said I mustn't look like a scrawny rooster with thick legs, because only a symmetrically developed body and an unscarred face will attract a rich wife when my career starts to decline. But she forgot that a possessive mother drives brides away. She's a real slave-driver, but I don't mind, since I benefit from it. As I said, I took up wrestling two or three months ago, and that has really made my arms and upper body strong, for I don't do anything halfheartedly. I may end up wrestling full time when I start losing races to younger men."

"I'm beginning to respect your mom. You look fast and powerful. You should try other forms of self-defense as well. But I'm wasting time. I'll be back right away."

When Surra returned from the shower, she was naked. With her head down, she shyly and self-consciously approached where Dai lay on the bed. He saw her strong muscles play under a smooth, beautiful skin as she glided closer, and he couldn't see a gram of fat anywhere. Dai's breathing stopped involuntarily at the sight of the goddess he had never even dreamed existed under the garments she had been wearing to keep the cold weather at bay. He had never seen such a magnificent, superbly developed body on a girl, and he told her so with undisguised admiration in his voice.

She heard the sincerity in his voice when he told her he was the luckiest man alive to see and touch such a truly amazing body. He exuded an aura of honesty, strength, and stability she hadn't sensed in anyone before, and that was a

91

major part of what had attracted her to him. She instinctively felt she could trust him with her life. She blushed furiously and advanced quickly to embrace him.

He jumped up, completely ignoring the towel and the injuries to his face as he folded her magnificent body into his arms, as if afraid she would disappear the moment his breath and eyes returned to normal.

"You have an exceptionally well-muscled body for a runner," she told him in a breathless voice. "I, too, have been training hard every day for a decade or more to develop and stay in shape. When I was in my midteens, I was assaulted and severely injured. I'm determined that no one will ever do that to me again. When you feel a little better I'll teach you some of the dirtier tricks I have learned throughout the years. You shouldn't be so easy to beat up."

"Thank you. I know this may sound insincere since we only met a few hours ago, but I already wish we could be together permanently. You are the type of woman I've been dreaming to meet, but you must know that an athlete can only be competitive while still young enough to be tough and dedicated, and I really enjoy running. I also like the prize money and only have about five or six years left before I must seriously consider other options for a more permanent career."

He sighed and added, "If I may, I'd like to come back periodically to check if you're still unmarried before I settle down, because I will never forget you. What made you decide to give a beaten-up guy like me a glimpse of the real you?"

Surra liked the earnestness she could read in his eyes and his tone of voice. She laughed easily and replied, "I felt attracted to you from the moment we met, and you reminded me of someone I was fond of long ago. Feel free to drop in any time as I probably won't be married. I won't bother you with the details, but I'm used to the fact that I won't have children because of the injuries I sustained in the attack, and that's what marriage is for, isn't it? In the meantime let's see how we get on in the next few days.

"Sorcuk won't be able to get your travel permit issued today, even if she tries hard, which I doubt. I'll take you around to an animal merchant or two in the late afternoon so you can see if you like anything they are offering for sale to gullible and unwary buyers.

"Oh, you recover ultrafast…or was the medic that good?" She laughed delightedly as she became aware of his surgation, and gently drew him down on the bed. He immediately forgot all about his injuries.

Kyr was drumming insistently in his head as only she knew how to, and he awoke with a start. He sat up, a headache beginning to form, and before he remembered where he was, he asked aloud, "Now what?"

It's already midmorning! Are you enjoying her company so much that you can't get back here, sleepyhead? Kyr asked sarcastically. *Look at the time!*

He looked at the bedside table. There was a note with his watch, which read almost ten o'clock. Surra was gone, and the bed was cold where she had slept. His head started to throb again, but he asked Kyr what was going on.

We are worried about you, stupid. The note delivered this morning said you would be back by nine. What's keeping you?

I was sleeping like a log, he replied, *and I still don't feel well, especially not now after this rude awakening. I'm supposed to check with the clinic this morning. As a concerned mother, Tumarok should accompany me.*

Then move your lazy butt, boy. I'll tell Tumarok to get ready.

The note said that Surra was on the early shift today and would contact him at the hotel to let him know when they could meet later in the afternoon. There were cereals and milk in the kitchenette, if he felt like eating. He should try to leave her apartment unnoticed, the note went on, as she must try to keep her untainted reputation in pristine condition.

Dai swallowed a couple of headache tablets, showered quickly, and dressed. He would eat with Tumarok at a restaurant around noon rather than waste more time. As he dressed he found a bug in the collar of his overcoat. What did Sorcuk think she could gain, or did she want to implicate him in the attack at the palace? He wasn't going to be a pawn in any nefarious scheme she had concocted. From now on, he wouldn't trust her with the time of day. He wished he knew what she had in mind and the reason for it. Since he was a stranger, it would be very difficult to ask questions, and he couldn't ask Surra, her own sister, without a valid reason. But he could ask Kyr to dig into Sorcuk's thoughts if she showed up at the hotel.

He would have to get rid of the listening device quite innocently after his visit to the clinic, because a guy like Pob shouldn't even think about bugs. After listening intently for footsteps or conversation in the corridor outside the apartment, he carefully opened the door, peeped around cautiously, and then quickly stepped outside. He couldn't be too sure he'd left the building unobserved, even though he was certain nobody saw which apartment he came from.

A beggar scrounging in some rubbish bins gave him an idea for getting rid of the bug without arousing suspicion. When he arrived at the hotel and entered his room, he said hello and asked to be forgiven for being late. He explained his reasons so everything would sound normal to anyone listening in, but he quietly told Kyr about the bug in the coat's collar and asked her to have Tumarok comment on the shabbiness of his clothing and order him to get rid of it. She did so in a convincing way, but told him they had to visit the clinic first, then eat and buy new clothes.

First he checked for bugs, but both rooms were clear. Then he searched systematically through pockets and secret hiding places in the overcoat and clothes he planned to discard with the wired coat and put the contents on the bed. He dropped the offending coat temporarily in Tumarok's room and then shifted his bed to pry up a floorboard as quietly as possible. The owners of this old hotel had conveniently installed false wooden floors instead of expensive under-floor heating that would have made its guests a bit more comfortable in winter. When he'd arrived two days ago, he'd made good use of this economizing by carefully loosening a board to hide his lethal equipment and extra funds. Now he hid Tumarok's weapons and treasure in the more than ample space. The things he had taken out of his pockets and wouldn't need right away went into the hiding place as well. He carefully replaced the board.

He kept the money Tumarok had given him to purchase various articles for their journey and donned the offending overcoat again. Kyr would hide under the already made-up bed and escape through the partly open window if necessary. He promised her a fresh, fat chicken when they returned.

At the clinic they were told that the blood tests didn't reveal anything unusual, except that he had been given an overdose of the Happy Drug. The medic on the day shift checked the artificial skin on his face and declared that all was well and that Pob should only report back if anything out of the ordinary happened. There might be some mild itching, he said, but the artificial skin should start to peel off on its own within six to nine days.

After lunch and nonsensical talk between mother and son, they bought a new overcoat, as well as some rugged outdoor clothes and boots for both of them. He dressed in his new warm clothing and bundled the old clothes into a disposable bag in the dressing room. Then he deliberately asked for a needle and thread to mend tears, should the need arise. This was meant for listeners, but the real reason was to sew secret pockets in the new clothes, and he bought suitable cloth for that purpose. At the first opportunity, he gave the bag with the old clothes to an astonished beggar.

Now he and Tumarok could openly discuss plans for getting out of Bojon. He had forgotten the picture Sorcuk gave him at the airport but found it when checking his old clothes again. He gave it to Tumarok now with the proper explanation. For the first time he noticed that Tumarok's eyes were sky-blue like her father's, while the picture showed light-brown eyes. He drew her attention to it.

Tumarok almost cried. "You know, for the first time I really believe the story you told me. I suppose I wanted to before, but now I'm convinced. There can be no mistake. I take after her, don't I? I mean, I look like her, even the general build, except I've got hard muscles, and she looks more soft and feminine." She smiled and impulsively hooked her arm through his, and a warm smile spread over her ancient face.

He squeezed her arm and smiled too. "Careful, girl, don't let your portrayed image err. Always wear a sour expression and be serious—a possessive mother doesn't smile often except at someone else's expense. We may be under surveillance and can't take chances at this stage." He told her about Surra and how she could help them if they befriended her, but didn't mention their personal relationship. He described Surra's role as

95

that of a reluctant watchdog.

As they wandered from street to street, he at last found an outdoor-sports and camping-equipment store. They entered and told the overeager salesman they were thinking of camping out for a week or two and wanted recommendations on what they would need. If he would be so kind as to make them a list, they would ponder it tonight and come back the next morning. Dai knew exactly what they needed but figured it was a good policy to express ignorance in the event someone sniffed around afterward. This way they could buy a few extra things and make it look as though they were suckered into spending a few extra credits.

Against one wall, looking like a trophy, hung a rare Krotan war bow, complete with a full quiver of arrows. The rare trees from which the wood for the bows came would only grow in ancient Krota; they simply didn't take in any other soil or climate. Dai would have done just about anything and paid pretty much any price to acquire this valuable relic of a bygone era, but he concealed his eagerness. It had to look as if the bow was foisted off onto him; otherwise it would be overpriced. From the discoloring of the wall paint behind the bow, he knew it had been there for years. It would be unusual for anyone, except a few archers or collectors, to even inquire after the price of such an item. He looked at it frequently until the salesman finally sensed that here at last was a naïve shopper he could con into buying the ancient item nobody ever so much as glanced at for more than five seconds.

"I see you are interested in the old bow and arrows, sir," he said with a trained salesman's enthusiasm. "It's a rare specimen and you won't find it anywhere else. It's useful for hunting small game or birds around the camp without scaring the rest away. You look strong, so you can easily learn to use it. Shall I take it down for your inspection, sir?"

Dai almost laughed. He knew that very few people could bend the tough wood back far enough to let an arrow fly far enough to clear their front foot. Even the string was of tough, special steel wire. You'd have to have power in your shoulders and arms, and it would take months of practice for even a very strong novice to be fairly accurate with such a heavy bow.

"I don't even know how to hold such old things," he lied.

96

He eyed the crestfallen salesman. "It looks so old it could break if anyone with the know-how tried to bend it. I'd rather buy a small gun if it is permitted without a proper license." He nevertheless stepped nearer to the bow and caressed the tough old leather. It would require attention to make it pliable again, but the Krotans still knew the secret of making these bows and quivers last for a couple of human lifetimes.

"Mom," he said without looking at Tumarok, "do you think that Uncle Seerpil may be interested in this old thing? Perhaps we could buy it for him as a present, for he collects these useless things."

Tumarok didn't know a thing about bows and arrows, but her wits were sharp and she sensed that Dai wanted it for some reason—perhaps as another weapon, as the salesman suggested. She shrugged her shoulders as if resigned to his whims and said yes, they might as well surprise the daylights out of "your Uncle Seerpil," if it wasn't too expensive.

The salesman, sensing a sale, named a price, but Dai shook his head sadly. The price was reasonable, but under the present circumstances, he couldn't divulge that he was keen to buy it because someone might inquire later about what they intended to purchase. "I'm sorry, but my uncle isn't worth that much money or the trouble of carrying it all the way back home."

Dai feigned lack of interest and turned away. "Would you make up that list of the camping equipment, please? My mother and I will look at it tonight, and if we decide it isn't too pricey to camp out, we will see you in the morning."

He took another look at the bow and shrugged his shoulders as if to say it was a pity it was so expensive. He knew he had to show a reluctance to buy it. He could always get it just before they left, as if he had changed his mind at the last moment. The possibility that someone else would buy it within the next few hours was very small indeed.

The salesman excused himself, saying it would save a lot of time if he fetched already-printed lists on which they could mark off the recommended items, since the price for each item was also listed.

They waited longer than seemed necessary and had just decided to leave when the salesman returned, almost running with haste.

97

Smiling a salesman's smile, he said, "I'm sorry I kept you waiting, madam and young sir, but I spoke to the manager, and he agreed to let you have the bow at half the price if you purchase all your equipment from us. It seems that someone pawned the bow many years ago and never returned to claim it. He said that if you buy an antigravity sledge from us to carry your equipment, we will throw in the bow and arrows as a gift. Can you give me an answer right now?" The salesman handed Tumarok the lists. Feigning disinterest, Dai turned to Tumarok and winked at her.

She knew that she, as the supposed mother, should make the decision. Hoping that she correctly interpreted the wink, she shrugged and said, seemingly reluctant, "Okay, if we can afford it, we might as well take it, but the sledge will be pulled by a pony or a horse. I think that calls for two shafts." She knew that much at least. Shoving the lists back into his reluctant hands, she ordered, "Write the price of the bow and the sledge down somewhere. We will look at it, add it all up tonight, and decide if it isn't too expensive for our budget."

The previous evening at the hotel she had learned her lesson about being too generous with someone else's money. She wondered why Daiyus was interested in the old bow. It really seemed ancient and not in the best condition.

The broadly smiling salesman saw them to the door and assured them that they were getting the best equipment at the best prices, and that his store supplied the best antigravity sledges at the most competitive prices. He wouldn't mind if they compared prices with another shop.

After bidding him good-bye, they sauntered back to the hotel. Dai told her that the old Krotan war bow was very rare, and nowadays they only made a lighter version of it for sportsmen, for few men had the power of the old Krotans to bend that particular bow. It was a sought-after item for the Fighting Priests, as well as for every collector of ancient weapons, but sellers usually wanted an arm and a leg for it, for the powerful bow was virtually priceless. One very seldom came across one for sale, and it was a deadly weapon in the hands of an expert, which he was. It took strength to use one, but it was silent except for the twang of the released string. He couldn't seem too anxious to buy it, he said, because some nosy Bojon official or priest might inquire what they were shopping for.

It was almost four o'clock when they returned to the hotel. Along the way they stopped at a butcher's shop to buy a chicken for Kyr. Dai knew what she preferred when she didn't hunt for herself. The leftovers wouldn't be a problem, for Kyr would take it out when she stretched her muscles tonight.

Surra was waiting for them in the lobby. Dai introduced her and told "his mom" that Surra had kindly offered to take him around to look at pack and riding beasts. They proceeded to the lounge to get to know each other better over a leisurely drink. Surra said her weekly two-day break started the next day, and would Mother Fov mind if she monopolized her son for the two days? She would, of course, return him to the hotel every evening.

Dai's heart warmed to Tumarok when she touched Surra's arm and said with a warm smile, "Of course you may, Surra, but only after we purchase the camping equipment tomorrow morning." She, too, had the feeling that they should be ready to move at short notice. "He heals fast and his face should be less painful after two days. I will see to it that he trains hard to make up for lost time when we leave. He needs the company of beautiful women like you now and then, and I must learn to let go sometime. I sometimes feel his need to be distracted by young girls, because I'm too much of a doter, but I sense a deep sadness in you that touches my heart. Please come and see me whenever you feel like talking to an old woman, even if it is in the middle of the night."

Although she thought she might as well play her role to the full, the offer was sincere, for her heart went out to Surra. She couldn't explain the odd intuitive flash, but she knew she had an inborn empathy for people and animals. The instructors at Operations emphasized that an agent didn't last long if he or she became attached to anyone or anything, and they discouraged such tendencies rather ruthlessly. She had tried in vain to suppress the trait.

Surra seemed happy that she and Pob's mother had hit it

off, and she thanked her for the kindness. When they finished their drinks, Tumarok asked to be excused and said she would call for her own supper and that Pob mustn't worry about her. But the two of them courteously accompanied her to her room because an "older woman" mustn't overstrain herself with packages while climbing stairs.

Dai quietly let Kyr know about her meal and asked her to scan Sorcuk if she showed up, for he thought she had some underhanded scheme up her sleeve. In turn, Kyr told him that his current companion had shielded her thoughts but that she could sense no treachery, only anger that was directed somewhere else. It could be important, and the lady might tell him if he played his cards right.

As they descended the stairs, Dai chuckled quietly, as though enjoying a private joke. When Surra asked what was up, he said it was the very first time his mother actually liked another woman at first sight. He was pleasantly surprised and very pleased.

"You mean you actually meant what you said about coming back in five years' time?" Surra sounded surprised.

"I meant it with all my heart, Surra. I've never met a woman as lovely and as sincere as you are. I feel comfortable with you, as if I've known you all my life. The couple of years that separate us mean nothing to me. What would it matter in another thirty or forty years anyway? I want to be your friend, at the very least." Dai meant what he said, and he wondered what her reaction would be if she knew his true identity. Perhaps he would tell her someday.

"If we weren't in public and everyone wasn't staring, I'd jump into your arms even if we rolled down the stairs and hurt ourselves. But let's save that for later. I want to show you some animals for sale, because my dear, lovable half sister said I must tell you to purchase and not lease animals. It's a condition before the permit to roam the countryside is approved and issued tomorrow."

The night before, Dai had gotten the impression that the half sisters didn't get on well, and now it seemed as if Sorcuk had made the decisions regarding this so-called emergency. She couldn't be the head of security, could she? But before he could ask the obvious question, Surra continued.

"I can't figure out her reasons for stipulating this expensive, and in my book, unfair condition. It makes me angry just thinking about it. Perhaps she's just being spiteful because you would have to resell them at a loss. It could be that she thinks you could lose them in the wilds, and she doesn't want any merchant in Bojon to sustain a loss. As if they would! Is this training that important to you? I mean, is the prize for winning the race important enough to spend a thousand or more credits just to prepare for it?"

They had reached the lobby, and Dai took the opportunity to think about it before he replied. For the umpteenth time he wished he had Kyr's ability to read minds because he didn't think it was spite, but he decided to drop his question about Sorcuk's real position. It was quite obvious that her opinions or decisions counted. There was much more to it than met the eye, but he decided he wasn't interested since he would be out of there within the next two days.

In the street, when they were out of hearing distance of passersby, he said, "I agree that it's a condition that stinks to heaven, but I don't think we have much choice. I can always arrange to ship the animals home or even give them to a farmer if I don't like them." He couldn't tell her that he intended to set the animals free if they couldn't cross the mountains with them. "I must start training in the next couple of days, and I must really train hard, since the race in Bireria will be one of the toughest of my career, but also the most rewarding in terms of money and prestige. The prize money is more than enough to pay for the expenses. Besides, I love the competition and enjoy measuring my stamina against others. Ah yes, I must add, for your ears only, that I have this inexplicable feeling that I must get out of Bojon for a while until this problem of who is responsible for what is sorted out."

"Okay, but I still feel that you're being taken advantage of because you're here at an inopportune moment. It makes me angry. I can't see what can be gained by it, or who, except the merchants, of course, and that's rubbish."

Kyr had told him that Surra was angry about something, and she sounded upset about it, too, he thought now. That showed him she cared. "Don't let it upset you," he said. "I agree that it is inconvenient and unnecessary, but don't let it spoil our couple of days together. It just isn't worth worrying about. I have learned that what one cannot change, one must accept with as much good grace as is possible at the time."

"You're right," she replied. "Okay, let's leave it there for the time being."

They took public transport to the western edge of the city and then proceeded on foot to the recommended animal merchant. Dai wasn't very keen to look at any animals at this time of the afternoon because the light was failing rapidly, and he said as much.

"I called to make an appointment for tomorrow morning, but he said that he would be away all day tomorrow and the next. I suspect that this particular merchant is a con artist, so if the light inside his barn is too dim, tell him so. Just be very firm, and we'll see if he changes his mind. If he doesn't, you can be sure that he is dishonest. There are others we can pay a visit to if he decides to be unavailable tomorrow."

Dai didn't like the fawning, oily manner in which the shifty-eyed owner greeted them. He reluctantly shook hands, trying hard not to show his distaste. The light inside the barn was very dim indeed, and the merchant apologized, saying it was to help the livestock keep calm because bright light bothered them. Like hell it does, Dai thought, and like hell you care.

He stayed back a little, trying to accustom his eyes to the dimness so he could determine whether it was worth returning in the morning. Then, from an almost-dark stall just in front of him, a scarcely audible voice whispered in a little-known language, "Greetings, Dai. This despicable shyster is the biggest swindler in creation. Don't allow him to sell you anything now. Insist on coming back in daylight. It's a standard trick to get rid of inferior stock to the gullible at the most inflated prices. Make a bid on me, too, or help me escape this filthy prison if you can't afford his high, exorbitant prices. He has a few decent ponies and horses that are worth rescuing. I'll point them out tomorrow."

He remembered the whisperer. It was a female Permerian by the name of Ekaasi, of the race thought of as man-horses from the far-off semidesert of Krisa. She was a high priestess of that rare breed of unsurpassable intelligent beings that looked half human, half horse, but wasn't related to either. He had met her on an assignment there when she volunteered to guide him to the hidden fortress of Alisun, a vicious murderer for hire. What had brought her from her native land more than halfway around the world?

While Dai felt sick to his stomach that Ekaasi was ill-treated, he whispered back in the same language that it wasn't his intention to purchase anything in the dark. He increased his pace to catch up with the other two and said it was too dark to see anything clearly, and he wasn't interested in buying anything without decent light to properly see by because his funds were severely limited. Perhaps he might come back in the morning to see if there was anything of interest. Privately, he thought he had glimpsed one or two animals that might be worth his while to swindle the swindler out of.

Caught unprepared, the merchant gulped audibly in the semidarkness. It was clear he hadn't expected a fussy client, or perhaps he was misinformed. He replied that, unfortunately, it was difficult to change plans at this late stage and asked if he could just show the lieutenant and Mister Pob a few animals of very good quality at very fair prices, on his word of honor.

Dai declined in no uncertain way. He said he would like to take the merchant's word of honor, but unfortunately, he couldn't afford to squander his or his mom's limited funds on anyone's word, however honorable. He would make his purchases somewhere else in the morning because he knew his mother would not accept any animal that was not properly inspected beforehand, even if it was at a giveaway price.

Realizing that he couldn't pull the wool over this particular customer's eyes and that he was throwing easy money to his competition, the merchant reluctantly agreed to try and postpone his trip for a day, but it would mean he would have to call right then to make the necessary arrangements.

On their way back through the barn, Dai heard Ekaasi chuckling to herself and realized she hadn't lost her sense of humor. Her language was very difficult to learn, and it was unlikely that Surra or the animal merchant had mastered it or perhaps even knew it existed. He sang to her in a soft voice that he would be back as early as he could make it and that they must act as complete strangers. Kyr might want to visit her during the night, so she shouldn't be surprised.

She wisely didn't reply, and he kept on singing until they

exited the barn.

18

"What are you singing?" Surra asked once they were outside.

He stopped abruptly. "Oh, sorry, it's an unconscious habit to quiet spooky animals when I'm near them. It's only the tone that matters and not the words. I was thinking of what may be the best to buy. My mom is still strong, but she would need an animal that rides comfortably and also has stamina to keep up with me until we set up camp in the evenings. A pony or two could be used to pull a sledge, but we still have to decide how long we will stay out there. I am hoping this mess will be cleared up within a week. We must plan carefully for some work in the mountains and hilly country, for that is what we came here for. I need to reach peak condition five weeks from tomorrow. That will be just two days before the race."

He turned to the merchant. "I'll be back as early as possible, Merchant Caclo. You may have horses that would do and perhaps you can arrange for someone to stand in for you if you can't manage to postpone. I'm sorry for the inconvenience, but thank you for agreeing to try and postpone your trip to accommodate me. We didn't bring excessive funds with us as we didn't know we would have to buy animals instead of renting a hover car. I think my mother might want to come along, as well, to give her approval." He decided he might as well act as if he believed the crafty old crook. It might serve to catch him unprepared if he thought he had a polite but dense customer who wasn't too bright upstairs.

They had supper on the way back to Surra's apartment. She offered to pay for it, but he said the alleged shortage of funds was for the ears of the dishonest animal trader so he would not be too avaricious when they discussed prices in the morning. Surra laughed and said she was beginning to enjoy her association with him and was learning something new in the process, as well, but she was still angry that he was being forced to purchase animals. He should have been allowed to rent a hover car so they could return to civilization every evening.

When they neared her apartment block, he followed some distance behind to make sure no one was following or observing them. He also made sure he was unobserved when he quietly slipped into her apartment.

After they showered, she insisted on showing him a few self-defense techniques, including hand and knee strikes, while they were naked. She said she could better explain and demonstrate kicks and punches by pointing to the location of a nerve center or specific group of muscles on his or her body that the punch or kick should temporarily disable. He couldn't help but marvel at her firm, beautifully muscled body. It was truly unique.

He forced himself to act slowly and clumsily, as if all this was new to him. He wished he could show her better and more vicious ways that could save her life, but he had to stick to his role as the innocent; he couldn't confide in her until Tumarok's safety was assured. What he also couldn't tell her was that he had a strange feeling—or perhaps it was a premonition—that he must stay in Bojon for as long as possible. Perhaps it was to protect her, but his gut feeling was that what was happening here had to do with what he and Kyr were investigating on the other side of the planet.

They made love spontaneously and passionately, unleashing all inhibitions, his body throbbing for hers. She seemed hungry for genuine affection, and he gave it freely. He reluctantly left her to return to his hotel just before midnight.

Instead of being tired, he felt very much alive and alert. He scanned every shadow and corner as he slowly walked back to the hotel. He had an uncomfortable feeling that Sorcuk or someone else was up to something ruthless to serve another purpose and that it somehow included Tumarok and himself, but the thoughts didn't distract his attention from his surroundings.

He concluded that they must buy today whatever they would need so they could run at a moment's notice. Once they were out in the country, they could live incommunicado and hide from public view at will because he knew how to throw pursuers off their track. Knowing the principles of how a thing worked made it easy to hide from anything but ultrasophisticated heat-tracing equipment. Even those instruments or their operators could be deceived, given the right circumstances at the right time, but it would be easy to trace heat emissions in Bojon at this time of the year, especially through the satellites that circled the Earth.

When he was a block away from the hotel, he decided he could relax, since no one in their right mind would lurk around in this bitter cold to waylay innocent victims, who would be scarce anyway. He didn't consider newly acquired enemies and their friends who might harbor cruel, unjust hatred. As he passed the dark alley that connected the rear entrance of the hotel to the main street, two grinning men stepped from a dark doorway into the light from the street lamp in front of him. Two more stepped from the alley to cut off retreat.

The appointed leader, or spokesman, said in a mocking voice, "You kept us waiting in the cold, Lover Boy, and that's bad, real bad. Now you're going to pay for it, Pretty Boy!"

Dai almost sighed audibly. He detested cheap theatrics from grown men, for it showed juvenility. "What do you want?" he demanded because he knew it was the expected response of a frightened man. They apparently failed to notice that there was no fear in his voice and likely misinterpreted the slight shuffling of his feet for balance as nervousness or fright.

"Listen to Pretty Boy, men! 'What do you want?'" he mocked in a shrill voice. "We want to rearrange your pretty face and put you in a medical institution like you did to our friend, ex-Sergeant Mohaz. You flattened his favorite tools, and they had to be amputated to save his life. He'll be in bed for weeks, and we're going to do the same to you, Pretty Boy. We're going to rearrange your face first, as our friend intended to do. We'll teach you a lesson you'll never forget, Lover Boy. You can try to run for it if you like, but you won't escape our reprisal."

Dai sighed audibly. "With friends like you, he likely needs a few enemies. Does your mother know that her naughty boy and his idiotic, perverted sidekicks are out to catch their deaths in this bitter cold?" He was angry because he abhorred stupidity, and self-imposed vendettas were utterly stupid in his book. These men were likely told that he was a real sissy and an easy pushover, which made them decide to waylay him. Cowards were always on the lookout for decent people they could bring down to their low level with violence, and they usually hid behind authority. He wouldn't permit these bullies to beat him up, and he also knew he couldn't let them live to spread the word that he wasn't what they thought he was. He was ready.

"I'll make you eat your words, Sissy Boy. Grab him, boys!" the cocky spokesman suddenly yelled, probably, Dai thought, to add the fear of the devil to their quarry's quaking mind and make him cringe.

Of course the "boys" behind him would do the grabbing and the holding. He therefore thrust his arms up over his head in a powerful circular movement and took a fast step backward. As the "boys" bumped against him, grabbing where his arms should have been, he grabbed them behind their necks with the same movement and pulled them to the front to bash their heads together with every ounce of power in his arms. Their heads met with a dull, sickening thud, like two pumpkins being bashed against each other. Quickly, he took a step forward and propelled the bodies into the instinctively raised arms of their utterly astonished friends, who'd expected a leisurely, enjoyable beating up and certainly not this kind of knowledgeable resistance from their intended victim. It was the last mistake they would ever make.

The hoodlums instinctively grabbed their dying buddies, slipped, and fell with the bodies on top of them. Dai shifted a fast step or two forward, broke one man's neck and jaw with a well-aimed heel, then dropped down to his knees and crushed the leader's Adam's apple with the hardened edge of his right hand.

He verified that all four were dead, quickly dragged them into the dark alley, then paused to listen if anyone had raised the alarm. No direct evidence linked him to their demise unless someone had witnessed this brief encounter, but that was unlikely this late at night and given the bitter cold.

After a few minutes, when he heard no raised voices, he started to think of the consequences if bodies of chums of Mohaz were found near the hotel in the morning, and he knew that he had to act quickly. Sorcuk, or whoever was the driving force behind the delaying tactics, might pounce on this killing to further delay or arrest him and Tumarok on suspicion. He couldn't take off unprepared, because that would cause unnecessary hardship for Tumarok.

The park would be the ideal place to hide bodies for a

while, but it was too far away to carry them one by one. To confuse investigators he should dump the bodies separately at four different locations, but first he must remove identification documents, if they were stupid enough to carry any on an escapade such as this.

He found documents, as well as weapons, on every one of them, which he dumped in one pile. He looked around and noticed a number of trash cans farther down the alley near the hotel's kitchen door. He opened a few until he found enough used but clean enough plastic bags to hold the guns and documents. He filled the bags with the confiscated items and hid them under old rubbish stacked against a wall out of casual sight.

Dragging would leave signs behind for any observant passerby to see and report, but there was no blood, so he shouldered a body and walked westward for two blocks before he lowered it, feet first, into a nearly empty rubbish bin. He took each body cautiously in a different direction and dumped it where it would not easily be seen. It took him about an hour, and he was sweating profusely in the cold when he returned to the hotel with the bags of weapons, papers, and wallets.

The night receptionist and the security guards were nowhere to be seen, and he entered the hotel unobserved. He ran silently up the stairs, thankful that he didn't have to use the icy-cold fire escape, because he couldn't risk knocking on the window if Kyr was out. He unlocked his door carefully, opened it silently, and stared right down the rock-steady barrel of his former stun gun.

"Sorry. I dared not knock," he whispered. "Where's Kyr?"

"She said you were in trouble and went to investigate," Tumarok whispered back. "If you were okay, she would go for a run in the park, for she is stiff from lying around all day. Did anything happen?" she asked and returned the stun gun to its holster.

He closed the door and told her what had happened in the street. "I hope I'm wrong, but I keep getting this feeling that Sorcuk is up to something and that she plans to make us take the rap for some underhanded scheme she is involved in. And ever since I entered the lobby I've had an urge to take our weapons, along with these I just confiscated, and go right now to

110

bury them somewhere in or near the park where I can retrieve them when we leave."

"You look tired, but I think you must not delay a second longer than necessary. Kyr said she got impressions from passersby in the passage that something was up concerning us and that we should be ready to decamp at a moment's notice. You can use my dagger to dig, and I'll keep this stun gun since you said it can't be detected by commercial instruments. We can buy a selection of hunting knives at the camping shop later today. Perhaps I should stay here and guard the money."

"Yes, that will be best. Are all your weapons with the money?"

They were, but she kept the paralysis bombs, saying they might come in handy if they were forced to leave and were pursued by a bunch of security personnel. He packed every weapon, except his own hunting knife and Tumarok's dagger, into a small sack with a broad strap he could sling over a shoulder.

He dressed in his old tracksuit and well-used training shoes but kept his thermal underwear on, so Tumarok didn't turn her back this time. He asked her to tell any unexpected visitors that he was restless and had wakened her to tell her he was taking a short run to check if the stitches in his face would hamper training.

A careful scrutiny from the windows revealed no movement of snoops braving the icy, early morning wind. She said she would wait up until he or Kyr returned. She didn't tell him to be careful, which he appreciated; it showed she was more mature than her years, or otherwise didn't care, which he couldn't believe.

He ran past the park to the stream where he had washed the day before—or, rather, two days before, because it was almost three o'clock in the morning. He had remembered a jumble of rocks near an old weeping-willow tree, and the small flashlight in the sack would dispel the darkness under the branches.

When he reached his destination, he silently prowled around for a few minutes, listening and sniffing for even the faintest smell of smoke to make sure no one was camped nearby. He could see well enough in the bright starlight, and the matted leaves and soil around the bare tree were not disturbed. No one had been around for quite some time.

He paced off eleven steps from the old tree directly away from the stream. There he dug a deep enough hole for the sack and its contents. He carefully replaced the cut-out square of grass and soil after filling and stamping the soil underneath to the correct level. The rest of the soil he threw into the brook for the water to disperse. Once done, he selected the heaviest flat rock he could carry and carefully placed it over the spot. He placed two other flat slabs nearby and scuffed the dead grass and leaves so it would look as if someone had decided to have a chat with friends in the sun.

This place was obviously not popular at this time of the year, but it didn't matter if the weapons were found and removed; he would have the Krotan war bow. Of course, any and all weapons would be useful if they had to defend themselves. He grimly reminded himself that enemies had supplied weapons before and would again if need be. He would ask Kyr to check the area before he retrieved these weapons.

Merging with the shadows, he silently prowled around for the next ten minutes to make sure he really was as alone as he thought he was. Then he jumped back over the brook and hurried back to the hotel. He would only have two or three hours' sleep, but a couple of hours was usually enough to keep him going. He ran silently so as not to attract attention, but he met no early risers or anyone crazy enough to go for a jog so early in icy weather.

19

Kyr homed in on him before he reached the hotel, and he slowed to a walk when she asked him to. She told him she wasn't going back to the hotel for the day because the Bojon Royal Security was going to cordon off the hotel, allowing no one in or out until their rooms had been searched for hidden weapons. He and Tumarok definitely were the selected targets.

The information came from the temple cats, who'd overheard some of the Aikon priests discussing it as a precautionary measure. The cats were not loyal to the not-so-honest Aikon priests, but they enjoyed the safety and quietness of the temple and would perform the usual services required of them. The priests wanted to make sure that Pob and his mother took no better weapons than knives with them into the wilds to avoid any of them getting hurt if the pair resisted arrest.

The moving force behind this outrage was the Aikon high priest, Heltos, and Sorcuk, who seemed to be his accomplice. They planned to murder the king, because he was hampering a search for something in the mountains of Bojon, and then manufacture evidence to lay the blame on Surra, Pob, and his mother. The latter had to be out in the wilderness, where no one could vouch for their innocence, and, being strangers, would not cause any grief to locals who might get interested in the case. During a special session with the king tomorrow at ten o'clock, the Aikon high priest would prophesy that the king's daughter and accomplices intended to murder him. The king would be coerced into signing an order for their arrest, after which he would be killed outright by the high priest and Sorcuk. Dai, Tumarok, and Surra would be blamed, hunted down, and killed without a trial so that Sorcuk could be crowned as the new ruler of Bojon.

Dai wondered how he could warn Surra. He just couldn't go up to her and tell her that her sister planned to have her murdered. As was his intention anyway, he would take his "mother" along today because now he couldn't leave her by herself to defend herself. How could a woman as lovely as

Sorcuk be so evil as to sacrifice her own flesh and blood to further her own ambitions? What was wrong with her?

Kyr remarked sarcastically, *Idiot! It still hasn't registered on your stunted perception that Surra and Sorcuk are the king's daughters, has it, you stupid moron?*

He stood speechless and frozen like a statue, his bemused brain blank with shock. He had told Kyr about finding Ekaasi a prisoner for sale at the animal trader's pens and had given her mental pictures to get there. Now Kyr said she would stay out of sight at Caclo's stables and talk to Ekaasi to renew their friendship. She took off at a leisurely trot, saying she would meet him there later in the day.

It took quite a while before Dai could rationalize his casual involvement with two Bojonian princesses. He now understood how and why Sorcuk could so casually dismiss him; he was just a lowly commoner in her eyes. Surra was somewhat of a puzzle, though. On the surface she seemed so sincere and straightforward, but she must have wanted to laugh herself silly when he told her he would come back for her when it suited his timetable.

He blushed hotly in the icy morning and thought about the arrogant stupidity of youth and wondered how he should handle his relationship with Surra when they met later that morning. He shrugged his shoulders, losing his temporary paralysis, and silently ascended the fire escape.

But the shocks were not yet over for the night. Hearing the murmur of voices in Tumarok's room, he went directly to the connecting door and knocked. Tumarok told him to come in, which he did, and he stopped in his tracks when he saw that she was embracing Surra.

"Come and sit down with us," Mother Fov's voice ordered in no uncertain terms. "We have been praying that you would finish your practice run sooner. Surra has urgent news, but you had better hear it directly from her." She patted Surra reassuringly on the back and drew her down on the bed as if ready to protect her, and motioned Dai to the chair.

"I was telling your mother the story of my miserable life," Surra said. "But first I must ask your forgiveness for the unintentional deception. Everyone in Bojon knows that we are the king's daughters doing our duty the same as anyone else, and it now seems that we have unconsciously accepted that even newcomers know it. You have to know part of the background to understand the current situation, but I'll make it short. There isn't much time left to organize a getaway, and I can always fill in gaps afterward.

"As I told you on the first night, someone hurt me terribly when I was sixteen years old. I was impregnated by another teenager, a young nobleman I was very much in love with. I managed to keep my pregnancy concealed, but when my son was born, someone told my sister about the boy and the baby. Of course she ran straight to her mother, and they made much out of it to our father. There was a terrible scene before my father had the nobleman arrested. He was viciously beaten under the supervision of my stepmother and half sister before being thrown into the old, abandoned dungeon in the palace.

"I don't know how he escaped, but he did. His family disappeared at the same time, and I think his father had a hand in his rescue. My baby son also disappeared the moment my sister reported his birth to my father, and I never found out what happened to him or my lover. Years later I learned that my half sister acted out of jealousy and hatred carefully cultivated by her insane mother.

"Meanwhile, Sorcuk and her mother had me trussed up, and after the men were ordered out, they started to beat me up, telling me I had disgraced the royal house. Where I found the courage I don't know, but when I just looked at them without so much as a groan, Sorcuk lost control and started to stab and cut me up. Even her unstable mother vomited and took off in a hurry because she couldn't deal with all the blood. When Sorcuk came to her senses—or rather, by the time Father was told what she was doing to me and forcefully had her restrained—I was near death.

"Father retained the best surgeons to sew me together. That's why you don't see any scars on me. Ironically, the next year Sorcuk married a prince from another country, but she couldn't conceive. When it was proven that she was barren, the prince sent her back. Sorcuk was never the same after that and couldn't start a serious relationship with anyone. My father offered just about the whole royal treasury for the whereabouts of my son, for he knew that Sorcuk had ruined my reproductive ability, but no one ever came forward with news or tried to claim the reward.

"My father couldn't have more children because a few months after Sorcuk was born, he was thrown from and dragged by his horse, and somehow his ability to reproduce was ruined. Sorcuk's mother went 'round the bend when Sorcuk returned with the news that she was kicked out because she was sterile. She became a drug addict and an alcoholic.

"One day, with drug-induced bravado, she bragged how she had murdered my mother to become queen in her place and had paid a groom to cause the accident in which my father was nearly killed because she wanted the throne for herself and her daughter. She and the groom were tried, found guilty, and executed. I tried to forgive and forget, but it seems that Sorcuk learned only too well from her mother, or perhaps the delusions of grandeur and invincibility are hereditary.

"About two hours ago, I was awakened by an insistent knocking on my door. It was an old priest who is related to my late mother and who really loves me. He showed me the sign to be silent, murmured in a slurred voice that he was so sorry, wrong apartment, closed the door, and then checked my apartment with a bug detector. He then beckoned me outside. He told me my apartment was rotten with every kind of listening device and that even sounds from the toilet were being transmitted somewhere.

"Remember you said something about reading or hearing about a cat's claw? I asked this old priest the day before yesterday if he could check it out for me. He told me that the cat's claw was used in primitive times by the Aikon priesthood in a ritual called the 'Offering to the Gods,' a ceremony to torture and eventually kill a victim on the altar. He said he was meditating in a dark corner of the temple last evening when Heltos, the high priest, and Sorcuk came in furtively and seated themselves nearby. Instinct told him to remain quiet and motionless if he wanted to live. He thus overheard what they said and came to me when he could leave safely.

"The Head, as he is called by lesser priests, assured Sorcuk that her sterility would be reversed, but the price was the lives of her father and sister, as ordained by the gods. Her first act after taking the throne must be to issue an edict that appoints the head of the local Aikon priests as coruler, as she must have the power that only the gods could provide through the high priest. Then she must marry the person the gods would point out during a very special ceremony to be held in the main temple at an auspicious time. It seems that my poor, delusional half sister was influenced to believe all that rubbish, and I'd like to know what Heltos has concocted and for what purpose. He has more power than he can handle as it is.

"It was obvious they had been plotting for a long time and that a person by the name of Morcun was involved from the very beginning on the assurance that he would be given a safe haven and anonymity. Unfortunately for them, the idiot accidentally killed himself in a botched attempt to enrich himself while killing and robbing a paymaster of a foreign power that had a network of agents in Bojon. The agent under his control, of whom you have a picture, would have been killed or arrested in that office, and she would have 'confessed' that she and I were responsible for the king's murder."

20

Tumarok grunted inaudibly, thinking her intuition had been right as usual. It had been a setup, all right. A good thing Daiyus and Kyr came to her rescue, or she would have been cold meat. But Surra was still speaking.

"Pob, you and your mother are unfortunately in the wrong place at the wrong time and conveniently on your own. Sorcuk, who is normally quite bright, was told to make you two the tools, with me as the plotter, of course. You will be subjected to all sorts of petty persecutions and inconveniences today to force you to leave Bojon without the promised permits. Tomorrow at ten o'clock, when you and your mother are out there where no one can vouch for you, the head priest will have a divination session with my father and reveal, with a shocked expression of course, that you and I are behind the botched attempt on his life. He will be coerced to sign a document for our arrests, and it will contain a clause that will be our death warrant if he is killed, which he will be the moment he signs.

"What I want to ask you is this: would you get a mount for me, too? I want to go with you whenever you leave today, disguised of course. I need to try and rescue my father, but won't involve you two. I'm hoping my father and I can plan something to stop the corrupted high priest Heltos—and Sorcuk. I promise that I will give you a map and directions to a secret escape route through the mountains. Just get me a horse or two, please."

Tumarok looked at Dai with a penetrating stare. "We will help her, won't we, and we might as well tell her, don't you think?"

Surra looked mystified. "Tell me what, please?"

"Yes, we will help her rescue her father," Dai said, "but I will have to get hold of Kyr to obtain permission. Don't look so mystified, Surra. There isn't time to explain right now, but you'll see for yourself this afternoon, and we'll explain everything at the first opportune moment. Will you trust us until then? You need all the help you can get, for I don't think you will be allowed an audience with your father at any time.

"My experience—sorry, not that of a runner—tells me that there will be all kinds of obstacles put in your way, and you might even be arrested to stop you from being seen or making a nuisance of yourself. The guards would have been tripled at least since the botched attempt, and perhaps most are already on Sorcuk's or the priest's payroll. Are there secret passages and entrances to the palace, or do we have to use disguises or force to get past the guards?"

Surra looked bewildered, but answered, "I don't understand, but I trust both of you. It's an instinctive feeling that has never been wrong. I don't want you to risk your lives for me or my father, but it would be welcome if you can handle a gun as I need someone to cover my back. Yes, it is an old, old palace and it has a secret escape tunnel, peepholes, and doors, which I learned as a kid. I can get us inside if the passages weren't blocked off in the meantime. I haven't visited the palace for a dozen years, so I don't know. I do not think Sorcuk knows about them, for she never had an inquiring mind, nor was she at any stage in her life interested in those kinds of things. She likes to think she is in control, though.

"I have a handgun, and I will try to get one or two more today so you can defend yourselves if necessary. Can you handle a handgun, Pob?" She looked at him seriously.

"Oh, for heaven's sake, I've detested that name ever since Sorcuk had the temerity to call me Pobby. Please call me 'Dai' from now on, both of you. We can get hold of handguns, Surra, but could you perhaps get me a rifle? It needn't be very powerful, but it must be accurate, and plenty of ammunition if it's the percussion type that fires solid projectiles with unnecessary violence and noise." He looked at his watch. "It's time for you to depart. Use the back way, please. We may be receiving the first unwelcome visitors at any moment and they mustn't find you here. As soon as we are allowed to leave the hotel, we will visit Caclo and see what we can get. We'll find another horse trader if he hasn't got anything decent."

Surra kissed both of them and said she would be at her apartment around noon. They were to ring the bell in code: two short rings, pause, one ring for exactly three seconds, pause, and then one short ring. She would be ready and would come down immediately if she was alone. Otherwise she would meet them at Caclo's at five o'clock. If she wasn't there by six, they should leave without her.

Surra checked the passage, then took the inside fire escape down to the rear of the building.

Dai had just politely requested Kyr to ask Karna for permission to rescue the king before he took Tumarok to safety when there was a thunderous knocking on his door. He quickly went through to his room and Tumarok silently closed the connecting door.

"Don't break the door!" he yelled, sounding as annoyed and grumpy as anyone just rudely awakened at this hour would be. He felt real anger rise and tried to control the illogical feeling. He still had the tracksuit on and hastily untied the laces of his running shoes and stamped a couple of times on the floor as if putting them on.

"Who's there?" he demanded at the door.

"State security," was the savagely uttered answer. "Open up immediately for an emergency search!"

Dai opened the door and four men rushed past. Now his anger was real. "Not even as much as a courteous 'please' or 'thank you.' I wonder if anyone in backward Bojon has ever learned that there is something called manners?" he commented sarcastically. He was suddenly fed up with arrogant bureaucracy and felt like inviting trouble.

Something in his attitude must have sounded a warning bell, for the leader turned around and said apologetically, "Sorry, sir. We are cold and tired and upset. We have been running around in circles for hours in the bitter cold, trying to make sense out of four dead colleagues discovered in the area around three o'clock this morning by refuse removers. We were still trying to puzzle out the motive for their deaths in four different locations when we were ordered to drop everything and search this hotel room by room and confiscate firearms, licensed or not, which also doesn't make any sense."

He turned back to his men. "Use the detectors. That will be good enough. We don't have to turn everything inside out since firearms are made of metal."

As the man turned away, Dai responded, "I beg your pardon for being so grumpy. I was beaten up about thirty-six

120

hours ago by one of your colleagues, and my face still hurts like blazes. It didn't permit me to get much sleep, and I feel like taking it out on just about everybody at the slightest chance. I have a knife here somewhere, or perhaps I left it in my mother's room." It served no purpose to make a decent man an enemy for doing his job, Dai thought.

The leader smiled abruptly. "That doesn't count as a weapon, sir. Our orders are to confiscate firearms. It doesn't make sense, but I have to follow orders even when I don't like them. I'd like to know what mentally disturbed idiot dreamed up this crazy idea so early in the morning."

Dai could have told him, but he resisted the impulse. Two of the men carried small metal detectors, which he realized were sophisticated instruments. He thanked his lucky stars that he had yielded to the urge to hide their weapons. He just hoped there were no metallic coins in Tumarok's loot. He asked the leader if they would be interested in free coffee and breakfast from the hotel's kitchen. The men stopped in their tracks with grateful smiles, and he knew he had said the right thing.

He immediately called for coffee and six man-sized breakfasts, after which he knocked on the connecting door and told his "mother" to dress quickly and come over for an early breakfast in his room. The four men, who had finished their scan of the room, sat around until the breakfasts and hot coffee arrived.

Having found nothing in his room or on his person that could be considered a firearm, they scanned his "mother's" room thoroughly while apologizing for the intrusion. They thanked him again for the unexpected breakfasts and coffee before they left, and he knew he had made four new friends, which might ease today's harassment somewhat. His watch said six thirty exactly.

21

After Dai and Tumarok showered and dressed, they packed their personal things so everything would be ready for a quick checkout. Dai didn't want to check out right away since the baggage would be an unnecessary hindrance and would draw the attention of the city's riffraff, who might perceive them as an easy target. They could handle the rabble, but they didn't have a bag for Tumarok's purloined money and jewels that was big and strong enough to withstand rough handling. It would be safer under the floor until they acquired a strong backpack and were ready to leave.

The streets were almost deserted, but public transport was available and they took the hover bus to Caclo's corrals. They arrived there a little before eight and found the merchant up and waiting.

Dai introduced his "mother," who treated the merchant as if he were the answer to an old woman's dreams and the most respected person on earth. She knew how to "butter up" a wily old rogue to make him forget about exploiting customers in the present circumstances.

Caclo thought that he was losing touch with reality, for he felt attracted against his will to this old lady. He had never heard of the term "empathy," which some very special people were blessed or cursed with. This is a cultured lady, he thought, and she has good taste, but he wasn't about to wave good-bye to a sucker's credits just because he liked someone. The chances that he would meet her again were virtually nonexistent, but, for the first time in his life, he felt slightly guilty about presenting inferior stock at inflated prices for her approval. He salved his sudden, inexplicably uneasy conscience by assuring himself that business was business.

Dai wasn't surprised that Caclo steered them directly to the corrals.

As they passed the barn, Kyr told Dai, *You have Karna's blessing to get involved in the rescue up past the top of your head, for the king's well-being is more important than getting*

Tumarok to safety right away. He said the Council has evidence that Heltos is a participant for personal reward but not a major player in the multinational and perhaps multiplanet complot we were investigating before we were ordered to rescue Tumarok. It is not clear at this stage what exactly the aim of this conspiracy is, but it may be to exploit this world's resources for the personal gain of a few avaricious individuals, or perhaps it may just be a smokescreen for something entirely different.

Karna thinks that if the king were to disappear for a while, it might rattle the obnoxious priest and force him into indiscretion. We must ensure that neither Heltos nor Sorcuk is killed in the rescue operation, and we must not hurt them seriously, for they might divulge important information at an unguarded moment. For that purpose, some of the local temple cats are invading the palace at this very moment to keep watch, listen, spy, and report on thoughts and conversations not concerning the usual everyday events, especially those of Heltos and Sorcuk. They will also warn us of danger when we enter the palace tomorrow. Karna said the Council suspects that Heltos may know more about this plot, which could provoke conflict and set the world aflame, than may be evident from his odious personality.

The Council hopes Heltos will panic when the king goes missing and get in touch with his contact, thereby identifying at least one. The contact can then be investigated and linked to others. Our orders are to first take the king, his daughter, and Tumarok to safety, then to return here to investigate and provoke Heltos into indiscretion. We need to identify all the local players and get rid of them if they're a menace to society in general.

Oh yes, the three mountain ponies with Ekaasi are the best Caclo has to offer. The sorrel and the gray horse in the farthest corral are well-trained draft animals and worth rescuing as well. Buy them and Ekaasi. The wild one with the sorrel and gray is ruined and will never recover from the abuse it was subjected to by cruel captors. The rest are just good-looking rejects and only good for dog food and the glue factories.

Caclo had taken them to the enclosure next to Ekaasi and the mountain ponies. Dai noticed that the ponies were well muscled and their short legs thin and out of proportion to their powerful bodies. He was familiar with this type of mountain pony and loved them at first sight. They were tough, honest, and known for their stamina. Even with little fodder, they could outstay any other known creature, unless they were sick or very old.

Caclo noticed his casual observation and drew his attention to the sole occupant of the enclosure. It was a big, shiny, well-groomed brown gelding that drew the inexperienced eye because of its size and well-muscled appearance. Dai didn't have to examine the swollen hocks to see that the horse would be crippled and almost worthless after half a day's ride, but he appeared to listen intently to the merchant extolling the horse's virtues and good looks. He glanced sideways at Tumarok, who gave the impression that she was taken in by the sales pitch, and decided it was the right time to reexamine the ponies and the Permerian in the next enclosure.

As intended, Caclo noticed the distraction and immediately took the bait to draw Dai's attention back to the piece of magnificent-looking uselessness. "I see that you are looking at the ponies with the thin, short legs," Caclo said. "They are nice to look at, but they are not in the same league as this magnificent saddle horse. Compare this one with one of them. He is almost twice as big, and just look at those long legs. Why, he could run circles around all three of those ponies and carry three times the weight as well. This beauty is priced at only eight hundred credits, and you could buy those three plus the half horse anywhere for a mere six hundred. They're not nearly as valuable as this powerful one."

He paused for effect, then looked confused, as if he hadn't heard correctly, when Dai immediately said, "I'll take them."

Caclo's jaw dropped open and shut again with an audible clang. He gasped. "Wha-wha…*what* did you say?"

Dai had a problem keeping a straight face but managed to say in an innocent voice, "I said that I'll take the three ponies and the useless half horse for a mere six hundred credits, as you said." He heard Ekaasi's snort of derision but still managed to keep his face relatively straight. Tumarok started to shake and turned away, but she couldn't control herself for long. It started off as a girlish giggle but quickly became uncontrollable laughter at Caclo's uncomprehending, gulping face.

Unexpectedly, Caclo started to chuckle. Then he grabbed the corral fence and roared with laughter. His flabby potbelly hopped up and down. After some time he managed to control himself enough to gasp out, "By the gods, boy, you really caught me nicely in my own trap. Okay, you can have them for six hundred, but they're worth a lot more. Now what else can I do you in with?"

Dai smiled ruefully. "I'll pay you a fair price for them. The Permerian female is as intelligent as we are and should not be treated as an animal. She must be set free. I'll pay you a reasonable price for the gray and the spotted sorrel in the end corral, too, without inspection. I think the other horse with them could be used for breeding purposes if its breeding essentials are still intact, but I'm not interested in it except that I feel sorry for it. One can plainly see it has been mistreated for the amusement of savages.

"I saw a dusty grav-sledge in your barn last night. Is it in working order, and can I buy it and other equipment at a decent and honest price? Please understand that we'll be forced to resell them at a huge loss in a couple of weeks, but we're willing to pay what everything is really worth."

Caclo turned to Tumarok. "Lady, you have a son that I can like, and that's not an easy thing for me to admit. I am putting my life in danger by warning you, but you seem to have made enemies who maybe want to track your whereabouts for their own ruthless purposes. The reason I tell you this is that I thoroughly hate the arrogant, preaching, know-it-all, interfering Aikon priests and what they stand for."

He turned to face Dai. "Also, the princess has always treated me like a human being on the few occasions we met, and I could see that she has taken a liking to you. After you left last night, an Aikon priest came by and very arrogantly told me to sell you the equipment he had brought with him. I did not want it and told him that I already have more than I can sell before they rot. He threatened me with dire consequences and made me pay for the equipment too.

"When I questioned the reason for his insistence, he said it's none of my concern, but the guilty look in his eyes made me think that the equipment is suspect, even though it seems to be good quality. He ordered me not to sell you a gun for any price under any circumstances, but he didn't order me not to sell you additional equipment. He said he would know if you didn't take his saddle, bridles, and harness, which made me think that a tracking device was hidden somewhere so they could know where you can be found at all times. I don't know how to locate it, not even what to look for. I'm fearful and afraid of what they want to do to you two, but I really don't know what to do. What have you done to them that they hate you so?"

Dai made a show of bewilderment. "I can't imagine why," he lied. "We are strangers, and I came here to do some training. Okay, let them find us if they want to find us! It could be that they want to blame some mischief of their own doing on us when we're not here to defend ourselves. Let's check the grav-sledge and have a look at the 'holy' equipment, and then we can argue over the price. We also have to get camping equipment and supplies, and since we didn't plan on this enforced stay or on camping out, we obviously have to watch what we spend."

A plan for the "holy" equipment was forming in his mind. "Maybe I should take that wild horse along with the gray and sorrel. I'll release it if I can't handle it, but it's not worth more than ten credits, as you well know. It will be wasted money in any event. It seems to have accepted the company of the other two, and I feel sorry for it."

Perhaps Caclo was influenced by his liking for the "old" lady, but he sold them everything they wanted at what Dai knew was a reasonable price, without too much quibbling. The big sledge had been unused for some time, but it was still functional and could be pulled by a human or an animal. Caclo said both the gray and the sorrel were trained to pull grav-sledges. Dai bought the old sledge, though it wasn't quite big enough to carry fodder for the animals, plus provisions for four persons for at least two weeks and the camping equipment. He decided he would buy one of the same size or slightly smaller, depending on the price, at the camping shop to carry the equipment and perhaps a passenger or two if necessary. Injuries in the wilderness were not uncommon, so extra space was always welcome.

The money he had in his wallet seemed to be just enough. Caclo privately congratulated himself on a shrewd deal, taking just about all the money the boy and his mother had. He didn't feel guilty, which wasn't unusual, but, to ease his newly acquired conscience just a little, he promised to include enough grain for free so that the animals could have a nosebag feed every night for two weeks. Natural fodder might be scarce that time of the year, so Dai asked Caclo to include five bales of dry fodder, just in case the grazing was inadequate where they camped; it wasn't unusual for large stretches of grassland to be devastated by fires in the dry season. Dai paid the "last" of his money for the fodder.

22

Dai asked Ekaasi and Kyr to keep an eye on the merchant and monitor his thoughts and those of any visitors while he and Tumarok went to buy provisions.

The salesman at the camping store appeared delighted to see them. Yes, he said, they kept rugged clothes of all sizes for the outdoors. Tumarok guessed Surra's size, and they bought warm things for her and some outsized warm clothes for the king as well. Dai didn't know if the king was fat, thin, tall, or short, but assumed he wouldn't be very active during their journey, so he could sit or lie on a sledge. Outsized clothing would not be a handicap but would instead be rather comfortable and warm. It was an unnecessary expense, but he couldn't be sure they would have time to pack the king's clothes if anything went wrong. The new grav-sledge, a little smaller than the one bought from Caclo, was piled with equipment by the time they were finished "being fleeced."

Dai obtained a special waterproof wrapping for the war bow and kept it, the knives, and some equipment that could be used as clubs in the front of the sledge in case they were waylaid before they could retrieve their weapons. He told the salesman that, although it was a waste of money, he wanted three emergency medical kits since he was prone to hurt himself when he trained in rough country. The salesman directed them to a shop that specialized in provisions for the camper.

As they left the provisions shop, both noticed that they had acquired a tail who must have thought he was following two innocent, unsuspecting tourists. In a whisper Dai asked Tumarok to look out for other, not-so-clumsy stalkers, since this one might be a decoy to rivet their attention. She smiled broadly and said she was always ready and willing to try out the stun gun, and she still had five paralysis bombs in her pocket. Any attackers were in for a nasty surprise.

Dai was beginning to regret his decision to go on a shopping spree before taking the grav-sledge to check out of the hotel. He should have expected to be under observation, and he didn't think it wise to leave Tumarok alone with a fully laden sledge outside in the street. But he had a few hidden gadgets that had to be retrieved personally, since they would explode if anyone else touched them. Perhaps he should check if Surra was home first so that she could keep watch with Tumarok.

His orders were to see to Tumarok's safety, and at that moment, he completely forgot that she was trained to take care of herself and that the cautious stage was a thing of the past. Their harassment had started the previous night with the priest at Caclo's, and even if this inept spy was a decoy or an opportunistic thief, he could be manhandled if he tried to help himself to something. Dai was trained to be protective and he liked his charge, so he was in a bit of a quandary.

He had just decided to check if Surra was already waiting for them when a calm voice spoke in his mind. *Hi Dai! I'm called Porrig because of my short temper. Kyr asked me to keep an eye on you and her Cookie. Look up here on the balcony you're passing under. Mind if I jump onto the top of your trolley so that we can talk? It will be easier to keep watch from there.*

Dai looked up and saw a huge temple cat perched on the edge of a deserted balcony. It was the biggest red-brown cat he had ever seen, and he was impressed by its powerful physique. It had to sport at least forty kilograms of muscle, he mused as he replied, *Sure, go ahead, and welcome. Are you one of the cats monitoring the activities in the palace?*

I'm too restless to skulk around in dark corners, the cat replied. *I like the courage I sense in both of your minds. If you and Kyr agree, I'll come with you, for I think you could use an extra scout, which is what I'm good at. Will you have me?*

The cat jumped onto the load and almost disappeared into the dent he made in the covering canvas. *Oh, by the way, ignore the wooden-headed priest who thinks he is the world's greatest pursuer. He was told to watch and report if any one of you acquired firearms so they can jump on you quickly. There are a couple of petty criminals, or as you would call them, "chicken thieves," who are interested in what you've got, but don't worry about them. I sense that Tumarok is a match for all of them together, and I might even pitch in, but only in an emergency, for Heltos must not find out that you have feline friends. Go ahead and check out, and don't worry about the trolley or Tumarok.*

She is quite capable of taking care of herself, and I'll give her a hand if need be. I'll talk to her and introduce myself.

Dai replied, *I already like you. You are the first feline I have come across that has a natural, dry sense of humor, even if you don't realize it. Thank you for coming, and yes, an extra scout might mean the difference between life and death. Kyr and I can only do so much, and we have to sleep sometime.*

He secured a thill to a pillar right in front of the hotel and looked around carefully. The street was busy at this time of day, and he was fairly certain that no one would have the courage to bother Tumarok in front of the hotel. He grabbed a rucksack and entered the lobby.

Porrig stretched out on his belly on top of the load, ready to warn Tumarok of anyone who approached her with malicious intent. He spoke to her as she seated herself on the steps near the wall, with the grav-sledge in front of her. Her hands were casually pushed into the opposite sleeves of her overcoat as if for warmth, but her right hand rested on the butt of the stun gun, ready for anyone dim-witted enough to grab anything from the sledge.

Dai went directly up the stairs after a quick look in the lobby to check if any suspicious characters loitered around. His manner changed the moment he started up the stairs. His steps became firm and his back straight. Pob's characteristics were gone from that moment. Dai preferred his own natural guise when action started, and he didn't have to concentrate on what came naturally.

He sensed a presence when he approached his room. He silently went past the door and opened Tumarok's door noiselessly with the key he had kept for security reasons.

There was nothing left in her room that could be disturbed, but the connecting door was open. He remembered closing the door after they had moved her things to his room, but not locking it. Dai's memory training allowed him to automatically recall every previous action, even a week past the event. His life had been saved on many occasions by this hard-practiced skill. Now he noiselessly closed and locked the door to the hallway. Then he carefully palmed the hunting knife he carried in his sleeve in place of the stun gun, reversed it, and gripped the blade in his right hand, ready to throw.

He approached the open door stealthily. Lowering the knee of his right leg to the floor, he looked around the doorframe at knee level, which was not the usual level one would look for a peeping Tom. He was ready to throw the knife in self-protection if necessary.

Surra was the last one he expected to see, but she was sitting in a chair, facing the outside door with her drawn gun pointing at it, and she looked tense. A sixth sense must have warned her, for she quickly looked at the connecting door. Dai quickly withdrew as her head started to turn. From behind the safety of the doorframe, he asked, "Is it safe to show my face?"

He heard her deep sigh of relief. "I thought you would never come. Did you lock the other door?"

"Yes, I did. I suddenly had a feeling that I should not open the door to my room. Would you have shot me if I came in fast?"

"I'm so nervous that I might have. I don't know. I think I was ready for anything because I can't trust anyone anymore. I, ah, used unusual means to unlock your room to see if your luggage was still here and was praying that you would come back sooner.

"As I told you, it's my two days off, and fortunately I went directly to the armory to get a rifle this morning. The old man there is a loyal friend, and he was shocked to see me. He told me that a directive was issued this morning for my arrest on suspicion of being involved in the attack on the king. He had orders not to sign out any weapon to me, but he was willing to do so if I asked. I declined because I love the honorable old man. I think that Sorcuk or Heltos may be afraid that I might discover their plans for me. I suspect that they have one of their teams waiting for me at my apartment. That's why I waited here instead."

While she was talking, a plan formed in his mind, and he asked, "Do you need anything from your apartment?"

"Yes, some warm clothing, walking boots, blankets, personal things, and documents. There are a few personal documents I'd like to destroy or take along if I can. It might not be possible to get anything without opposition, and I feel reluctant to kill colleagues who might not have a clue why they were sent to arrest me."

"Okay, but first I have to check out of here. Will you trust me? I have to ask you to do a few things on faith until I can explain in detail."

When she nodded, he took the last tube of aging cream from its hiding place and told her what to do with it and what it did, also not to use much more than half the tube because he wanted some for himself.

While she applied the cream, he went downstairs and checked out. He settled his account and told the new girl on duty that he would return the key when he brought his luggage down within the next ten minutes. He returned to the room and found Surra laughing at her own image in the bathroom mirror.

"If I live that long, I hope I won't age like this in real life. It really is something! Not even Sorcuk will recognize me."

"You'll have to change the manner in which you walk and really concentrate on changing your voice when you speak. Remember to keep your eyes down and try to mimic my mom. Her real name is Tumarok. As we said earlier, we'll explain everything when we have time. Just take our word that we will do all we can to help you and your father."

He handed her his tinted glasses and told her to put them on. He asked her to leave through the back entrance and wait for them on the corner of the alleyway and the main street. He closed the door after her, pushed the bed away from the loose floor plank, and threw the bags of money and jewels into the rucksack.

After handing the key to the receptionist, he joined Tumarok, secured their baggage under the sledge's waterproof cover, and told her about Surra. Then Tumarok watched him while he rubbed the last of the aging cream onto his face and hands and put the empty tube in a pocket; he would bury it somewhere outside the city, together with the other accumulated empty tubes. He threw a scarf around his face to hide his rapid aging from curious onlookers and wondered how the plastic skin on his damaged face was going to fare and if the aging cream's inventor had taken that into consideration. Then he unfastened the sledge, grabbed a thill in each hand, pumped both a few times to elevate the sledge to the required height, and got going.

23

As they came around the corner, Surra stepped hesitantly into the street. Tumarok immediately embraced her and took her hand. She told Dai that they would follow a few steps behind the sledge. He heard them talking as if they hadn't seen each other in ages.

The unusual sight of the grav-sledge in the middle of the city drawn by a sprightly old man drew curious glances. Tumarok overheard comments that it was a bit odd for strangers to travel somewhere at this time of day. She thought it might be a good idea, when curious people were near, to tell her "sister" that it was unfair that they should go back to the farm so late in the afternoon and that it was going to be a long, cold walk when the sun went down. Surra quickly caught on and loudly agreed.

The apartment building was on a quiet street not far from the busy business area. Dai stopped the sledge around the corner and, seeing no one around, handed the shafts to Tumarok. He told them that he was first going to check if anyone was watching the entrance. He strolled casually around the corner and scrutinized the street in front of Surra's apartment building. Again detecting no overt watchmen, he went back and pulled the sledge to the front. He dropped the shafts without grounding the sledge, saying they might have to depart in a hurry. If Tumarok agreed to keep an eye on the sledge, he would accompany Surra in case unwelcome visitors were waiting for her inside. Porrig said he would warn Tumarok if anyone approached with dishonest intentions.

Dai removed his scarf and Surra burst into laughter again. He smiled, thinking it was good that she could see the funny side of things, since her life had been turned completely upside down. This little bit of distraction eased the tension he had sensed in her.

He took her hand as they entered the building, telling her to follow his lead and not utter a word unless he directly asked her a question. He spoke quickly. "It wasn't my intention to mislead you, but I can fight without conventional weapons, so don't worry. A few days ago we were going to leave quietly without any fuss. That's why I had to permit that maniac to beat me up. Sorcuk or Heltos prevented us from leaving, and now I'm going to make them regret that mistake.

"I was sent to rescue Tuala, whom you now know as Tumarok. She was forced by Morcun into being an assassin for an organization called Operations. My real name is Daiyus, but you call me Dai, as I asked this morning. Sorcuk and the priest want to tell all and sundry that I am the one called Dart, but they conveniently failed to remember that Dart is an avenger, not an assassin."

Surra smiled and said, "This is my lucky week. I will not question anything you say or do and will follow where you lead without question. I learned to love you both in just two days. Tumarok has shown that she truly cares about me. I won't question her past, for I feel deep down that she is a true friend, as are you."

Dai said that she must have official visitors waiting, since the street and building were far too quiet for this time of the day. Just before they arrived at her door, he whispered for her to be quiet and gestured for her to move against the wall a few steps past the door.

He knocked loudly. There was no answer, but he could hear a faint murmuring, as if two or three individuals were discussing something. He waited about eight seconds and knocked more loudly, calling out in a loud, quarrelsome voice a name that suddenly came to mind, "Open up, Keenalam. Don't pretend you're not there!" He continued to knock insistently.

The door was suddenly yanked open by a huge man, who snarled, "Bugger off, you drunken idiot. You've got the wrong damn door, and you're messing up a security operation."

The big man seemed to suddenly change his mind about chasing the old intruder off. He abruptly grabbed at Dai to pull him into the apartment, perhaps to teach him a lesson or maybe to ease his own accumulated boredom of waiting too long in silence. But the big lout was completely taken by surprise when the "drunken idiot" brushed his muscular arm aside, grabbed *his* wrist instead, and swiftly entered the apartment willingly. Before he could recover from his bewilderment, he was propelled into his two buddies, who stood by with anticipatory grins on their faces. Dai didn't kill, but put the three to sleep in less than two seconds with controlled, accurately placed punches.

When he turned around to call Surra, she dived through the open door into the room with gun in hand. She rolled and quickly came to her feet and then crouched in the standard way, holding her gun with both hands before her. Dai was amused. "That roll-dive into a room will get you killed one day when the goons are ready and waiting for you like these three. It is impressive but way too slow. You have to enter with your gun already cocked, but on your feet in a crouch below belt level because eyes usually focus at chest height. It gives you a split-second advantage."

Surra didn't blush. "I'll think about it. I thought Blorck was going to pulverize you and I might dissuade him in time. I was ready to wound him to save you from another beating because he, too, has a reputation for viciousness, and no one has bested him before. How did you do it, and so fast? You were scarcely inside when I followed."

"Practice, Surra, practice. I was taught well, as you can see. You can start packing." He assembled his bug detector and checked the apartment while Surra hurriedly threw things into a travel bag. He found several bugs, but they were all in the big man's pocket, along with a somewhat older type of detector. Assuming no one was listening, he said, "These bugs are presumably disabled, as they'd want no recording if they were invited to misuse you first. They'd want to be able to say you resisted this sham arrest. Calm down and take your time to pack. Make sure you take only the things you really want. I took their guns, and I won't hesitate to use them if there is no other way."

Surra's breathing slowed a little, and she gave him a brief hug. "I suppose I'll have to get used to the idea that you *really* can fight. It will take some time to believe what my eyes saw. I've got dark glasses so I can give yours back so your young eyes can be disguised."

She proceeded with her packing but was less hurried and more selective in what she packed. She finished in less than ten minutes, and he added two of the confiscated guns and spare ammunition before she closed her bags. He put the other gun and a spare clip in his overcoat pocket. These men seemed to prefer the older, heavier, noisy type of percussion handguns, but he knew how to use them. Perhaps they were fond of creating a racket or hurting their eardrums when they used a gun, Dai thought; it could satisfy their appetites for violence to see their victim jump with fright.

He carried Surra's bags to the entrance and found Tumarok there with two unconscious bodies she had dragged inside the little foyer.

"According to Porrig, these are the 'chicken thieves' who followed us," she explained. Then she smiled sweetly. "They're going to experience awful headaches, and perhaps it might dissuade them from pursuing their petty thieving careers."

Dai also smiled, then grabbed the thieves by their collars and dragged them into Surra's apartment. *Let's give them bigger headaches when they wake up, and give these security dogs a chance to vent their frustration on these sleeping sports when they wake up*, he thought. It might delay them giving the alarm for a few minutes. He draped both bodies over the big bully's legs before he closed the door softly behind him.

He loaded Surra's bags and told the women to make themselves at home on the sledge because he was going to run with it to gain some time before half the security force came after them. The city would be an unhealthy place in an hour or so when Blorck and his chums woke up. When he saw Surra's inquiring glance, he explained that the grav-sledge was easy to run with because of the neutralized weight.

Tumarok looked at Surra. "Jump on and let him run. He needs the exercise. There's more than enough space for both of us. I've never been carted off by any man, and I might enjoy the experience."

Surra smiled with genuine affection and jumped onto the sledge.

Dai started off at a trot to warm his leg muscles. He gradually increased speed until he achieved a comfortable pace he could maintain for hours if need be. People would remember a fit old man running with two old women on a grav-sledge and which way he went, but they would even if he walked. He couldn't do anything about it—they had to get to the countryside without delay. The hunt for Surra and the Pabruk mother and son would be on as soon as those guys woke up and reported

136

in.

The sign at the bus stop said, "Only five hundred meters to Caclo's Corrals." Dai was still breathing evenly when they arrived at the corrals a couple of minutes later.

24

True to his promise, Caclo had everything ready. He recognized "Mother Fov" only, and Dai wondered why his face looked pale and why he couldn't look her in the eyes when he greeted her. As they had planned, Tumarok explained that her son was delayed. Her friends, whom she didn't introduce and who only nodded at Caclo without uttering a word, had volunteered to help her get going and keep her company for the night.

"My son will meet me over there tomorrow sometime." She pointed westward, the opposite direction of the palace, toward a smooth, bare conical hill resembling a giant dunce cap that stood alone in the vast, undulating grasslands dotted with clumps of low trees and bare patches. Dai thought the land looked like the hide of a roughly sheared sheep with scabies.

They had decided on this subterfuge to temporarily mislead pursuers if they questioned Caclo, but Dai intended to take the abused horse in that direction and let it loose with the tracking devices Caclo thought were embedded in the equipment. Trackers wouldn't be fooled, but tracking equipment was another story.

They distributed the packs between the two sledges, which left plenty of space for passengers on both sledges whenever someone grew tired of being in the saddle. Although Tumarok said she was taught to ride, she was far from being accustomed to riding, or even staying on a horse. Dai suspected she would be stiff and sore after a day in the saddle.

Unnoticed by Caclo, Kyr and Porrig hid on the old sledge and quickly made themselves comfortable. Tumarok and Surra were mounted; they had volunteered to lead the horses harnessed to the sledges so Dai could lead the wild one away and do some scouting.

When everything was ready, Tumarok thanked Caclo and bade him farewell. The other two only partially raised their hands in a token salute as if they didn't care one way or another. Ekaasi trotted to one side as if she couldn't care less. She had the wild one on a tight leash and cheekily waved a derisive good-bye to Caclo, who turned a blind eye in her direction.

Dai had chosen the best of the mountain ponies, a gray stallion, because he was the heaviest and would do most of the riding. He rode over to Ekaasi and explained his reasons for buying the wild one. He told her that Caclo had warned of tracking devices planted in the equipment. He figured that instead of going to all the trouble of tracking them down and disposing of them, Sorcuk and her accomplices might just use the signals emitted by the tracking devices to guide a homing missile. Anything could be blamed on people who could not be traced. He intended to let the wild horse go with the halter still on and the tracking devices attached to the end of an almost severed leash, which would break off easily when it snagged on something.

After thinking for a moment, Ekaasi said she could handle the wild one and would take it closer to the ugly hill. It was callous, but if they used the missile before the leash snapped, the horse would at least be out of its mental misery.

About a kilometer outside the city limits, Dai halted the procession in a screen of trees and dismounted. Ekaasi tied the wild one securely to a bare tree and came up to them. Then she held out her arms to Dai and he quickly ran to her with a warm smile. Her equestrian body was as big and hard-muscled as Dai's mountain pony, and with a torso longer and more heavily muscled than Dai's upper body mounted on her forelegs, she was much taller than he was. She picked Dai up high off the ground as if he weighed little more than a cat. He was really glad to see her and loved her fiercely, as she well knew. He embraced her as tightly as she held onto him.

When Ekaasi let Dai down, he introduced her to Surra and Tumarok. They bowed slightly, which he had told them was the accepted way. To his surprise, Tumarok asked to be called "Tumar" since it was shorter and less formal than "Tumarok." Ekaasi looked intensely at her and asked her to come closer. She held her calloused hands out to the girl, and Tumarok took them without hesitation.

"I sense in you a power for good that is chained and suppressed, Tumar. It must be set loose, but the time is not yet. I, and others, will help you when the time is ripe, but you have a lot that must be learned before I can aid you." She sensed Tumar's desire to hug her, so she let go of her hands and picked her up as easily as she had Dai.

Tumar was surprised at the gentle strength in the muscled arms and the softness of the small, hard-looking breasts. The short golden hair that covered Ekaasi's upper torso, as well as her big equestrian body, was smooth and silky to the touch.

Sensing the question Tumar suppressed, Ekaasi said, "Yes, girl, as you can feel, the soft pelt keeps me warm in this cold climate and cool in hot weather, but right now it needs a good brushing. My bare face and hands are used to all kinds of weather, and only my ears need some kind of covering in extreme conditions. I usually bind my hair over them."

Tumar felt herself blushing when Ekaasi put her down.

Ekaasi then held her hands out to Surra. Giving her a brief hug, she told her, "You and I will have to talk sometime during the next few days after you have rescued your father. Oh, don't bother about me knowing about it. You will come to know soon enough that I know more than any human, and before you ask, no, I can't read minds. I'm a diviner priestess, as Dai will tell you. We don't have time right now for a long chat."

Both Surra and Tumarok were pleasantly surprised to learn that Ekaasi and Dai were old friends and that she spoke a number of languages.

Dai had moved away from them to listen intently, while the cats used their senses to check that the area was free of other humans before he used his detector to locate the tracking devices. He found two—one embedded in the stuffing of a saddle and another sewn into a bridle. He cursed softly under his breath as he found it difficult to remove them without damaging the saddle or bridle.

Then he double-checked everything, excluding Ekaasi and the cats, scanning himself, Surra, and Tumar; the animals; and the equipment they bought in town, as well as the sledges. He found a third tracking device attached to the old grav-sledge, but eventually was certain he had found all the devices. Dai felt his ire rise at this low-down, underhanded treachery, but he now understood why Caclo had looked so pale. They must consider themselves outlaws or fugitives, he thought grimly.

He put the tracking devices in a pouch and knotted the

string of the pouch to the end of the wild horse's leash. Ekaasi would cut the leash almost through, an arm's length from the knot, before she released it. The pouch would catch in a bush or bunched grass soon after the wild one was let loose, and the rope or pouch should then snap off.

Dai filled a big canteen with water and handed a knapsack of food to Ekaasi, for he knew she was starved for decent food. In the knapsack, he also included a hunting knife and a set of brushes he knew she would appreciate. She hung both items over a shoulder by their straps without looking at the contents. He asked her to set the wild one free as soon as she felt it wouldn't return to the city.

Surra started to tell Ekaasi how to get to the palace and where they would try to make camp, but Ekaasi politely told her that Kyr would direct her to where they were when she decided to return. There was no need to rush back. She was going to enjoy her freedom first by galloping all over the countryside after setting the wild one free. She would enjoy the sorely needed exercise.

Dai handed Ekaasi the other two confiscated guns and spare clips on the off chance that she must defend herself. She stowed everything in the food bag, which she again hung over her shoulders. Then she gave Dai a powerful hug before leading the wild one away at a trot, which gradually increased to a gallop as the wild one accepted her gentle encouragement and guidance.

Dai led his charges to the park, where he retrieved the stashed guns without incident. He gave Tumar her own weapons and put the spit gun and spare clips in his own pocket. The rest he stowed in the new sledge under the tarpaulin where they could easily be reached.

As the sun set, they climbed the fairly steep hill to the edge of the woods on the northwestern side of the palace, which sat in the middle of the flattened hilltop, about ten acres of fairly level ground. The elevation provided an excellent view of the city and most of the countryside, but limited looking down for any great distance. To the north and northeast, the view was soon obscured by broken, hilly terrain and dense overgrowth. After Dai had a careful look around to memorize details, they moved deeper into the dense forest to escape the suddenly strengthening, colder breeze.

Surra had described the terrain around the palace as about a two-kilometer-thick strip of dense forest, which surrounded the walls of the palace on all sides and had lost the planted-by-man image ages ago. On the west side, it was bisected by a broad, paved road that connected the palace to the city. The forest had been very well preserved and was home to a variety of animals and birds. Hunting on the hill and in the forest was prohibited, but it had not been enforced for the last ten years or so.

The city of Bojon was situated toward the southeastern end of a vast, roughly oval valley stretching north to south. The valley, called Bojon Country, was some three hundred kilometers across at the narrowest point and about a thousand between the farthest points. It was surrounded by high mountain ranges varying from six to ten kilometers high, isolating the inhabitants from the rest of the continent. Access was mostly by air; although a few high passes had been used in bygone eras, they were mostly impassible in winter because of the deep snow. The plateaus, or mountaintops, were perpetually covered by ice and snow, and possibly a glacier or two in remote regions. The river, which started in Bojon, accommodated traffic all year round but wasn't deep enough for large ships. The mountain chains were separated by deep canyons that were mostly unexplored and had never been thoroughly mapped. Some active and a few dormant volcanoes kept most of the known canyons warm throughout the year, allowing ancient life-forms such as giant reptiles, cave bears, mastodons, and saber-toothed tigers to survive, even though they were extinct or almost extinct elsewhere. Perhaps villages existed in some of the canyons, but it really was a no-man's-land that none of the adjoining countries wanted to take responsibility for.

Broken terrain and flat grasslands met here, where the city was situated. The terrain to the east of Bojon was mostly flat grassland, with farms and farming communities up to the Eastern Mountains. West of the city stood the one peculiar-looking hill in the almost flat, broken terrain—a wilderness of gullies, dry open spaces, sparse patches of grass, clumps of thorny trees, thickets, areas of scattered boulders, and the like. It was a place for wild horses and wildlife that fed on grass and leaves. It was thought it might contain mineral wealth, but no prospectors had yet been allowed to look around or even been interested enough to ask to look around.

The north and northeast was a hunter's paradise. It was mostly broken country consisting of a mix of trees, thorny thickets, boulders, hillocks, raised ground, small shallow valleys, and the ancient highway that came from somewhere deep in the unexplored mountains to the northwest. Dai wondered why nobody, on record, had had the guts to go and look for the origin of the road during the last couple of centuries. It was really strange, but he didn't ask, for it had nothing to do with the present situation. Still, it was puzzling, and perhaps someday, when he had nothing better to do, he would come back to take a look.

Surra explained that the palace was previously a fort built three and a half centuries earlier around a strong, permanent spring that had never run dry in recorded history. The spring was also one of the sources of the Hetnog River, which ended in the ocean two thousand kilometers away. The hills on both sides of the spring had been flattened and made into one over time, and the hard rock was used to build the great walls around the former fortress, while the rubble filled the hollow between the hills. Later on, low walls were erected to protect the spring, and then the fort was extended over it so that now the water source was under the palace where it could be reached by a wide stairway. The creek, which ran down to the river on the east side, had once been an entrance, but Surra's grandfather had it sealed with heavy, impervious metal bars that were too hard and thick to be cut by conventional equipment.

The secret entrance, which was really a forgotten escape route, was built to look like a part of the northern wall on the corner formed with the west wall. A self-lubricating lock was enabled or disabled by pressing a series of faintly discolored stones in the correct sequence. According to legend, she said, the natural crack in the rock that formed the start of the passage was covered by rock and concrete slabs during the building of the fort to level the ground above. The intention was to use it as an escape route in the event the fort was overwhelmed, but the passage was only used by smugglers and criminals to escape. After about thirty years, it was blocked at both ends. When it

143

was rediscovered by chance during the building of the palace a century later, it was enlarged in secret by the then king's personal guard, and the perpetual self-lubricating doors were installed.

The narrow passage, which started out as a prehistoric, meandering crack in solid rock, was extended to continue inside one of the palace's inner walls, going past all the old important conference chambers and a couple of bedrooms and ending in the throne hall. The secret doors were thick and sounded like solid rock when knocked on, but they were designed to open noiselessly. From inside the chambers, the doors could be opened by pressing the five protuberances that were part of the royal emblem.

Surra made them memorize the sequence for opening the doors: four, one, three, two, five, counting to the left from the right-hand side; to lock a door again they would just close it. The outer rock door responded to the reverse sequence, and she would show them the naturally colored stones to press from outside and inside when they entered in the morning.

That night, they stopped well inside the forest in a naturally open space. In the next clearing, Dai hobbled the horses and ponies so they could graze on the sparse, dry winter grass. Porrig volunteered to stand guard and watch the horses till after midnight, when he would go into the forest to hunt. Dai said he would take over if Porrig would wake him up.

The women had never camped out and didn't know what to do or where to start. Dai explained how to pitch a tent as he erected the one they would share. Once their camp beds were inside, he prepared a quick meal from tinned provisions over the quick-heating camp stove. After they ate, he said he would provide the means to clean their faces, but not until after the rescue the following day because in his experience, the aged faces had a shock value that slowed an adversary's reaction time for a vital instant. Tumar endorsed that statement with a naughty grin, telling Surra about the vulgar tracker-priest in the park.

They went to bed early since they had to be up and going by seven in the morning. Surra had told Dai that it could take more than an hour to negotiate the tortuous passage, and he thought it prudent to allow three hours for the whole trip since there might be unforeseen delays or obstructions.

Dai elected to sleep under a tree in his sleeping bag, for he was used to it and didn't expect rain. If they had to leave in a hurry, it would be easy to just throw the bag on a sledge. Kyr told him that she would crawl into the tent with Tumar and Surra for a change, but knew the more likely reason was to guard them; Kyr took her orders from Karna seriously. Dai sensed that she had also taken a liking to Tumar.

25

Dai awakened with a drumming in his head. The pattern was hesitant, so he knew immediately it wasn't Kyr. Then he recognized Porrig's "voice," or more accurately, mental wavelength.

I'm sorry, friend Dai, but Kyr said it was safer to wake you up this way. I think it's past midnight, and Kyr said that Ekaasi was on her way. She is near and has something to tell you. Everything else is quiet. I will go and hunt now.

Dai still felt tired and needed more sleep to recover fully, but he crawled out of the bag and had a good stretch to get his blood circulating properly. Perhaps his subconscious mind had done some homework, for he had a sudden inspiration. *Don't be sorry,* he told Porrig. *You're a powerful guy, and I like having you around. Your mind-send feels as if it is bouncing around in my skull. I think you should consider changing your name to Koro, as it rhymes with Kyr and it means "powerful." Porrig sounds a bit juvenile for a big guy like you.*

The cat responded, *I really like that name! It feels like me inside. You hear that, Kyr? You can guard the princess and your Cookie from now on, like you want to do. I'm going to stay, with or without your permission. I'll look after Dai.*

Kyr chuckled in Dai's mind: *Now that's what I call manly assertiveness. I'm getting along in years, Koro, and I may slow down a bit over the next year or two, so I would appreciate some help to look after the overgrown ex-idiot. I welcome you, but I'll scratch your eyes out if you let any harm come to him. Now leave me alone to doze in peace. Go try your luck at catching your own breakfast and bring me the leftovers if you are lucky. Prove your hunting ability to me or let me know if you need more guidance. Congratulations, Dai! You don't deserve it, but you've attracted a competent companion, at last…Now Ekaasi wants to talk to you privately, so hurry up!*

Did he imagine it, or did Kyr's mind-send have the beginnings of the fierce mating desire? It disturbed him, for it was not yet time for her mating madness, but he didn't have time to ponder more because he had to see to their safety on this bitterly cold morning. His watch said one o'clock, and he took stock of their surroundings. There was a stiff breeze from the southwest that intensified the cold.

He started a special breathing exercise to generate warmth in his cold body while he alertly walked to the next clearing. The breeze didn't penetrate here as much as it did at the camping site, but the ponies and horses had bunched together for warmth under a leafy tree. They snorted in a defensive manner, and he quickly moved upwind from them so as not to spook them. When they recognized his scent, they ignored his presence and went back to slumbering on their feet. He reminded himself to give them some oats come daylight.

It was cold and lonely, and he slinked around silently, circling the camp a few times in ever-wider circles until he was satisfied that no danger was lurking around. He relaxed, but kept moving to stay warm and awake because he hadn't gotten any sleep the previous night and not much the night before that either. He had gone without sleep for long periods before, but he knew that involuntary mistakes occurred when he wasn't able to sleep enough, and he couldn't afford to make mistakes with two lives depending on him and perhaps a third later today.

He didn't check his watch again, for he knew that prying eyes would be drawn by its luminous face if he drew his sleeve up to see it. He was sure no one was near, but he didn't want to ignore ingrained discipline, since that might become a habit.

He guessed it was after two o'clock when he heard the faint, uneasy, hesitant call of a lost giant desert quail—out of place in this country since they were only found in Krisa. He twittered the answering call to guide Ekaasi to him. He smiled grimly; it reminded him of the perilous mission in Krisa when she had volunteered to accompany and guide him. During the most dangerous period, when Kyr was away on an even more deadly spying mission, Ekaasi had forced him to practice both calls until they were perfect. When they were forced apart to separate or confuse pursuers, they couldn't call out loudly to find each other again. He then found out how much he had come to depend on Kyr's abilities.

He repeated the call at intervals to guide her and also to tell her it was safe to approach. Three minutes later he heard her soft hoof falls approaching and stepped into the clearing for her to see him. He wished he could see as well as she did in the starlight without the moon to illuminate the landscape.

She hugged him again and said she was feeling a bit tired. Caclo hadn't allowed her to exercise, and she was going to lie down where the breeze would not bother her. Then they must have their long-overdue talk. She went into a dense thicket near the ponies because she knew they would warn them if they heard or smelled an intruder. She said as much to Dai, although she knew he already knew it, while they made themselves comfortable.

"Okay, now I can tell you what brought me here and why it is important for you to understand certain prophecies of the elders of my tribe," Ekaasi began. "It has to do with what you and Kyr were investigating.

"But first…I led the wild one westward at an easy gallop to that misplaced hill Tumar pointed to. A few kilometers from the hill, he seemed to get new life and began to act as if he knew where he wanted to go. He tried to jerk the leash out of my hand as he increased his pace. I thought I might as well cut the leash, and I tried to make him stop, but he wouldn't respond and acted as if he had gone completely crazy.

"I struggled to try to control and bring him to a halt, but eventually he kicked me so hard in the ribs that I involuntarily let go. He took off like a demented demon at full speed in a northwestern direction toward the far mountain, as if he had a destination in mind. When I recovered my knocked-out breath a little, the wild one was already two or more kilometers away. I thought of a few unkind expletives to describe his ungrateful behavior because at that moment, I didn't know that the poor, abused animal had just saved my life.

"I was just wondering if I could catch up with him and whether it was worth the effort, when I heard a peculiar whistle in the sky. Instinct made me drop to the ground and curl up for protection. Before I had time to put my hands over my ears, there was a thunderous detonation, and I knew the wild one had been blown into a better life.

"When my ears recovered somewhat, I investigated. There was a large, shallow hole in the earth, but I couldn't find even one hair of the wild one. It could have been a two-hundred-kilogram warhead someone activated in a panic to get rid of us. They might have thought we were escaping and perhaps were nearing the range limit of their detection instruments. I extinguished a few small fires in the sparse grass that might have spread when the wind increases. So the wild one is mercifully out of his misery, and we may be presumed dead. To get back to the reason I came to this miserably cold country, however—"

Dai interrupted. "You could have been killed before you reached the hill and released the poor thing! Ekaasi, I'm sorry I put your life at risk. No wonder Kyr calls me stupid." His head was almost level with hers when he stood up, so he had to bend just a little to hug her intensely, pushing his cheek against hers.

She patted his shoulder. "I know you didn't do it intentionally. It was one of those unforeseen things. I don't know much about tracking instruments, but I do know they have a limited range. Unfortunately, the thought only entered my mind after that poor horse was blasted out of this life. Maybe an observer panicked, or perhaps they thought we were far enough away for the blast to be unobserved. Anyway, I was lucky this time. Now back to my story.

"Half a century ago, one of our sages went into an involuntary trance and predicted that a good many years into the future, the writings and relics of a bygone era would be discovered in the mountains around Bojon by a young prince of the realm. Ruthless, greedy humans would set off a destructive global war in an attempt to find and steal this legacy from a forgotten, very powerful race of irresponsible humans. Those ancients had a thriving, rich civilization where no one was short of anything, but they destroyed themselves and most of the earth in a power struggle through rampant greediness, lust for power over others, and plain, unadulterated stupidity.

"When rumors of the discovery began to filter through to us, the old sages gathered to check the prediction. The most senior one was assisted into a controlled trance and divined that, although the prediction was true in every way, there was a slim chance that the war could be prevented by you and the temple cats with the assistance of a few others and me as adviser and tutor. They sent word to the Council of the Fighting Priests, who should have given you a full briefing so that you knew what was at stake.

"Guard your tongue in Surra's presence, and don't ever let slip that you know her son is alive. Her baby was taken away and raised by a priestess who now lives in one of the canyons to the north. There is a real probability that Surra will be so overeager and impatient to see her son that she will put his life, and ours, at grave risk. I will tell her when the time is ripe, and it might be wise for you to pretend that you didn't know about it if she confronts you. It won't hurt her to wait another week or so before we have that talk I promised her.

"It was her son who discovered the artifacts, but others were present, too, and saw them. One of them tried to sell the information to the wrong person. For his effort he was tortured for details and killed afterward.

"Rumor has it that the treasure was discovered in an almost inaccessible place and is extremely difficult to find. It is also rumored that the priestess, who is also a scientist, knows the location and is relocating some of the major artifacts to an unknown destination. The dangerous inventions are supposedly booby-trapped to make it difficult for unscrupulous people to tamper with them until she and her accomplices decide what to do with them.

"We understand that these are only rumors and probably devoid of the truth. She is very wise, and we suspect she has been doing her own divinations for many, many years. I don't know how our sages found out, but we know that she is very much afraid, although not for herself.

"The sages emphasized that the young prince must be protected at all cost, but they deemed it wise not to tell me why he is so important that he must be protected until Bojon is made safe. Surra is important for a different reason, and we are to protect her at all times, but she must also be taught to defend herself better. That pleasant task is yours because I have a different body and therefore different methods, unsuitable for humans to imitate or copy.

"The king must be brought to safety, as he is the one who must transfer knowledge and complete the prince's training. Even though it is not crucial that he survives, we must help him to the best of our abilities. He must be told that he is important to give him a reason to struggle to stay alive. That's your responsibility, too, by the way, but you must choose an opportune moment. I can't do it because, as you know, I'm incapable of answering questions with anything other than the honest truth"—Ekaasi giggled like a human girl—"whereas you were taught to lie with a straight face.

"Now get moving—the sky is paler. We will talk again, for I have only given you a brief outline. I will look after the ponies and the camp until you return, with or without the king."

26

Dai yawned uncontrollably a few times as he gathered firewood on the way back to the temporary camp. When breakfast was almost ready, he asked Kyr to wake up Tumar and Surra. Kyr told him to deal with them himself because they were already awake, decently dressed, but unwilling to stir. She was going out to hunt, as that bungling Koro had wandered far away and would be lost without her guidance. Dai again detected the subtle stirring of her mating urge, as he had so many times before, but this one was way out of period. Perhaps it was because of her advancing years. Since by tonight it would control her, he only hoped it would stay away until the king was rescued. Otherwise, without her and Koro, the task might be more difficult.

He removed the pan from the fire so the meat wouldn't burn, then opened the tent flap. The two women were smothered under blankets and even had their heads covered.

When they were done eating, Dai sent a call to Kyr, hoping that she still kept track of him.

Of course I do, stupid, she replied. *Koro eventually caught a hare, the lucky guy, but he ate the whole thing and can hardly move. I found a cold partridge trying to stay warm underneath a bush, and that's enough of a meal. We'll meet you by the wall because it's closer for Koro, and I can drag him by the tail if I must.*

She chuckled in glee, and he knew she had cut Koro in on the thought exchange. Poor guy; he wasn't used to the wilds, but he'd learn quickly under Kyr's exasperating but expert guidance. She'd let him make small mistakes like this one so that he'd learn to think for himself and heed her advice when it was offered. Dai had liked the casual way Koro joined them and was beginning to enjoy the cat's company, but he didn't let the thought surface, for Kyr might be offended. He loved her with his whole being but thought she deserved to be less active, for she was getting on in years, although she wouldn't admit it.

He made sure the fire was doused and then set a fast pace for the nearest wall. He could only hope that the secret passage and doors were still undiscovered and not blocked or booby-trapped. They would gain some extra time if they could secretly spirit the king away without being seen, and their disguises should throw any observer off their track. Dai was alert as always, but now he was just a bit more careful, since he took his role as protector seriously. He had cautioned the women to be silent because any unusual noise would immediately alert anyone who was used to the silence in the woods. He noticed that Tumar copied him without being told, and that her tread became softer as they progressed.

He had looked upon her as a city-bred child, even though he was only two or three years older, but she had quietly proved him wrong on a number of occasions. He was beginning to develop a healthy respect for her unusual attention to detail and other abilities. She had a remarkable analytical mind and unusual adaptability, or perhaps it was training or survival instinct, he thought.

In contrast, Surra just concentrated on keeping up with him, and she walked as noisily as a horse on a paved road, even though she was very fit. She would be harder to teach because she exhibited the typical inattentive deafness and blindness of a person who grew up in the city.

He stopped suddenly, and Surra bumped into him with a soft "umph." He turned to them with a finger on his lips and pointed to the ground in front of him. "Fresh tracks," he whispered. "Someone is scavenging around, perhaps a poacher, because there are older prints from the same boots. We must be careful and quiet because we need to see the prowler before he senses us. I don't want to kill an innocent person, but we must treat him as a potential enemy."

Dai immediately noticed that Surra now paid attention to where she stepped. He realized that although she had been taught to track game, it hadn't yet penetrated her mind that they were now fugitives and must make it a habit to be wary at all times. He also noticed that Tumar looked alert, listened, and scanned the area around them. He approved. She would be an asset in the wilds when properly trained.

The tracks were going toward the palace walls, but then

veered away sharply. He noticed that deer tracks also went that way. He whispered, "This intruder can also read tracks, for he took off after a deer that passed a little earlier. Therefore, we must trick him, because he will notice our tracks if he comes back this way." He pointed to the tracks and explained what he saw for Tumar's education. He liked transferring some of his knowledge to a pupil who was eager to learn.

He noticed that both women were now wary, and indications were that they would stay that way. He was relieved but didn't show it.

To make their footprints harder to read, he chose harder ground when he found it, but it was difficult. He searched for a certain kind of bush, and when he came across it, he carefully broke a medium-sized leafy branch off from the inside. He explained that if he broke the branch off from the outside, it would be noticed by a tracker. He intended to wipe their tracks out carefully when they were near the wall, just in case the hunter got curious if he came back that way. Illegal hunters tended to investigate anything out of the ordinary, since it could compromise their safety; they usually knew the penalty for being caught.

Kyr told him that she and Koro were waiting near the northwest corner and that the gorged Koro looked a bit better after some exercise. Dai looked for hard ground and found an outcrop of flat rock. He had Tumar and Surra step onto it and proceed to the now plainly visible north wall. He walked off the outcrop with short steps in a northerly direction and then walked carefully backward on his own tracks. This tactic often baffled trackers if meticulously done.

Where the women had stepped off the ground, he walked backward and very delicately removed all tracks leading to where they waited with the cats.

"How far are we from the entrance?" he asked Surra.

"It's right here," she whispered. "Do you want me to open it?"

"Not yet. Is it safe to do so, Kyr?" he whispered so that Surra would know why he'd stopped her, although it might baffle her how he communicated with a cat.

Kyr lifted her head in a slow semicircle as if she was sniffing the air. She told him the hunter was about two kilometers away. Dai told Surra it was safe to open the door, which she did. When the ancient door had opened noiselessly, he asked them to step inside while he very, very carefully obliterated their tracks. He dropped the branch inside a small cubicle behind the entrance and then closed the door.

It was pitch-dark, and he activated the battery-operated lamp he'd brought along. Surra pointed to five protuberances above the door that looked like naturally colored stone and said they had to be pressed in the correct sequence, but with power, not just a touch.

Dai asked Koro to go first and act as scout. If he found anything that didn't smell right, he was to report it and wait right there until Dai checked it out. He asked Kyr to act as rear guard, on the off-chance that someone might follow them.

He had Surra walk behind him and Tumar after her because the passage was very narrow and he wanted Surra's guidance when necessary. The floor was dusty, and only Koro's tracks spoiled the thin film, but Dai stepped warily, as was his way. He looked at his watch—the first time since leaving the camp—and realized with a shock that it was past nine. Surra told him it took almost forty minutes to reach the palace from the passage's entrance.

After walking for some time, they passed a colored line that went from one wall to the ceiling and down the other wall to the floor. When Dai asked Surra about its significance, she told him to immediately douse the light and stop because they were near the first secret door and light might shine through a crack. The line was a warning. He looked at his watch before extinguishing the lamp and saw that it was almost ten minutes to ten. It seemed that his insistence on getting started at seven had brought them here just in time.

Surra felt for Tumar's hand, which she guided to Dai's belt. Then she squeezed past Dai and asked him softly to hold onto her belt so she could guide them. She held the fingers of her right hand lightly against the right-hand wall as they proceeded slowly. When she felt a protuberance, she stopped. Dai had counted thirty steps from the line.

After listening attentively, she slowly opened a peephole. The room was empty, but she double-checked. As they passed every room after that, they checked it thoroughly. The dining room and the old entertainment hall were devoid of life, and to her the palace felt empty. All the bedrooms were empty and only the king's bed had been slept in.

"The palace is deserted," Surra whispered. "I don't even see a loitering guard. The next and last is the throne room. We should find my father there unless we are too late and he has already been murdered."

Dai automatically counted his steps again and had almost reached thirty when Surra came to a standstill. She opened the peephole very slowly. Dai's watch indicated two minutes to ten. He shared the peephole for a moment with Surra before he made room for Tumar to have a look at the layout of the fairly large room or small hall.

In the room, the king sat on the throne, halfway on his back with his arms draped over the armrests, looking half-asleep but watching something on his left side—the picture of someone waiting unenthusiastically for detested visitors or an unpleasant interview. The secret door was on the right side of the throne but opened a little way behind it; the back of the throne was two meters from the wall. The throne was in the center of a raised floor more than a meter higher than the main floor and four meters from the three room-wide steps connecting it to the lower floor.

Double-entry doors were about thirty meters directly in front of the throne, and anyone who entered would be visible from this peephole. The room was ten meters wide, austere, and nearly barren of furniture. The present and previous monarchs hadn't wasted anything on showy decorations, he thought. Perhaps the throne room wasn't used often.

Dai had a sudden premonition he couldn't ignore. It was an acquired intuition that had saved his life many times.

"May I borrow your stunner?" he asked Tumar in a whisper. She handed it over without a word and sat down on the dusty floor to rest her feet. Surra followed her example and left the peephole to Dai.

27

Dai asked if the door could be opened and held in check with fingers to prevent it from swinging wide open. Surra said yes. A coiled, perm-greased gadget between the hinges assisted it to swing outward quickly but quietly. There was a hollow at the top where fingers could be hooked in to prevent the door from swinging open prematurely. Dai used his fingers to find the hollow, then held the door in check as he opened it.

He saw the king glance impatiently at his watch and again look at something on the left armrest where his hand had rested. Dai checked his own watch and saw that it was four minutes past ten. The sham divination was supposed to be just after ten. The high priest and Sorcuk were very late, and he wondered if the king would be irritated when they arrived, even if it was his own daughter.

At six minutes after ten, the king arose angrily. He was just about to take the first step down when the double doors were flung open and the high priest marched in airily, without announcement, with Sorcuk in tow. He carried a sheaf of papers in his left hand.

Dai realized it was a deliberately planned, discourteous gesture to provoke the king to anger.

The king paused and said angrily, "Both your timepieces can't be that wrong at the same time. Get out, both of you! I'm not interested in the lies you're about to dish up."

The king took the first step down, but Heltos bowed and said in a condescending and insincere tone, "I beg your forgiveness, Your Majesty, but I decided to make the divination beforehand. Unfortunately, it took longer than I anticipated and—"

"You both stink of deception, and you lie glibly as always, you evil-smelling fraud," the king interrupted angrily. "Do you really expect me to believe that utter nonsense? The reason I waited this long, you foolish conspirators, was to find out what hellish brew you've concocted this time. Sorcuk, don't you realize that Heltos is just a scrawny, brain-dead, murderous pretender who wants to marry you for his own evil purposes? You will be dead within a month after your so-called 'ordained' marriage.

"I saw you two arrive long before ten, and then you stood outside, peeping through the keyhole like naughty children, whispering and assuring your stupid selves that nothing could go wrong with your murderous plot if I got impatient enough. I know what you two are planning. Now get out before I ask the guards to throw you out, and don't come back—ever." He looked at Sorcuk, loathing plainly visible on his face, and asked, "What have you done with my daughter, you crazy hellcat?"

Heltos was caught off guard by the king he thought he was leading by the nose and exposed in front of the gullible woman he was using to further his own ambitions; his face was a study in red and purple splotches. Dai thought he imitated a freshly landed fish, the way his thin-lipped mouth opened and closed as if his nose was clogged. He sputtered as he tried to speak placating words, but and he couldn't get a word out.

Sorcuk's face contorted with hate, and she replied with venom in her voice, "I have news for you, you pudgy old drip! She, together with her boyfriend and his ugly mother, became ghosts late yesterday when they thought they could outrun a two-hundred-kilogram blast missile. Their atoms are scattered all over the country to the west. Now you only have one daughter left, you wife-murdering beast."

She smirked when she saw the king's devastated face. Then she snatched the papers out of Heltos's hand and demanded, "Now sign these documents, or I'll kill you, too. You're not fit to be king!"

But the king looked her straight in the eyes, took the papers, and tore them to shreds without looking at them. With a sad voice he told, "You're going to kill me anyway—if you can, that is. I'm so sorry you inherited your mother's insanity and let yourself be deceived by this rotten, stinking, bogus priest. I realized you had a kink in the top story when you and your mother used that lame excuse to cut up the daughter I loved with all my heart. But I gave you the benefit of the doubt at the time because my blood flows in your veins. Now I can see the madness plainly in your eyes, and you must be restrained." He threw the shreds into her face and yelled, "GUARDS!"

Sorcuk's laugh sounded shrill and nasty. Dai detected an insane note in it, and her eyes now plainly showed the madness that was previously held at bay. Poor girl, he thought with sorrow; the scheming priest is preying on her desperation to be a mother. He must be held accountable. Right now I can only give the bastard a fierce headache, but I'll come back for him.

"Scream as loudly as you want, you old goat!" Sorcuk yelled in a completely out-of-control voice. "Your so-called loyal guards have all been bought or replaced. Everyone will be deaf to your frantic yells." Sorcuk turned her face toward Heltos and pulled a knife out of her belt. "He knows too much. We must cut the swine's throat right now, before he can escape."

Dai now saw her face clearly through the opening and couldn't believe the metamorphosis. Her lovely face was transformed to an evil mask by madness—or was it hatred? Spittle streamed out of the corners of her mouth, and her eyes were wide open and staring, as if she had been drugged; but her vicious gestures and body movements weren't impaired.

As Dai cautiously opened the secret door, Heltos eagerly reached inside his robe and brought out the ceremonial cat's claw. He grinned evilly in anticipation as he saw the king's eyes on the murder weapon, but both he and Sorcuk froze in shock when the king calmly drew a handgun from the sleeve of his ceremonial robe and pointed it rock-steady at Heltos's now shock-contorted face.

The king sighed heavily. "I thought I recognized you! As you can see, this time I'm prepared for your treachery, you phony! If you have a bogus prayer to offer to any of your false gods, say it quickly."

The king hesitated a moment; it was clear that he didn't want to shoot his own daughter. The pause gave Dai the chance to shoot the priest and Sorcuk in the head with the stun gun. He was ready to paralyze the king's gun arm, but the king looked bewilderedly at his own gun and then at the two falling. Dai suppressed a smile. The stunner was an almost silent weapon, and the king wouldn't have heard it hiss. Instead of keeling over, Sorcuk and Heltos deflated like rubber dolls at the astounded king's feet. Dai was quite sure that neither Heltos nor Sorcuk would ever know that they had been hit by a mini stun bolt.

Tumar saw the humor in the situation and smiled. It

seemed Dai also believed in giving his enemies excruciating headaches whenever he could.

Dai pushed the door open the rest of the way and called out, "Don't shoot, sir. We're on your side." He put his hands in the air to show his peaceful intention, but was pushed out of the way by Surra, followed almost immediately by Tumar.

Before Surra could open her mouth, the king dropped his gun and rushed to her. "What have they *done* to you, sweetheart?"

Surra embraced her confused father. Tears were streaming down his face and into her hair, and she had to use all her strength to break his embrace.

Dai dropped his arms and returned the stunner to Tumar. He was truly amazed that the king had recognized his daughter through the old-woman disguise.

"I'm sorry, Father." Surra touched her face. "This is not real. It's artificial skin to confuse my enemies. I'll explain later, as we don't have time now. Oh, this is Daiyus—call him Dai—and this is Tumar. Meet Hespus, my father. We came to spirit you away for a while until things can be sorted out. Dai will tell you about the conspiracy and the reason we don't want Heltos or Sorcuk killed."

"Sir, we don't want anyone to know that we've been here, if at all possible," Dai said. "The reason I only stunned Sorcuk and the high priest before you could shoot is that they must not be harmed, at least not yet. We are trying to identify those who are behind this attempt to usurp your throne. Your enemies are determined to do away with you, and if you disappear, it may prompt Heltos to give away a name or two and reveal the identities of other plotters who want to take over your country. Please trust us. I'll explain everything as soon as we get you to safety."

"You came as if in answer to my prayers," Hespus said. "I didn't know where or to whom to turn for help after I found out that Sorcuk wanted me dead. Yes, Dai, if Surra trusts you enough to show you our secret way, I'll trust you with my life." The king shrugged and gave a wry smile. "I don't have a choice anyway because there are plenty of ways to murder me, which I can't prevent if my guards can be lured or scared away so easily. Just tell me what I need to do and what I can take along."

"Sir, you'll need warm clothes without the royal emblem and warm walking boots. We only need some long-range weapons for defense and hunting. I assume you have some in your personal armory, sir, and I'll fight my way bare-handed to the armory if need be."

The king smiled. "There's no need to fight, Dai. The armory is next door, a part of my bedroom. Come." He turned toward a door Dai already knew led to his bedroom.

"I'll follow in a moment, sir. I just want to rearrange the high priest a little more uncomfortably. He deserves to wake up with sore, screaming muscles." Dai was comforted to hear the king laugh naturally. *The old man is not a coward, but with a daughter like Surra, I didn't think he would be*, he thought. Dai was known as "The Avenger," but he wasn't a vengeful person. The name was invented to put the fear of the devil into the minds of evildoers, but now, as the would-be victim of these two plotters, he felt he owed them a few extra discomforts, if only petty and minor, in retaliation for the inconveniences they had all been subjected to.

He draped Sorcuk over the throne in such a way that she would have a sore neck, aching back, and leg muscles to complement the headache for a few days. One leg was draped over one armrest of the throne at an extreme angle in a shamelessly revealing posture that would immediately draw the eyes of anyone entering the throne room and hold the attention for quite a while. *She wanted the throne, so let her have it!*

He rearranged Heltos on the steps as if he were peering up at the shameless, indecent exposure on the throne above, but in a severely twisted position that Dai knew would cause agonizing pain and cramping muscles when the priest twitched or tried to move. *This heartless, scheming high priest deserves every minor and major agony I can possibly arrange*, he thought with satisfaction. *He only thinks of himself and his own selfish desires and has no mercy for anyone else in that twisted mind of his.*

28

When Dai entered the bedroom, the king had already changed into warm, nondescript clothes and boots. He was telling Surra, "...for your own safety, you were conditioned not to remember, but a trigger was implanted that would cause you to remember when you heard of my death. Go ahead. The built-in biometric identifier inside will recognize your handprints and eye pattern. I chose that as a verifying check because it can't easily be duplicated or faked out. One's eye pattern disappears a very short while after one dies."

Dai saw Surra at the door of a huge walk-in safe. He could see she was hesitant, but she put her left eye up to a hole through which a dull red light was shining. She pulled her head away after two seconds, and the red changed to green. Surra smiled as if relieved and put her right eye to the same hole and then held her left hand on a scanning device on the left side of the door. After a series of loud clicks, she pushed the sliding door to the right, the opposite of the normal direction, although there was a deep groove for that purpose on the right side.

The king saw Dai and explained, "My strong room was sensitized to Surra's eye patterns and handprints when she was twelve years old. Her left or right hand can open the door, but if she lost one eye, it must scan the remaining eye twice for recognition. She was then hypnotized to forget it completely if she was tortured for information and to remember it when she heard I was dead. If I cannot return to this palace, I wanted her to know that she can open this private armory. Oh...ah...yes, as a last safeguard, if the door is opened to the left, one must stand to the left and let someone you dislike intensely do it. There will be an almighty outward blast on the right-hand side.

"I was reluctant to trust Sorcuk with any information about the secrets of the palace, and today I was vindicated in that. Now go in and help yourself to whatever you want. I will take my old percussion-type hunting rifle, which uses solid projectiles. It's got quite a kick, but it will stop a giant reptile in its tracks. There should be a thousand rounds of bullets in a box underneath it."

Dai was surprised at the extensive collection of old and modern hunting weapons in the vault. It would be the envy of any one of the many collectors he knew, a few of whom thought they had large collections. The collection lacked only the blaster type of rifle, but the previous kings and Hespus were obviously interested in hunting weapons only. Dai wasn't surprised to see a large number of old bows and arrows. He wasn't envious, but he would have liked to add some of them to his slowly growing collection.

For now, he wanted to be able to stop an airborne tank if necessary, so he chose a heavy energy-bolt gun he knew would stop a mammoth or a giant reptile with ease at four hundred meters, and a long-range light-energy rifle complete with a sophisticated rangefinder telescope for hunting, which could be adjusted for night use as well. He saw night-vision helmets and took four of them, for they would be invaluable if they had to play hide-and-seek at night.

He noticed that Tumar, after thinking briefly, chose the same types of weapons and realized that she knew their uses and followed his example. His opinion of her increased, and he was grateful for the backup she would provide. He suddenly realized that he had grown to really like her; she was a rare type of competent girl who gave thought to whatever she was doing without being loquacious. She was indeed an extraordinary individual.

Surra chose a rapid-fire energy weapon that wasn't really effective or accurate at a range greater than a hundred meters, but it would be fine for defense.

Dai carried the cases of ammunition and recharge magazines out of the gunroom. He knew he was strong enough to carry all of it on his back if necessary. Then he thought of Ekaasi and selected a short energy rifle that used the same recharge magazines as the light hunting rifles. It had a strap for easy carrying over a shoulder, as did all the rifles—which made him want to pat the king on the shoulder for the thoughtfulness.

Although Ekaasi abhorred killing, she needed something better than a noisy, inaccurate handgun to discourage attackers from a longer distance. He knew she could use a rifle because he had taught her, and she had used one effectively on a number of occasions. She was an excellent shot and would kill

163

when the situation demanded it.

The king produced three extra-strong backpacks from a closet, and Dai gratefully packed the boxes into two of them after he had pushed a magazine into every gun. He asked the king if the percussion gun was his favorite, and receiving a yes, packed the heavy box of ammunition into the third backpack. He would carry two of the heaviest backpacks, Tumar the other one, and Surra would carry a rucksack with extra clothing for her father and two guns. Dai suspected that the king wasn't too healthy because he was somewhat flabby, but he was strong enough to carry his own rifle over a shoulder through the winding tunnel and the two kilometers to the camp. He knew he must be diplomatic and try not to inadvertently damage the older man's pride.

Kyr flashed him a warning that two guards outside the throne room were thinking of entering because it had been too silent for too long. The high priest had told them to wait outside and guard the entrance, but to be ready to assist if he called. They were talking about taking a quick peek to see what was going on.

Dai asked Kyr to close the secret door and that she and Koro then come to the bedroom. Then he asked Tumar to incapacitate the guards with her stunner when they came through the double door.

Tumar nodded, smiled grimly, and moved to the still-open bedroom door. She was happy she could do something, for she had felt like excess baggage until now. She opened the bedroom door enough to have a full view of the double doors to the throne room, drew the stun gun, and sat down to wait, ready to disable the guards the moment they entered. She knew that the guards' eyes would be riveted on the Sorcuk display on the throne, for she had taken a peek and grinned at the arrangement. It drew *her* eyes, all right. Dai really was a naughty boy, she thought, but she knew that his intention was to attract attention to the throne so they would have a slight advantage if they were still here when someone came along to investigate.

Kyr told her the guards had taken a quick look through the keyhole and were debating whether to enter, since they could only dimly see Sorcuk and the priest lying alone in the room in what looked like very awkward positions. They couldn't get a clear view because something, maybe a cobweb, half-obscured the keyhole. Then Kyr warned that the guards had at last mustered enough courage to enter.

Tumar saw one of the doors being pushed open slowly and a head appear. Then the mouth in the head called out loudly, "Your holy eminence, are you all right?" She heard a low muttering before the door opened cautiously and both guards entered. They approached the throne slowly, their eyes riveted on Sorcuk, who was sprawled on the throne in a very unladylike posture.

Tumar saw that they didn't even spare a glance for "your holy eminence" on the steps. Perhaps even they thought the unholy priest deserved stiff muscles. Then she gave each guard a neck shot so quickly that they dropped almost simultaneously. She had decided that they should wake up a little before the other two; perhaps they would like another look at the princess before they thought of restoring her modesty.

A neck shot was the correct choice, Cookie, Kyr thought to her.

29

Dai asked Tumar if he could have two of her mini bombs. The existence of the secret passage would be surmised because of the king's disappearance. Dai wanted to prepare traps in the event that the secret doors here or in the throne room were discovered and broken open. He told Surra and the king that the traps could be disabled by cutting a certain string before the door was opened, but it had to be done from inside the tunnel.

He showed Surra how and where he'd set the trap in the throne room's secret door; it would go off if anyone opened the door from the throne room side. He would attach the one in the king's bedroom as they left.

Dai locked the king's heavy bedroom door and gave him the key. It was only of nuisance value, but it would delay pursuit long enough. Surra made doubly sure that the armory was securely locked before she opened the secret door in the king's bedroom.

The king gallantly offered to carry Tumar's heavy burden. Tumar, sensing that he wasn't healthy and fit, gave him her best smile and said coquettishly, "Oh no, sir, I'm not as old as I look. It isn't that heavy anyway."

They all laughed. The king felt better, and Dai wanted to kiss Tumar. He realized that her unconstrained empathy for all creatures was almost as instinctive as breathing. Nobody in his or her right mind could dislike her.

Kyr went in first to lead the way. Her role as advance scout was to make sure that no unpleasant surprises had been set up in their absence. Surra followed, then her father and Tumar. Koro entered last. Dai closed the heavy secret door, and Tumar turned on one of the camp lights the king had provided. Dai connected the bomb. It was a bit awkward in the narrow passage, but Koro, Dai, and Tumar backed up toward the throne room so that Surra could show her father how to disconnect the tiny bomb. Both of them had to be prepared if one of them returned from outside or had to make the doors safe again.

After about forty minutes, Kyr warned them to stop and extinguish the lights because someone was examining the wall outside for a secret entrance. Surra stopped in her tracks and switched her light off. The king bumped into her, since Kyr had not included him in the mind flash, but he knew instinctively that he had to be quiet. In a whisper Surra asked Tumar if the cat had really spoken to her.

"Yes, it's quite a story," Tumar whispered. She sensed that the king was mystified, but he kept silent. "They only speak to a person if they trust him or her completely. Count yourself one of the rare, lucky ones, because not everyone can communicate with them or understand them."

Oh, shut up, Cookie, you embarrass me, Kyr admonished. She included Surra in the exchange, who chuckled softly.

Kyr added that the person outside was the same individual whose tracks Dai had found earlier. Although it was awfully difficult, she included the astounded king in this communication, since it would save a lot of whispering that might be heard outside. Koro sensed the drain on Kyr's energies, and, unasked, synchronized with her to boost her power to communicate with a difficult one such as the king.

Kyr said the hunter had come across their tracks upon his return and decided to follow them out of inquisitiveness. He was the avaricious type and thought he might profit if he found information about the track-makers that could be sold to the right party. Now he was wondering if they had been pulled up the wall or if there was a secret door, since he found no scuff marks where the tracks ended abruptly. He also couldn't find evidence that the tracks were wiped out, and he was mystified.

Koro brushed past their legs to join Kyr. Dai remembered that there was enough space in the cubicle just inside the door to accommodate all of them in a sitting position, and he softly suggested that they shrug the backpacks off and sit down to wait. He silently dropped his packs and felt his way to Kyr and Koro, who sat in front of the door as if they were staring straight through the solid stone at the nosy interloper. Dai sat down and opened his mind and thoughts to them.

If he opened the door and shot the person outside, he thought, they would have a body to hide, which would be difficult and time-consuming without leaving some sort of trace. Any knowledgeable tracker would be able to figure out what happened for weeks to come. If the man didn't turn up at his destination, someone might be sent soon to look for him, which might lead others here.

They could ask Ekaasi to come and chase the guy away, but that would also draw undesired attention to their whereabouts. No, it might be more difficult, but they must wait for the nosy hunter to get going. Perhaps Kyr and Koro would agree to hurry him along and discourage him from returning to the woods any time soon.

Dai heard the silent cat-laughter and received a picture of two cats scratching and biting a man's backside while he galloped at top speed, screeching his head off. He approved and almost, but not quite, felt sorry for the man. He agreed that the greedy person deserved every scratch and bite he would get in his rear.

Yes, he will sleep on his stomach for weeks, we promise. We desired to do the same thing to Heltos, but this one will do for practice.

Dai quietly whispered to his companions that they had to wait for the interloper to leave, but it shouldn't be long. His eyes were adapted to the dark by now, and he could faintly see what he was doing. He passed his flask to the king and asked him to take a few sips of water even if he wasn't thirsty. The women did the same, and when Dai received his flask back, he poured some water into a flat metal dish he always kept with him for Kyr. He made sure the cats drank enough before he took a few mouthfuls. He didn't think the subdued lapping noise the cats made could be heard outside by human ears.

He sat flat on his buttocks, since that was the most comfortable position he could assume without tiring his legs. He let his mind go quiet—that is, he suspended thought, as he was taught long ago by Karna and other mentors. It was supposed to relax his body completely so his energy levels could be preserved or renewed.

He felt a peculiar, inexplicable wrench in his brain, as if a little muscle was being torn. It was followed by such a brief moment of disorientation or dizziness that he dismissed it as imagined until Kyr told him that the interloper was leaving. The quidnunc had decided to follow the tracks to see where they came from; he hoped to learn something he might be able to sell, or perhaps he could help himself to a few things if he was lucky enough to find an unguarded campsite.

Dai quickly pressed the stones in the memorized sequence. The cats were out as soon as they could squeeze through the opening. Twenty seconds later they heard an agonized scream of pain, the first of many, almost continuous screams that rapidly faded away. Koro let Dai know he had never enjoyed himself so much and that he never thought any human could run as fast and furiously as this one.

Dai smiled and thought how Kyr and Koro seldom could relax completely or enjoy themselves, especially Kyr. The faintly growling undertone in her mental communication told him that *that time* of the year had arrived for her, which initially was the reason for Koro's requested company. It would start in all its madness in an hour or so. She was old and now conceived infrequently, and even though she still got the urge at almost regular intervals, as was their nature, it would gradually diminish over the next few years and then stop completely. He silently wished them happiness, although he knew it would be a violent one-night affair and a two- or three-day recovery period, if not more.

30

Dai carefully obliterated their tracks near the secret door before he led them away. About three hundred meters from the wall, he found the poacher's rifle and the small deer he had shot. When the cats had pounced on him, he had abandoned everything to escape the furious felines. Dai left the rifle where it was and didn't even bother to conceal their tracks since the ground was hard and the poacher wouldn't be back soon. It was awkward, but he shouldered the deer, for it would otherwise be wasted. Surra had said that to her knowledge there weren't any large carnivores in the forest.

When they neared the camp, he whistled in a peculiar way. It was not really a whistle, but it sounded that way to anyone not schooled in the Permerian language. The answer came in exactly five seconds, which meant everything was in order.

Ekaasi met them as they entered the camp. Dai introduced her to the king, and she offered him the usual half-bow acknowledgement with her front legs slightly crossed. It almost looked like a curtsy, but Dai knew that to a Permerian it meant the same as a handshake to humans. He approved as the king offered a half bow in return, since that was the correct response in a polite greeting between equals. Perhaps the king had met a Permerian before, or else he was well informed.

Ekaasi looked the king up and down. He was on the plump side though not yet obese; but lack of exercise was obvious in his posture, and the brisk two-kilometer walk had made him short of breath. With her training, she immediately identified that the king had developed a heart condition, but it was not too serious yet.

"Glad to make your acquaintance, Hespus," she said. "You've been careless with your health and are developing a serious heart problem." She gave him a warm smile. "You've grown a bit too much in the wrong direction, I'm sorry to say. I'll look around for some herbs to help curb your appetite until you can be treated properly at a clinic. Sorry if I sound too abrupt, but I always get directly to the point. It saves time."

She looked at Dai and asked in the same tone of voice, "When did you last have a proper night's sleep?"

Dai knew she wouldn't ask such a question without a valid reason. He therefore replied with the truth. "About four nights ago, I think, on the way here, but I had about four hours' sleep two nights ago, and about two hours last night." He wondered what she was leading up to.

"So you could go on for another twelve hours or so without falling over your feet. I can sense that you are nearing your limit of endurance without proper rest, but we may have to leave tonight. Make the king comfortable so he can rest, and you might as well clean up your faces. I don't think satellite technology has improved so much during the last week that they would recognize your faces from up there, but wear hats anyway, like hunters. I'm going to take a walk around." She turned to leave.

Dai said, "Wait a moment, please. I brought you something better and less noisy than those awkward handguns. You have used one before, and King Hespus had enough ammunition in his personal arsenal that you can practice on a few innocent rocks if you feel like it." He passed the short rifle to her. "It's loaded, and I'll give you extra clips the moment I can put these rucksacks and this deer down. On the other hand, I think I'll put the box with the recharges under the seat on the big old sledge so you can help yourself whenever necessary. I don't think we'll be attacked today unless someone followed our tracks from Caclo's."

Ekaasi accepted the rifle and flung it over a shoulder. "Thank you, Hespus, Dai. I'll keep the handguns for backups. Although I dislike the things, it's better to have more than one just in case. I'll see you all later," she said as she walked away. Soon she was hidden by the vegetation, but they heard the *click-clock* sound of her hooves for a while after since she wasn't trying to be silent.

Dai produced a camping chair for the king and then filled two small basins with water. He opened his last tube of mask remover, squeezed a little into his hand, and handed the open tube to Surra. "Squeeze about half of this into your hand, pass the rest to Tumar, and then rub it gently in both hands to get an even distribution. Close your eyes and rub it thoroughly all over your face and then hands. After a minute, wash your face with this soap and dry. You do the same, Tumar. The gray in your hair will wash out with any kind of soap or shampoo."

He rubbed his own face very carefully and rinsed under a trickle of icy water from the tank on the new sledge. His face was still painful and he didn't want to damage the artificial skin. Then he set about preparing something to eat because it was well after midday. He didn't look at the women as they washed their faces.

To make conversation, the king said, "You had me fooled with that old face, Dai. It's remarkable. I still wonder how I recognized my own daughter. Where did you come across that half-horse creature, and will she recognize you?"

Dai straightened, looked intently at the king, and said, "This disguise cream is top secret, sir, and it has saved more lives than I've had breakfasts. Please don't mention it to anyone. Yes, Ekaasi is a sensitive and will recognize me with any disguise. Have you met her kind before?" He continued preparing the light lunch.

"No, but I've heard about them. She is the very first I've seen in the flesh, but I've been taught about them and had them described to me. There are no pictures or information about them in any libraries."

"Sir, I'm not lecturing, but your response to her polite curtsy was the only correct one. It's their way of acknowledging an equal, but you'll have to earn her respect if you want it." He noticed that Tumar and Surra were listening intently while they were washing in the cold water.

"She will turn her back on you and completely ignore you as if you don't exist if she hears you calling her a half horse. They have no horse blood in them and are not related to humans, either. If you are permitted to touch one of them, you'll find their body hair so soft and silky, you wouldn't believe it. As a matter of fact, they have no respect for us warlike, greedy humans, but they will help and guide humans if and when they deem it necessary, and if they consider the human worthy of help.

"They are of a completely different evolution and are dying

out because they have lost the urge to breed. They are highly intelligent, more so than the brightest human I know of, and they specialize in the sciences of the mind. They have developed their mental abilities to a very high degree, and the wisest human is still a child compared to one of them. It seems that the more interested one becomes in developing the mind, the less one is interested in procreation. Most of them live for a few hundred years. I understand that it's a consequence of their highly developed minds being in tune with nature.

"Ekaasi is a hundred and sixty-two years old, and she is acknowledged as a priestess and a seeress in her country. She came halfway around the word to enlist my help to rescue you and Surra and to tell me why it was necessary. As a seeress she knew I would be here at this time to rescue Tumar. She even knew she would be captured by unscrupulous horse hunters, sold for a mere pittance to an animal trader, and that I would find her there.

"According to the prophecy, she wasn't to resist being captured, and I now know that our lives were saved by that act." He told the king about the tracking devices and the missile striking the wild horse. "Now you know why Sorcuk bragged that we were dead. I sincerely hope they won't find out soon that we're not.

"Ekaasi didn't tell me why you and Surra are important, but she told me that relics, buried by a previous, forgotten civilization were recently discovered in the mountains up north somewhere. The treasure of artifacts, if studied and understood, could change the course of our civilization or destroy it if unscrupulous people get hold of it, she said. A few greedy individuals found out about the cache and will stop at nothing to get their hands on it. For some obscure reason, they recruited the corrupt Heltos to help them establish a base from which they could operate to locate the invaluable relics. It seems he jumped at the chance to further his own nefarious plans and went to work on Sorcuk for that purpose." He paused to make sure Tumar and Surra were still listening, then continued.

"Apparently Heltos's quick solution to his instructions was to kill you both and take over the governance of this country before one of you finds out about the alleged treasure. We don't know who the instigators are, but we think that if we make life difficult and uncertain for the high priest, he might be panicked into revealing a name or two, which can be followed up and linked to others.

"We have enlisted the help of the local temple cats to prowl around in the palace and eavesdrop on conversations. They should not be noticed or suspected by anyone except a sensitive, in which case they will make themselves scarce as they are as intelligent as you and I, sir, and will let us know if anything of importance is said or happens in the palace. A cat understands human speech, provided the words are accompanied by clear mental images. Heltos will be kept under observation day and night, if at all possible."

"It's only humans who can't understand cats, or any other animal for that matter. A few individuals are born with the rare talent to communicate with them, but it's a talent that needs coaching and guidance. Very few Temple Priests have that ability, and it seems that the rest of them aren't even informed that a human can communicate with cats. The general impression the average person has is that cats are guardians of valuables in the temples, which is also true. I won't go into their reasons for that voluntary service."

Dai stopped to serve lunch. The king was in deep thought and absently thanked Dai when he gave him a platter of food. Dai had just started to wash the dishes when Ekaasi arrived with a bundle of herbs clutched in one hand.

"The girls can wash the dishes and start breaking up the camp, for we'll have to move by tonight," she said. "I received a message that a man is being chased by Heltos's underlings, and you must leave immediately to rescue him. It is thought that the man accidentally overheard Heltos mentioning a name to a confidant, so Heltos ordered that he be killed immediately. He may be wounded, so you must take a first-aid kit along. He managed to escape beyond the gate and is running eastward toward the stream with two sentries in close pursuit. A cat followed them and may contact you to guide you if necessary."

Dai took her to the old sledge, where he pointed out where he kept food for her and magazines for her rifle, and told her to help herself to whatever she needed. Then he told her in her own language what he had told the king with the girls listening in. She approved and said she would tell them a bit more over

174

time to prepare them for the true story.

Dai slung the light hunting rifle over his shoulder by its strap and put two spare magazines in an outside pocket. He made sure the first-aid kit had everything, including bandages, before he put it into a knapsack, which he slung over a shoulder and then strapped firmly to his back. The forest was too dense for a horse to run, and he didn't even think of taking the stallion. Luckily the already-gutted deer wouldn't spoil quickly in this weather, he thought.

31

He ran hard but silently so as not to unduly alarm any wild creatures, which might attract undesirable attention. He reached the north wall sooner than expected. As he had noticed earlier, vegetation along the walls was cleared regularly, which left an almost bare passage about thirty meters wide.

Dai ignored the silence as he increased his pace, fearing that he might arrive too late, but he tried not to think about it. The lesson he had learned long ago was that it was quite useless to speculate on what might be and what might have been.

As he reached the corner formed by the north and east walls, he slowed to a walk and quickly but carefully looked around the corner below belt level before he resumed his run along the east wall. Then he thought he heard something that sounded like enraged pig squeals far off in the distance, but it was very faint. He stopped to listen intently but his breathing came too fast for proper silence, so he took a deep breath, opened his mouth, and stopped breathing; but his heart still pounded too strongly in his ears.

He mentally shrugged his shoulders. If he was too late, he was too late, and as Kyr had told him a few hundred times while scolding him, it is plain stupidity to rush in blindly anywhere. He decided to continue in the cleared space along the wall until he reached the stream that was supposed to flow about halfway to the next corner, or until he heard something clearly or found tracks.

He jogged slowly and silently so his breathing could normalize and listened for any sounds that did not belong to the woods. His eyes roamed restlessly from in front of his feet to the woods on his left, and farther away to where he could discern a narrow footbridge over the not-so-very-broad stream. Now the dense wood abruptly made way for an area of scattered trees and almost hip-high grass to the bank of the stream.

He was about two hundred steps away from the footbridge when he heard a brief outbreak of enraged, grunting squeals of wild pigs some distance to his left. He stopped in his tracks. Their first inclination was to attack, no matter the cost. He had twice been treed by small families of these lean, omnivorous pigs and knew how vicious they were by nature when they were suddenly disturbed or when they smelled blood. They always attacked first. If you were caught on foot without a handy tree nearby, you were torn to bloody pieces in moments. Dai couldn't think of a more brutally savage death. Once aroused the pigs were not easily discouraged, and most of the time they could only be stopped by killing the entire herd.

Nothing moved or looked out of order in the cleared area next to the wall beyond the footbridge as far as he could see, so the man he was looking for might be the cause of the pigs' bloodlust. He thought he was exactly opposite the place where the sounds had come from, in a patch of bushes and low, stunted trees about three hundred meters away. Perhaps there was a solid rock shelf not too deep under the soil level in this particular area, which usually was the cause of such stunted vegetation.

Wherever possible, he thought, he must take a circuitous route with tall-enough, scalable trees nearby. He saw that it wasn't always possible, but since he had no other choice, he left the clearing and began to steal along silently, as if he were hunting. He was thankful that the wind was blowing in his direction, but he still made very sure he wasn't making any kind of sound, not even brushing against a blade of grass. From experience he knew the pigs had a keen sense of smell and hearing, especially when they were browsing, and he wanted to see them before they became aware of his presence. His eyes flashed constantly in all directions as he tried to pick a route clear of obstacles, but when he neared his objective, he ensured that he always knew where the nearest climbable tree was. The rifle was still slung over a shoulder; it would be useless to try to shoot them when they charged, since the animals were fast and the herds were usually quite large.

He had reached the area of the stunted trees, but a row of dense, thorny vegetation higher than eye level obscured his view. Now he could smell disturbed dust and hear the gnashing of teeth and low, labored grunts and low squeals just behind the thicket, as if the pigs were trying to climb a slippery surface and kept falling off. The breeze wafted their distinct odor, mixed with the scent of water and dust, toward him. He guessed they were less than fifty steps away. The nearest trees big enough to make it impossible for a pig to reach him were about eighty steps to his right. They weren't very tall, but he would be out of a pig's reach because their bodies were too heavy to jump higher than their own knee height.

He knew the direction of the breeze could change any time, at the whim of capricious nature, but it was unlikely to flutter much in winter. He nevertheless checked the next big-enough tree before his next move. Its stem was thick enough not to bend, but there were no branches strong enough to hold his weight. He looked farther to the right, somewhat closer to the stream. About fifteen meters farther, but closer to the thicket that barred his way, was a larger tree with several branches thick enough to handle his weight.

He looked around for something more suitable, but was alerted by a changed note in the pig squeals, a challenging sound, which he knew meant the breeze had swirled, taking his scent to them for a moment. Without hesitation he sprinted for the second tree and prayed that the pigs would be delayed in the thick brush for those vital seconds he needed to reach sanctuary. He didn't see the well-trodden game path near his target tree until he almost put a foot in it.

His vigilance saved him. When he was a step away from the path, out of the corner of his left eye, he saw the huge boar charging out of the brush-and-grass tunnel about three meters away. Such was its speed that it would have run Dai's leg from under him as he put his foot down, had he not put it down just short of the path and let out a furious "Ay-yaaaah!" then jumped high over the boar and continued his furious sprint.

Dai thought the startled boar had confusedly tried to stop to work out this unexpected noise and appearance and that a few others had run into the boar, because he heard the furious squeals of a short fight. They were amazingly fast, and he knew that some of the following pigs would avoid the melee and continue after him when they heard his footfalls. He jumped for a branch to pull himself up and felt a pig knock a heel forward with its snout, but he had a firm grip on the branch and pulled his legs out of the way. He quickly got his feet up on a branch and climbed as high and as fast as he safely could, ignoring or not feeling the scratches.

When he looked down, he saw that the pig had knocked itself out on the trunk of an adjacent tree, but it was already drunkenly getting back onto its feet with a bleeding snout. He let out a sigh and said a prayer of thanks that he had made it. Death had been cheated again by the narrowest of margins. He was about two meters above the ground, just high enough to be out of their reach.

The pigs were now squealing furiously beneath the tree, and some were on their hind legs leaning against the trunk, vigorously trying to reach his nearest foot with teeth protruding from their enormous, wide-open jaws. He turned his head the other way and saw to his amazement that he was about ten steps away from the edge of a large, dusty clearing that ended on the bank of the stream. It was obviously a gathering place trodden by animals coming to drink over many years.

In about the middle of the clearing lay a single, recently fallen old tree. It was badly rotten in some places, and it was plain to see that it had been uncommonly big before it died long ago. A man was climbing down from the highest, still-stout branch, fearfully looking around. It was evident that one of his arms was useless.

Dai shouted in the Bojonian language for him to stay where he was. The pigs were very fast and might catch him on the ground. The man stopped as if shot, and Dai saw that he was looking at two bundles of bloodied rags on the bank of the slow, but strong-flowing stream. He understood then and shouted that he came to help, but that he must first get rid of the pigs.

With his left hand, Dai held on to the main stem above his head to be sure he wouldn't slip from his precarious perch, since he wasn't far above the pigs. To prevent his gun from inadvertently falling, he carefully wrapped the strap of the loaded rifle around his right forearm and slid it off his shoulder. Making sure he was still secure on his perch, he pushed the barrel up and held it with a finger of his left hand behind the sight and then, with his right hand, took hold of the rifle just behind the trigger guard.

He flipped the safety catch off with his thumb. He couldn't

179

aim, so he pointed the barrel down above the eyes of the boar trying to reach his left foot, about thirty centimeters from its snout. The soft hiss of the bolt went unheard in the continuous pushing and squealing beneath the tree, as the pigs bumped each other out of the way or tried to climb onto others to get at him. The big boar, which he knew was the leader, suddenly froze and with stiffened legs dropped on its back among his subjects, who ignored him completely. Another took its place without so much as a glance at the fallen leader. Dai shot it by just pointing the gun at the head. He continued to shoot those that obligingly presented themselves.

There were only three younger ones left alive when they seemed to realize that the bodies they were trying to climb over meant that they were being decimated, or perhaps they were tired and had lost their bloodlust. They grunted, as if wakened from a blood-filled nightmare, and suddenly took off as one with tufted tails held straight up into the late afternoon sky, perhaps as a token of surrender. Squealing with all their might, as if stuck with something sharp in the rear, they pelted through the clearing without even looking at the object of their previous attention and continued along a game trail into the woods.

Suddenly there was an almost deafening silence. Dai was only too happy to let them go their own way. He abhorred unnecessary killing, even in self-defense, but he preferred to stay alive and in one piece. He counted eight carcasses before he stepped down onto one. Keeping the rifle ready in case the pigs changed their minds about running away, he entered the clearing and walked toward the man still perched on the branch.

He stopped for a moment to listen intently. He knew the pigs were fast runners, but he was surprised to hear a brief squeal farther away than expected. He relaxed.

"It's okay to come down now," he told the exhausted man, who looked middle-aged. Before the man could ask, he introduced himself as Daiyus and told him that someone had asked him to come and look for him.

The man didn't ask questions, only replied, "Thank you for coming in time, sir. My name is Murima, and until today I was the alternate cook for the king. With Heltos on my tail, I have nowhere to go except back to my village northeast of here in the high mountains, but I don't think I dare go back there right now either. May I come with you, sir? I am wounded, but not seriously, and I can still cook without too much inconvenience."

"You're welcome to come with me, and you can still cook for the king if you like. Sit down and I will tend to your wound first. We can exchange tall stories and even outright lies afterward as much as you like." Dai smiled to indicate that he wasn't serious. He was certain Murima must have a lot of questions but was in too much pain to talk, and he knew how to put him at ease.

Murima removed his jacket, slowly sat down on the trunk of the fallen tree, and put his blood-soaked jacket down next to him. Dai noticed that his shirt was saturated on the left shoulder and side, but the blood had already dried, which meant a not-too-serious wound.

Dai loosened the first-aid kit on his back and put it down on the trunk. Then he shook four pain tablets out of a small bottle. It was two too many, but Murima looked the stocky, sturdy type who was too proud to groan aloud. Dai offered all four tablets in the palm of one scratched hand and his flask with the other. Murima gratefully swallowed all, but continued to swallow another few mouthfuls of water, indicating that he was thirsty but in control.

Dai admired and respected courage in any human or animal. He nodded approvingly and said, "Keep the canteen with you and drink some more. Your body is dehydrated by now. I'll refill at the stream before we go. You call me 'Dai' from now on, and I'll call you 'Murima.' I know you have many questions, so I'll explain while I examine and clean your wound.

"You may not believe this, but temple cats in the palace let one of my companions know that a man was being chased out of the palace grounds by Heltos's guards. They said he may have information we would like to have and that he may be wounded—therefore the first-aid kit. I grabbed a rifle and the kit, and here I am. Unfortunately I didn't think of bringing anything stronger than water in the rush to find you.

" Okay, I've soaked your shirt with a cleaning solution, and now I'm going to peel it off slowly. It will hurt, and your wound may start bleeding again, but it is necessary to clean it properly to prevent a possible infection. Bite on the strap of the flask if it will help, and scream as loud as you like, for we are alone. Then tell me what happened to you before you were chased out of the palace and if any strange names were mentioned by anyone."

32

Dai knew it would help Murima if his mind was occupied with something else, and he wanted names if there were any to be had.

Murima replied, "Go ahead and pull. I've been wounded before, and I'm not a sissy. Yes, the high priest Heltos mentioned two names and that's why he wants me dead, but let me tell you what happened. I have the late-afternoon shift this week to cook supper and wait until the king retires, for he usually wants something to eat or drink before going to bed. I relieved the morning cook earlier than usual because he sent me a message that he wasn't feeling well and asked if I would take the shift before noon. The king's lunch was ready when I arrived, but no one came to fetch it at noon or later, which was out of character—but it's not my business to go and ask the king why he doesn't want his lunch.

"It was too quiet in the palace, and I started to worry, but I could not venture beyond the kitchen—" Murima grunted and drew in a sharp, deep breath as Dai yanked the shirtsleeve off the shoulder wound. Dai had soaked a pad with blood-coagulating solution and had a bandage ready. The wound was just in the thick muscle of the shoulder and had gone cleanly through, missing bone. He pressed the pad with thumb and forefingers on both sides of the neat hole.

"Sorry about that. I'll press this pad till the bleeding stops, and I've added something to numb the pain. Luckily it's not serious, and it nearly missed your shoulder. When the bleeding stops, I'll clean and bandage your shoulder properly. Please continue."

Murima swallowed a mouthful of water, cleared his throat, and continued. "We are not allowed to wander in the palace unless we are summoned, so I sat quietly in a dark corner near the door, waiting for the time to pass so I could start making supper for the king. It was almost three o'clock, and I was wondering why the king doesn't eat his lunch before it spoils, for he enjoys food. Then I heard grunts, curses, and real nasty swear words as shuffling footsteps approached the kitchen. I knew the voice to be that of the high priest Heltos, and I was petrified. He was not allowed to enter that side of the palace. But I just sat there, stunned by the language coming from such an exalted personage. I couldn't move and couldn't think of anything to do or say. My mind was a total blank, which was as unusual as the foul words uttered by the high priest.

"He continually cursed as he shuffled into the kitchen with his eyes closed. He hung almost limp between two guards I have often seen accompanying him. They guided him to an armchair in a corner we sometimes use to take a quick nap between meals. They didn't see me, and one fetched a glass of water, which he gave to the high priest. After slowly emptying the glass, he told the other guard—I forget his name—to take a hover car or anything fast to the temple and tell the apothecary to give him the best pain tablets or concoctions they had to stop a throbbing, nauseating, blinding headache, which he described in very unpriestly words, and to tell him who it is for and to hurry his lazy butt.

"To hell with 'high priest'—I'll call him Heltos from now on and nothing else! The foulmouthed, scrawny pretender doesn't deserve respect." Murima sounded disgusted and stopped to take a deep breath.

Dai saw that the bleeding had stopped. He smeared disinfecting ointment onto another pad and firmly bandaged the arm while Murima continued.

"Anyway, the guard asked, 'What about Princess Sorcuk?' Heltos told him to get the same for the stupid bitch. Those were his own words, Dai, and I just can't respect him anymore. Then he harshly told the man to move his ass if he valued his life. The guard ran out of the back door like a scared rabbit with a wolf after him.

"Heltos then told the remaining guard, and again these are more or less his own words, not mine, 'I can't even think with this bastard of a headache without making it worse. I wonder what caused it. Now that we're alone, I can tell you that Sorcuk and I confronted the king, late as recommended, and that irritable bastard told us to piss off, mind you. Sorcuk then told me we might as well kill the old goat and get it over with. All I can remember before you found us is that she took her knife out and

I the claw. I don't know what happened then and why we and the two who were supposed to guard us blacked out. Now the son of a bitch has disappeared, and nobody saw him take off. He must be hiding somewhere in a secret room or his armory. If we don't find him by tonight, you must summon everyone you can to scour the town and the countryside for any sign of him at first light.'

"Heltos then retched and asked for more water. He groaned and moaned and cursed his throbbing head again and just couldn't sit still for a moment. After he had his water, he continued, 'I suppose I must report our temporary setback to Blerts and Maursig on Shaytan, but it'll have to wait until this pain is tolerable. Where is that lazy bastard with the pain relievers? Maybe it will help if I eat something.'

"The cold lunch was next to me, and when the guard looked at it, he saw me and shouted that the bloody cook had heard everything that was said, which made me remember those two names. Heltos then yelled at him to kill me, to make sure that I don't escape.

"I sped out of the back door without hesitating a second. I still keep fairly fit and made for the gate with the guard after me. As I started to draw away from the unfit, winded guard when we neared the gate, he shouted for the gates to be closed quickly, but perhaps he didn't have the authority to order them around or they couldn't hear his gasped words. He then started to shoot at me, and the bewildered gatekeepers ducked into their cubicle to get out of the way. From out of nowhere, two other guards joined the chase, and Heltos's personal guard ordered them to bring evidence that I'm dead before they dared return.

"I sprinted through the gate as they, too, began to shoot. I felt pain in my left shoulder, which encouraged me to speed up. I turned left to run along the wall, thinking I could lose them in the woods once I was on this side of the stream. As I ran over the footbridge, I took a quick glimpse back and saw only the two unknown guards after me. I had gained some distance, and they only shot at me now and then, hoping for a chance hit, I think.

"I turned along the stream but was getting tired and my arm started to throb almost as much as Heltos's head. Nevertheless, I had to get away if I wanted to live. I stumbled into this clearing, and before I was halfway through, the wild pigs entered from there"—he pointed to the path next to the stream—"and they immediately charged since I was soaked with fresh blood. I barely managed to reach this old tree. I ran up the main trunk until I found this branch with the fork I could reach. I felt a bit dizzy by then, and I was afraid I would faint.

"The pigs were in a mindless frenzy and jostled each other out of the way to get at me, but of course their hard hoofs caused them to slip and fall off when they rushed onto the main trunk, which enraged them further. They squealed all the time and they just kept on trying to get me, and then my pursuers entered the clearing. They obviously are, or rather were, city dwellers because they stopped to laugh and jeer at me; they enjoyed my predicament immensely. It was obvious that they didn't even give it a thought about why wild pigs would want to attack me. The pigs didn't notice them at first until one of them thought it would provide greater amusement if he could incense the pigs more. I don't know what he intended, but he aimed at the herd and wounded one of the pigs.

"Because the percussion pistols the guards prefer make such a loud noise, the pigs immediately took notice of them and charged. The laughing simpletons just stood petrified and only realized they should run after it was way too late. The pigs caught up with them quickly and tore them to pieces before turning their attention back to me, as I knew they would. I knew I would have to sit still and endure until they lost interest in me. It felt like hours before you showed up."

33

Dai wound the bandage tightly about Murima's upper arm and shoulder, but both knew the wound would be painful and bothersome for a few days. Then he asked Murima to hold his arm against his chest so he could immobilize it. The latter started to shiver uncontrollably, so Dai quickly removed his own shirt and helped the protesting Murima to don it over the tightly strapped arm. He explained, "I have this leather tunic that ties around the waist and around my neck. I know how to keep warm, and you only have that woolen jacket, so don't worry about my comfort. I want to pass on those two names, so excuse me a moment while I try to concentrate. Don't talk, please."

Dai sat down on the tree trunk and opened his mind to Kyr, but her presence wasn't there as usual. Without quite knowing what or why he was doing it, he instinctively reached out with his mind to seek her, something he had never even thought of doing before. He was astounded when he found her, but a wild, raw, seething urge flooded his consciousness, and he was inexorably drawn into her mind to become part of her wild, uncontrolled emotions.

Dai felt himself go quietly mad, and he nearly fell off the tree trunk in shock. Then the turmoil in his mind was driven out by calm, strong, but controlled thoughts from an unruffled mind. A clear mental voice, which he immediately sensed belonged to a lady cat, said in his reeling mind:

I'm sorry that happened, Dai. Kyr felt her natural mating urge stir strongly while you were connecting the bombs to discourage intruders from investigating the secret escape route. She asked my permission to replace her contact wavelength in your brain with mine so that you would find me if you had urgent information to transmit to Karna…yes, Kyr had us contact him before. I sense that you don't know what I'm talking about. Well, what comes to mind is that brains function on different wavelengths like individual radio comm-units. Each one of us, humans included, has a slightly different wavelength. Otherwise our chaotic thoughts would intermingle, and we wouldn't be able to distinguish our own thoughts. When we mind-talk, we more or less synchronize our wavelengths.

She should have told you about the switch and how it works. I don't know what happened after she spoke to me, but something may have prevented her from telling you, or maybe the mating madness came upon her too suddenly. During this time we lose our ability to rationalize or think two coherent thoughts in succession, for we become one-track-minded. It's our chemistry, and the undeniable urge controls our bodies and minds during this time.

Unfortunately, we are born this way and not one lady cat can postpone or control the mating madness when it comes. In the heat of the moment—excuse the pun, but it's true—she made a little blunder and inadvertently awakened your natural but untrained ability to search with your mind. She went into the gripping madness of her mating period very fast, which is not unusual in older ladies, and I don't think she knew she had made a mistake. Without the proper training, you'll get trapped by another mind, as almost happened just now. Don't try to do it again before you have had some training. The ability can't be suppressed without permanent damage now that it has been awakened.

I followed the cook, trying to penetrate his clogged mind to learn what he accidentally overheard, but he is one of those individuals whose thoughts are naturally closed to us, and no thought as to why Heltos wanted him dead surfaced. I alerted Ekaasi about the cook's plight and was on the lookout for you while I followed closely behind him and his pursuers. I was trying to force my way past that inborn disbelief in the cook's mind, but the concentration nearly got me killed when the pigs charged his pursuers. I was caught in between them.

I almost made it, but unfortunately, I'm old and slow, and the leading pig nearly tore my leg off as I jumped onto the first branch of this tree. Luckily it let go when it smashed snout-first into the trunk, and I scrambled up out of the way. My leg throbs with hellish pain, which prevented me from being as alert as usual—otherwise I would have spared you the ordeal in Kyr's seething brain. On the other hand, perhaps it is fortuitous that it happened now instead of later. I'm in this tree next to what's left of the humans, and I can't get down by myself. Tell me what the cook overheard so that I can give the information to the relay team right now to pass on to Karna while you come and help me down.

Dai gave her the two names and then located the tree where she had taken refuge. It wasn't high off the ground, and a younger cat could easily have jumped to and from the branch she was clinging to. She was about fifty meters away, and he could clearly see that she was gray with age. A bloody hind leg hung down at an awkward angle.

When he saw the broken leg, he ran to her, concerned because he knew she was enduring incredible pain. He marveled at her ability to stay so totally in control while she had gone to great length to educate him. She looked at him with calm yellow eyes. *Just help me down, Dai. I can get by on three legs.*

Why didn't you speak up sooner? Dai asked. *Or do you like to endure all that dreadful pain? I will give you half a pill to dull the pain, but it will make you sleep. I once gave it to Kyr out of desperation, and it worked better than expected. I know how to set that leg. I'll set it first and then take you with me. You will not be in the way, and we will look after you until you can walk without pain. If you have a real compelling reason to want to return to the palace, I will carry you as far as the gate and ask a guard to look after you.*

Dai knew that half of an ordinary pain pill would do what he said since he had administered it many times before to Kyr and other injured cats.

You are a good human, and I can see why Kyr loves you, Dai. You have compassion and an appreciation for what humans call animals but what you see as people of a different evolution in dissimilar shapes. I can sense that in your mind, and I like what I see. I am old and have not much longer to live, but yes, I will come with you. Perhaps I can stand in for Kyr and he who was renamed Koro, as they are, eh, well, otherwise engaged. I cannot repair what Kyr inadvertently let loose, but I will teach you how to use that ability without getting into too much trouble. I'm ready. Ah yes, they call me the old lady, but my name is Skrot. It means "lady" in cat language.

Dai gently lifted her from the fork of the low tree. He asked

189

her to tell him if he did something that caused additional pain. He had carried an injured Kyr many times, and he would always remember her scathing remarks when he inadvertently erred, so he did everything with deliberation and as gently as he could.

Dai didn't even think of laughing when Skrot told him that Kyr had trained him well. He put her down with care on the broad trunk of the fallen tree and did what he had to do, with an interested Murima looking on without comment. First, he gave her half a pain tablet, which she chewed with disrelish, and then lapped up some water Dai provided.

As Dai was telling her how she behaved like a real lady, her thoughts always calm and controlled, she abruptly passed out. The pain pill, meant for humans only, did that to cats, and many times he was grateful that he had discovered that property. Fortunately, Skrot had only a shallow wound, but her lower leg was broken in several places. He cleaned the open wound and then quickly set her leg before he bandaged it thickly. He knew it was excruciatingly painful and would be so for weeks, for an old cat healed slowly—even more slowly than an old human being. Perhaps Ekaasi would know how to ease her pain, but he knew that animals had developed the ability to live with pain because they didn't have any other choice but to endure.

34

Dai tore the bloody section off Murima's old shirt, dragged it through the dust, then let it catch on a snag at the other end of the dead tree. It wouldn't fool any outdoorsman, but he was leaving a message to trick any expert into believing that he was dealing with an amateur.

The relatively clean part of the shirt he knotted to use as a sling, together with the strap he had secured the first-aid kit with, to carry Skrot. When asked, Murima said he was okay and ready to travel. The sun had dipped behind the western mountains, and Dai knew it would be completely dark by the time they reached the corner of the north wall on this side. He slung the rifle over his right shoulder, asking Murima to hook his good right hand into his belt and to hang onto him if he stumbled in the dark. He was thankful that Murima was not the loquacious type.

Dai used both hands to hold Skrot steady in front of him, but a handgun was within easy reach should he need it. Even at a fairly fast pace with no incidents, it took nearly two hours to reach the camp through the almost lightless woods. It was pitch-dark under the trees, and Dai belatedly wished he'd had the foresight to bring one of the night-vision helmets with him. He could only faintly see where he was going by the light of the bright stars of the clear, icy winter night, but the exhausted Murima kept stumbling over every obstacle.

He was about two hundred steps from the camp when he stopped dead in his tracks. Murima felt him stop and suppressed the grunt of pain the jolt caused. Dai whispered close to his ear, "Something's wrong. The fire is too bright. Let's go back a bit. There is a big tree where you and the cat can wait out of this icy wind. I want to do some scouting to make sure we're not walking into a trap. Can you handle a gun?"

"Yes, I grew up in a small village, remember? Every boy learns to hunt as soon as he can hold a gun steady."

When they reached the tree, Dai gently put the cat down on the bed of dry leaves. He slung the rifle and first-aid kit from his shoulder and even removed the flask so he had nothing on his body to make a noise. He handed the rifle to Murima, since it would be difficult to steal along silently with it.

"I don't want to be shot by you," he whispered, "so I'll either call out your name or, if it is not safe, I'll hoot like a night owl, like this." He hooted softly. "Sit down behind the trunk so you are not silhouetted by the faint light of the fire. If anyone comes too close without saying your name first, don't call out, just shoot to kill. Can you see well enough in this darkness?"

"Yes. I'll be okay. I just feel a bit tired."

Dai checked again that nothing on his body would make a noise then became one with the night. Without meaning to and without knowing what he was doing, Dai sent a questing thought into the darker shadows around the camp, searching for strangers that should not be there. He was shocked when he felt a mind quite near that seethed with chaotic thoughts of lust and murder. The shock made his mind recoil, for which he was thankful. He didn't know what Kyr had done to his brain, but he silently thanked her. It was a curse, but it was also a gift, for he would have walked right into the man without knowing he was there unless he had sensed him when he got closer.

Dai bent down very low and stole closer with a hunting knife in his right hand. He wished he had a cat's ability to see in the dark and read thoughts without getting sucked into a mind. He brushed the thought aside and concentrated on being noiseless in every way.

Then he smelled the man's unwashed, sweaty odor and saw his vague outline against the firelight. The man was watching the camp intently instead of being alert to his surroundings, which accounted for his mischievous, perverted thoughts. Dai didn't mind the inattentiveness; he appreciated negligence in enemies and opponents. He would have used the silent stun gun if he still had it, for he didn't kill unless he thought it absolutely necessary. This figure lurking in the bushes obviously had no such peaceful intentions, so Dai came up silently from behind and grabbed him with his left hand over the mouth, pulling him backward in one quick, smooth movement while ramming the knife high up into the ribs more or less where the kidneys should be.

Dai did it expertly and fast, so his victim only had time for a soft groan through his nose before he collapsed limply. Dai quietly eased him to the ground, pulled the knife out, and wiped the blade on the man's clothes. He wondered how many more were on watch and observing Surra and Tumar from an exposed position instead of looking out for their own lives. For the moment, he could only assume that these men were after Tumar and himself and that they must have used a tracker. Anyone sent by Heltos would not have searched for them so soon in this direction.

He looked toward the campfire. The king still sat in the chair, but his head was bowed and his hands clasped, as if in prayer. The women sat next to him with their heads bent down. Their dejected attitude clearly spelled deep concern. It would be clear to even an amateur that they were being watched and that whoever had caught them was dense enough to think they were waiting for a blind idiot who walked around in his sleep. They must be another batch of Mohaz's stupid bedfellows, he thought, and very sure that they were dealing with dolts.

Dai almost smiled as he saw Ekaasi tending the unusually big campfire. That alone was a giveaway. A Permerian would never tend a fire or even start one unless it was for a very specific reason. Whoever guarded them was well hidden, probably on a sledge, but he must get rid of sentries before he attended to them.

He would have had no trouble getting rid of watchers if he had a cat, even Skrot, to locate them for him, but it was no use wishing for the easy way when there was no choice. He was afraid to try the dangerous mind search again, so he started to circle the camp to his left, bent over in a stalker's crouch and very alert. He had only one life, and if that was lost, everything else might be lost too. Certainly Ekaasi, the king, Surra, and Tumar would be killed. He was taking a perilous chance with a circuit so close to the fire, but judging from the late sentry's attitude, he didn't think the lookouts would be very far from where they could watch the goings-on in the camp. They wouldn't want to miss out on the fun if the women's guard or guards started something, or if, he was sure, the effeminate "Pob" wandered into the camp without being detained. They should be easy to find against the light of the fire.

Dai couldn't guess what story had been dished up to the ambushers, but he knew they expected an inexperienced, noisy clod to walk into the not-very-subtle trap, assuming they thought of him as the dense runner. He therefore stayed close to the ground, even if it made progress slower; he had done this sort of thing many times before without Kyr's aid.

Dai smelled the next sentry long before he located him. He had completed about a third of the circuit when a shift of the slight breeze brought him a whiff of stale sweat, unwashed clothes, and reeking footwear. He knew that human nature was such that a person couldn't smell his own odor unless he deliberately checked, and surely this one wasn't even aware that he ponged like rotten cheese. Dai sat down slowly. He listened and waited without moving for the sentry to give himself away.

He didn't have long to wait. About ten steps to his left, the sentry had decided that his bladder was bothering him. He emptied it noisily into an open space, not even into a bush or against a tree trunk to dampen the loud, splashing noise. It was apparent that he thought he was all by himself in the woods and that everyone else and every woodland creature was deaf. Dai was on him before he was halfway finished, and he died with a slight grunt, clutching his favorite tool tightly in total surprise.

Karna had made Dai practice hundreds of times how to approach and kill a sentry with a knife in the dark. He knew just where to jab the knife into the back of a victim to paralyze him. Dai didn't like it, but Karna had drilled it into him that it was utter folly to feel remorse or pity for an enemy, since that same enemy wouldn't give him the slightest chance if the roles were reversed.

Dai twitched involuntarily when the calm voice of Skrot shattered his intense concentration. *I sense the presence of one more sentry on the other side of the camp a hundred steps directly across from where you are now. I can only sense his presence, not his thoughts. I'm barely awake, but I will guide you as best I can. I can sense the repulsive thoughts and hatred for you from three more lying in ambush within the camp, but I assume you'll want to take care of the out-sentry first as he is more dangerous. Go now, Dai! I will let you know when you are near and when to be cautious. I'll try to be more alert and do my utmost not to drift off again, for you may need my aid.*

35

Dai knew from experience that half a pain pill would let a cat sleep for about three hours and leave it groggy for at least another half an hour after that. He didn't realize that time had passed so quickly, and he still wasn't sure if it was self-elected adversaries he was pursuing so carefully and warily. He mentally shrugged his shoulders. He only had one life, and others depended on him. It paid to be extra careful when your only life was at stake.

He said, *Thank you, Skrot, I would really appreciate your assistance*, and returned the way he had come at a silent but faster pace. He was taking a chance, for even the faintest noise carried on a silent, icy night like this. He counted seventy steps and then stopped to check the surrounding area carefully before proceeding. Now he'd have to take care so as not to step on a dry twig or leaf.

About thirty steps in front but a little to your right, Skrot's mental voice said. *He's heard a noise and he's very alert, but at the moment he's looking directly at the girls by the fire.*

Dai sank to his heels. Although he didn't feel it, he knew the cat was looking through his eyes, and until he could see the sentry, she could only guess at the distance separating him from his intended victim. He squinted until he saw a slight movement. Then Skrot spoke again.

That human is an old woodsman. You stopped just in time, and he may hear you if you move closer. He thinks he has heard something and is ready to fire at any sound or movement. Thickhead Murima here has fallen asleep, and he snores like a pig with a blocked snout. It may attract attention, and the rifle has slipped from his hand onto me. I'm still wrapped in the sling and can't move or breathe properly. Please come and remove the rifle. You might as well use it, as it is the only way you'll safely get rid of this one, for you won't get close to him. I get the impression that the other three are also very much alert, as they are accountable to someone who expects positive results from this invasion of your camp.

Dai could use the noisy handgun to kill the watchman, but that would alert everyone in a circumference of two kilometers or more. The rifle with Murima was equipped with an expensive telescope that was as good at night as it was in the daylight, and it was silent enough. The slight zip sound wouldn't be heard more than ten steps away in this stillness.

Suddenly the woodsman stepped out from the shadow under the tree, and now Dai could see his silhouette in the starlight. The silent way the man moved and the wary way he scanned the area all around him made it quite clear that this was a wily old fighter who intended to stay alive. Dai instinctively felt that the man was the type who could not be coerced into unarmed combat. He was strictly a gun man, or, Dai thought wryly, he would stick to his guns.

It was an intuitive feeling that Dai never ignored. He soundlessly reversed on hands and toes until he was behind foliage before taking his eyes off the man. Then he turned and skulked away, taking great care that he didn't brush against or step on anything. He didn't stand fully upright until he was sure he was well hidden from direct sight. Even then he still moved stealthily to where he had left Skrot and Murima. He didn't call out because the cat told him that "Thickhead" was out like a light but wasn't snoring so loudly anymore.

He arrived as silently as he'd left. Murima was leaning with his back against the tree, his head on his chest. The gun had slipped out of his lax fingers, though fortunately was still on his outstretched legs. Only the barrel rested on Skrot's ribs, and her breathing was labored.

Dai silently lifted the gun away, but he didn't wake Murima because he didn't want to embarrass him. The four painkillers he had swallowed and the loss of blood, under normal circumstances, would have had him in dreamland in less than thirty minutes. Only the constant exercise and a strong constitution had kept him awake that long.

He silently asked Skrot if she needed attention, as she had awoken sooner than he'd expected. She told him she had a tough old body and was still comfortably wrapped in the sling. He could finish the job first and then come for them. She would stay with him and guide him. He thanked her, carefully adjusted the strength of the scope for night sight, and left as silently as he could.

When he figured he had crept to within sight of the woodsman, Dai brought the scope to his eyes every few steps. As soon as he saw the alert sentry clearly, he stopped and carefully knelt down on his right knee. With an elbow on his bent left knee to steady the rifle, he checked the man out through the scope. He guessed he was about fifty, and he alertly held a rifle, ready for use, that was almost identical to the one in Dai's hand. This was the type of man he would have welcomed as a friend, he thought, and felt momentary regret as he pulled the trigger for a head shot.

Dai approached the woodsman's body and turned it on its back. He felt that the woodsman shouldn't have died ignobly like this, and he straightened the body before he took the rifle. It was a newer model than the one in his hand and might come in handy as a backup.

Then the cat told him she had the impression that one sentry was on top of a sledge, another beneath the second sledge, and a third in a tent with human female things.

He considered his next move. The normal inclination would be to approach the welcoming fire, but who could have a plainer warning to stay away? He was afraid that Ekaasi might run out of firewood, and then he wanted to kick himself for his forgetfulness. The slightly hesitant, jubilant morning song of a desert quail welcoming the new morning, no doubt out of place about halfway around the planet from its native habitat and totally ignorant of the time of night, drifted out over the too-brightly lit clearing. Now Ekaasi would know he had cleared the area around the camp.

Dai saw Ekaasi hesitate as if in thought, throw the sticks she had in her hands into the fire, and then move a few steps sideways toward the sledges. It was a warning that Dai must pay attention to the sledges. Dai wasn't aware of it, but lack of sleep was beginning to take its toll. He could have communicated with Ekaasi through Skrot, but it never occurred to him that it was the logical thing to do. His tired mind was back in the semidesert with Kyr away on a mission.

Dai closed his eyes and pictured the area around the camp. There was an old, stunted, dying tree to his left, near the edge of the clearing and about thirty meters from and slightly behind the sledges, which were parked side by side. He had broken dead branches from it earlier and had absently noticed that there were sturdy branches a little higher than the sledges. They might still support his weight, and he should be able to look down on the loads of both sledges through the scope.

Dai stooped over to search for the tree, which might be silhouetted by the firelight, but didn't see it. Nobody on either of the sledges would be able to see him where he was, beyond the edge of the trees and shrubbery, even with a nightscope, but he was still careful as he slunk away to search for the old tree. He was glad they had picked up the abundant fallen branches around the camp the night before.

He found the stunted old tree about eighty steps to his left. He leaned the sentry's rifle against a low branch before he silently scaled the tree, carefully avoiding brushing against branches. As he ascended branch by branch, he kept an eye on the clearing, but if anybody noticed him, they tactfully looked away. He paused on every branch to check the sledges and the tent, but he didn't notice any hidden ambushers until he could look down on both sledges.

One man was lying on top of the tarpaulin on the old sledge, wrapped up against the cold in one of the new blankets. Even his head was half covered. Dai was annoyed. The bloody cheek of it! Disregarding the property of others like a bloody thief! Now he would have to throw the blanket away. The one in the tent was out of sight, since he might have made himself comfortable on one of the women's beds, and Dai was in the wrong position to see anyone hidden in or under the sledges.

Now Dai was really aggravated. What the hell were these people doing here anyway, and who gave them the right to do as they pleased? A pervert like Mohaz wasn't worth all the lives wasted on his behalf so far, but unfortunately, like attracted like, and they clearly didn't have much sense. Or perhaps this madness was linked to Heltos and to what Dai was investigating. It made a crazy sort of sense.

A shot in the head just above the ears should kill the man instantly, and the chances were negligible that he would shudder or go into spasms that might alert his buddies. The closer sledge wasn't piled quite as high as the old one. Dai climbed down slightly to a level where he could at least miss the tarpaulin, for he didn't want the equipment and provisions to be spoiled with blood. With the nightscope he could see where the man's head protruded a little from under the blanket. He made sure his aim was in the correct area and pulled the trigger. The ambusher sagged down as if going to sleep on his face. Two left, he thought, and sighed. Killing had become too much of an everyday affair; he wished there were easier ways to permanently get rid of noisome people.

He left the woodsman's rifle propped against the tree and quietly moved away to get behind the sledges. Skrot told him that she sensed the ambusher under the sledge nearest to him was getting a little impatient after the long wait for their victim to return from his alleged run.

Dai wondered if every single one was a friend of that crackbrain Mohaz, or if Heltos and his accomplices in the temple had sponsored this invasion? It didn't make sense, but he vowed to settle accounts with both megalomaniacs when he returned to Bojon. Four already dead, and now another six! The numskull wasn't worth all the unnecessarily lost lives…or were there other reasons or motives behind this seemingly senseless persecution? It couldn't be connected to this so-called treasure, could it? He wished he had the answers, but he felt sure it all was connected in a sort of crazy, illogical way. He was suddenly aware that fatigue was responsible for this idle speculation. The sooner he could finish them off, the sooner he would get some much-needed rest.

36

It was awkward to crawl silently with the rifle gripped in one hand, but he had no other silent weapon for long-range use. He came to a decision, got onto his feet, and crouched low while he approached the sledge from behind a tree, as usual moving like a shadow without the slightest sound. As he came from behind the protection of the tree, he could make out the silhouette of a person fidgeting uncomfortably while lying on his stomach under the new sledge.

Dai wondered why Ekaasi was again stoking the fire, adding wood as if the supply was inexhaustible and she wanted the heat to reach everyone in the camp to save blankets. Like so many times before, Dai appreciated her thoughtful warning, but she already knew he was here. He wondered dully what could have changed in the few minutes it took him to steal up on the sledges from behind. Dai was too tired to think of asking the cat to query this new development, and he was too dull with fatigue to puzzle it out, so he concentrated on what he came to do. He needed to sleep for an hour or more to clear his mind, but first he must get rid of these infernal busybodies.

Dai didn't want to mess up the women's belongings by killing the man directly inside the tent. He decided he must somehow induce the man to leave the tent. Was that individual the type who would rush out to investigate if he heard an alarming noise? It would serve Dai's purpose finely, for he could shoot rapidly even at shifting, dodging targets. He pondered tiredly for a moment. Maybe he should make use of that possibility.

The impatient watchman under the sledge was lying with his face toward the fire, where he had a clear view of the whole camp. Now he pushed his legs wide apart as if to ease a cramp in a leg or his ample buttocks. Dai tiredly thought it was a tempting target in a perverted sense, and the bolt, if correctly placed, would go right up, but it would exit through the man's chest or throat instead of the head. It was not what he wanted. What he wanted was a noise startling enough to draw the other watchman out of the tent without giving him time for thought.

He shifted aim slightly and burned the man's bulging left buttock. He was more than gratified at the hearty shout of pained surprise from the recipient, but his eyes were on the tent. As the remaining man thoughtlessly rushed out of the tent to investigate, Dai shot his first victim in the back of the head and the man popping out of the tent in the chest and again through the head as he fell down.

Dai tiredly came to his feet, but to his surprise, Tumar jumped up and yelled, "Look out! On top!" and she pulled the stun gun and shot in one stunningly fast and smooth movement, as if she'd been practicing daily for this particular moment. For a fleeting moment he thought she was shooting at the already dead ambusher. He was taken by surprise when another one, whom Skrot had somehow missed, tumbled head first from the smaller sledge. *This man must have been highly trained for me not to have heard him rise*, he thought dully. He felt grateful to Tumar.

The man fell headfirst onto the hard ground, and Dai heard a very distinct *crack*. Apparently, the man had risen silently with his face toward Dai, ready to shoot, and Tumar's bolt had hit him right in the back of his head, causing him to fall forward and break his neck. Now he knew what Ekaasi had been trying to make him aware of.

Tumar yelled, "There are three more around the camp. Did you find them?"

"Yes, I did, thanks!" he called out as he walked to the fire. "I owe you, Tumar. I didn't expect another one up there. I wonder how the cat missed that one."

Seeing the uncomprehending looks on their faces, he explained, "An old lady cat followed the man I went to rescue as he fled the palace, and she got hurt. Her name is Skrot." He quickly related the gist of the story in as few words as possible.

"I'll go and fetch them quickly, then I suppose we have to hightail it out of here. I'll pull that one on top of the old sledge down when I get back. Pity the new blanket was wasted." Wistfully he thought about missing more sleep tonight, but he stowed the rifle on the sledge next to his sleeping bag. As he passed the stunted tree, he retrieved the woodsman's rifle, which he took with him.

He homed in on the tree and as he silently approached, Skrot told him that "Thickhead" was again snorting his dense head off, scaring the nearby animals away. Dai reluctantly woke Murima by gently tapping him on the left leg with his hand. Murima woke up with a few loud, gargling snorts and a startled grunt. Dai gently told him, "I'm sorry to have to wake you, but it seems that we have to shift camps in a hurry. The enemy knows where we are."

"Oh, I'm sorry. I didn't realize I had fallen asleep."

Dai smiled in the dark. "You wouldn't—and don't apologize. You've had an overdose of pain pills, remember? They have that effect on the body, and I really was surprised you stayed awake and lucid for as long as you did. You must have a very tough constitution." He took Murima's uninjured arm and gently assisted him to his feet.

After Dai picked up the cat, Murima rested his hand on Dai's shoulder. Progress was easier, and they reached the camp in a few minutes.

Ekaasi supervised the women as they took the tent down. The king was brewing tea on the fire, for he knew that Dai would be desperately tired by now, and he had developed a high regard for the young man. He had even asked Surra to kick the cadaver rolled into the now-spoiled blanket off the sledge to save Dai the trouble, which she did.

As Dai introduced Murima to everyone, Ekaasi also sensed the fatigue in Dai. She knew they all depended on him for their continued safety, so she firmly told him, "After you've had the tea Hespus so thoughtfully brewed, climb onto the sledge and sleep until I wake you up. I will lead, and the girls will drive the sledges. Hespus says there's a big cavern about fifteen kilometers from here that he knows from his hunting days. We should be safe there for a day. Sleep now and leave the rest to us. Okay?"

Dai nodded. "Yes, thank you, girls! But first things first. Surra, do you know if these men were friends of Mohaz?"

Surra nodded. She had been unusually silent, but he was too tired to wonder about it. Then she added, "Five of them were from Sorcuk's squad and two were priests. They were after you, as Pob. I just don't understand how or why such lowlife psychopaths like Mohaz attract such loyal friends. I'm not sure why the priests accompanied them. One was a well-known woodsman, and the one Tumar killed was well educated and high up in the temple hierarchy."

Dai dully thought that he had decimated Sorcuk's squad. "So maybe that's why Skrot didn't sense him. Some of them know how to suppress their brainwaves for long periods so that no sensitive can pick them up. In effect, they become invisible as eyes tend to pass over them, which mine did. Do you need help to hitch the horses?"

"No," Ekaasi answered firmly. "You go and sleep right now. We may need you sooner than expected, and we want you fresh and alert."

He asked Ekaasi to have a look at the lady cat in the morning. He was very hungry, but more tired than hungry. If the others could go without food, so could he, and it certainly wouldn't be the first time. Dai staggered slightly as he stood up and went to the big old sledge. He shifted enough cargo to the center so that he and Murima had enough space on the sides to crawl into sleeping bags without any danger of falling off. He opened the sleeping bag on the left side for Murima to crawl into, handed him a stiff pillow, and then put Skrot on a soft cushion next to his spot and crawled in. He was asleep as soon as his head touched the cold pillow.

37

Dai sat next to a clear, cool stream with a tin beaker in his hand. He dipped the beaker into the slow-flowing stream and swallowed the cold water in two huge gulps, but remained thirsty. After the third beaker, he wondered why he couldn't drink enough and what kind of water this was that couldn't quench his raging thirst. From somewhere a gong started to clang, and he threw the beaker into the stream in disgust. What kind of water was this anyway? He started to run. He would be late for lunch again and would be punished with extra work and fitness classes without food until supper time.

The gong was damn insistent, he thought, which was unusual. Maybe it's an emergency, but it's the lunchtime gong, so what's going on? Dai reluctantly woke up to the insistent clang of an empty pot being drummed against the side of the sledge by Ekaasi. It was still dark, and the sledge was still parked.

He fixed a half-open eye on Ekaasi. "I thought you said I can go to sleep? So what changed your mind?"

"You did sleep. You slept for sixteen hours, but now you must get up and eat. It's about two past noon, and we must prepare to depart. We are in the cavern Hespus led us to. Kyr said she and Koro will be here around sundown; they are following a search party headed this way. She says it's only one of many teams sent out by Heltos to find the king. The party picked up the trail from our camp, but the bodies baffled them. Some of them know about this cave but are nevertheless following the horses' tracks to be sure we kept to the trail, but they are only hoping that the king may be one of us. We have two to three hours, or perhaps more, to prepare for battle or to depart—whatever you decide. Now wake up properly and get up."

"Can I have some water, please? I'm dying of thirst," he said.

When he crawled out of the sleeping bag, both Surra and

Tumar were there, each with a beaker of water. He thanked them and drank both before he moved away from the sledge toward the fire, where Murima was stirring a stew, using only one arm a bit awkwardly. The pain in the left arm obviously hindered him, but he didn't wince when he used it.

Murima looked up and smiled. "Thank you for coming to my rescue, Dai. It seems that I neglected to properly express my appreciation yesterday. The lady Ekaasi dressed my wound again this morning after we parked here. The pain is under control for she slapped a thick dressing of herbs on it, and now I can use my hand to hold things without pain. The princess really is a good marksman. She shot a buck that took off suddenly from almost underneath the sorrel's hoofs. It made him rear, but he didn't bolt. I think this stew is ready. It's from the smaller deer you hung on the side of the bigger sledge."

Surra laughed. "Ekaasi was scouting ahead, and I was so nervous that I almost emptied the magazine into the bolting thing. It was pure reflex as a result of my nervousness. What Murima means is that the poor thing had four holes in it when we picked it up."

Dai smiled happily. "That's good shooting, even as a reflex. My stomach is so empty it complains continuously. The stew sure smells delicious, and if you don't dish it up right now I'll hit you on the sore arm until you do."

"I can hear it screaming, Dai. I'm very happy that I'm alive to cook for you." He filled a tin plate to capacity and passed it on with a knife and fork.

As they ate, Dai looked around the cavern. The entrance was quite huge but looked as if it was almost closed by boulders. Dai estimated the cavern mouth to measure about twenty meters wide and six or seven meters high.

"This particular cave is still used by hunters and travelers as a stopover or refuge, especially during storms in the summer," the king said. "It was used as a fortress until about ninety years ago, which is why the floor is so level. Those huge boulders were stacked about four meters in front of the entrance as a sort of bulwark and windscreen."

Dai thought it was a bit reckless to use such a well-known place as a refuge, even temporarily, but he kept his opinion to himself. He enjoyed the stew and complimented Murima. When

205

he had eaten himself to an almost standstill, he washed the plate and then went to the entrance. He realized that, even if they started now, they wouldn't be able to elude the group of king-hunters. There just wouldn't be enough daylight or time to confuse a decent tracker, and some might be mounted or leading mounts so they could follow fast to harass fugitives.

Outside he looked around for inspiration, but ideas just wouldn't come. The terrain was flat and denuded of any cover for five hundred meters. If they dawdled, they could easily be besieged and starved out or killed as they left the cave. He looked farther north and saw that the terrain became wild and rugged, but the sledges could be elevated high enough to pass through the rough country. Northeast and eastward, the country became more open and flat, so that was not an option. They should go directly north if they could, he thought.

He went back and asked the king and Murima if they knew anything about the terrain to the north. The king said he remembered it was rough, but not so much that the horses couldn't pull the sledges over or around obstacles. There was a deep cutting that used to be an ancient road about twenty to thirty kilometers from where they were, but the sides were too steep for the safety of the sledges and horses. He didn't know if there was a way down unless it was farther to the east, where the terrain flattened out. Murima said he only knew some of the country near the mountains in the northeast.

Dai made up his mind. "I'll go back two or three kilometers and delay them as long as I can, if I can't discourage them. Ekaasi, can you take the sledges north? I might catch up before you hit the cutting, but if I do not, look for a place under cover to stay tomorrow during the day. Skrot can guide me in. If Kyr and Koro aren't too tired, they can help me." He looked at the others. Ekaasi nodded, but Surra had a strange look in her eyes.

"You'll need someone to watch your back when you're busy," she said. "I'm trained for this type of situation, Dai, and I'll go with you." Seeing the objection in his eyes, she added, "I'm serious and I won't be in the line of fire for most of the time. I'll stay behind cover and watch to make sure no one sneaks up on you. We might even encounter the cats and ask them to act as additional lookouts."

Dai looked at the king, who nodded. Then he looked at

Ekaasi, who said, "She won't come to any harm if she stays out of the fight. Take her with you, Dai. I know you will see to her safety. I'll take care of things while you're gone."

38

As they left, Tumar came up to them and offered him two of her three paralysis bombs. Dai smiled.

"While the three of us are together, I want to tell you a few things I'd like to teach both of you." He proceeded to educate them on proper breathing rhythms while walking and running.

"I'd like to take each of you out with me when I go on a scout or hunt, but not both at the same time. I need to teach you how to survive in case we have to separate for some reason."

Surra gave him a strange look, but she nodded and followed him. They walked briskly for a while. Dai let his new, untrained ability range around the area, and to his joy, he reestablished contact with Kyr and Koro. Kyr said they were still about seven or eight kilometers away and that the company they were watching, eleven in all, was moving slowly. They planned to arrive at and surround the old fortress-cavern after dark, since they were fairly sure the king would be there. She had already told Ekaasi.

Dai told Surra what Kyr had said.

"When we came this way, I noticed outcroppings—one can't really call them knolls or small hills—no more than two kilometers from here," Surra said. "From this side, it's at the beginning of a small, shallow valley. Actually, it's more a depression than a valley, about two or three kilometers long. We can ambush them there, but they might expect it and be wary. This wide trail passes conveniently between two of the highest knolls. There are struggling thorn trees and dense thickets all the way to the two knolls. The depression is free of vegetation for more than two kilometers. It's as if someone cleared the area for farming a long time ago, but not so long ago for vegetation to grow high again."

"Kyr said there are eleven of them," Dai said. "I suspect that one is a tracker." He stood in thought for a few seconds. "They would expect an ambush at those points, so we'll use another place. Let's jog to get warm. We have plenty of time."

Surra's strange looks were finally explained when they

started to jog. She forgot all about her breathing rhythm as she told him, "I think Tumar is in love with you. Did you see the way she looks at you and follows your example all the time?"

So that's her problem, he thought. *She's jealous of Tumar for no reason at all.* Without stopping or turning his head, Dai replied, "I don't think so. She was trained from childhood to survive, and it has become habit. I do the same, but it's just not as obvious. I noticed that she watches what I do, the way I walk, and then she imitates what she feels is right, and she learns quickly. She hasn't had any training for the wilds. Anyway, even if that is the case, she is a client of the Fighting Priests, and as such I will never end up in a relationship with any client, even if they force themselves on me. They are sacrosanct until I deliver them to their destination. Only then do they cease to be a client," he emphasized.

Surra said, "Okay. Hey, I was wondering…have you ever made love in the wilderness in freezing weather? I think it would be pretty erotic to have only certain body areas exposed to the bitter cold and to 'get down to business' while we wait for our victims. I would like to try it that way while we have the chance— would you?"

Dai stopped and embraced her. She was a lot of fun, and he told her so. But first they had to find a suitable place to ambush the would-be hunters. They jogged again, faster, hand in hand.

When they reached the knolls, Dai saw that this would be the obvious location for an ambush and therefore should be avoided. He climbed the nearest one and looked around. The highest point on his left was only one huge boulder surrounded by vegetation, and the bare, well-used trail passed between it and the outcropping where he stood.

He scanned the area to his right. About two hundred steps away was a flat knoll with a few large boulders, barely visible in the surrounding dense vegetation and trees. It was the most unlikely place for an ambush and therefore the best. The trees were too stunted and wouldn't offer any protection against a volley of bullets or bolts. He told Surra what he was observing, because she needed to learn to assess the possibilities of a defensive or offensive position.

Dai looked through the scope of his rifle but couldn't see

any movement along the trail. He could only see for about three kilometers, but it was an adequate distance, giving him more than enough time to fulfill Surra's fantasy.

They inspected the knoll and found it adequately fortified by boulders that protected them from a frontal attack. The breeze blew from the west, and the dense foliage of a clump of bushes lower down on the eastern side offered relief from the iciness. He looked for an opening to the center, which he soon found after breaking off a few branches. They started kissing and were both fairly worked up before baring anything. It was chilly, but they didn't feel the cold. Afterward it got cold again pretty fast. Surra laughingly joked, "It's so cold out here, your eyes freeze shut when you blink."

Dai put his arms around her from the back and said they needn't yet go on watch. Kyr always knew how far she was from Dai, and she or Koro would warn him when they were close by. He smiled as he told her that Kyr was also teaching Koro the ways of the wilderness and other things so he could adapt to their established ways and routines. She turned around and kissed him, returning his tight embrace.

All too soon, Koro let him know the search party must be in their sight. He let Dai have a picture of how he saw the outcroppings. Dai would have been disoriented if he wasn't used to Kyr's pictures from ground level, for the outcrops looked like huge hills in the far distance.

Dai quickly told Surra that the cats were only about a kilometer away. They picked up their rifles and ran bent over to the top. The sun was close to the western horizon; it would be dark in little more than an hour. Dai made sure Surra was well protected, although she was able to see the entire arena—which her instructors at Bojon Security always called the operational field. Then he settled down comfortably and told Surra she should look at the enemy through her scope and memorize the position of every individual, especially when they dived for cover. If or when that happened, she should still have a mental picture of where an individual might be for the next few moments, or even longer, and she should fire in that immediate location into any position that looked like cover, but remember that her rifle's effective range was less than a hundred meters. When their enemies started firing, he said, she should stop looking and hide behind the boulder. He wanted her safe and alive, for she had a formidable task ahead of her to rebuild Bojon.

Through the scope Dai looked at the one in front who walked with his eyes mostly on the ground in front of him, but he saw that the man's eyes ranged warily from his feet to the outcroppings, which must have been visible in fine detail at that distance. Dai once again felt a reluctance to kill someone he knew would have spent many years accumulating the knowledge of scoutcraft, but he also was the most dangerous. Dai adjusted his scope to five hundred meters and took careful aim. The scout had his head turned to a large individual who must be the leader, and he pointed to the outcroppings. Dai assumed he was telling the leader it was a likely point for an ambush if any could be expected. The leader laughed and shook his head. It was obvious that he dismissed any thought of an ambush, and Dai understood his reasoning.

He kept a running commentary all the time to educate Surra, who said nothing. Maybe she knew all this in theory, he thought, but now she would see it in real live action. He told her he was going to kill the scout first and then the leader, and also explained why he was doing it in that sequence and at three hundred meters. Her rifle would only be effective at a hundred meters or less, and she should always keep that in mind.

He adjusted the scope to three hundred meters. It would still be a long shot for most individuals, although it was an easy range for an energy hunting rifle. When they came into the three-hundred-meter range, he aimed at the scout's head and gently squeezed the trigger. He immediately shifted his aim to the big man and shot him, too. They dropped almost together, and the rest of the company dived for cover without hesitation.

He killed another one who popped up to take an incautious look at the two outcroppings. Subconsciously he kept track of the number of shots fired from this particular clip until he knew there was only one shot left. He took another clip from his pocket, put it within easy reach, and told Surra to count her shots so she could reload when it was time. When he fired the last round, he would do a fast change of clips.

Surra crouched behind a boulder well away from Dai. She could see the arena very well, but Dai's position would draw the fire when they located him. She would only join the action if they came within a hundred meters and stormed their position.

Dai fired sporadically whenever there was a movement or when someone rushed closer, and he didn't take his eyes from the field except to blink quickly now and then. Surra knew he had killed another three by the time Kyr and Koro quietly announced that they were joining them. Dai didn't look at the cats, but Surra noticed that both looked a bit haggard and thirsty. She asked if they'd like some water. Then she quietly told Dai that she would crawl over to fetch the metal saucer he always carried with him for that purpose.

Dai shot twice before she returned the dish to its clip on his belt. She did a quick calculation: "There should only be four left, I think. Why don't you finish them all off quickly?"

"No, there are six left. I missed a few times to discourage them." Solid bullets and energy bolts suddenly ricocheted from the boulder that sheltered them. The pursuers had at last located them. "And I wounded another just before they found rocks to hide behind. Someone has taken over the leadership, and I think they will rush closer in a few moments, but they will weave as they run. That gun of yours may come in handy after all, if you will get back to your position quickly."

She wondered how he knew she didn't have her gun, because he had not once taken his eyes from the arena.

He's young in years, but he's an old warrior, Kyr thought to her. *Although he can't smell as good as cats can, he's better at effectively using all his senses together than any human I know of because I taught him.*

Surra realized she was an open book to the cats, but she didn't mind. She was learning that she must think and listen if she wanted to survive long enough to reach old age.

Before she reached her gun, Dai fired five times rapidly. Then he changed clips before it was necessary. She was now behind her boulder, as she thought of it, and moved swiftly to grab her gun. She peeked out cautiously, but there was no one to see.

"They were rushing closer, and I think I got another four," Dai said, "but I may only have wounded some of them. They're about a hundred and twenty meters from us and are progressing quickly, weaving a lot, and fast. There are fairly large rocks scattered there, and they may snipe from there, I think. Be very careful, please."

No, you killed four and wounded the fifth. Surra was made party to the silent communication, and by the different tone, she knew it must be Koro who included her. It was at that moment she started to love the cats.

Koro continued. *The surviving two, who are both wounded, although not very seriously, are discussing ways to withdraw and run because they have at last realized that this is a deadly serious game and not an outing as they believed. They have lost heart and are wondering who the deadly marksman could be. Ah yes, they are going to leave their guns and emerge with their hands up. They have realized that they will be dead anyway.*

Dai said quickly, "You speak to them, Surra, but don't show yourself. It will confuse them no end. Tell them you won't be lenient with the next group, and they must leave you alone or face the consequences. You don't like to be followed or tracked because you like your privacy. Lay it on thick."

As he spoke, the two men got up slowly with their hands above their heads to indicate that they held no weapons. One of them called out, "We surrender. Please don't shoot. We are wounded. Who are you?"

Surra called out, "Start walking back the way you came. You may take one gun. You don't deserve to live, but tell whoever sent you that I won't take pity on anyone who comes after me again. I like my privacy, and if I want anyone with me, I'll send him an invitation." She paused.

"We were sent to look for the king, not you, lady—"

Dai shot so close that he burned the speaker's ear. The individual ducked and started to run at full speed without saying good-bye. The other survivor lost no time in racing him to get out of range. Both ran like jackals, darting from side to side as if they expected to be shot at, and neither stopped to pick up a gun.

"The way they are hopping and skipping along with such abandon," Dai said laconically, "no one would guess that they are wounded."

Koro chuckled as he told both of them, *What that character thought was that the lady could shoot damned accurately and that she only missed by a mere fraction. He ran instinctively, and he keeps wondering who the heck the lady is and where she came from. He has no idea that she is the king's daughter because word is out that the other daughter is dead.*

Watch your language, youngster! Kyr admonished severely. *It's permissible when you address Dai, but not when you include a human female. Remember that!*

Don't worry, Kyr, Koro. I'm used to much stronger descriptive language than that, Surra thought back, *and it doesn't matter if he uses common slang in a situation like this. I love both of you, and you can use any words you feel like in my presence.*

She's starting to treat them like human companions, which is a good start, Dai thought. She has the instincts of a real good leader, and she is very serious when she thinks at them. To change the subject, he thought, *It's getting late and we should be going. It may be hours before we catch up with Ekaasi. Kyr, is there anyone left alive? If not, we can start jogging, for I don't want to waste time collecting weapons we don't need. And it would be a dead giveaway as to who we are if we do so.* He waited, since he knew that both cats were reaching out to check for brain emissions on the battlefield.

He didn't ask if the cats would be comfortable bounding along with them. Kyr knew him very well, and she would have told him if they had any pains or wounds that would hamper them. He made his way down the hillock with the others on his heels. When they reached level ground, he started to jog, slowly at first so Surra could establish a breathing rhythm.

39

The sun would set in a few minutes, and darkness would soon follow because of the high mountains. Dai asked Kyr to talk to Ekaasi or to the old lady cat so they could run in the right direction without diverting to the cave to locate and follow the tracks.

After a few seconds, Kyr told him that Ekaasi would follow the North Star as soon as it became visible, and if it didn't, she would borrow Tumar's compass. Kyr now bounded to the front so Dai could follow her. When they were up the slight incline and on the low mesa above the cave, she left the trail, which veered slightly to the east.

Like a good scout, Koro had slowed his pace until he could guard their rear. Although chances were slim that they would be followed, in the wilds, as Kyr had explained to him, nothing should be left to chance. Koro let his senses roam backward, to the sides, and to the front, even though he knew Kyr would also be doing that. She had told him that only hungry predators hunted in the cold of winter and that reptiles went through a process called brumation—similar to hibernation, but rather than living off fat, their metabolism slowed.

It was completely dark when Koro almost yelped in fright and surprise as he detected a big predator lying in wait a little way ahead. He clearly sensed the starving thoughts and the craving to kill any prey to still the pangs of its raving hunger. He didn't know that Kyr had already warned Dai about twenty seconds earlier and that they were giving Koro a chance to become aware of its existence. It was part of his training to make him vigilant at all times.

Dai calmly thanked him and asked him to warn Kyr and to tell Surra to slow down to a walk. He felt the cat's proud thoughts, but he and Kyr were well versed in the art of thought suppression. When Surra slowed down, he did the same and unslung his rifle from his back. He adjusted the scope for night sight and tested it by looking at where Kyr had indicated the predator crouched on a rock, getting ready to attack as they passed.

He stopped and asked Surra to adjust her scope and look at the rock outcropping in front of them, but slightly to the left on top of it. It was part of her training, as well. When he heard her slight gasp, he asked in a whisper if she would kill it. Surra nodded, not even thinking that Dai couldn't see her head in the pitch-black darkness. Kyr sensed her acceptance and warned him that Surra was going to shoot and was taking aim.

He trained his scope on the gaunt saber-toothed tiger, ready to shoot if Surra's shot missed or if she only wounded the cat. He knew she could shoot, but this was a test to see if she could stay calm. He heard a quiet, single cough and saw the tiger plop down as if tired. He approved when he heard a second cough as she made sure the tiger was actually dead. He realized she wasn't the overconfident type who took it for granted that they were deadly shots.

"Very good," he said and walked closer. "You've been taught well." He kept the scope trained on the cat to check for movement, but there was none. His night sight wasn't affected, and he scaled the rough boulder quickly. He expertly removed the tail skin with his hunting knife and joined her again.

Surra had watched him through the scope of her gun. "Why did you do that?" she asked.

"An old custom," he lied. "I will dress it when it's dry enough and then I will make it into a belt or a headband and present it to you as an initiation gift. You kept calm and passed the test. I knew you would, but it's still a custom."

Surra said nothing. She thought it silly but nevertheless felt a glow of pride. "Make it a belt," she said. "I would feel a bit silly and primitive if I wore it around my head in public. If we make it through this, I will wear it with pride, provided it doesn't smell."

Dai laughed and wrapped it in a rag. He would salt it in the morning and leave it out to dry. They started to jog a little bit faster because Kyr said Ekaasi was about ten kilometers ahead of them. Dai would have liked to run, but he knew Surra would not be able to keep up for more than two hundred meters at that pace.

As it was, Surra lasted for about five kilometers before Kyr told Dai to slow down to a walk. Surra wasn't complaining, but the cat sensed she was reaching the limit of her endurance. Dai thought Surra had done very well. He slowed to a walk and then stopped. He told her to take a mouthful of water, swirl it about for a few seconds, and then spit it out. Then she must take small mouthfuls at intervals until she felt she'd had enough.

He filled the saucer for the cats and then drank his water as he had instructed Surra to do so she didn't think he stopped for her benefit. He had found that pride played a dominant role in most people's lives, and Surra was a proud, if not stubborn, individual; Kyr also knew this from reading her mind. When the cats had finished, Dai picked up the saucer and started to walk. They were warm from the jogging, and to cool down now would be a mistake. Quietly, he asked Kyr to let him know when Surra had recovered.

Meanwhile, he told Surra she was doing extremely well. They would walk for a minute or two before gradually increasing the pace again. He took her gloved hand in his, and they walked a bit faster until Kyr told him he could start jogging again.

They repeated this routine five times before they caught up with Ekaasi. It was well after midnight, and the terrain was relatively rocky. Surra was extremely tired by this time but didn't complain once.

Ekaasi said they were near a deep cutting and should explore it a bit to find a way down and across. She'd only had a quick look because the king was tired, and she wanted him to sleep to avoid overtaxing his heart. While Ekaasi was talking, Dai bundled Surra into his sleeping bag with shoes on, and she went to sleep almost immediately. He knew she was fit, but even so, she might be stiff in unaccustomed places for a few days. The king was already asleep in the place prepared for him, but Tumar and Murima were wide awake.

Ekaasi said she had found a large overhang where the sledges and horses would be sheltered from the cold and from observation by satellites or from aircraft during the day. There was even a bubbling brook and sparse grass to keep the animals occupied.

Dai took the reins of the sorrel and followed behind the other sledge. The cats had jumped aboard, and they stretched out comfortably near Skrot and Surra. Dai suspected that the cats were exchanging information or comparing notes.

When they reached the camping spot, Ekaasi said she would scout to the west along the cutting while Dai saw to the well-being of the animals.

He approved the choice of the overhang. There was evidence of occasional use by animals, and it was high, deep, and wide. The surrounding dense, thorny brush had no openings other than the wide entrance on the hard ground at one end. He unhitched the horses and ponies and showed Tumar how to apply the hobbles. Then he asked if she would keep watch with the cats while Ekaasi rested when she returned. Ekaasi had only had a brief rest that morning, and it wasn't enough, since she, too, had to be wide awake in case they needed to defend themselves.

It wasn't necessary to stay awake, he told her. One cat would always be on watch and drum her awake as soon as anything that might be a menace approached within five hundred meters. However, she must have her weapons on hand and ready to use at a moment's notice. Then he told Murima to retire as well and that his taking over the cooking job was much appreciated. The cook gratefully crawled into his sleeping bag.

Although Tumar would have liked to accompany Dai, she was too disciplined to say so and understood that someone should keep watch with the cats at all times. Dai looked tired, and she knew there would be plenty of opportunities to learn later. She helped him gently maneuver the sledges so their rears were against the back of the overhang before being grounded. Parked that way, Dai explained, they were ready to move out at a moment's notice. He took the tiger tail from his rucksack and sprinkled it with salt while giving Tumar a brief recap of how Surra had killed the tail's owner. Then he hung it over a rail on the old sledge to dry.

Ekaasi returned within a few minutes and quietly told them that the way to the west was blocked about three kilometers away by a steep, high plateau, and she didn't think they would find an easy way to cross the cleft to the west. Dai must check toward the east along the cleft, she added. Hespus called it a cutting but it wasn't manmade, only man-used—or man-misused, if she knew anything about humans, present company excluded.

Dai hugged her and told her to eat and then go to sleep,

for the cats would be on watch and pester Tumar if necessary. He might not be back by sunrise, but he'd try his best to find a way across. He made sure he had some dry rations to eat in his rucksack in case he was delayed. Then he refilled his canteen at the source of the brook, where it bubbled out at the base of the overhang, and left at a jog.

When he reached the cutting, he scanned it up and down through the scope of the rifle, as a night-sight helmet would have been too much of an encumbrance. He agreed with Ekaasi's observation. Westward, the cutting looked like a deep slash in solid rock that had been filled up and leveled to create a highway in ancient times by a long-lost civilization. Subsequently, nature had taken over, and scattered, scrubby, hardy plants grew between the cracks in the hard-looking surface. The rocky sides were sheer, as if a giant grinder had been used to make the old roadway inaccessible except from either end.

About two kilometers eastward, the northern wall of the cutting looked somewhat lower. It then curved gently toward the north, so he couldn't see any farther. If he had a rope with him, he could have gone down to the level roadway and progressed much more easily and faster, but he didn't, and he wasn't going back for one.

Dai ran where he could along the edge of the cutting and walked where he couldn't run, until his way was blocked by dense, thorny brush and an assortment of huge boulders. He veered away until he found a way past, but the dense obstruction along the edge continued, sometimes wider and sometimes so narrow he could almost sense the closeness of the cleft. It would've been better to negotiate this broken terrain during daylight, he thought, but he had no choice. His eyes were accustomed to the darkness, and he could see well enough in the bright starlight to avoid falling over rocks and other natural obstacles even while he was running.

He was past the curve in the roadway before the dense brush ended. He turned northward and found that the ground gradually sloped down to the east. He nevertheless continued to the north until he found the cleft again. It was now shallow enough for a very fit man to jump down, if he could see where he would land. Dai looked to his right and could see only a large, sloping, flat outcrop of rock about a hundred meters away. He guessed it was sometimes used by predators as a lookout point. On impulse, he decided to climb the few meters to the top. Perhaps he needn't go farther if he could see what was off to the east.

He could smell lion as he bent forward to keep his balance on the short, steep, and somewhat smoothened incline, but it was an old scent. When he reached the top, he looked down to locate the other side of the cleft so he could follow it through the scope. The cleft flattened out rapidly and gradually became part of the flat grassland about five hundred meters east from "Lookout Point," as he thought of this outcropping.

He looked farther toward the east, as it was a habit to thoroughly scan the area around him. He stiffened when he saw a startlingly brightly lit spot less than three kilometers away. He could distinguish a brightly illuminated tent behind a floodlight and a grounded hover car near the tent. If it weren't for the very bright lights, he would not have seen it, for it was barely discernible at this distance in the darkness. It could be a hunter's camp, but he didn't think so. Only a very obtuse hunter would advertise his whereabouts so flamboyantly during the night.

He scanned the roadway in the center of the cleft back to where he was. It was surprisingly solid, and he didn't see any obvious obstacles. Whoever constructed this road ages ago knew how to build for keeps, he thought. The scope lost its focus when he brought it too close to where he stood on the lookout point. He swung the rifle to the west, thinking he might as well see how the road looked back toward their temporary camp before checking the opposite side of the cleft right across from him. It might be prudent to cross where the ground was the hardest or rockiest.

He ducked low when he saw a hover car slowly approaching, scarcely three hundred meters away. A dish rotated lazily on top of the roof, and he knew the occupants were using infrared to scan for sentient life. That meant his body heat would be detected at any moment. He scrambled down the shelf, but it was already too late. A bolt from a large-caliber energy rifle sizzled high over his body just as he scampered down the side away from the car on hands and feet. He knew that the dish operator wouldn't be able to distinguish shapes, so he flopped down the sharp decline as a wounded animal would.

The car put on a burst of speed and stopped opposite the lookout rock. Dai remembered that he would also be hidden by the edge of the cleft, so he crawled a bit closer. They might be from the camp down there, and he was angry. Only an inexperienced or cowardly hunter from the city would use a large-caliber rifle like that to spoil a large portion of his prey, unless he hunted solely to satisfy his killing lust.

He flattened down near the shallow edge of the cutting, which was overgrown with short grass, and crawled behind a fairly large rock that would shield his body heat to some extent. The solid sides of the cutting must have petered out or were buried under soil here, he thought, and then concentrated on the car. He heard a door open and a querulous voice complaining, "You're wasting time, Grut. We're late, and you know how the gross Carros hates to be kept waiting. He'll take it out on our hides."

"I'll only be a minute, Gommy. I know I got him, and it must be a big predator. I want his head." The voice was gruff, jubilant, and loud.

"What if you only wounded him, huh Grut? He could be lying in wait for you to get closer. They are like that, you know. It'll be full daylight when we return this way, and you can look for him then. If you don't get back in the car right now, I'm not going to wait around for you. Carros can have your eggs, but I'm still fond of mine."

Grut hesitated. Dai could almost hear him thinking. His type would not confront a wounded predator at any price at any time, and maybe this Gommy knew it and had given him a way out without showing him up as a coward. He heard, "You're right. We are running a bit late." The door slammed hard, and the car moved off at a faster pace.

40

Dai glanced at his watch. It was about a quarter to four, but the sun wouldn't be up for another four hours. To cross the cutting in this wide-open wilderness in the light of day with trigger-happy and perhaps murderous hunters nearby would be taking one hell of a chance. This Grut might just be the kind who kills for the fun of it, and he would get away with murder out here. He wondered how anyone in their right mind would pick a cold winter morning like this for a meeting in the middle of nowhere. It smelled fishy, and he felt a sudden urge to try to find out more.

He was up and over the shallow drop to the roadway before the car was a hundred meters away. He sprinted along the patchy road, but the car slowed down after a few minutes, enabling him to catch up. Perhaps the occupants also didn't want to be too early for their meeting with this feared Carros. The dish had stopped revolving, and Dai assumed they had turned the infrared display screen off.

He caught up with the car and then kept an estimated fifty meters behind at an easily maintainable pace. He knew that even if the infrared scanner was still switched on, it couldn't detect his body heat in this particular spot at this distance due to some peculiarity of the antigravity generator.

Perhaps his mounting fatigue or the coldness of the morning, or both, made his thought process a bit sluggish. Two hundred meters from the camp, he suddenly realized that sentries would be posted even at this hour of the morning. Criminal activities called for tight security everywhere, at all hours. His fast running pace became a bent-over jog as he looked for cover. The area around the tent had been thoroughly cleared, so there wasn't enough cover for a mouse under the overly bright floodlights. He kept the car between him and the brightly lit tent, for he very much wanted to hear the conversation and he was willing to take a chance. Sentries should be cold and worn out after being up all night, or so he hoped.

As the car grounded and was switched off, an extremely obese man waddled from the tent as if he had been waiting just inside. Dai was shocked; he had never seen an individual with such a vast globular circumference. He had to be supported by an antigravity belt because he looked like a giant ball with a small knob on top for a head and two appendages at the bottom to propel him forward and perhaps backward. Two short, slab-like arms with pudgy fingers protruded from below the head and just reached the special holsters with guns stuck into them on top of the broad belt, which looked embedded into the middle of the globular body. Dai didn't venture to estimate the weight of the "ball-man." *Oh, wow!* he thought. Without that belt, his legs would fold or break and he wouldn't be able to move. He must have a *very* personal servant!

"You cut it so fine, Grut, that I was on the verge of getting angry. What kept you?" He glared at Grut and Gommy. He had an unusually deep voice, but it suited him, Dai thought. Here was a man used to power and command.

"Uh, we thought that we should scout around a bit as you wouldn't want us here too early, Carros," Grut replied and received a murderous look from Gommy.

Carros laughed a deep rumble. "You're an old accomplished liar, Grut. It's more likely that you wasted valuable time as usual by shooting at shadows and widely missing them. Perhaps one day you might hit one by pure accident. Come on in and have a drink to drive out the iciness." It was an order, not an invitation.

Dai was torn between the need to scout around to put any guards to sleep and the need to hear what was being said. The first and more urgent need lost out when he heard Carros rumble that he called them here at this hour because he wanted their talents and men in on the search for the escaped king. Dai pricked up his ears, then moved closer and crouched so as not to miss anything.

"When you leave, you must immediately mobilize your men, dogs, trackers, and whatever you may need. Have them patrol this cutting and ten kilometers past this spot twenty-four hours a day, and that means every centimeter. I don't think he can cross the steep part, but nothing must be left to chance. Have men posted where they are in sight of each other and

223

have the means to communicate with each other, including night vision. You know how to do it, but concentrate more on this side from where the steep part of the cutting ends, and do it by first light today."

Carros paused…and a strange female voice shouted in Dai's head, *DANGER BEHIND YOU!*

His head rang, but he felt the slight displacement of air above and behind him at the same time. He ducked and dodged half a step to his left with a fast shift of his right foot to get his head and upper body out of the way, simultaneously twisting his hips to turn around lightning fast. His subconscious mind must have warned him not to get the artificial skin on his face damaged, for without thinking he blocked the descending butt of a rifle with a raised left forearm.

The arm went numb, but without conscious thought, he grabbed the butt with his right hand, twisted his hips, and kicked his assailant right over the heart with the toes of his right foot, driven by all the power he could muster in his leg. The silent attacker let go of the rifle as the wind was knocked out of his body. He couldn't breathe, so he couldn't yell. Silently he keeled over and curled up in a fetal position in an effort to regain his breathing ability. Dai hit him hard just below the ear with the butt of his own rifle. He heard a dull crack.

Dai's head spun with the pain in his damaged muscles, and he hoped his forearm wasn't broken. He grimly suppressed the urge to yell heartily, but it wouldn't do to warn the neighborhood that he had arrived. He let go of the rifle, and it fell against the now-limp body. Then he unslung his own rifle one-handedly from his shoulder, rested the point of the barrel against the temple of his erstwhile assailant, and pulled the trigger to make sure the man was permanently out of circulation and wouldn't bother an innocent eavesdropper again. There was a dull "plop" sound, and he hoped no one heard it or the dull crack when he broke the man's jaw.

The voice spoke again in his pain-filled head. *It's okay, Dai. The three inside haven't heard a thing. Too busy feeding their greedy maws. There are two more guards, one about a hundred meters to the west and another about the same distance to the south. The one you just disposed of saw you running after the car and moved closer, then hid to catch you off guard, for he had a bizarre sense of humor. He was guarding the old road. I'm sorry, it took me quite a while to get through to you. Go take care of the guards. They're vicious riffraff, and everybody will be glad to miss them. Then you might as well come back to rescue me while you're in the vicinity. I know the whole plot and who is involved, so don't worry about missing any information. I'm a captive inside the tent and destined to be murdered.*

Dai felt the presence withdraw from his head. Stranger things had happened to him, and he didn't question the authenticity of the sender. No human had been in direct communication with him before, and he was filled with wonder at one with such a powerful mind. Being used to mind talk with Kyr, he could feel the difference between honesty and lies, and this one was genuine. He wondered how she knew his name, but that could wait. It was time to get going and ignore the pain, as a wild animal would.

His left hand was too numb to hold on to anything, so as soon as he was away from the extremely bright lights, he rested the rifle's barrel on the elbow of his throbbing arm to look through the nightscope. The scope wobbled slightly, but he could see well enough. He lifted his elbow with the gun on it, slowly scanned the area to the left of the tent, and saw the guard. He was looking toward the tent and probably wishing he could get his hands on a bottle, Dai thought as he pulled the trigger. The guard collapsed in his tracks, as anyone shot right through the head would. His rifle made a soft cluttering sound, but Dai didn't think anyone heard it.

He waited a few seconds to listen and then swung the scope to the right and almost completed a full circle, but he didn't see the other guard. All his senses were alert as he slunk silently through the twilight zone into the darkness, so that anyone would be silhouetted against the illumination around the tent. He found the remaining guard in the twilight zone on the other side of the tent, lifting a bottle to his lips. As he shot the man through the back of the head, Dai thought that even if it was so bitterly cold, it was dim-witted and dangerous to drink on duty.

He didn't check the sentries. Only an instantly dead body dropped as limply as they had. It was painful, but he cradled the

225

rifle in the crook of his left arm as he silently walked to the entrance of the tent. The rifle in the crook of his arm had fooled many adversaries over the past four years because it wasn't an ideal position to shoot from accurately—or so people usually thought. The pain in his left forearm had decreased somewhat, and his fingers had enough life again to hook over the top of the barrel just behind the scope. It caused pain, but he was trained to live with it.

41

No one noticed him as he appeared in the tent's extra-wide entrance like a specter. He stood so that the rifle was casually pointed in the direction of one of the occupants and so he could swivel his hips just that little extra distance, as he had practiced and practiced until he was sick of it, but which had served him very well before.

He flicked his eyes over the interior of the huge, brightly lit tent. Grut and Gommy sat on a hard bench against the right wall, and Carros faced them. The moment he saw the round, sweating face of the obese Carros, he recognized him as the one known as Car Bolloth. Against the rear wall was a black-clad bundle chained to a canvas camp bed, but the flashing green eyes told him that the old woman was very much alive. She nodded faintly, and he knew she was the one with the powerful mind who had spoken to him. He smiled and nodded his head in her direction, then cleared his throat noisily. He almost laughed as Carros jumped around as if suspended like a balloon, and the other two leapt straight up as if stung simultaneously in the butts.

"Excuse me, *Mister* Bolloth, gentlemen, for arriving unannounced, but there wasn't time to request a formal invitation. I dropped in because *Mister* Grut here is such a lousy shot, and his action actually invited me."

Grut's mouth dropped open in incomprehension, and he shook his head as if clearing water from his ears.

"Yes," Dai continued, "you thought I was a defenseless predator about three kilometers back, and you shot at me because it made you feel like a man. It's a good thing your friend Gommy prevented you from investigating, otherwise this helpless predator might have ripped your guts out for the carrion eaters."

He turned to Carros and said with a smile, "I have the king you are looking for and also his other daughter, the sane one called Surra. Oh! Pardon my terrible manners! Vermin like you call me 'Dart,' and you may address me so if you like." He saw the shock on all three faces, but he wasn't finished.

"I came because I want to invite you, Grut the Coward, to take another shot at me, but expect me to shoot back this time. Just grab a gun whenever you feel lucky and start shooting if you have any guts left." He saw Carros peep manifestly past him and said, "Ah, no, *Mister* Carros, that's real naughty! The guards you brought along are citified and, like *Mister* Grut, useless out here in the wilderness. They're out cold, so to speak, and won't interrupt us at an inopportune moment."

He saw the astonishment on Carros's face, and turned slightly to face Grut again, wrinkling his nose while keeping check on Carros out of the corner of his left eye. He made sure the gun was pointed directly at the overgrown criminal boss's head while giving the impression that all his attention was centered on the visibly quaking Grut. "I smell something awful, Grut. What's the matter? Can't you even control your bowels, or is it an automated response?"

He saw the lardy Carros pull both guns out of their holsters, and quite fast. He must've thought that Dai's attention was firmly fixed on Grut. Dai shifted slightly and pulled the trigger with his forefinger. The bolt burned a small hole in the center of Carros's forehead as he made a backward somersault, with the gravity belt supporting his center of gravity. The guns clattered out of his lax fingers, and his head slumped forward, but he stayed upright.

Grut and Gommy made use of this opportunity to draw their handguns, but that was as far as they got. Dai swiveled his hips again and pulled the trigger twice. Both men fell back against the tent.

Dai turned toward the woman and sincerely apologized. "I'm sorry, lady. I didn't know what else to do. Anyway, Bolloth's enemies and many innocent people might sleep more soundly when they find out that he is no longer with us. How did you know my name?"

"Don't bother with apologies, Dai," the woman replied. "Bolly didn't deserve such a quick and clean end, as he specialized in gruesome torture and messy deaths. I wonder if he knows yet that he's dead. Come and unlock this contraption that keeps me chained to the corner of the tent. The key is on Bolly's belt. It's the short, flat, red one. I'll tell you everything

228

later. First you must remove these cadavers from the tent. Then you must select things you may need, like medicines and supplies. He's got the very best of everything. Then you must break up this camp before dawn and load what you don't want and the bodies into Grut's car and send them south, east, or west. We might as well make use of Bolly's outsized car because it can't be detected or tracked by satellite or other sophisticated equipment, since it is equipped with an illegal nullifier. The car is not even registered anywhere in any country. It's nice to be so powerful and influential that you can get anything and do anything you like without being called to account in this life."

Dai unlocked the chain belt around the old woman's slender waist and helped her to her feet. She didn't weigh much, he thought.

As if reading his thoughts, the old woman said, "Thank you, Dai. Would you please remove these malodorous bodies so I can prepare a decent meal in peace and comfort for the first time in three months? Mind communication with another human takes a lot of energy from a starved body. Yes, Bolly denied me food while he stuffed himself in front of me—and took pleasure in it. That's why I look like an old hag. I'll tell you a few things you need to know after you've dragged them outside. There's a small grav-trolley outside that'll make it easier. Carros Bolloth had everything to make life comfortable for himself, and now he only has his evil reputation and misdeeds to explain in the afterlife."

Dai pulled the late Carros Bolloth outside by his gravity belt. His sphincter had relaxed in death, and the rotten stench was awful. Dai thought that without the grav-belt, he would have had to laboriously roll "Bolly" outside. He cut the rope near the tent flap and looped it through Bolly's belt, then attached the other end to the handle of the cargo door on Grut's car. Then he adjusted the belt and let go. The buoyant globular body drifted upward like a balloon. Now it wouldn't be wafted away by the icy, early morning breeze that had sprung up, as if trying to cleanse the reeking tent.

The gigantic gravity car was covered by a camouflage net under a cluster of old trees about fifty meters from the tent. It can't be just a car, Dai thought. It was as big as a bus, and he marveled at the luxurious interior and comfortable seats, as well as the sleeper-bench to one side. Everything, including the doors, was oversized. Bolloth had traveled in style and lived in extravagance, and this luxurious "bus" must almost be as fast as an aircraft, judging by the streamlined design. It must have cost a fortune and taken a lot of clout to build and equip, Dai thought, but he didn't envy the late owner.

He found the grav-trolley inside the bus and took it out through an extra-large cargo door in the rear. He quickly removed the bodies of Grut and Gommy from the tent and put them inside their own grav-car, then did the same with the three guards.

When he returned to the tent, it smelled clean again because the old woman had slashed the back side opposite the entrance to let the icy air waft out the odors. She had prepared a huge breakfast for two. She pointed to a basin, and while he washed his hands in hot water with sweet-smelling soap, Dai thanked her for her thoughtfulness.

To his amazement, the woman said, "My name's Nogalithe, by the way. I'm a Diviner Priestess, or rather, one of them I should say."

Dai was caught off guard. He knew of the Diviner Priestesses—they were deemed part of the organization of Fighting Priests—but he had never met one in the flesh. They were initially trained by the Temple Priests and then passed on to the Fighters, or the other way around. He wondered how "Bolly" was able to take a Diviner Priestess prisoner because they could fight like tigresses.

Nogalithe continued, "There is a satellite-connected comm-unit in Bolly's car, and we can call Karna from there instead of using the normal relay. I know you have memorized his number, and Bolly's comm-unit has a scrambler. I will talk to him and give him names, dates, and places. To ensure that no one can understand, I will speak in the old language, as we always do when communicating top-secret information. Now, come sit down and eat, boy."

Dai was impressed. He had learned the old language and used it, but he was not yet much of an expert. It was a forgotten language known only to the Fighting Priests and a few librarians.

Between bites, the priestess told him, "Carros Bolloth—I

called him Bolly to annoy him—had me abducted a little more than three months ago. He required a diviner to predict the outcome of his nefarious ventures but couldn't buy the services of one, since there are no dishonest diviners, so I permitted myself to be abducted. He wanted advice on the best course to take, and the best choices to make. You see, as a result of his greed, he managed to get himself involved up to his eyeballs in an interplanetary conspiracy to steal the treasure of the ancients. He was caught in a vise, because this is much bigger than he was capable of handling. It made him more vicious because he was fighting to preserve his life.

"He thought he was very clever, but I knew he would kill me the moment he had no further use for me. What he didn't know, of course, was that I knew many years ago that he would abduct me and for what purpose. That is one curse that I abhor about this talent. We always know in advance what will happen to us. All other predictions are just likely probabilities, because everyone can make choices. If an individual takes another course, the probabilities change based on their choice.

"Anyway, Bolly starved me and threatened me with all kinds of dire fates if I gave him false information. He couldn't know that I could read his desires under certain conditions, so I usually predicted what he wanted to hear, with a few warnings here and there to make it sound genuine. I have known for years that I had a date with destiny out here and that he'd be the instrument to bring it about. I also knew that he would die here by your hand, but I told him he would find his true destiny out here. He, of course, interpreted that as meaning the old artifacts left by a forgotten civilization would be his.

"I have to stop talking for now. You must load everything you can use on the bus, as you call it, and the rest on the grav-car, then send it on its way before first light. We mustn't leave any evidence that Bolly was here. Otherwise this wilderness will swarm with his chums, and we don't want them underfoot...or overhead, for that matter."

Dai hurriedly loaded just about everything he could on the trolley and dumped it in the bus. The pain in his left arm had subsided. He carried the weak priestess to the bus and made four more trips before he dismantled the tent and forced it into the storage compartment of Grut's car. He made sure that

Carros was well tied before he adjusted the gravity belt to maximum lift. He opened the driver's door and activated the car, programming it to fly southeast, then disengaged the automatic collision evaders, since it would be better if the car crashed in the mountains, and set the height selector to a hundred meters, which would avoid just about every obstacle except a high hill or the mountains.

Gommy's body was the smallest and nearest, so he maneuvered it over to the speed-pedal and positioned it so that a little push would topple him onto the pedal. He made sure everything was ready, then, while holding the door open with one hand, pushed the limp body forward. The door slammed as the car took off at top speed. Bolly's body behaved like a balloon behind the car. Dai felt like rubbing his hands together, and he watched for a minute or two while the car climbed until it was out of his sight. It would speed on until it crashed into a barrier, such as the Eastern Mountains.

Dai closed the door of the bus after him and did a quick mental calculation; it would be about noon at his home base. He dialed a number, which was answered almost immediately by Karna, as if he were waiting for the call. Dai identified himself with his code name and said he was handing the comm-unit to a priestess named Nogalithe.

She activated the conference-call facility, and Dai listened to the dialogue in the old language while he sedately drove the bus along the road. He heard astonishing things about the conspiracy, and some of the names mentioned sent shivers up his spine. It seemed that even the ruling priest of their country, an older man named Hedra, was involved. Dai had met him on a number of occasions, but he'd never liked the cross-eyed man with the oily, insincere manners. He could never figure out the reason for the dislike, for there were others with similar manners who he liked. It was just an instinctive distrust, but he'd never told anyone about his feelings because he thought them juvenile.

42

Nogalithe was still talking when Dai contacted Koro, who had taken over the watch from the old lady cat. When Koro confirmed that Dai was almost parallel with the camp, he lifted the bus over the edge of the cleft.

Koro had warned Tumar not to open fire when she saw a grav-car approach, but Dai grounded the huge bus before the opening in the bush because he didn't think there would be enough space in front of the overhang. He would activate the nullifier with the remote control when he left the bus because he didn't feel like draping the huge camouflage net over it without help. The nullifier would make the bus invisible to the naked eye on ground level and from the air.

Just before Nogalithe handed the comm-unit back to him, he heard her say, "No, I had to wait till now to report back, otherwise my suffering would have been in vain. I had to gather all the names before you could take action, otherwise they would have put two and two together and had me killed before I could complete the job. As it is, I still don't know who's the elusive leader—the mastermind behind this plot."

Karna told Dai, still in the old language, to take the royals and Tumarok to the priestess on the mountain as soon as he'd had some decent rest. There he should make sure that the discovered artifacts were still safe, and then return and rid society of the unscrupulous characters in the palace and Bojon. They were, as he put it quite bluntly, "redundant." The priestess Nogalithe would guide and aid him, since she was still a member of the Fighting Order, which didn't surprise Dai at all.

He asked for more aging cream to be delivered, and Karna said he would find a courier to bring it to the coordinates where he was talking. It would take at least a week to organize, and by then Dai would be back unless something more urgent happened while he was on the mountain. Dai thanked him and replaced the handset of the comm-unit.

"Why didn't you tell me that you are still a Fighter?"

"What purpose would it have served?" she countered. "Anyway, I'm not an active member anymore. While we're still alone, I'll stay here to recover and wait for your package. There will be a few things for me as well. I think your Permerian friend will stay and keep me company. I have met her kind and know that they detest air travel, and perhaps I can persuade the cook to stay as well. I need a few good meals to regain my lost youth. Ah yes, don't be surprised. I am a Diviner, remember?" She smiled for the first time, and Dai saw that she was still attractive. Her eyes didn't show age.

"Okay, I'll talk to them when they wake up. I should probably take a nap as well so that I'll be well rested when I take the rest of the party up to the priestess on the mountain. Hopefully Murima can give me an idea of where the priestess is located."

"No need to even ask him. Kyr will lead you directly to her. Please don't ask me to explain. It will take too long," she said somewhat sharply.

Dai managed a lopsided grin. "Okay again. I just wish I had all the answers, like you apparently have. It would have saved me a lot of grief in the past."

Dai landed the car and deactivated it. Nogalithe patted him on the shoulder and asked him to introduce her to the approaching beauty. Dai vacated his seat to open the door for Tumar, who whistled appreciatively and innocently asked him where he'd bought the vehicle. Ignoring the question, Dai introduced her to Nogalithe, then told her the bus had come with the priestess, that he had just taken the job as driver because he was too lazy to walk back.

Seeing the very skeptical expression on Tumar's face, Nogalithe said, "He's just shy about his persuasive powers. Actually, the previous owner didn't even put up an argument when we took the car—or, as Dai calls it, 'the bus.' He even let us have his supplies."

Tumar knew she was not going to get the full story right now, so she said the cook had started a fire, and they were invited for early morning tea, which should be just about ready. Dai locked the door and took the car's ignition key and remote with him. He was always careful, especially out here in the wilderness, where one couldn't take anything for granted.

He supported Nogalithe as she walked, for she was very weak as a result of the deprivations and three months without any exercise. Tumar quickly draped the priestess's other arm over her shoulder. Nogalithe thanked them while they slowly walked to the inviting fire. When Murima saw her, he produced a chair from somewhere behind him. Nogalithe sat down next to the fire and said, "I've had very little food and no exercise for three months, but I shall have my strength back in a day or two after a few good meals. I'm not *that* old yet."

Dai introduced the cook, who said, "You take all the time you need to recover, Lady Nogalithe, and I will produce the meals. Just let me know what you want, and I will see what I can do with what is available."

After drinking her hot tea, Tumar said she was going to catch a few winks since it was almost daybreak. The priestess said she didn't feel like sleeping yet and would keep Murima company until she felt tired. Dai saw that Surra was still sleeping, so he took another sleeping bag and stretched out next to the sledge on the hard ground. He was tired, and the sun would be up in an hour or so. He still had a lot of lost slumber to catch up on.

Dai was shaken awake around midday by Surra. "Sorry to wake you up, Dai, but it's getting late and I want to see my son. Ekaasi told me that my son is alive and in the care of the priestess on the mountain."

When she saw that Dai was fully awake, she handed him a beaker of strong tea and continued. "My father, damn him, said he asked the priestess to take the baby and my boyfriend and look after them. He said he couldn't take the chance of letting me know where my son was, and he is right—triple damn him. All that money he spent on sham searches was just to keep that worthless priest and Sorcuk off the trail because my father distrusted Heltos from the very beginning, even before he became high priest and toadied up to my half sister. I wonder if I still have feelings for Gemur after all these years. And what will I do about us?"

"Don't give it a second thought, Princess. I'm not interested in any thrones or in ruling unruly people. I'm not cut out for such things and would rather take a more direct approach. Just remember this. If you ever need my help, even ten or twenty years from now, just ask a temple cat politely if he or she would send a message for me to come to your aid. If I'm still alive, I'll come as quickly as I can. That is a solemn promise, Princess."

She kissed him and replied, "Thank you, Dai. My father told me that he considered asking you to take over the throne with me until my son is ready to rule. I'm willing to do it even if I still love my old boyfriend."

"He makes quick decisions, doesn't he? If you want me dead within a year, ask my mentor, Karna, to force me to do that. I thank you both for the honor, but I can't sit still for long, and I hate giving judgments. I have been training for the life I lead since I was two years old, and I don't think I can adapt to any other kind. It's ingrained in my restless nature, and I somehow sense that it's not my destiny to sit on a throne and degenerate into a fatty with a false smile and good intentions. I love you deeply, Surra, but it's the love for a very dear, close friend. Can you understand that? I don't know if I can explain it any better than that."

"Yes, I do understand. If I don't love that boy anymore, will you visit me every now and then? That is, if we come out of this crisis alive."

"I'll see to it that you survive, Surra. Of course I will visit you, even if you're still in love with the boy, who will be a man by now, I should think, provided of course that you invite me. I infrequently get a chance to take a few weeks off, but if I'm in the vicinity, I will definitely stop by to say hello."

"You do that, Dai, and you will always be welcome, even without an invitation. But come, I'm impatient to meet my son."

Dai had finished his tea by then and hoped for something to eat before he left, for it would be a long trip to the mountain and back.

Kyr sent a thought to him: *I waited until Surra had her chat with you. Ekaasi, the old lady cat, and the dense one will stay here with the priestess until we come back. They think they can safely stay here for a week or so, as Ekaasi had wiped out our trail from the edge of the cutting. The king thinks that very few hunters know about this overhang and the water. Koro refuses to stay if you don't stay, which is correct. Skrot will roam with her mind even when she sleeps, and she doesn't need much food or*

236

attention. She will warn Ekaasi or Lithe if something needs
attention, and Lithe knows how to free her mind to keep watch
as well. She can shoot, too!

Dai saw that it was not yet noon, but Murima had lunch
ready. The king was silent and deep in thought, but Dai saw him
look inquiringly at Surra, who shook her head slightly before
sitting down to eat quite close to him, as if afraid that he'd run
away. The king seemed a bit disappointed, but Dai couldn't care
less. What happened to this small, isolated kingdom wasn't his
responsibility after he had neutralized the threat—assuming he
was successful.

After lunch was over, Nogalithe told him that her colleague
on the mountain might need Bolly's supplies to feed them all,
unless Surra's boyfriend had turned into a good hunter or she
had an arrangement with the villagers to bring what they
needed. Dai told Surra and Tumar to load their personal things
and anything else they might need for a lengthy stay, just in
case.

Dai denullified the bus and loaded the king's personal
things. He thought about possibilities. Just about anything could
happen before and after they reached their destination. He had
to prepare for any eventuality. He rummaged until he found their
already heavily packed backpacks. Then he went to the bus for
the trolley and loaded spare blankets, the camp stretchers not
required by Nogalithe and Murima, sleeping bags, and even the
war bow and quiver—because it was so rare and valuable, he
didn't want to leave it behind, even for a few days. He left his
hunting gun and a few hundred rounds for Ekaasi and for
Murima in case he wanted to hunt or if he had to defend the
camp. The king said he had no use for his gun up in the
mountain so that could stay as well. Dai packed the woodsman's
gun, together with all the other weapons and ammunition into
"Bolly's bus."

He saw that Tumar hadn't brought any of the special
clothes they had bought "for hunting." Those clothes were
essential for hiding and camouflage in the event they had to
abandon the sledges to hide. He dumped all the clothes—his
and hers—into another bag and onto the trolley. He thought he
had just about everything except some dry rations, which he
gathered and packed on the trolley. Then he pulled the loaded

trolley into the bus and secured it.

Dai hugged his friend Ekaasi, said good-bye to the others, and thanked Skrot for staying to look after the people. He told Murima what he intended to do with the tiger's tail, and Murima said that being a country boy, he knew about curing and tanning and would see to it that the tail was properly cared for.

They boarded the bus, and Dai strapped Koro right in the back in case the cat panicked or became ill, for he was not used to the slight swaying of an air car. He then made sure everything else was behind and under the baggage net or strapped down, for he didn't want any accidents.

Kyr took the other front seat and told him she would guide him. She curled up comfortably, as if going to sleep, but Dai knew she was trying to establish contact with the priestess who lived on the mountain. He didn't know how she was doing it, but he knew she would be successful. He strapped her down and told everyone to do the same, for they were going to encounter dangerous air currents in the mountain valleys and canyons.

He activated the bus and slowly moved it away until he was over the cutting and well away from the temporary hideout. Then he gradually increased height and speed until the bus was moving at top speed, which was a surprising five hundred kilometers per hour. Bolly must have had this bus specially built or modified, for the best grav-cars had a top speed of only two hundred kilometers per hour. If all went as planned, they would reach the northern mountains in less than two hours.

43

When the bus was lifted out of the clearing, Ekaasi turned to the priestess and asked in another language, "The priestess who goes by the name of Justina is your sister, isn't she, and is she also Dai's mother?"

Nogalithe instinctively knew that Ekaasi wanted the truth because she loved Dai and knew he had more hidden talents and abilities than he knew about. She effortlessly switched to Ekaasi's native language to exclude the curious Murima.

"You are extraordinarily perceptive, and I can see what your questions lead up to, colleague. No, I didn't tell Dai about it because, as you may have deduced, he has certain blocks in place, and for a very valid reason. I'll leave it to his mother to decide what to tell him and when to lift those blocks in his brain. But I might as well tell you as much of the story as I know.

"I'll trust you with her real name, which is Lur, because I know you will not reveal it to anyone. She married a very special young man by the name of Ogath at a young age. He had very unusual talents, but he became a deep-space pilot because his passion was to explore the universe. Lur has more than enough talents herself, and while her husband trained with the Explorers, she studied with the Fighting Priests to develop her mind and body. She believes that mind and body must be fit and act as one unit and not separately for the best results.

"She was so dedicated that after two years the Fighters declared that she could start teaching them. She was then allowed to study in the local temples under special teachers, for she had two very rare talents—for healing mind and body and foreseeing the future. Actually, the trait for prediction is dominant in the females of our family, and I can foresee the probabilities of the future just as accurately as she does.

"Anyway, the head priest in charge of the Temple for Science at the time, Hedra, became besotted with her when he met her after she became renowned for her accurate forecasts and the healing of difficult cases, but she made it quite clear that she was married and not at all interested in him or any other man.

"To make a long story short, one day, on what was by all accounts a routine training flight, her husband, together with the entire crew of his ship, mysteriously disappeared. She couldn't prove anything, but she knew very well that Hedra was behind the disappearance because he was responsible for the Explorer program as well. She loathed his insincere, self-satisfied condolences and the drooling, disingenuous concern about her loss. She was pregnant at the time, but not yet visibly so. One night she left, because she feared that the lustful, hate-filled Hedra would kill her and her unborn son, for she'd told him that she detested him and his nauseous advances. She was accompanied by a young Kyr, who chose her as a friend, as they sometimes do when they find a compatible, honest, and sincere human.

"When Dai was two years old, Lur put blocks on certain centers in his brain, and only she can safely remove them. She feared that Hedra would murder the boy out of spite or jealousy if Dai showed certain inborn traits that could make Hedra suspect he was her son. Then she asked Kyr if she would be a friend to her son and take him to Karna. We can, of course, talk directly to Karna, and always could ever since we were born. We are triplets, you see.

"On Karna's insistence, we have always kept it a secret that we're family. He said it was for our and his protection because he had many enemies. Karna, of course, knew the whole story, and Lur asked him to protect the boy but to never let him—and especially not Hedra—know that Dai was her son or our nephew, but to treat him as an orphan found wandering by a temple cat and brought to him by chance.

"So now you know that Kyr is guiding Dai to his mother, and she will decide whether it is time to remove those blocks and tell him. By mistake, Kyr almost removed a block on one of his untrained but natural talents a few days ago when she was in the grip of early mating fever, but the damage was covered by Skrot to the best of her abilities. So you see, I could not have told Dai a thing without perhaps doing a lot of irreparable damage."

Ekaasi was thoughtful for a while. "Yes, you are a wise woman, since you may have deprived him of some of those blocked talents, and his mother was also wise in isolating those talents until he was mature enough to use them wisely when trained. I had a glimpse of what they may be, and I was impressed. He is unique in that very, very few human males are born with strong natural psychic abilities."

They were silent for a while, and Murima brought them some tea. They thanked him for his courtesy, and then Ekaasi told her story in a thoughtful manner.

"Two years ago, an invader by the name of Alisun appropriated a corner of Krisa, our country. We asked the Fighters for help to remove him and his army, because we are a peaceful race and know nothing about warfare. Only Dai and Kyr were sent to help us because Dai had been searching for the same person, on orders of the Fighters—Alisun specialized in murdering priests, especially political priests, for a price, of course.

"We were taken aback and felt insulted that the Fighters would send someone so young, and only one, to remove a notorious criminal known for his viciousness and strength and a horde of equally vicious cutthroats. Pity for the sincere young human moved me to volunteer to accompany him, ostensibly to show him the way, but in reality I thought I might be able to keep him out of trouble. I definitely would not have volunteered had I known at the time that he was not yet eighteen years old, for I'm more than seven times his age.

"Kyr and I immediately became friends, and of course, as cats will do, she read my outer thoughts. She gave that peculiar mental cat laugh and told me to take it easy and to not show my concern, for he was an old warrior and only young in years. She said many criminals had misjudged his abilities because he looked so innocent, and they didn't take him seriously until after they were dead, which was an asset the Fighting Priests fully exploited. Kyr bragged that he succeeded where others failed because he was exceptionally intelligent, strong, and fast for his age.

"We were attacked a number of times by an assortment of opportunists, bandits, and roaming bands of Alisun's raiders. When we could do so, we avoided a fight. Dai could keep pace with me for long distances, and although I would not admit it, he could outstay me. I quickly changed my mind after Dai saved my life twice in one day. I came to love the courteous boy, and I had the opportunity to repay him by saving his life a couple of times. He taught me to shoot and a lot about fighting, because we are not an aggressive race, and I taught him to live off the land using tubers, roots, berries, herbs, and so on. He is a quick learner, and he knows which herb has what medicinal or nutritional value.

"We were together for about eight months, and I lost count of the number of times we saved each other's lives. In the end, he killed Alisun in hand-to-hand combat, which lasted for about two hours. Alisun was a bear of a man and skilled in dirty fighting methods. I thought of it as an old bear fighting against a lithe temple cat, and the temple cat won when the bear became tired and lost his concentration for just one moment.

"After we escaped the fortress, Alisun's accomplices and minions hunted us relentlessly, but Kyr warned us well in advance every time. Dai had two broken ribs, infected wounds all over his body, and a high fever, which I couldn't cure with the regular herbs. Sick and battered as he was, Dai fought when we had to, and he showed me how to hide our trail when he wasn't feverish. I never would have dreamed that a young human boy could be so hard to kill. He and Kyr are a formidable team, if not unbeatable.

"I nursed him as well as I could and almost had a heart attack when I found out that he had just become eighteen years old. Kyr, of course, laughed her head off and told me that I thought in human terms. When Dai's injuries began to heal and the fever left him, we set about hunting the late Alisun's friends and minions to clear Krisa permanently of the murderous scum. When the last one was disposed of, I reluctantly led him back to our place of learning. By then I wished that he was a Permerian and would stay with us.

"For one so peaceful and dedicated to learning, I enjoyed fighting alongside Dai. He inspired me, you know, by just being his normal self, and his attitude was, well, always polite and considerate, even against our enemies. He never boasted or displayed his abilities until it was called for. Then he climbed in tooth and nail like an angry wildcat defending her young. I learned quite a lot from the young man.

"Anyway, while we played hide-and-seek when Dai was

seriously injured, I tried the usual method of stimulating certain brain centers to speed up healing. It was then I discovered the blocks someone had put in his brain at various centers. The sophisticated way in which it was done told me that whoever did it was more skilled than I was, and that really surprised me. It made me realize that they were put there for a purpose and that I must leave them alone until I knew more.

"I studied this phenomenon intensely during this past two years and, as we did with Tumar this morning, I can now remove the blocks safely if I have to, to help defeat these corrupt, powerful individuals who care only for their own rampant greed and for nobody or nothing else. I will remove those blocks if Lur doesn't."

Nogalithe answered, "I think Lur will remove them now, for Dai obviously has matured, and he needs some of those talents to survive the coming conflict with these very powerful criminals. I told her so just now. That's the main reason I made him take Bolly's bus; otherwise this journey to the mountains would have taken weeks and a lot of hardship and perhaps fighting for days, instead of an hour or two. If you would help me recover my lost mental and physical energies, we will be ready to help when he comes back; it took the last of my reserves when we removed those hideous, implanted compulsions in Tumar's brain on Kyr's insistence. That beautiful child was grossly misused by those monsters of that organization for their own profit, and it makes me shudder. They should all be executed, for much of her mental potential was ruined, perhaps permanently."

"Of course I will help you, and I know how. I wish I could have gone with them to help, but my big body would suffocate in that thin air. We must help Dai in all that we can, and I know that Tumar's help will be vital in the end. I also know that the world may be devastated if she and Dai are not successful up there in the canyons and here in Bojon, for those unscrupulous, depraved human beings who started this will stop at nothing, nor will they be stopped by anything except death."

44

Kyr asked Dai to slow down when they approached the mountain. Then she told him to fly lower, for she was looking for a reference point—a deep, narrow cleft with straight, black walls. The opening was about a hundred human steps wide.

Dai found it after about twenty minutes, and as he turned toward it to enter, Kyr told him sharply to fly on; it was only a reference point, she reminded him. Dai suppressed a rejoinder and flew on about fifty meters above the rough terrain at sixty kilometers per hour.

Then Kyr said the second opening from the cleft was a deep U-shaped canyon. This canyon led to the back door of the place they had to reach, but they would encounter extreme wind shear at this time of the year. She explained that she was acting on and relaying instructions from the priestess as she received them. Dai silently told her that he understood.

He found the canyon. It looked more like a sharp cleft in a high plateau, about five kilometers high. Close up, it was wider than it looked from a distance. Distant peaks were white with perpetual snow, and judging by the crevasses and other distinguishing features, it was clear that a glacier was part of the distant mountain range. He knew it would be extremely cold on top of the plateau, and he was glad they were not on foot.

It would be an arduous task to climb up that wall to the top, he thought. He knew the king would not have made it, as the air would get thinner as they neared the top. Climbing and walking at that elevation was difficult for a lowlander, and it would be a death sentence for one with a heart condition. He was suddenly glad that fate had provided them with this particular grav-car, for it even had an oxygen bottle with a mask, probably for some ailment the extremely obese Bolly had suffered from time to time.

As he turned the bus into the canyon, Kyr told him not to lift up to the rim because the air was very turbulent and dangerous up there. They had to reach a wide, flat ledge on the right side about twenty-five to thirty kilometers on, in a quiet corner about halfway between the canyon floor and rim. The walls would change from brown sandstone to brownish-black basalt a few kilometers before then.

Everyone except Koro had relaxed and unbuckled their straps when they found that the bus was so strong, it glided smoothly over the broken terrain. Now Dai told everyone to strap down immediately and make sure the straps fit tight. Tumar leaned over and adjusted the straps to make Kyr safe but comfortable. Everything was done in silence, and Dai buckled up hastily with one hand before he activated all collision evaders, of which the craft had an astounding fifteen, not the standard five or six.

He lifted the grav-car to a height of two kilometers and tried to maintain a speed of about sixty kilometers per hour. This height, which was about halfway to the top, gave him the safety margin to compensate for extreme up- or downdrafts and crosswinds. He kept the grav-car in the middle of the canyon, which he estimated to be five hundred meters wide. The wind that howled down the canyon was so strong at times that it pushed the vehicle backward. Dai manipulated the throttle to keep the bus going forward slowly. He thought fleetingly that it would be extremely dangerous to return the same way with a gale-force wind behind.

The first strong updraft hit the grav-car just around the first bend, and he fought to keep the bus level and in the middle of the canyon. Only the width of the canyon saved the bus from being dashed against the left wall. The collision evaders forced the craft above the rim of the canyon, and Dai had a momentary glimpse of an ice-covered plateau that gradually sloped down toward the northeast and ended abruptly at the edge of a vast, dark gorge.

As the vehicle automatically dropped down again to its designated height after passing the updraft, he thought grimly that this was going to be a more dangerous journey than he had anticipated. How in creation was he going to land the bus in this strong, almost gale-force wind without smashing it to little pieces?

Not to worry, Kyr told him calmly. *The canyon widens at our destination and forms a recess, creating a quiet harbor against the wind. The ledge is lower down and you can land with your eyes closed…if you were that stupid. Just be quick to pull the throttle back. Ah yes, behind the ledge there's a wide cave where you can park. We are to follow the natural tunnel on foot. I'll tell you the rest after we land.*

Dai was too busy fighting the capricious wind to think of a suitable sarcastic retort. Unbeknownst to him, Kyr was not as casual as she pretended to be. She was coming home to her chosen companion after so many years, but her homecoming was not the peaceful one she'd always looked forward to. Lur was making desperate plans to either fortify or abandon her home because her archenemy, Hedra, had at last found her.

As Lur communicated to her, someone who knew about Lur's connection with the village had been coerced, paid, or compelled to talk about the healer in the northern mountains of Bojon. It could even be the individual who had tried to sell the information about the legacy left by the ancients. The noxious Hedra had put two and two together, and he and some of his fellow conspirators had arrived this morning at dawn at the village, which they quickly surrounded with their troops. They had begun a bloody questioning orgy, but one of the villagers had escaped after faking death. He was dragged away with the other bodies to the edge of the village. He then crawled and stumbled his way to a farm where they kept a few ponies. He rode bareback to warn Lur of the murderous invasion. He had reached her about an hour before Dai flew into the canyon. Now Dai's expertise was desperately needed to drive the invaders out of the village and the canyon.

Kyr knew that Dai must not be distracted, for he needed his full concentration to keep the grav-car and passengers safe, so she told Tumar of the complication.

Tumar knew that Surra was anxious to meet her son and could understand how she must feel, so she approached the problem from that angle. Dai should be left alone for now, and she couldn't speak to Surra or the king without breaking Dai's concentration. She thought at Kyr, *Surra might lose her head and complicate things if we talk about it. Maybe you should ask the priestess for advice. Ask her when she expects her enemies to arrive and can that brave man tell her how many to expect? You can bring Dai up to speed after we land safely.*

Kyr agreed. She knew that the valley on the other side of

246

the mountain was already veiled in twilight, the same as this canyon, since it was near evening, and night came early and fast here. Perhaps they had the night to prepare an ambush. She stopped talking and didn't include Tumar when she conversed with the priestess. A few minutes later, she told Tumar that they must wait for Dai to land. She would then tell him, and when they reached their destination, all of them together would discuss the problem.

It was nearly dark when Dai saw the broad ledge three hundred meters below in the strong headlights of the bus. Some ages-old volcanic activity had perhaps made a gigantic bubble that had burst and rapidly cooled to form this quiet corner pocket. He pulled the throttle back sharply when the bus abruptly sped up as it nosed into the almost windless pocket. The collision evaders brought the vehicle to an abrupt halt.

Dai was tired from the seemingly endless fighting against the wind—although it had only lasted for about forty minutes he saw when he glanced at his watch. He eased the bus onto the ledge before the cave to check the entrance in the almost-blinding headlights.

The entrance was wide enough, but the floor of the cave initially sloped sharply downward behind the almost-level ledge. He slowly eased the grav-car through the opening and then saw that the cave was huge, like a spaceship hangar. It must have been a remarkably big, final belch of the ancient volcano, he thought tiredly. He hovered for a while, looking for a level space inside the gigantic hall to put the grav-car down. He found it near the opposite wall, where the tunnel started. He put the bus down with a sigh and grounded it.

He activated the dim interior lights as he switched off because they didn't consume much power. Then he removed his strap and turned to the others with a grin, although he noticed the seriousness on Tumar's face. As the king and Surra unfastened their straps, Tumar told them what Kyr had told her to say about the interlopers.

As expected, Surra immediately said that of course they must hurry to help because her son would be in danger. Dai asked for silence so he could think about the complications. After a while he silently asked Kyr to ask the priestess how far it was to where she was and if she knew of any obstacles in this

247

tunnel, assuming that it led the right way.

After a moment Kyr said the tunnel held no surprises. The priestess lived in a series of natural hollows converted to rooms in the main cave on the other side of that same tunnel, a little more than two kilometers away. They were at the rear entrance, which nobody but the priestess and the two boys knew about. Surra's old boyfriend had reported that he couldn't see any fires, but the priestess said it was of no significance.

Then Kyr told him, as instructed by the priestess, *Mother Lur instructs…*

Dai stiffened and then slowly keeled over sideways. Tumar's reaction was fast. Before Dai fell out of his chair, she grabbed him by the shoulders and eased him down on the floor beside the seat. She had straightened his body by the time Surra jumped up with her flask.

Kyr sharply told them to relax and wait a while. There was nothing wrong with Dai that a few minutes of sleep wouldn't fix, and could they see about something to eat meanwhile? It was going to be a very long night. And could they please remove the straps from the patient Koro?

Reluctantly the two women checked the supplies and somehow managed to gather a few things that looked edible, which they put down on the long convertible bench against the side, wondering what to do with it and how to open the cans. It served Kyr's purpose of keeping them from disturbing Dai.

Then the king took a hand. He set up a fold-back table and showed them what to dish up and how to do it, as he remembered from his younger days and his numerous hunting trips.

Tumar smiled when Kyr told her "Cookie" that she would eat with Dai and Koro in about half an hour's time when he woke up. The boy needed to rest about that long, and then he should eat to regain his depleted energy.

What Kyr didn't mention, and what was of no concern to anyone but her and Dai, was that certain hypnotic blocks were being dissolved, and his brain must be given time to assimilate and adjust to the liberated abilities. That cue that she'd passed on to Dai's brain was implanted before he was two years old, together with the knowledge to control and utilize the talents. Lur would teach him more if she could stay alive long enough to

248

release the rest of his inborn talents, but right now a few must be released so that Dai's subconscious mind could adjust to it before he met his mother.

Dai wasn't even aware that he was unconscious for about an hour. When he opened his eyes, he wondered what he was doing on the floor, and Kyr quickly told him the reason, before Surra and Tumar saw that he had recovered.

Dai realized that his senses were enhanced and his brain was functioning a bit differently. He felt more alive and aware. He could talk directly to Kyr and Koro without the usual concentration and was aware of their cat thoughts. He reached out to the women and then quickly shied away before their very private thoughts could pervade his mind. Skrot had showed him how hazardous that could be, and he instinctively felt it was a dangerous and forbidden area.

Then a new mind synchronized with his and Kyr's. Dai didn't recoil, for he instinctively knew who it was. He said, *Hello, Mother. Thank you for keeping me safe all these years from Hedra and others. I missed you, although I didn't know what I missed. Now tell me what I need to know.*

Lur knew what he meant and replied, *I think we are safe for the time being, though this canyon is a dangerous place at night. First eat something to restore your energy and then bring everyone here, as I don't think you can stop Surra unless you can physically restrain her, which is unwise. You were wise in not touching the girls' minds, as they both are sensitives and will know. Oh yes, Nogalithe is my sister, and she and Ekaasi, whom I have yet to meet, removed the hypnotic inhibitions and commands from Tumar's brain this morning. She won't be influenced by anything you may reveal anymore. You and I will have a private talk later.*

Lur left abruptly, and Dai felt empty, but not for long. As he started to get up, Koro rubbed against him and told him he was hungry.

When the women realized Dai was awake and getting up, he could sense the comradely love and concern of both.

"Are you okay?" both of them said together and then laughed.

"Yes, thank you. I just had to take a short nap and didn't know that I wasn't lying down. I'm hungry and I smell food..."

The women and the king knew he was talking nonsense to put their fears to rest. Perhaps he was stressed with the constant fighting and concentration to keep the grav-car intact, they thought. They somehow sensed a difference in him, but their wildest guesses couldn't come anywhere near the truth.

45

While Dai and the cats ate, Tumar remarked, "There is something different about you. What happened?"

Dai looked at her and shrugged. Then he replied, "You are quite perceptive. I feel different, but I don't know how and why. Perhaps it's the stress I was under to get us here safely or the challenges and strange circumstances we will face in this place, wherever this place is. When I have eaten, we'll pack the trolley with the essentials and move on. Decide what you'll need for the next few days and put it near the trolley." That should keep them busy for a while, he thought.

When his hunger and thirst were satisfied, he opened the rear of the grav-car and retrieved the trolley. He packed their ammunition and guns on it. Then, leaving enough room for the king to sit in, he filled the remaining space with supplies and their personal belongings. He gave each of them a powerful torch from Bolly's stores.

At first the king refused the seat, but Dai teasingly said he was going to set a fast pace to keep up with Surra, which would unnecessarily overtax the king. He would be no extra weight anyway, as Dai would only guide the trolley in the right direction; so he might as well take it easy and enjoy the ride. They would need everyone who could pull a trigger the next day or two, and he would prefer to have the king rested and ready for a firefight.

The king had to agree with the logic and reluctantly seated himself. He felt better when Kyr sat down next to him. She closed her eyes because the strong reflected light blinded her night sight. Koro said he would scout ahead and warn of obstacles, if any, but he wanted to be out of the bright light.

Dai took the ignition keys and the remote with him. He activated the nullifier before he led the way at a pace he knew would be easy on Tumar and Surra, who followed behind the grav-trolley with their lights a bit dimmed and aimed at where they would step. At times he had to slow down to negotiate fallen debris, but the tunnel was mostly smooth, as if water ran through it from time to time. He allowed his still-unfamiliar senses to range ahead so he could get to know how some of them would serve him; he was worried that they were unblocked at the wrong time and that he wasn't yet shown or taught properly how to use them. He liked the idea that he could establish contact with a person or animal and perhaps divine their thoughts when necessary, but he needed a lot of practice before he would feel safe and confident.

After fifteen or twenty minutes, he sensed the presence of four humans and a horse straight ahead. Kyr told him he was correct, and he thanked her out of habit. When he felt he was close, he called out, identified himself, and asked if he could approach. It was a habit, but also a courteous gesture.

Lur came rushing out of the darkness. Dai sensed her intentions, so he stopped the trolley and met her a few steps away. He held his arms open, and an astounded audience saw a still-beautiful, well-built woman run into his arms. Dai didn't remember his mother, but inside he knew who she was. Kyr meowed for attention and forced herself in between them. Dai laughed, as he intuitively knew that Kyr had come home. He let go of his mother, who stooped and effortlessly picked up the purring cat in her arms. She continued to stroke Kyr's back while she greeted King Hespus by name as if he were an old acquaintance. Dai introduced Surra, Tumar, and Koro, in that order.

Then a young boy of about twelve came shyly up to them and introduced himself as Krekur, as Lur—or Lady Justina, as he knew her—had previously instructed him to do. Dai immediately saw the resemblance to Surra, who looked very pale and whose eyes were locked on the boy.

Dai stepped back a few steps and pushed Surra lightly on the back toward the boy. "I'm not the only son who doesn't remember his own mother, Surra," he said encouragingly.

Krekur gave her a shy smile and hesitantly moved forward. Surra dropped her torch and ran to him with an exclamation that was half cry, half sob, but filled with immeasurable joy. She folded her arms around the boy and picked him up. The boy had no choice but to put his arms around her neck to keep from being suffocated, and he had the sense not to struggle against the embrace. Surra didn't hear Lur asking everyone else to come into the living area.

The king preceded Tumar and Dai to a fairly well-lit rocky chamber. A fit-looking young man, whom Dai estimated to be about thirty years old, got up from beside a fire and smiled with his eyes on Hespus. To Dai's surprise, the king went forward and embraced the younger man, who returned the gesture.

Then the king let go, turned around to Dai and Tumar, and said, "This is Gemur, the father of Krekur. Meet my rescuers, Tumar and Dai, Surra's friends." He turned his face to Dai. "I will tell you about him when Surra joins us."

Tumar and then Dai shook the man's hand. Dai immediately liked the firm, confident handshake. He noticed that Kyr and his mother were absent and that Koro had sat down in a corner away from the fire. He let Koro know that he showed good sense to keep away from human traffic and clumsy feet.

Although the room was warm, the king was icy to the touch, for the forced inactivity had not warmed his blood. Gemur took him by the arm and seated him next to the fire in the rough chair he had just vacated. Then he poured hot tea for them all, even for the battered bundle of a man lying on the other side of the fire on a rough leather stretcher.

Dai's opinion of Gemur jumped a few notches higher when Gemur asked the injured man if he was still comfortable and if he needed anything else. He saw Dai looking and introduced the battered man as Laecur, a brave man from the village down in the valley.

Dai thought his mother had taught this one well. His experience with the few so-called nobles he had met was that they were so supercilious and head-in-the-air that they fell over their own feet. He detested that species. They treated ordinary people, who sometimes were nobler in character than they themselves, as dirt and only suitable for menial work. Dai went over, sat down on the floor, and lightly touched the injured man's hand.

"I recently met another brave man by the name of Murima who comes from a village here in the mountain, which he didn't name. I think it might be the same village. My friends call me Dai, and I ask you to do the same. I greatly respect courage in any man, and it seems to me that your village produces real brave men."

The man nodded and whispered, "Thank you. I know him.

253

Short but not too stocky, and he loves to cook. We hunted and were naughty together when we were kids, but he wanted to work in the city 'cause he likes a lot of people around him. The village was too quiet for him."

Dai went back to drink his tea while it was still drinkable. He knew that up in the mountains, the boiling point tended to be low and liquids cooled rapidly. As it was, it could barely still be called tepid. He hastily swallowed the tea and then went back to sit on the sandy floor next to Laecur. He needed information—urgently.

"I know that you would rather sleep, Laecur, but I must know the strength of the force that arrived here and any relevant information you can remember. We must prepare to greet them when they arrive."

Laecur didn't have to think. He said, "They arrived in six huge grav-cars just after eight this morning and quickly surrounded our village. I estimate about sixty, excluding the corpulent leader and his six mates. The troops are equipped with the usual weapons, such as assault guns and what are called hand-thrown shatter-bombs, knives, and some had clubs with which they were ordered to beat us until we told them where the priestess was hiding out. I will leave out the sordid, grisly details of our torture. The burly old political priest who acted as if he owned the world ordered the dead bodies to be taken out of the village, which included me. He said he wanted to overnight in the village and wanted the place clean and odorless.

"I had almost reached the farm where we keep mountain ponies, about two kilometers from the village, when I saw one craft take off sluggishly. It behaved as if it was heavily overloaded, and I hid while it flew up the valley and picked up speed as it climbed. The driver must have been inexperienced or drunk or crowded, for I saw the car crash low down against the cliff on the right-hand side of this canyon when it was caught in a downdraft about a kilometer past the farm.

"Six troopers were sent on foot to investigate. I don't think there could have been any survivors because the car was at least eight hundred meters high, and it came down fast and hard, as if under full power. I would say that there are fewer than fifty troops left, again excluding that vicious old priest and his

254

cronies. Perhaps some of them had already left on foot, which means they could be here by midmorning. If they leave the village at first light in the morning, they might make it before dark if they force-march. If you can spare a gun, I am a good shot, sir...eh, Dai."

"I'll see about it. Sleep if you can. I have some spare blankets, and I will bring you one just now. It may be too warm, but it's comforting." He left to fetch the trolley, where there should be some sleeping capsules in the emergency first-aid kit.

Surra was sitting on the trolley where the king had sat, and she still held her son tightly on her lap. Dai apologized for disturbing them and said he needed the supplies. Surra ignored him or didn't hear, so Dai took hold of the trolley handle and pulled it into the lighted cave where the others were. The opening was wide enough.

Surra seemed to wake up when Gemur shook her by the shoulders. She looked at him, gave a low moan, let go of her son, who gratefully scurried away, and wonderingly put her arms around Gemur, hugging him tightly.

Dai smiled secretly as he started to unload the trolley. He carefully put the ammunition boxes and guns on the other side of the room away from the fire. Then Tumar joined him, and they soon had everything neatly packed to one side. He couldn't find sleeping tablets, so he asked Tumar to put one of the blankets over the injured man.

Then Lur came in with Kyr still held comfortably in the crook of one arm. She had the boy by one shoulder and brought him to the king. "Hespus, talk to your grandson for a while," she said firmly. "It's time you get to know him."

46

Dai mentioned that he wanted to go back to the grav-car for more supplies and that it would take less than an hour. Lur told him that she and Kyr had just been scanning the valley with their senses. They detected eighteen troopers about twenty kilometers away who wouldn't move before full daylight because the strange murmurings, cries, and sounds of the valley during the night terrified them. They wouldn't sleep much and would be exhausted by morning.

It was not yet six o'clock and, yes, some luxury supplies would be a welcome change from the plain country fare they were used to. Then she and Dai would have a serious talk before they made any decisions. There were plenty of other caves they could move to, and this one could be blocked to keep the grav-car from prying eyes.

Tumar accompanied Dai, and they were back within the hour. They had overloaded the trolley with just about everything, including some extra sleeping bags they had found under some expensive booze, of which they had also brought a couple of bottles along for their medicinal value. Lur told him to leave everything on the trolley since they might have to move out.

Then she asked Tumar to excuse them, for she and Dai had to talk for a while in private. Kyr told them she would go on watch at the entrance in a few minutes and perhaps ask her "Cookie" to join her in a while. Tumar joined the king by the fire and made some fresh tea. She was proud that she could do that after Murima had only once shown her how.

Dai and his mother left immediately. Lur led him to another room not too far away. The room was already well lit and warm, so Dai switched the torch off and put it on a rough table. They sat down on the rough bed.

"Your thoughts are correct, my love. I want you alone to explain everything, but I'm not going to use many words. You need some hurried training for that sense Kyr involuntarily stirred. If you accidentally merge your mind with another, you've had it and that's that. That is a fate the old lady cat saved you from in the nick of time. You must synchronize wavelengths with another mind, which makes all the difference. What I want to do is show you how to synchronize your mind with mine, and then I'll quickly transfer some of my memories. The thought transference will take only a few minutes instead of two or three days of normal conversation.

"Yes, I want to hold you like Surra held her son, but we don't have time, as that murdering deceiver, Hedra, found me after all these years. I don't know how that happened, but I suppose it had to happen sooner or later. He may be one of the planners, or perhaps just a stooge for those who are determined to steal this inheritance of the Old Ones. I don't think it will deter him, or any of them, to know that those relics are time bombs that can destroy our world in an eyeblink. Yes, it is Hedra who arrived at the village with a few of his closest associates. I think they are just fronts or executives for a group of powerful people who can afford to let someone else do the dirty work and take the rap if anything goes wrong with the theft of the relics.

"I'm going to give you just a short explanation. My sister, Nogalithe—yes, she, Karna, and I are triplets. Anyway, after I'd asked Kyr to take you to Karna, Lithe and I forecasted the future. We had an uneasy premonition that something portentous was going to happen soon and that we were going to be involved in it. Thus we divined our individual roles, including yours, in that probable future, and it's the reason we are at our particular places at this particular time. It was not easy to accept, believe me. I had to come to Bojon and introduce myself to Hespus and offer my services as a healer so I was there when Surra's son was born. When Sorcuk heard about the baby, she went over the edge out of—can you believe it?—uncontrollable, terrible jealousy, which had been carefully nurtured and blown into full flame by her crazy mother from childhood. Hespus asked me to look after the injured Gemur and the baby and take them out of the city. He provided an armed escort, and we went to the village at the end of this valley. When Gemur could walk again, we settled here. That's it in short.

"About eight, nine months ago a man came for help. He and a friend had been climbing one of the most difficult peaks in this region about a hundred kilometers from here. His friend slipped, fell, and was seriously injured. He left his friend, who was unconscious, in a tent they had erected in a cave they used as a base and then came for me as fast as he could, for he knew of me and more or less where I could be found. Unfortunately, they used a two-man grav-scooter, with side panniers only, that was long overdue for service. It gave up the ghost just after he and I left here to tend to his friend.

"We came back then, for we needed some camping equipment, but my wards insisted on going along. We ran most of the way, but it took us just about three days to reach his friend. It was near evening, and we camped in the cave, where I tried to treat the critically injured man. He was in a serious condition. Legs, arms, and ribs were broken, and he was dehydrated after being in a coma for four or five days without attention. I knew that even if we had arrived three days earlier, he wouldn't have survived. I made him as comfortable as I could and eased his pain as much as I could under the circumstances. The descent to the canyon floor was too dangerous to attempt at night, but the man died quietly during the night.

"Just before daybreak there was an unusually violent tremor. As it stopped, there was a tremendously sharp crack, as if someone had fired the older type of concussion cannons nearby, and then we heard the crash of falling rocks nearby. Krekur, being a boy with an inquisitive mind, was out as soon as he could see properly to look at the rockfall before breakfast. He returned out of breath and said the rockfall had uncovered a long cave filled with a collection of weird-looking gadgets and machines.

"We had a look after breakfast. A boulder from very high up must have been dislodged by the tremor and fallen in just the place it shouldn't have. It created an opening in the four-meter-thick outside wall of a lost, sealed vault carved or melted inside the solid rock, exposing an unpleasant surprise. I have had some training in old languages and could decipher some of the inscriptions, which seemed pasted to the wall behind the machines. It warned that the cave—they used a word that translates as 'cache'—must be sealed by the discoverer if his civilization was not an advanced and peaceful one.

"It emphasized that the scientific gadgets were very sensitive, powerful, and utterly perilous to handle. If dropped or tinkered with, the planet would be destroyed or pushed from its orbit, which had happened and which had decimated and all but destroyed their civilization. One gadget could be used for peaceful purposes, but would cause tremendous damage if used by a warlike culture and unscrupulous people who didn't heed the dire warnings. It emphasized that it would be equally dangerous to try to destroy the machines, for the substances incorporated into some of the gadgets are very powerful, and the chain reaction would blow the planet apart or burn the atmosphere if activated, accidentally or intentionally.

"I had a feeling that there might be other vaults or chambers nearby, and then I read a rather big inscription with no gadget before it in some sort of alcove that could have been the ancient entrance. It warned that the perilous scientific gadgets should be left on their special resting pedestals untouched until such time as they could gently be removed and placed onto a wandering asteroid or exploded in outer space. It recommended that the finder confine himself to the implements in the larger vault, where useful inventions of their civilization were on display.

"I was filled with dread, so I kept the knowledge to myself. Perhaps there are so many wonders in there that scientific researchers could be occupied for a few centuries, but I know that this civilization is not yet ready for it, except for a few individuals, but they are innocent researchers and may blabber about it in the wrong company.

"I might take the knowledge of the location from the boy, and his father as well, if I deem it necessary. I have not yet decided, but I think it would be the prudent thing to do since I already did something against my ethics, though I now know I did the right thing. I sensed that the man who came to ask for our help contemplated selling the information to the highest bidder. Back here I hypnotized him, without his or my wards' knowledge, of course, and implanted a totally different location for the accident and the rockfall. Gemur accompanied him to the village, but it seems he couldn't keep his mouth shut, or perhaps he feared that we might keep the find to enrich ourselves. Greed will find many excuses.

"Anyway, we went back within a week and caused another rockfall to bury the entrance, but an opening remained that we filled with soil and debris. The soil was for a rare, hardy sapling tree so we could find the entrance again. The idea was that we would go back after a time to evaluate the importance or the danger of the cache before we decided what to do with it and who, if any, we could trust with it. I also wished to find a clue to the whereabouts of the other vault, but before we could return, the canyons began to swarm with searchers, and we stayed away. Fortunately metal detectors won't locate the machines or gadgets in the vault, for we tried. It seems they are made of more durable material than metal.

"Make yourself comfortable now so I can teach you how to synchronize with my mind and other minds, because you must know how to let your mind range like Kyr and her kind. I'll implant the knowledge to control and direct the search talent in your brain. Even a very sensitive mind must not be able to detect yours when you search, and you must know how not to accidentally merge with another. Relax your mind and body as Karna taught you."

Dai did so, and his mother showed him how to let his mind roam to search for the presence of life forces with his finer senses and how to avoid being trapped or detected by synchronizing a thought tendril with the thoughts emanating from that mind. She took his mind, literally, to the village, and he perceived the noxious Hedra, who sat in comfort while the villagers were mistreated and abused worse than slaves. Dai had a glimpse of the depraved thoughts in that perverted mind, and he involuntarily recoiled from synchronizing with it.

Lur showed him how to block or send a blast into the mind of one who tried to penetrate or influence his thoughts. She taught him various skills that she had mastered over the years, and his mind absorbed it all like a sponge. He would remember and practice, for Karna had taught him well.

When she was finished, she let him have a glimpse of her earlier years, before he was born, after his father, Ogath, and his ship vanished without a trace. She let him have a few glimpses of how the disgusting Hedra tried to woo her before and after the disappearance, and how she knew, but couldn't prove, that he had a hand in Ogath's disappearance. She also showed him what she'd done to his mind to protect him from Hedra and others so he could receive a normal, full education and a life free from Hedra's wrath.

Dai was taught by Karna and his other mentors not to be vengeful, but he vowed now that he would have the full story out of Hedra before he killed him slowly, if he got the chance. He was very pleased to find out that Karna was family, and he resolved to treat him with more respect from now on, even though he already loved the older man like a father.

He was still bemused when Kyr brought Tumar to join them. Lur thanked her for coming and said they must discuss the defense of this cave. The others had to be given time to have their reunion and could be informed in the morning. Dai roused himself from his reverie to give his attention to the discussion.

"I have a plan, Mother," Dai said. "It calls for me, Koro, and Kyr, if she wants, to go after the baddies who are on their way here tonight and put the fear of the Evil One in them. I really don't like the thought, but it might involve a lot of killing and harassment to make them dread this valley; but it can be done, as the darkness can be used as a friend. I will take enough supplies for a week and will try to harass and delay them as much as I possibly can. You and the others can fortify this cave, but it's better to move to a not-so-well-known location. Do you know of a better defensible place?"

Before his mother could reply, Tumar angrily interjected, "I'd rather go with you. I have enough training to be useful, and you and the cats have to sleep sometime. You promised to train me, remember? Now is the time to start."

Lur sensed Dai's objection and said, "That is good sense. I agree."

"This harassing could be dangerous, and as a client, Tumar is under the protection of the Fighters. As such, I am obliged to put her safety first until she is reunited with her family. There is nothing I can do about it, but she can defend herself along with the others when, and if, you are attacked. I was going to train her on the way here, but that was before we took Bolloth's bus."

Without warning, Tumar moved to punch him hard on the chin. She was very fast, but that faint, sharp inhaling of breath before the punch warned him, as it had warned him countless times before. He deflected the fist, but stopped the ingrained automatic retaliation reflex in the nick of time.

261

"Don't do that again, girl," he warned, and then sighed heavily. "You are very fast, Tumar, but I'm a trained killer with fast, automatic reflexes. Please remember that, because I very nearly wasn't able to stop myself in time."

Tumar wasn't put off. "I'm sick and tired of being treated like a hot-house plant that can't be exposed to a bit of cold weather," she said forcefully through her teeth, but not loudly. "I'm a trained killer as well, and I learn fast, as you bloody well should know by now if you had eyes in your head. I declare myself delivered, and I therefore cease to be your client. Believe…me…I…am…going…with…you!" she said in a measured tone as if she were driving it into the brain of a moron.

"Wow!" Lur said. "I suggest you take her with you, Dai. She will be quite safe because Kyr has taken a liking to her. And she's right, you know. You and Kyr are old campaigners, but this valley is a harsh place, and even the cats will not be safe. Sometimes large reptiles from the hotter canyons wander into this valley because it, too, is warmed by the hot air from a residue of old volcanic activity. Even predators walk warily in this canyon valley. It's another reason why I chose to stay in this cave, because very few strangers dare come this far. I suggest you teach Tumar whatever you can, and when you return, I'll take my time to teach her what I just taught you, because many of her talents were ruthlessly suppressed by her mentors. I will explain it to Karna, don't you worry. It's a well-kept secret, but he, Lithe, and I could mind-talk with each other from our very earliest years. But never talk about it—both of you. That's an order. It will endanger our lives, and enemies might try to blackmail Karna through one of us."

Tumar was still glaring at him, but suddenly Dai smiled and said, "Okay, Mom, but I was surprised to learn that Karna is my uncle. I already love him, since he always treated me fairly even when he ruthlessly drove me."

He turned to Tumar. "My mother should know what she is doing. You're welcome to come along. I saw you follow my example when we rescued the king, so I'm aware that you don't need lengthy explanations. Just remember one thing. Obey my orders on the instant, or you may die. If I shout 'dive,' you dive into a prickly pear or a thorn bush without hesitation if it's in the way. We can always remove the thorns later, but survival comes

262

first and injuries or inquiries second.

"If you want to learn, you start right now! When you want to punch someone, don't warn him or her by drawing in a sharp breath and then holding it in before you punch. Rather take a deep breath slowly, then blow it out sharply while you punch. Okay?"

"Okay," Tumar said and nodded at the same time. "Now come and show me, *this once*, what I should leave and what I should take along."

"Son," Lur told him, "you have a very decisive companion who knows her own mind. Teach her well, or you may regret it." She hooked each with an arm and held them close to her as she moved back to the others, where Dai located their packed rucksacks.

47

Dai found the special clothing they had bought and gave Tumar what she had bought for herself. He asked Kyr to tell her to ask Lur where she could take a quick shower or bath so she wouldn't attract wild animals with their keen sense of smell. Then she must don her new thermal underwear, socks, the clothes, and the soft shoes. He didn't think it advisable to whisper instructions to Tumar since they could be overheard, which might be embarrassing. Kyr must have also told his mother at the same time, because Lur beckoned to Tumar to follow her.

His mother had told him that she, Gemur, and the boy had guns they used when they hunted. He told Laecur that he could use the gun he had confiscated from the woodsman, if necessary, and the king that Tumar's hunting rifle would be left behind if he wanted to use it. He and Tumar only needed short-range firepower.

He put the heavy energy guns and enough recharges for them with the backpacks, as well as the war bow. He took his own new clothes and asked Gemur to show him where he could wash or bathe. Gemur took him to a room where water formed a pool. He said it was almost hot because it bubbled up from below and was presumably heated by extinguished volcanic activity or a leak from a hot underground stream. He didn't really know or care, but it was preferable to icy mountain streams.

Tumar was waiting for him when he returned. He told her that their initial loads would be heavy because of the food and ammunition. They would take the night-vision equipment and use it to avoid unpleasant surprises, since the heavy rifles weren't equipped with nightscopes. After saying good-bye to everyone, they each shouldered a heavy backpack and a bag with ammunition. Koro came out of the corner and stood next to Dai as if awaiting the next command.

Dai hung the war bow and arrows onto his other shoulder. Gemur asked why he was taking the ancient bow along, so Dai told him that the primitive weapon would sow terror among the enemy troopers and confuse them to no end. Terror was a terrible weapon to use, but it evened the odds somewhat against superior numbers.

Lur accompanied them to the exit, where Dai handed her the keys and remote for Bolly's bus. She hugged each one of them, including Kyr and Koro. The latter remarked to Dai that he found human behavior strange, but it was comforting, and he would get used to it in time.

Dai donned the night sight and looked around for beacons to find his way back. He told Tumar to do the same and to check backward from time to time so she could find her way back without getting lost. Then he told his mother again that she must move to an easier place to defend because the brush and boulders that obscured the entrance also impeded the view deeper into the valley. They must have a long-distance view of visitors, at least three hundred meters, and there must be no or very few places where attackers could conceal themselves.

Lur said there was a place about two hundred meters above and to their right. She would see to it that they moved there at first light, and he would find them there when he returned. There was an easy way to block and conceal this entrance, which she'd also see to after they had moved.

Dai said good-bye and then asked Tumar to stay about five steps behind, with Kyr, and to cock her rifle and keep the safety catch off, but not to point it at his back. When silence was necessary, he would communicate with her through Kyr. Kyr would explain the way to walk silently and their usual methods, as necessary.

Tumar murmured, "Okay." With Koro as the advance scout, about five steps in front of Dai, they began their dangerous journey to discourage the enemy from visiting this part of the wide canyon.

Dai set a fast pace on the too-well-used rocky path down to the bottom and the main trail. It was not easy, since the rucksacks tended to make noise, but he first wanted distance. He would have run if he were by himself with just the cats, but Tumar must be taught—and fast. His plan was to start harassing the enemy early in the morning if he could reach them before first light, and he also had to look for a safe place to hide their rucksacks after he had located them.

As they progressed downward it grew strangely warmer, and Dai found the tight, warm gloves a bit bothersome, but he endured the slight discomfort because it might get colder toward morning. He scanned the area around him with his awakened talent, and he felt Kyr's and Koro's presence; Kyr had taught Koro what to take notice of with his senses and what he should ignore. Kyr synched with Dai and showed him how to let his senses range far ahead, as far as they could reach, then start a zigzag pattern backward to where they were, continue to the rear as far as he could go, and then reverse. She also showed him what she had been teaching Koro.

The night-vision equipment enabled Dai to see some distance ahead, but not too well where starlight didn't penetrate. He felt the familiar exhilaration as he listened to the night sounds, felt the breeze on his skin where it was exposed, and smelled the scents that wafted to his nose on the wind. He had mastered the knack of seeing, hearing, feeling, smelling, and even tasting all at the same time when he was in the wilds, and he felt totally alive, like a wild animal. He turned around and told Tumar in a quiet voice to try and do the same while they were just walking along or resting. The cats would warn them of any approaching danger, and she must try to develop her senses of seeing, listening, feeling, and smelling—even try to taste the smells the breeze brought. It would take a while, but it was worth mastering, he told her.

48

Dai walked softly, slowly, and warily, as he wanted to adjust to the nightlife and sounds of this wild canyon. They reached the sylvan main trail, in about the middle of the canyon, after fifteen minutes. The warm breeze made leaves rustle just enough to impair normal, insensitive human hearing. Dai grew too hot and stopped to remove the gloves. He heard Tumar sigh softly in relief as she did the same.

He turned to her while he put the gloves into a pocket. In a quiet voice he said, "No wonder the giant reptiles in the reputedly steaming canyons somewhere in this region like to wander around even in the middle of winter. My mother says that one or a pair of them wander into this canyon at least once a year and then must be driven off or killed when they start to terrorize the villagers and their livestock. I have heard that some of the carnivorous species are quite fast. Luckily I have not come face-to-face with any so far, and I hope my luck holds. But we should expect snakes; they are everywhere in a hot place like this.

"In this heat we must take a mouthful of water as often as possible, even if we don't feel like it. Dehydration is a serious problem because you are not aware of it, and it impairs your reactions rather quickly, which can be quite hazardous to your health. Maybe we should take our thermals off at the first opportunity where we can do so in privacy. Just hiss when you want me to stop or if you want my attention, or you can ask Kyr to tell me what you want. Okay?"

"Okay," Tumar replied in a whisper. "I detest snakes. I had to kill one about a year ago, and it gave me goose bumps all over just to touch it to drag it away."

"The cats and I can smell them most of the time. You will learn to distinguish the snake smell under certain conditions, and the cats can even hear them slither. Be especially on the lookout when you have to pass under a low overhead branch, since the huge constrictors usually lie in wait there to drop on unwary prey. I have an idea that we will find huge forests and giant trees in deeper dips farther on, where the canyon becomes a valley. Oh, ah…my mother showed me how to communicate like the cats do. I'd like to try to communicate directly with you when I get the knack of it, with your permission of course, but only when absolutely necessary. I have not yet had enough practice, but I can detect both cats when I want to."

"Okay, let's try it sometime, but not tonight, please. I'm still trying to practice what you told me earlier. You must bear in mind that I'm citified and have to adapt bit by bit. I'm scared of all the strange sounds around us, since I do not know what kinds of animals are responsible for the noises, how far or how near they are, and I'm watching you closely for clues. I want to learn quickly, but there's too much information coming at me too fast."

"I'm sorry," Dai said. "I didn't realize I was being pushy. Walk closer to me and ask any question you want, but not loudly, because sounds carry easily. I'll ask Kyr and Koro to warn us when to be quiet. I'm exercising my detection sense to get familiar with it, so please don't take offense if I don't answer immediately. Just grab my hand or give me a jab in the back if you urgently need my attention."

She nodded and followed his example when he took some water. Then he walked on, wary but alive in every atom of his being. The valley was full of the familiar vibrant night sounds he usually heard only in summer, but now and then he detected an unfamiliar sound.

He identified closer or single sounds for her, and he didn't have to repeat anything twice. The time flew by without notice, and he found that he liked her company, although it slowed him down a lot compared with his and Kyr's usual rapid progress when it was just them. But he had an inkling that they were forging a formidable team.

Dai had a sudden presentiment that they were being watched. He held up a hand to stop Tumar and let his senses scan all around. He found the crouching tiger about two hundred meters in front of them—just as Koro informed them that he sensed a big cat lying in wait ahead on an overhead branch. It was too big to be family. Kyr complimented both of them—in her sarcastic cat manner, since she had detected the tiger two minutes earlier.

Dai quietly told Tumar of the ambush and thought quickly. They must be near the enemy encampment since they had been walking for more than two hours. Then he had a sudden inspiration. He asked the cats if they could link with him—which they did so effortlessly, he was surprised. He told them he wanted to try to persuade the tiger to ignore them and stalk the enemy troops, who must be near enough. If the tiger could be persuaded to stalk and attack them, the survivors would rush back to Hedra, and it would inspire fear of the valley much faster than they could accomplish on their own.

Kyr said she was the best qualified to do this, and they must follow her lead so they could learn, but she would have to draw on their mind energy to control and direct the woodlands tiger from another canyon.

Somehow Dai relinquished control of his mind and felt Koro do the same. He was fully aware of what was happening and knew he could disengage his mind any time he wanted to, but he trusted Kyr and wanted to learn. When Kyr synchronized with the savage brain, Dai became aware of the familiar pangs of gnawing hunger and the intention to relieve the raging hunger with hot flesh torn from a fresh kill, which he would seize in a few heartbeats.

Kyr ignored those intentions as she took control of that brain and subtly planted a suggestion that the approaching prey was inedible and likely to cause severe cramps and convulsions. There was easier, juicier prey slumbering farther along the path, and the tiger just had to go to it and then rush in and kill to its heart's content before it settled down to gorge itself. When Kyr urged the predator to act right away, Dai found he was drooling, as if he were part of that savage brain. He felt the mighty muscles gather, and he felt as if he himself were jumping from the limb with lithe grace and trotting along the path in search of the prey he knew was quite near.

Kyr slowly withdrew from the savage mind as the huge tiger rumbled deep in its throat and broke into a run. Dai broke the link when he felt Tumar shaking him urgently. He wanted to be angry, but he knew it was his own fault for not thinking of warning her. He said patiently, "I'm sorry, Tumar. I should have warned you, but I'm still used to being with Kyr on my own. I guess I must come out of the groove and think and act as part of

269

a bigger team from now on. Anyway, we persuaded that tiger to leave us alone and to go on to search easier prey, namely the sleeping troops farther on. It should save us a lot of trouble."

"I'm sorry too, Dai. I saw you go stiff-like, and I didn't know what to do. I was ready to shoot but I waited. It was a relief to see the tiger jump away from us off that limb." Then Tumar laughed softly as she visualized the probable scene. "The poor devils. What a rude awakening!"

Dai told her they had done something he and Kyr had never tried before, and his undivided attention was centered on the task. He thanked her for her restraint and promised not to forget again.

Kyr interjected, *You also must remember, Dai, to think and act like the mind you're trying to influence. If it's savage, think and be savage. Never go contrary to the prime thoughts you encounter, just influence them the way you want to.*

49

They came upon the scene of the carnage an hour later. Kyr said the tiger was just ahead, so they must go slowly and be ready. A low ridge gave the impression that the canyon made a sharp turn to the right, but it only formed a protected pocket around a wide clearing through which a small stream murmured quietly. It obviously was a grazing and watering place for herbivores. There were small and huge boulders scattered on the other side of the stream close to the ridge, and also numerous fallen trees. This side had been trodden by countless hooves over time.

The tiger was still feeding happily, and when he became aware of the humans just about to enter the clearing, he charged immediately to protect his kills. Dai and Tumar fired simultaneously, and the tiger turned a somersault as both heavy charges hit it in the face.

"I was afraid I had created a man-killer, but it had the decency to wait for us," Dai said. "I thought the troops would kill it, but it seems I was wrong. Let's count and see if any got away."

Tumar was conditioned not to be nauseated by blood, of which there was plenty, but she still found it a gruesome scene. Dai had seen so much of the same type of thing happening time and time again all over the world—mostly caused or made by humans—that he had lost count. It had no effect on him at all.

They counted eight bodies, so at least ten had gotten away, Dai pointed out. He then collected rifles and ammunition. They stacked the weapons to one side, and he counted ten rifles.

"Two must have run without their guns," he remarked, "or otherwise they died earlier and their rifles were taken along by the others. We'll look for a place to stash these. I have learned never to discard a weapon you may need later on." If Hedra sent another party to investigate, the absence of the rifles and ammunition might cause raised eyebrows, but he doubted they would ever reach this area, with him in between to harass them.

He asked Kyr and Koro to scout for a nearby grotto, hole, overhang, or other hiding place where they could sleep till morning. He wrapped the rifles in a clean groundsheet used by one of the departed troopers and then tied the bundle together with a belt that was not wet with blood. He also found a clean rucksack for the ammunition. Then he skinned the tiger's tail and told Tumar the same lie he'd told Surra about the tradition of making a belt of the tail of the first tiger killed by a companion. It made them proud.

"But we killed him together," Tumar protested.

"Who can say whose bolt killed it first?" Dai queried. "Anyway, as you can see, it's a rare tiger, and you can wear the belt with pride. Surra is not the only woman who can shoot accurately, so why should she alone have something to show off?" He salted the raw side of the skin and carefully rolled it into a bundle, which he stowed in an empty pocket of his own rucksack.

"What can I say, except thanks a lot, Dai."

"You're welcome. Would you carry the ammunition, please? I hope there's a rill or a fountain somewhere ahead where I can wash my hands and face." He took the bundle of rifles by the belt and started down the trail. Only an exceptional tracker would be able to decipher the story of what happened here, and others could only guess. He didn't care either way because he intended to stop anyone long before he or she reached this place. There were always scavengers in the wilds, and they would clean up thoroughly and quickly enough to confuse anyone.

They had gone about two hundred steps when the cats told them of a hollow in an outcropping big enough for them to sleep in. It was about a hundred meters up and two hundred steps ahead of them. There was a trickling of water not far off as well.

Dai thanked them. As they walked along the trail, Koro suddenly appeared in front of them and said he came to show the way. The "way" was to their left and up toward a low bank of gray, crumbly-looking rock.

The "hollow" was a small natural grotto hidden behind dense brush. It smelled as if wild dogs had used it recently, but there were no droppings to sweep away. Dai thought it safe enough to start a fire to drive the strong smell away. He put his burdens, except his own rifle, upright at the back, and Tumar put hers next to them. The trooper's rifles would be safe there even when it rained.

He heard the trickle of water nearby, but went out to collect some firewood first. Tumar followed, but he told her to put her gloves back on because her hands were not used to hard labor, and the wood might have splinters or thorns, which could cause a problem. Then he showed her what to pick up or break off and what to ignore. He knew Kyr would keep watch as always and warn them of any danger. She was also teaching Koro their normal routine.

After he had started the fire, they went to the fountain to wash their hands and faces and to replenish their canteens. Dai also filled a small kettle with water for making coffee for a change. Tumar must get used to drinking the stuff black and bitter, he thought.

He glanced at his watch and saw that it was just past three. "I might as well make us some breakfast before we take a nap. You never know what will happen next, so you eat when you can and go hungry when you must. There is no set time for meals or sleep out here, but you adapt to the varying routine."

Tumar nodded and said he must tell her what he did as he was doing it and why. He did so while he prepared breakfast for them and the cats. Kyr settled down next to Tumar, as if she wanted to be close to the fire.

Dai hadn't forgotten to pack a tin plate and a small bowl for Koro, so he handed Kyr's usual utensils to Tumar and told her that she was responsible for Kyr from now on. He poured water for the cats, however, and then dished up breakfast for them all. When they were finished, they washed up and then took a nap.

Koro woke him up by jumping onto the sleeping bag. Dai nearly killed the cat in reaction, but he stayed his hand in time. He told Koro to wake him up by drumming on his head, as Kyr had shown him, but Koro said, *I thought it was too urgent to go to all that trouble. Next time I'll jump away. There's a walking snake thing coming down from up canyon and it may smell us. It's near and it's too huge for us to drive away.* He meant Kyr and himself.

Dai jumped out of his sleeping bag as if an uninvited scorpion had entered. Tumar was sleeping heavily, and Kyr asked him to let her sleep since he could kill the monster by himself. He thought quickly and asked Koro, *Which way is the wind blowing*?

Toward us. That's how I smelled it. Unfortunately it does not have a thinking mind to influence like we did with the big wild cat.

Dai thanked Koro and then poured water over the few remaining coals. He didn't know how keen the reptile's sense of smell was, or what kind this one could be. With a little bit of luck, he thought, it might pass them right by. He had read what was known about these primeval, nearly extinct species. Only a few remained in remote, hot valleys on certain continents, and they had never been of much interest to him because he hadn't expected to ever come across them. Now it was too late for regrets, he thought grimly.

Fortunately, this grotto was a bit out of the way and high up. The reptile might have helped itself to the remains of the troopers and the tiger, but it might not be gorged. Kyr stopped his thoughts by telling him that it might have a big stomach. Dai smiled and asked Koro to come with him to keep Kyr up to date so she could wake Tumar if need be.

Dai checked his watch and saw that it was nearly eight o'clock. He looked up and to the east, but he knew daylight came late to deep valleys, even though the sky far above had a tinge of morning in it. He had scarcely descended fifty steps when he thought he felt the ground tremble slightly, though he knew it was more of a vibration picked up by his keen ears. He had the night-sight equipment on, and he stopped; he could now see the trail clearly. He squatted behind a low bush and had just sat down when a two-legged gray monster with a long, muscular tail came strolling down the trail with ponderous steps. It was a powerful tread that Dai knew could change into a fast, thunderous run.

He estimated that its head was nine or ten meters above the ground. It had a huge, bony head set on a short, muscular neck, and it seemed to grin continuously to display a dental plate full of fangs. Its narrow shoulders ended in two ridiculously small arms for grabbing or eating, but Dai instinctively felt that this monster reptile was death incarnate, and he didn't want to mess with it, even with the heavy gun that he knew could drop an airborne tank out of the sky. He would just be a quick snack for the creature.

He willed it to pass, and it did. He was just about to sigh heavily with relief when the monster stopped, looked his way, and turned around with a quick jump. Perhaps it smelled or sensed something, Dai thought. He stiffened and tensed to bring the gun to his shoulder to shoot its big, ugly head off, but then a strange, rare coincidence occurred.

As it took a step in his direction, its head swiveled to its right as a large creature took off down the trail with a frightened snort and a clatter of pebbles. The monster turned back and started the chase with a surprising burst of speed, but Dai intuitively knew that he and the monster would meet again very soon. He let out a pent-up breath in a heavy sigh and hoped fervently that the meeting would take place during daylight. He watched as long as he could, which was only a few seconds. The creature was soon out of sight among the giant trees that bordered the trail, but not out of hearing range.

He smiled as he heard a thunderous crash and an angry bellow; the beast had run into a tree, perhaps on a tight bend in the trail. It seemed that the monster wasn't nimble enough to avoid obstacles, or maybe its eyes weren't good. With that awful mass at full speed, it wouldn't be able to avoid a rock wall if its eyesight was on the dim side, or perhaps it wasn't a nocturnal creature.

50

Dai collected more firewood on his way back to the grotto. It was time to move on, but they might as well have coffee again before they followed the main trail toward the village. Reptiles were cold-blooded, and he wondered if it would go all the way to the village. He didn't think to ask, but perhaps the village was well inside the warm canyon, which, given human nature, was probably the case. Nobody liked to freeze if it wasn't necessary. Anyway, Hedra's troops would experience the terror of the reptile before the villagers, and the latter should know how to deal with one since this wouldn't be the first one to come their way.

He started a fire and the aroma of the coffee awoke Tumar. "Ah, it's nice to wake up with a stiff body to the aroma of bitter coffee. Nothing can beat it."

"I have a little bit of sugar. Would you like some in your coffee? I also have some powdered milk, if you want both."

"Thank you. Save the sugar. It's not good for my figure anyway."

Dai poured her a beaker while she rolled out of the sleeping bag, yawned, and stretched to get her blood going and relieve the stiffness somewhat.

"I've hardly slept for four hours, and you look as if you have been up for hours already. Don't you sleep much?"

"I would still be asleep if Koro here hadn't woken me up to watch a big reptile amble down the trail toward the village. It's a first for me."

"I would have liked to see it, as well. I've only heard of them. Why didn't you wake me up?"

"Oh, you'll see it before long, and you needed your beauty sleep since we don't know how long we'll sleep tonight, if at all. We'll just finish the coffee before we run after the reptile to catch up with it if you like. It's cool outside, so put something warm on before we go."

She wasn't afraid of the dark or anything because she knew she would be warned by the cats, but the silence of the canyon just before dawn was strange and intimidating. She had never experienced anything vaguely similar. She was grateful that the water in the rill was not freezing cold.

They reached the deserted village late in the afternoon without encountering the giant reptile, other predators, or humans. As Dai expected, the village was well inside the canyon, and he couldn't see where the canyon ended. There was no sign of Hedra, the troops, the villagers, or the giant reptile, and no obvious damage to the houses. The eerie silence seemed unnatural.

Dai wondered what had happened here. They had seen the tracks left by the antelope and the reptile and a multitude of animals that had fled before the reptile. Had they come all this way for nothing? He looked around on the ground to interpret the signs. He showed Tumar what he saw and how he interpreted it. The reptile had reached here, all right, but it had found an empty village. It had not been tempted to knock the fairly large wooden houses down, but it had visited a few, perhaps to look into the open doors or to smell if anything was alive inside. Then it had wandered away, farther down the canyon, after the prey it couldn't catch.

Dai found the impressions left by the grav-cars where they were grounded, and he wondered what had happened to the villagers. Even the bodies of the dead ones, as reported by Laecur, weren't anywhere to be found.

The canyon here was still wide, and the sturdy houses were built in a circle about two hundred meters from the foot of a stupendously high cliff of solid rock, which Dai guessed to be at least two kilometers high. He wondered if the houses were far enough away to miss rockfalls, but figured they knew what they were doing.

The villagers seemed to be fond of a certain type of tree with a very peculiar smell. Each house had at least two—one in front and one at the back. Perhaps they liked the smell, or it had some sort of medicinal value. He shrugged. It was irrelevant, but the smell bothered him.

He concentrated on reading signs, which were difficult to distinguish because the ground was hard, as if cement had been mixed with the top layer to prevent marks from showing. He eventually followed faint scuff marks that led toward the cliff, until he came to a flat, solid rock that might serve as a bridge, over which a thin, broad stream of water washed lazily. It was a natural bridge and dam wall on a small lake from which the water spilled over.

Instinct told Dai to continue. Through Kyr he told Tumar to wait, then follow at least twenty steps behind, and to watch the bushes at the other side but not shoot to kill unless one of them was being shot at. He suspected that the villagers had a hideout inside a cave or a crack in the cliff, and this sheet of shallow water over the rock surface would be convenient for hiding their tracks.

He let his senses scan the bushes on the cliff side for signs of life, and he found it just as Koro told him that about a hundred humans were clustered in a cave a little to the left. One was on guard just outside the cave and one was on the other side of the stream behind a bush with long, needle-like leaves.

Dai thanked him, shouldered his rifle, and picked up Koro to carry him over the water. Koro was surprisingly heavy—about thirty kilograms of solid muscle and perhaps a little fat. Just as he bent over on the other side to put Koro down next to the suspect bush, the barrel of a rifle was jammed against his neck with the word "Freeze!"

Almost nonchalantly, but blindingly fast, Dai seized the barrel with the nearest hand, pulled it out of alignment with his neck, and jerked it sharply upward. A shot went off as the man's finger pulled the trigger of the old percussion gun, and Dai kicked the man in the stomach just hard enough to make him let go of the rifle so he could grab and rub his punished abdomen.

"That was naughty as well as stupid, mister," Dai told the gasping man in a conversational tone as he handed the rifle back to the wide-eyed, astonished man.

While this happened, Koro, with Kyr's approval, updated Tumar, who picked Kyr up and carried her over the thin sheet of water.

Dai continued talking to the man. "If you want to stay alive, don't push your gun against your victim's body. Stay at least five steps away to give yourself a chance to shoot if he or she doesn't want to 'freeze!' We just want to talk, not fight. I hear a few people running to investigate why you shot. Please tell them that we just want information. Laecur told us more or less what happened here."

The man had stopped gasping for breath. In an astonished voice, he asked, "We wondered what happened to Laecur because we didn't find his body. We thought he was killed."

"He is a brave and intelligent man," Dai replied. *I might as well butter these folks up*, he thought. "He was badly beaten up, but he came all the way bareback on a pony to warn Priestess Justina. I don't know how he stayed conscious, but he is definitely a tough and determined man!"

Dai heard three individuals coming up stealthily—or so they thought—but hearing his words, one of them spoke up. "That he is, and he owes his life to the priestess, as do many of us. We'll do anything for her. I'm glad he went to warn her. Who fired the shot?"

Out of the corner of an eye Dai saw his victim go red in the face, so he quickly replied, "He fired a warning shot, for which I'm grateful. We are not your enemies, and we just want to know where your attackers are or what happened to them. Oh, ah, I'm Daiyus, and my companion is Tumarok."

The spokesman introduced his companions and lastly himself as Mouf. Then he explained. "The big priest sent a company of his troops up the canyon yesterday as an advance scout to locate and apprehend the priestess. The rest of them, including him, would have started today just after first light. We didn't warn them of the dangerous beasts and reptiles that sometimes descend down the mountains this time of the year. A few survivors staggered back just after daybreak and told a likely story of being attacked by tigers as they slept and being chased by a giant reptile. The whole caboodle then got ready to kill the reptile when it arrived, but the cowardly priest and his gluttonous friends got into one of the cars, which upset the morale of the troops.

"The troops muttered amongst themselves, and when the giant reptile made its sudden appearance well after the sun was up, the car with the priest inside took off speedily. The rest piled into the remaining cars and followed. Not one shot was fired! We know how to handle the occasional reptile, and we just calmly walked away toward this cave, where we keep our surplus produce and weapons. You may have noticed those smelly trees next to our houses. Well, that peculiar smell confuses the senses of a reptile and affects its eyes as well, but we didn't tell the invaders about that, of course.

"The weapons we kept in our houses were confiscated by the troops, and they are now gone, along with the cars. We only have three old guns, but if the reptile is driven back by the cold, we should be able to kill it. Won't you stay with us for the night? It will soon be dark, and the reptile will be very hungry if it comes back. The reptile carnivores, such as this one, have voracious appetites and seemingly insatiable bellies. You won't be safe out there."

"Yes, the beast passed by our camp early this morning, just when the sky started to change color," Dai said. "I collected ten rifles and some ammunition from the campsite where the troopers were killed by the tiger and stashed the weapons in a small grotto about a hundred meters above the trail. It's just past the dip in the trail where the big trees are, and about straight up from a tree I slashed at ground level on the east slope.

"You will see where the reptile collided with one of those big trees on a turn on the west side of the trail. The bark is stripped about seven meters above ground level. It ran after an antelope it scared out of its hiding place, and it had just picked up speed when the tree got in the way. It's been a source of amazement to me how just about any animal or man will instinctively follow a trail when it goes in the right direction." Dai laughed. "I usually do the same, but I look where I'm going."

Mouf and the others grinned, then Mouf remarked, "Those things can run fast once they pick up speed. Their strides are long and they are therefore not nimble. If they start chasing you, just run straight and swerve to one side the instant it reaches down for you. Be sure to stay out of range of those awful teeth, as they can swivel their necks very fast to grab you as they pass. Fall on your stomach and get up fast again. Run for the trees if there are any when you're on level ground because that slows them down somewhat.

"I had this experience a couple of years ago when I lost my gun after I was caught in a minor flash flood. One chased me down a slope that ended against the bottom of a sheer, solid, high cliff like the one behind me. I dived behind a rock a few meters from the cliff, and it dashed what little brains it had against the cliff at full speed. I cut its throat and tendons with my

280

knife, which was the only weapon I had left. I wanted to make sure it didn't breathe again. Come, it's late and you two will stay safely with us tonight. It will be nice to swap tall stories with a stranger for a change." He looked down. "These are temple cats, but you don't act like a religious priest. How come?"

"They chose to forego laziness and be our companions," Dai said of the cats. He didn't elaborate because it wasn't anybody's business.

51

The cats, of course, were a source of wonder for the children. Kyr allowed the affection because she was used to being admired, but Koro took off, saying he was going to hunt because he didn't like dirty little paws on his clean pelt. Dai and Tumar were introduced to the villagers. When asked if Tumarok was his wife, Dai told them she had been abducted and he was an investigator hired to rescue her, but now they had teamed up to look for the rest of the gang before she went back to her family.

It was as good a lie as any other, and the questions ceased. Dai didn't want the real reason to be general knowledge, since it would entice all kinds of unsavory characters to come to the mountains. These villagers were too unsophisticated to deal with such scum.

Tumar showed good sense in joining the women and ignoring the men. Dai accepted a beaker of home-brewed ale and sat down to trade lies with the adult men while they waited for supper. He had just finished his ale when a lookout reported that the reptile had returned in a bad mood and was in the process of wrecking the meeting hall.

Dai grabbed his gun and ran in front because the villagers didn't have any heavy-caliber guns left. Mouf, who seemed to be the leader, told him where to shoot. Apparently, the reptile had two small brains, one in the head to control the upper part of the body and the other just above the root of the tail in the spine, and both must be destroyed to kill it quickly. It was best to disable the lower brain first, Mouf said.

The monster stopped its irritated destruction when it became aware of the approaching humans. Light was fading fast, but Dai could see well enough to shoot quickly and accurately. He knew he could stop a tank with the gun, but he was as amazed as the villagers when the reptile fell on its face without uttering a sound.

"Now that's what I call good shooting," one of the men remarked. "I can now see why they sent you to rescue the beautiful girl, Daiyus. Mouf, I volunteer to go get the rifles tomorrow. The soldiers had some heavy calibers with them, and I could use one myself."

Mouf laughed good-naturedly and replied, "We'll see. If you have so much energy, you just volunteered to help chop up this monster into little pieces and cart it off where predators and carrion eaters can dispose of it."

A groan went up from the group, but then the women clanged a bell to announce that supper was ready, and they rushed back to the cave. Dai liked this simple rural life, and he sometimes wished he was part of it instead of the dangerous existence Hedra and his ilk were responsible for.

After the meal, Dai told the villagers that he was after the priest, Hedra, who'd tried to enslave them, because he suspected he was part of the gang that had abducted Tumarok. It was unfortunate that the fearful coward took off so quickly, he said.

One of the women said she'd overheard Hedra telling his cronies that he intended to go to the palace in Bojon after he had settled accounts with Justina, whom he called Lur. Maybe he had run there when they left. Dai thanked her for the information.

Tumar became the women's center of attention. Dai knew they were pumping her for information about the abduction and rescue, but he didn't mind. He also knew that the men and women would compare notes as soon as he and Tumar left in the morning. He therefore asked Kyr to tell Tumar to lie her head off if necessary, but not to let slip anything about the treasure somewhere in the mountain or their real purpose in going after Hedra. Kyr kept him up to date with her story so he didn't say anything in contradiction. These people led a quiet, lonely life, and strangers were talked about for weeks after they were gone.

Dai had a knack for getting people to talk about themselves, and he usually learned a lot that way. He told a few lies about himself and gradually led the villagers to talk about their experiences, until someone remarked that they had better get some sleep if they wanted to remove the carcass in the morning before it made the area impossible to breathe in. When he finally got into the cold sleeping bag, Koro came in and stretched out next to him.

Rural people are early risers, but Dai awoke before the first one stirred to stoke the cooking fire. Koro was gone, but something else had disturbed him. He sensed Koro on watch near the water's edge, but the sleepy sentry there wasn't aware of the cat. Dai willed his mind-feeler to move on. He didn't quite know how it worked as yet, but he was thrilled that he could do so. He couldn't describe the feeling of liberty it gave him. He let his senses roam as far as he could toward the end of the canyon, as Kyr had taught him.

Then he sensed a multitude of minds. Kyr's and Koro's minds synchronized with his, and he got a clearer picture through the eyes of an eagle soaring high up, looking for an early breakfast. He thought he must ask Kyr how she did that, and she said she would show him when they had time.

It was dawn outside the canyon, and four cars and a light tank were slowly entering the canyon. Dai sensed that Hedra was not there and that they were sent to lay waste to the canyon to destroy the reptile and other predators. Kyr showed him how to recognize the leader and to sense and isolate his private thoughts, since this one wasn't one of the naturally shielded or educated types.

The leader was thinking derisively of the cowardly Hedra and his buddies, and of other priests of the ruling class who considered their hides too precious to put to any kind of risk. But they were always very willing to send others into danger, where no power on earth could make them go themselves until they felt it safe to be there. What was so scary about one huge reptile, a few assorted wild predators, and a handful of unarmed villagers? he thought over and over again. Using fifty troopers to do the job a single light-infantry tank could do in a few minutes, or using a tank when a few well-trained troops were sufficient? He still couldn't believe it, but he had to follow orders, however obnoxious and illogical.

Dai sympathized with the captain, who radiated decency, but he couldn't allow the slaughter of innocents because a power-mad priest had ordered it. It wasn't the first time he felt reluctant to kill a decent man, but there were larger issues at stake than a few innocent lives. He got out of his sleeping bag and told the villagers that the cats warned that a lot of troops were approaching. It was the only way to make the villagers

284

believe him, for they were almost superstitious about the abilities of temple cats.

Mouf asked him what they should do. It seemed that the role of leader had been temporarily palmed off on Dai.

Dai thought for a moment and then said, "We'll go to the bridge and wait for their arrival. Tumar and I will put the tank out of action, and when the troop carriers ground, we wait for the troops to start running about before we start killing them. If any want to flee, we allow them to do so. Those who are unarmed can later gather arms from the slain troopers when it's safe to do so." Then Dai raised his voice. "For heaven's sake, don't get reckless! You only have one life. Don't waste it by taking chances! Wait till I tell you what to do."

At the bridge, Dai picked a huge, solid boulder and told Tumar, "My boss won't look kindly on me if anything happens to you. You are very precious to me, so stay behind this boulder and don't expose yourself to danger needlessly, or my boss will knock my head from my shoulders to kick around to vent his ire. Keep in mind that I'm accountable for your life, please! I'm going over to that boulder"—he pointed to a smaller one to their right on the other side of the natural bridge—"alone, and don't start shooting at the tank before I do. Kyr will tell you when you can. After that, shoot only if they storm my position or try to cross over. Mouf, your men must disperse a little, as men bunched together make an appreciated target. Shoot only when you are sure of a target. Okay?"

Tumar agreed, and Mouf said he would share the boulder with her. He told the others to scatter around and find cover from where they could watch Dai for signals. It made sense to Dai, so he told Tumar to stay as a lookout, and when he signaled, she or Mouf could tell the men to come over the bridge to gather weapons. If a car was used to ferry troops to this side, she was to shoot it out of the air if she had a chance without endangering herself and if he didn't do it first.

"I hate being pampered," Tumar told him, "but this once I will listen to you because this is an unfamiliar combat situation for me. Stop talking, and go to your position before they arrive. Kyr says they are near, and it will soon be light, but the tank captain is using night-sight equipment."

Dai smiled and gingerly walked over the thin sheet of

285

water. Koro splashed finically after him, and he stopped to pick up the cat. On the other side he wiped Koro's feet with a handkerchief before he put him down.

52

The tank came slowly into sight around the bend in the canyon without lights, maybe in an attempt to catch the villagers asleep. The gunner of the tank's cannon started to fire at the dead monster, perhaps to make sure it was dead. After the third shot, he stopped and then fired a cannon shell into a house. The house burst into flame.

Dai carefully sighted on the driver's eyehole and fired two rapid shots inside the tank. Kyr must have told Tumar he was going to fire, for at the same time, she put two shots through the gun turret. She sure could shoot, all right, he thought, and then quickly ducked behind the boulder as the tank exploded quite violently.

Debris clattered all over the village and beyond. The leading troop carrier was disabled, and it settled down slowly on the ground as its automatic safety feature kicked in. The other three cars grounded quickly behind buildings and disgorged their troops almost as soon as those in the stricken carrier jumped out and dived behind the nearest available cover.

Dai sent a thought to Koro to run like hell to find secure shelter well away from him and to stay there until he was called. He expected the area around him to be riddled with bullets as soon as they pinpointed his position. He had already checked that there was no other cover for him, and he couldn't sprint over the open area around the village. Wryly he thought that the villagers had done too good a job of clearing the area for their imagined safety.

Tell Tumar that was good shooting, he thought to Kyr. *Then ask her to hold fire until they storm my position. I'll get my head down when they get too accurate. Don't allow her to take chances, please, even if you have to bite her.*

Okay, idiot. I'll look after her. I'm teaching her just as I taught you.

Dai wondered why Kyr called him by her favorite name out of the blue. He hadn't done anything out of the ordinary as far as he knew, but his attention was centered on the still-confused troops. He shot the first one who exposed himself by attempting to dart for the next cover. The open space between Dai and the troopers was at least a hundred meters long, so he didn't expect anyone would be stupid enough to try and dash toward him. Unless this group was by chance elite troopers, their shooting wouldn't be too accurate either, even over this short distance.

Perhaps that stupid soldier had acted on orders, Dai thought, for the next moment, he had to tuck his head far down as the boulder was peppered by a continuous, intense fusillade. Now they will storm this little old rock like a bunch of enraged morons until their magazines are empty, and then they'll have to reload on the run, Dai thought. He pushed the lever to rapid fire and shifted to the side of the boulder that still had enough cover to risk a peek.

As soon as the firing eased a little, he raised his head around the side of the boulder to have a look. He estimated that half the squad members were bundled about fifty meters away to change magazines, while the other half still fired sporadically as they ran toward his hiding place. This latter group was now the target for Tumar and those villagers who had weapons.

The troopers realized they had run into an ambush and stopped in confusion, only to be picked off rapidly by the villagers and Tumar, who appreciated stationary targets. Dai concentrated his fire on the bundle, and quite a few went down before he stopped to change magazines. It only took a moment, as he had been drilled by a relentless Karna to eject and slam a new magazine into the slot of any gun within a second. Karna had emphasized time and time again that a lone warrior just couldn't afford to take his sweet time to leisurely reload when an enemy was galloping up, intent on taking what was left of his pelt for a trophy.

Dai resumed firing. He didn't aim but knew his shots were still effective, for he had done this many times before. Then, all of a sudden, all the troops were down. Dai quickly asked Kyr to tell Tumar to watch them for movement and for her to tell Mouf and the villagers not to move yet. Then he was off at full speed, zigzagging as he ran, just in case some were hiding behind the buildings, which would be officers' tactics. He knew that a few, like Hedra, preferred others to take the risk before they made a belated appearance.

Tumar was thrilled to see him run at full speed. He reminded her of a leopard chasing a dodgy prey, but his head and eyes shifted quickly from side to side as he scanned the buildings. A few of the younger villagers cheered him on excitedly, forgetting their own safety, but Tumar and Mouf didn't. Mouf shot a trooper as he rolled over to take aim at Dai, and Tumar saw a movement at the damaged troop carrier.

She'd shifted her gun that way and pulled the trigger when a man in an officer's uniform stepped out from behind to take aim at Dai. She was surprised to see that Dai had also taken a shot at the officer at the same time, and that the shot had also gone home. Now that takes some doing, she thought with sudden envy, wishing her training had been just as thorough.

You wouldn't have liked it, Cookie, just as he didn't, Kyr told her. *Kama is a hard and relentless taskmaster, and he trained Dai to stay alive anywhere in any situation at all times. He loves the boy, you see! I thought more than once that Dai would collapse or get himself killed, but he was born to be as stubborn as one of those hybrids between a slow-thinking, hard-headed, long-eared stinker and a corrupted pony. As a city girl, you may not understand what I'm talking about—a cross between a donkey and a horse, which farmers call a stubborn mule. Now you know why I love Dai and call him an idiot. He's too stubborn and stupid to know when to quit, but he's a beautiful boy, isn't he?*

Tumar couldn't help but smile at Kyr's dry and somewhat scathing description, but she suddenly envied the close companionship between the two.

Dai had reached the nearest building, and he quietly approached the closest blind corner. He crouched and became totally still.

Now he stops breathing and listens, Kyr commented, as if she was lecturing Tumar, which she was. *Even if he hears nothing, he will crouch over so that he's lower down than any normal human would expect him to be, and then he will peep carefully around the corner before he scurries around it. Always do it the way no sane human would do it. It gives you that split-second advantage.*

Tumar grinned to herself when she saw Dai doing precisely that. She didn't realize just then that Kyr was training her by pointing out why things were done just a certain way, but she would remember.

Dai went around the corner and flattened himself against the wall. He had a clear view of all three grounded troop carriers, but he saw no movement. He ran to each in a rapid zigzag and peeped inside, but all were devoid of life. Apparently it was only the one officer who hadn't felt like joining the general assault, and perhaps he'd ordered it out of stupidity. He told Kyr it was safe for Tumar and the villagers to come out and collect weapons.

Kyr told him she'd just got a message that Karna would be there in twenty minutes in a small, two-seater ship to collect Tumar because her parents were in serious condition after an almost-successful assassination attempt. Tumar's father was fighting for his life, and her mother was in a coma. Would he please come and explain the situation to Tumar? She was all thumbs when it came to breaking bad news and didn't want to hurt her "Cookie" by being blunt.

Dai ran and asked Mouf to send someone to fetch Tumar's rucksack on the double, since a small spaceship would land in the clearing in a few minutes to pick her up. Mouf sent a strong lad with instructions to run like hell to quickly fetch the rucksack.

Dai said they could send the carriers loaded with the bodies away out of the canyon if Mouf and the others would quickly dump the troopers into the carriers, and then they would only have to get rid of what was left of the tank and the damaged troop carrier.

Mouf himself ran to drive a troop carrier nearer, and while the villagers rapidly piled bodies into it, after removing the weapons and ammunition belts, Mouf ran to fetch the next carrier.

Meanwhile, Dai took Tumar gently by the arm and asked her to walk with him for a while. He told her what Kyr had told him, but in a gentler way. Tumar could sense that he felt the loss as if it were his own parents.

Dai concluded, "I have met them only once, but at the time I wished I had parents like that, and I would have been proud of them. I didn't know then that I still had a mother. Anyway, Karna must think very highly of them and you if he uses a space-flyer to come and fetch you. I won't forget to take care of the tiger's tail, and I'll bring it personally if I can," he promised.

Tumar was very firm. "You've already taught me to care about others, and I will go, but I'll be back to complete my training. I cannot remember my parents yet, but I feel I must go to see them if your Karna deems it so important that he must come personally for me in such an awful hurry. It might just be what I need to be a whole person again. Just remember that you promised to teach me the ways of the wilderness, because I will be back, whether you like it or not. It doesn't matter to me where or when, or whether you are in the middle of a battle. I'll find you. You are the first person who treated me like a decent fellow human being, and I cannot forget it. It made such a difference to my perceptions of life that I feel no one else can teach me to be a normal human being. I sort of depend on you. Do you mind?"

"No, not at all, Tumar. You will be welcome any time. We make a good team." Dai suddenly smiled. "It will save me much embarrassment, because you will be such a wealthy, important lady that I will have to make special arrangements just to be admitted into your presence."

"That reminds me. I left the liberated money and things with Lur and asked her to keep them for you in case I do not return. Perhaps I had a premonition. Do whatever you want with it because I know you won't waste it. I'll miss Kyr because I have come to love her and to depend on her to guide me."

You won't miss me, Cookie, because I'm coming with you to look after you. How else will you find out where Dai is at the time you want to reach him, stupid? Anyway, I will be useless for a while because I feel that I'm with young, or as humans call it, pregnant. It might be just a single kitten, mind you, but somehow I know it will be my last one, and I know you will look after us. Dai won't miss me so much because Koro is happy to be with him, and they soon will come to know each other better. They suit each other, too.

Dai knelt and very gently picked Kyr up. "I knew we would part someday, but it doesn't make it any easier. I won't ever forget you because I love you with my whole heart. Koro must pardon me if I call him Kyr sometimes, for you have become a part of my existence." He pressed his face into her fur. "Of course you can talk to me directly from anywhere in the world, and please do so!"

He handed her to Tumar as Karna's small spaceship appeared in the morning sky and hovered above. Kyr asked Dai to tell the villagers to evacuate the clearing. Dai whistled and waved the villagers toward him, for they had cleared the open space of bodies in record time. As soon as the place was empty, Kyr told Karna to land.

53

The villagers stood in awe while the small ship landed silently without a bump. As the ramp came down, Dai walked forward to greet a stern-faced man of middle age. He now could see the resemblance to his mother, but not to Nogalithe. Karna stopped on top of the ramp for a brief moment to wave to the villagers in greeting before he came down all the way.

When he reached the ground, he held his arms open to Dai in an uncommon welcoming gesture. "Hello, Dai. I'm glad to see you still in one piece." A rare smile transformed his stern face.

Dai rushed forward into the proffered arms and hugged his uncle fiercely. "How else did you expect me to be, Uncle? I may call you 'uncle' privately, right?" he whispered.

"Yes, of course, but not where anyone can plant a bug. It's best that our friends, as well as our enemies, do not know about it. I have a few things for you, personally, but I must get out of here fast. I cannot endanger you and the people of this remote village in case I was tracked. Before you introduce your charge, there is a rumor that the location of the relics is known. Try to get there and check up, but don't be obvious, as it may be a ploy to get someone to visit the site. I'll try to get the satellites that can see and photograph these mountains shifted a bit in the next few days."

Just then the runner arrived with Tumar's rucksack and the rest of the villagers in tow. Tumar came forward shyly with Kyr in her arms and Koro at her heels. Dai introduced Karna to Tumar and Koro. When the latter sincerely told Karna that Kyr had told him so much about him, he thought Karna would be twice as big as Dai, Karna laughed and stroked Koro's back.

Dai shoved the rucksack into the small cargo hold. Karna said the package in there was for him and Lur, but he must get going because he and the ship were vulnerable on the ground. He shook Dai's hand, waved to the villagers, and turned around. When Tumar put Kyr down, she scurried up the ramp after Karna and into the cockpit.

Then Tumar leaned the heavy-caliber gun against the ramp and shyly put her arms around Dai's neck, who gave her a comradely hug. His heart skipped a beat when he felt her firm and shapely body pressed against his for a brief moment. When she hurried up the ramp, he approved of her taking the heavy-caliber gun with her. One should always have a weapon within reach, for anything can happen anywhere at any time.

Dai shouted to the villagers to get clear, as he did himself. He gave the thumbs up to Karna, who retracted the ramp, which was also the door, and then gently took the ship up a few meters on hover. The ship then drifted slowly down the canyon on minimal power; Dai knew Karna would fly well away from the vicinity of the canyon before he increased power and pointed the ship up into space.

Dai decided to wait until he was back with Lur before he opened the square box from Karna. He asked Mouf to select two men with stamina to go with him to fetch the hidden weapons. They might as well take those guns, too; otherwise they'd be wasted. It was still long before noon, and if they ran hard all the way, they could make the grotto before sundown, where they could overnight and return the next day.

Mouf called another man, who he introduced as Kuras, and told Dai that he and Kuras were the best runners and were ready to accompany him. Dai estimated the men's level of fitness. He noticed that both were about the same height and build as he was, and both looked fit. He was satisfied with Mouf's choice.

In the meantime, Mouf had directed the other men to chop up the disabled transport and the tank, which they would store deep in the cave for future use. Then Dai programmed the carriers one by one to send them on their way, flying on automatic until they were boarded by someone to stop them.

Dai fetched his rucksack and the bow. There was just enough space for the box in the rucksack. Although the villagers only ate twice a day—a huge breakfast and a late supper—he declined a late breakfast now because it would affect his stamina. Mouf and Kuras also declined; they, too, knew that food didn't digest well when the body is subjected to strenuous, prolonged exercise. They were used to sometimes going without food for a day or two. Dai sent Koro ahead to scout and then set a hard pace. Mouf and his friend didn't carry anything but knives because they knew how to live off the land, and they would have guns by evening anyway.

Dai's mind was partly occupied with the challenge of how to proceed without Kyr and Tumar. He had quickly gotten used to having Tumar around and liked her silent company. Now he missed her uncomplaining presence. While he thought, his senses scanned the path ahead and behind, even though he was aware that Koro was not alarmed by anything out of the ordinary; Koro still had much to learn before he became Kyr's equal. At least Kyr's sarcasm hadn't rubbed off. Still, he'd accepted that she used sarcasm to hide her humanlike concern; now he missed her honest comments.

He decided he must somehow enlist Mouf's help to make sure his mother and the others would be safe here while he had a look at the location of the relics. Perhaps it would be safer to first move them to the camp under the overhang and then move the camp every few days deeper into the country away from Bojon to avoid discovery. He could ask the old lady cat, Skrot, if she would stay with them so it would be easier to keep track of their whereabouts. He decided to talk to his mother and get her opinion.

He was just about to turn his head to ask Mouf for help in guarding the priestess when Koro said something huge was coming their way. Dai told Koro to come back and then held up a hand for his companions to stop while he listened. He quietly told the others that something huge was coming their way. He was trying to smell what it was, for the wind was blowing their way and his thudding heart impaired the keenness of his hearing. Mouf and Kuras also tried hard to stop their heaving chests so they could hear better.

Just then Koro came down the trail like a red streak and skidded to a halt just in front of Dai. He said the thing was as big as a village house, walked on four legs, was hairy, and had a thick tail in front that waved from side to side as if it were a snake between two downward-sloping horns or gigantic fangs pointing the wrong way. Dai described it aloud to the two men, saying he thought it might be a mammoth, but since he had never seen one, he wasn't sure.

Mouf picked up a handful of dust and threw it into the air,

then pointed to the left. "Let's go up a bit that way and wait for it to pass. It won't smell us from there. I think it's one of those rare visitors we call a 'phobos.' It uses that long nose as a hand. It is amazing what it can do with that nose-hand, but its smell and hearing senses are keen, so stay still. We can let it go by for the villagers to kill, for we need the meat. Most of our provisions were destroyed or taken by the invaders."

They scurried up the incline as quietly as possible. They had just settled down when the monstrosity came ambling into view. Dai had heard about rare sightings of mammoths in the cold countries, but he'd never expected to see one in the flesh, and he marveled at its enormity compared with other animals. He had heard of hairless ones way down in a southern continent, and if they were as big as this one, it would be a sight worth seeing.

Then something strange happened. The mammoth, or phobos as Mouf called it, stopped in its tracks and performed a very fast turnaround for its massive size. A huge tiger, almost a third the size of the phobos, came charging down the trail and leapt for the mammoth's neck while it was still turning around. The mammoth raised its trunk, the tiger collided with it, and as the tiger instinctively grabbed it with extended claws, the trunk curled around its neck. The next moment the tiger was dashed against the ground, and the mammoth knelt on it with unexpected speed. They heard the crush of bones and only a short agonized squeal as the tiger was crushed to death.

It happened so fast that Dai gasped in surprise. The mammoth must have heard the faint sound because it jumped up and stood on the tiger's carcass with its front feet while it turned its raised trunk in their direction. Dai could hear the deep sniff as the animal sampled the air, and he saw the massive ears tense and turn slowly back and forth like searching radar dishes.

It could be that the whimsical wind sent a whiff of human smell in its direction, for the next moment it turned down the trail again and started to run with the ridiculously short, bare tail held straight up skyward like a wild pig's. Dai looked at Mouf with a frown, but it was Kuras who supplied the answer to the unasked question.

"They are full of whims and tricks. I wouldn't be surprised if it turns around and trails us as soon as it is out of our sight. There's only one spot where it is vulnerable, and that's the small hollow just above each eye where the bone is thin. You have to be a brave marksman to hit that small spot when it's charging straight at you. The rest of the head is protected by thick bone. A shot to the body is stupid because the heart is protected by solid ribs and very thick, tough hide. The heaviest old-fashioned bullet guns won't even penetrate two centimeters into the skin, and it only makes the beast dislike you more. A high-powered energy gun might do the trick if you know where to shoot. This one must have had dealings with humans before, therefore its odd behavior. Also, that huge tiger is not one of the regular inhabitants of the canyons hereabouts or even a regular visitor."

"Then it's the second irregular one," Dai said. "One like that killed the troops, and Tumar killed it later. I have its tail in my rucksack to make Tumar a belt. Let's be on our way. Koro will warn us if the phobos comes back." They would have shaken their heads in disbelief if he'd told them that he would be able to sense if the beast returned. They needn't know about that ability anyway. "I think we'll reach the tall trees in just over an hour at the pace we're going." He silently asked Koro to scout ahead again.

All of them were breathing normally again, but Mouf and Kuras groaned in mock agony. Dai ignored them and scanned their back trail as Kyr had shown him, but he didn't detect the mammoth. He was thankful because he didn't like to waste a life unnecessarily. They returned to the trail and started to run again.

54

Daylight was beginning to shy away from the wide canyon when they entered the region of the tall trees. Ten minutes later Dai saw the marked tree on his right side. As he climbed to the cave, he picked up dry branches. The two men followed his example and they arrived at the cave with arms full of firewood.

Dai pointed to the rifles and then put his rucksack out of the way against the back wall. He strung the bow. It was about time he tried it out, for he wanted to get the feel of it. He slung the quiver over a shoulder and told the men he was going to see if he could bag something for supper. Mouf told him to take his rifle because it was time for the nocturnal creatures to start making a nuisance of themselves.

On impulse, Dai asked him to come along as a guard. He handed Mouf the rifle and said, "I'm taking my night-sight headgear, for it will be dark before long. In one of those bundles there should be three that I collected with the rifles. Take one of them and use my rifle, for I don't think it is good policy to use a strange rifle if you haven't tested it. We may just need the firepower in a hurry. The clearing where the tiger attacked the troops is just around the corner. The wild animals around here go there to graze and drink."

"That phobos has got me worried," Mouf said. "I think we should go and have a look at what's going on in the hotter canyons. Those tigers *never*, and I really mean *never*, migrate to the colder canyons in the winter. They are being disturbed, and we should go and check it out."

Dai heard the seriousness in Mouf's voice. He could make an accurate guess as to what had chased them out of the hotter areas, but he couldn't talk about it. Then he knew what he was going to do but said they would discuss it later. First they must go and get something before they starved to death.

Koro told Dai that he was going to hunt for himself along the canyon side nearby. Kuras said he would make a fire and have a look at the rifles in case some were damaged and perhaps try them out. Then he would start making porridge, and they had better bring back some meat or they would get no porridge. Dai told him to pay attention where he shot so he didn't kill the cat.

Daylight was fading, so they donned the night-sight headgear. When they reached the trail, Dai put an arrow to the string so he would be ready if they flushed out anything that looked good enough to eat.

He was pleased by the silent way Mouf trailed along, as if it was his natural gait, but then Mouf was a woodsman and had probably learned the hard way to move silently. He knew Kuras would be of the same mold, and either of them would be a good companion for the trip to the warmer canyons to investigate and drive the intruders away—if possible—and then casually check the location of the treasure.

As they stealthily entered the clearing, they were greeted by a thunderous roar, and the biggest black bear Dai had ever seen charged straight at them, as if it had been lying in wait. Without thinking, Dai drew the bow's string all the way back to his shoulder and let the arrow fly before the bear was in full stride. It was a lucky shot; the arrow entered the bear's chest at the soft spot just below the neck where it joined the chest. The arrow almost disappeared into its chest and the bear seemed to stumble. Dai dropped the bow and drew one of his handguns just as Mouf calmly shot the bear through the head. It tumbled head over heels and didn't even twitch.

"Hell! That was the best bow shot I have ever seen in my life!" Mouf's voice was filled with awe. "You are quite a surprise, Daiyus. You had a gun in your hand even before the bow touched the ground and just as the arrow entered the bear's chest at the right spot. I think my shot was superfluous, but I had to make sure, because that's a cave bear, the most dangerous predator I know. Damn! Something is messing up their private lives. Even in the hotter canyons, this one should still be hibernating. I'm going to have a look, starting tomorrow. Do you want to come along?"

"Of course, Mouf. That is what we are going to discuss tonight, but one of you should take the rifles back to your village, since the danger for your people is not over yet. I was going to ask you to send two or three men to protect the priestess as well. Ah! I see the bear was feeding on an antelope and that was why it charged when it saw us. It was protecting its prey. I was just starting to think that my chances of finding fresh meat had significantly diminished, but this looks like a recent kill and not carrion it scavenged on."

"Don't you know that bear meat is considered the best? It is much tastier than beef or mutton. I'll cut us some choice portions, and you can see if there's anything usable left of that buck. I'd love to brag with the bear's pelt as a coat or a blanket, but I think it's a bit dangerous to linger too long."

"I'll watch you work and I can help with the skinning, but give me the gun and I'll play sentry. I'll see if I can contact Koro and ask him if he wants some bear liver, and he can come and stand sentry as well." Dai took the rifle, then picked up his bow and slung it over a shoulder while he sent a mental call to Koro, who answered immediately and said yes, he would like to taste bear liver and brag about it when he could.

Dai watched an expert at skinning and picked up some tips. Mouf remarked that Kuras was going to be surprised to see the unusual skin, but he wasn't the type to be jealous. This was a prime skin and would dress well when dry. His wife was an expert.

When Koro arrived, he was given a huge piece of liver. After he had taken a few bites, he told Dai it was the best red meat he had ever tasted. Mouf laughed when Dai relayed the comment.

Mouf worked fast, and as he finished, Dai cut the undamaged hindquarters off the antelope carcass, skin and all. It was less messy that way. Mouf had wrapped his choice of the bear's meat in the skin and slung it expertly over a shoulder. Koro was finished and barely able to walk, but Dai said nothing; the cat would learn in time not to overindulge whenever he got the chance.

"If there is a next time, I'll be the one who hunts with you," Kuras remarked when he saw the soft, glossy black pelt. Mouf had brought enough meat for a dozen hungry people since scavengers would clean the bear carcass long before morning. Kuras happily prepared a huge supper and more than enough to provide for a cold breakfast as well. It was Dai's first taste of bear meat; he concluded that it was an acquired taste, but it wasn't bad at all.

While they washed up, Dai started the conversation: "I planned to follow the mammoth's trail back to where it came from, but I have an uneasy feeling that it's going to be a dangerous undertaking."

"I want to go with you, as I've already indicated," Mouf said. "It's in our interest to check out anything unusual in these canyons and stop it before it gets out of hand. I know these canyons well since I explored quite a few not too long ago. But I'll have to catch up with you later because I can't expect Kuras to carry all these rifles and ammunition by his lonesome self. Make it easy for me to catch up with you." Mouf grinned easily at Kuras. Dai thought a secretive look passed between them, but he could have imagined it in the dim light emitted by the fire.

He sensed that Mouf was a little too anxious to accompany him dismissed it as imagination caused by his tiredness. "Think about this," he said. "There is a pony about an hour's run from here. Laecur may not mind if you borrowed it for a few days. He won't be up and around for at least a week, and it can speed things up for you. You two can outstay a fit pony, and it can carry the load."

"With the pony to carry the load, I'll be fine alone," Kuras replied. He continued with a grin, "I know that Mouf likes to take a breather from his wrestler wife now and then, and it's about time he gets a break again." He grinned mischievously at Dai. "Did you know that the other day when she was annoyed with him, she hit him so hard on his head that he left a zero imprinted on the rock he was sitting on?"

Dai joined the laughter. He was a loner; still, these were the sort of companions he would like to have but rarely met, and this good-natured jesting meant their friendship was an old one. It also explained Mouf's seemingly out-of-the-blue eagerness to accompany him.

Mouf pretended to be offended. He scowled in mock seriousness. "I'm proud of her, I'll have you know. I like strong women, not the lean, skinny type you married. I haven't told anyone, Kuras, and don't you dare tell anyone else, that a week ago she chased a mouse that jumped out of a cupboard door, and when she cornered it, the terrified thing panicked and scurried up her leg in pure confusion. My girl screamed furiously and hastily clamped her legs together. She caught it just above

301

her knees and squeezed about two liters of water and a full bucket of fertilizer out of it. That's my girl..." But he had to stop and join them as they rolled in the dust, laughing their heads off. Dai could visualize such a scene, although he knew it was nonsensical talk between friends to while away the evening.

Koro looked on, not knowing or caring what all the merriment was about and not understanding what was humorous about the story. Then he remembered Kyr's admonishment and expanded the range of his senses to examine the night life, which was already in full swing around them, for signs of malicious intent toward himself and his companions. He moved away from the fire before he settled down, for his extended stomach was a bother, and he felt sleepy. He should watch his appetite, he thought as he yawned and promptly fell asleep.

Although Dai enjoyed the laughter that enlightened his rather grim life for such a brief period, he was alert and noticed the cat plop down and promptly fall asleep before his rounded stomach touched the ground. He sorely missed Kyr and her sarcastic comments, but she deserved a break and a long rest from this all-too-dangerous life.

Mouf was not finished yet. He waited for the laughter to subside a little and then continued, "Lorca—that's my wife's name, Daiyus—told me that her mother is stronger and not so sweet tempered. Once, when she was annoyed with something Lorca said, she hit her so hard on the head that she thought she permanently imprinted an outsized exclamation mark on the wooden chair she was sitting on at the time. She later realized it was a natural discoloring in the grain of the wood."

Dai knew it was just friendly fun, and he wished he had time to stay with these down-to-earth people, but time was pressing. After he had laughed enough, he proposed that they share the night's watch with him so they could get going an hour or so before first light.

55

It was still dark when they left. Mouf and Kuras had each picked a rifle and ammunition the night before. When they reached the pathway leading to Lur's cave, daybreak illuminated the canyon, and they removed the night-sight equipment from their heads. Dai proposed they have breakfast before they tackled the brief ascent so that Kuras wouldn't have to waste unnecessary time before starting back to the village. While they wolfed down the cold meat with sips of water, Dai asked Koro to let his mother know they would arrive in about ten minutes and that she must guide them to the pony and then to her.

When they reached the pony, Kuras mounted it and promised Mouf that he would give the bearskin to Lorca to dry and dress. He added with a grin that she had the build for it, anyway, and when Mouf mock-scowled and advanced on him, hurriedly pointed the pony down the footpath. Kuras waved back before the foliage engulfed him and the pony.

When the priestess came down and hugged Dai fiercely, Mouf looked completely confused. Seeing his astonishment, Lur told him that Dai was her son, and she asked him to promise to keep this a secret until they no longer had any enemies who would take advantage of the relationship.

She led them up an undefined route to the hideout, where she introduced Mouf to the others. When it was polite to do so, Mouf sat down with Laecur to bring him and the curious audience up to date.

Lur excused herself and took Dai to a bare room, where they sat on the cold floor to discuss Dai's plans and intentions. When Lur was satisfied, she took his face between her hands, looked deeply into his mind, and mentally transferred the location of the treasure.

Dai's plan was to make the invaders believe they were being attacked by primitives. He would use the bow whenever possible and get them to pass that false information on to whomever they had contact with. But if attacked in force, he and Mouf would defend themselves with whatever means was at their disposal. Primitives would happily resort to guns if they took them from their victims, and who was going to question uncannily accurate shooting or pass the information on when they were dead?

Dai then opened the parcel from Karna. They found two stun guns and a curiously thin but sturdy-looking hand weapon with a thin, finger-length barrel. On top was a sealed envelope on which Karna had written in his neat handwriting to not to touch the guns in any way before the letter was read. Dai opened the envelope and read the letter aloud.

"I assume that there is no need to rush things, so you have ten luxurious minutes to read this letter. You recently asked me to replace the stun gun you gave to Tumarok, but I could not send these top-secret ones with the courier. They are the newest developments and, as you can see, they are almost flesh colored but not quite identical. The one with the shorter barrel is for Lur. They are not loaded.

"The handles are sensitized and you each must hold it in your right hand, repeat, right hand, with your forefinger depressing the trigger until the severe tingling stops. Then you alone can handle that weapon, but only with your right hand, as it can only recognize the imprint of one hand. If anyone else picks up the gun and can withstand the severe tingling for five seconds, it will explode. The explosion will more than likely kill the person. We didn't have anyone test it longer than two seconds, of course. This new stun gun works the same as the older model, but it has twenty charges.

"The slender but deadly needle gun is yours, Dai, and you must imprint your left hand on it because you may have to use both at the same time on occasion. Again, don't touch it with the other hand! The needler, as we call it, has a double magazine and each side has two hundred charges. It was designed so that the user can spray a total of four hundred explosive poison needles in one minute if confronted by a hostile horde. It's deadly! The thumb lever up is single-shot. There are four extra magazines and five stun gun mags for each of you. Lur, you must let me know when you have used two or three, and I will bring or send you more as soon as I can. They strap to the forearms, and you must show your mother how to draw quickly. Regards, Karna."

Dai put the letter down a little distance from them and invited his mother to pick up her gun. The letter flashed into a brief flame just as he picked the guns up, one in each hand. He sensitized both guns at the same time; the severe tingling almost made him drop the guns, but he knew he wouldn't have a second chance and he determinedly held on. The previous stunner had saved his life many times, and it was worth enduring a few numbing shocks for another one.

Then he showed his mother where to strap the holster onto her forearm out of sight in the sleeve of her robe or any long, loose-sleeved garment she might wear. He explained how the holster worked and how it let the gun jump into her waiting hand if she used certain attachments. She must always keep the gun covered by a sleeve and not let anyone see it, as it paid to keep it as a surprise.

Meanwhile, responding to the curious questioning, Mouf had related the story of what happened in the village and the intention to investigate the unusual migration of the huge animals. When Dai and Lur returned to the warm room where the others were gathered, Surra said she was coming along to help.

Dai was taken by surprise, but he sensed instant hostility from Gemur, and before Lur could recover from her astonishment to warn Dai not to accept, he replied, "I admire your courage, Princess, and I thank you for your offer, but this venture into primitive country and precarious living is not for a loving mother who must survive long enough to bring this country back onto its feet again.

"Mouf and I will rely on each other to survive. He knows the canyons, the ways of the wilderness, and how to live off the land. We will be constantly on the move with little sleep, and the only bathing will be in streams if there is time and if it is safe to do so. You know the city like the back of your hand, and I would welcome your knowledge of Bojon if we were going there, but the intruders must be driven out of the canyons, and that requires a different kind of expertise and brutal tactics that you wouldn't approve of." He hoped that was clear enough to get her to stop acting on impulse.

Surra smiled unexpectedly. "Very well put, Dai. I'm still hurting in unexpected places from the running you subjected me to the other night, reminding me of your teaching methods. And I thought I was in shape? My father abdicated last night, and my first act as queen is to declare that you are never to address me by any title except in public when protocol requires it. When you return we work side by side to eradicate the enemies from my kingdom. As for you, Mouf, although you don't know the half of it, you will be putting your life on the line for our country. When you return you can ask for any reward, and I will give it to you if it is within my power." She looked him squarely and honestly in the eyes and smiled.

Mouf's face reddened. His eyes shifted and he stammered his thanks, saying he would think about it.

Dai exchanged their rifles for the hunting guns the ex-king had given to Tumar and the one he had taken from the woodsman. Then he said, "I am going to take the grav-trolley. I'm tired of carrying the gear on my back.

At this stage Mouf had to prove himself honest and trustworthy before Dai would part with any information regarding the real reason for this furtive, unlawful invasion.

"Please come with me, Mouf. I have special clothes that will fit you, if someone will show me where the personal things I brought are stored."

"Please show them where we put it with the trolley, Krekur," Surra told her son. "We didn't expect you back this soon, Dai."

They didn't have to go far. Although he changed clothes and discarded the thermal underwear in Mouf's presence, Dai, as was his wont, didn't let him or the curious boy get a glimpse of the weapons strapped to his wrists. Soon Dai and Mouf bade the company good-bye.

56

After Karna had picked Tumar up in the village, he headed directly for space when he thought it safe. He said he must show her what the planet looked like from a distance while the opportunity was there, and then went twice around the Earth in different directions so she could see the entire globe. Karna had sensed Tumar's intention to rejoin Dai, so this trip served as a test to see how gravity and weightlessness affected her and what her response would be to the great emptiness beneath and around them. Kyr, of course, had done this many times before, and she blissfully went to sleep.

It was midafternoon when he landed the small spaceship at the Fighters' headquarters. After he had moved the ship to its hangar, Tumar asked if she could be shown around because she was interested in seeing how candidates were trained. Karna showed her the various facilities and explained the purpose of everything. He added that the mental training was most severe and that new trainees were subjected to much, much more to determine abilities, weaknesses, and their suitability for the strenuous life as a Fighter.

After they had an early supper, Karna said they must go to bed early, for they would leave just after midnight to visit her parents at the medical clinic in a neighboring country. He asked a female assistant to show Tumar to the guest quarters and see to it that she had everything she needed. Tumar gave him her rifle with a smile and asked him to keep it for her, for she would be back for training if he would accept her.

Karna did not have to be a soothsayer to know that she wanted to be nearly as good as Dai was before she joined him. He sensed her sincerity and intuitively knew she was the ideal choice of a partner for Dai, since she had qualities that supplemented his abilities. They would make a formidable, if not unbeatable, team.

Kyr, who had gone directly to his office when they landed, told him his reasoning was on the right track. She followed Tumar, for she had become quite attached to the girl. She would look after and help Tumar when she could until after her kitten was born, before she would reconsider her role. She hoped that her last kitten would adopt Tumar as a companion even if it was not very bright, which some of her previous offspring fortunately had been. She would like to spend her few remaining years with Lur—peacefully, she hoped.

Kyr didn't regret her life with Dai. It had been an exciting, dangerous, trying, but joyful twenty years. Even the starvation and privation they oftentimes had to endure was essential to make Dai the exceptional young human he had become.

It was just before six in the morning when Karna parked the fast grav-car on the grounds of the clinic where Tumar's parents were being treated. According to the report Karna had received last night, her mother had regained consciousness for about half an hour the previous day, and her father was still holding on to life.

Kyr elected to guard the grav-car, since her presence in the hospital could cause an upset, and she was not fast and agile at present. It wasn't imagination, for as early as it was, she could feel the presence of a single embryo inside her, and it had to be taken into consideration; she didn't want to lose it through carelessness.

Tumar had regained her true memories when Ekaasi and Nogalithe had expertly removed the implanted false ones, but her recollection was vague and out of date. She was somewhat nervous and wondered what her response would and should be toward the parents she hadn't seen for more than a dozen years, and, to be truthful, still couldn't remember.

Karna was expected, and he took Tumar directly to her parents' private room. The guards, who were highly trained Fighting Priests, let them in.

As they entered, a nurse began to turn around to check the sudden, unannounced intrusion. Her body jerked in shock and her eyes widened for an instant at the sight of Tumar, who acted without the slightest hesitation, as Dai had impressed upon her: even as the nurse started to turn around, Tumar made a fast shift forward and knocked her out with a single punch. She shook her hand as if it were hurt, while her victim fell partly against the bed of the woman Tumar recognized from the photo Sorcuk had given to Dai at Bojon's aerodrome.

Meanwhile, Karna closed the door softly and calmly asked her what that was all about. The guards had belatedly jumped up and were about to tackle Tumar, who was inspecting the tray the "nurse" had deposited on the bedside table a few seconds ago, but Karna's calm voice stopped them before they were over the shock of seeing a stranger enter with speed and knock a nurse out cold without even saying, "Hello, excuse me."

"She's from Operations and definitely not trained to help people get better," Tumar said. "It seems that providence arranged for me to catch this assassin in the nick of time. Would you please have the contents of the syringes on the tray analyzed, for I don't think it's prescribed medical treatment." She turned to the guards. "Has she been here before?"

Both guards looked at Karna for guidance. "Answer her, please," he told them. "She's the patients' daughter and has the right to know."

"We only came on duty a few minutes before six," the older one answered. "We don't know if she was here during the night, but she wasn't here yesterday, and we haven't seen her before. She came in a few moments ago, just after the night shift left. We questioned her, and she said she was new and was transferred from another clinic yesterday. And sir, before you ask, she had just put the tray down when you came in."

"Thank you. Handcuff her hands and feet. I'll take her along for interrogation, and I might as well take the contents of that tray along for analysis. How are the patients doing?"

"The man is in a stable condition and the woman regained consciousness for about half an hour yesterday as reported, sir. The night shift said nothing else occurred during the night."

"You'd better put some sort of a gag in the phony nurse's mouth and cuff her hands behind her back so she can't reach her mouth," Tumar said. "She's very supple, so please bind her elbows, too, so she can't get her hands in front of her. Her operational name is Nogene, and she may have a poison capsule in a hollow tooth or under a fingernail. I held back a little so I don't think any teeth are broken. She's still breathing normally, and she may not be out for long."

The men hurriedly fettered the "nurse" and tore a towel to make a thick gag that could not be bitten through. Karna sighed inaudibly. Now the patients would have to be moved elsewhere.

Yes, he thought, in retrospect it's easy to see that all an inquirer would have to do is pretend he or she is from the Fighters, chat up the receptionist at an idle period, especially late at night, and then ask how the special patients are doing, or something similar. The bored night receptionist would reply with the truth without giving it a thought. The problem was that if they asked everyone not to mention any special patients, word would get out even faster.

Tumar turned her attention to her parents. Both seemed to be sleeping deeply. She felt their pulses to check if they were still alive. Her mother's pulse was strong but her father's was slow and sometimes erratic. She didn't know how to pray, but she fervently wished he would recover. After so many years of believing herself an orphan, she desperately wanted to embrace her parents and get to know them. She now understood how Dai had felt when he'd met his mother.

Karna said, "I can arrange for you to stay with your parents for as long as you want, but only during the day. There is a hotel about a kilometer from here and you can stay there, but now that Operations knows where your parents are, I'll have to arrange to move them quickly, perhaps as soon as tonight. I'd like to know what they have against your parents, or if it's just a spiteful deed their twisted minds devised to let you know they can get back at you."

"Thank you, sir. I have no money with me as I left everything with Lur before Dai and I went to the village where you picked me up. I'll refund every credit you have to spend on my behalf. I'll come back to sit with my parents until they throw me out tonight or until you arrange to move them. But I'll only stay until they regain consciousness, then you must enroll me for training if you deem me good enough. I'll take any and all tests you require."

"As a matter of interest, you're already qualified, based on Lur's recommendation, and you passed the final test when we went around the Earth, and you didn't succumb to space sickness while adapting to weightlessness for the first time in your life. You must learn to handle anything, including spaceships, for sometimes you may have to grab the first available vehicle to escape in the course of your duties. I expected that you'd want to join us, but you must bear in mind that some of the training you have had may put you at a disadvantage, though if you persevere as Dai and others did, including these two characters, nothing will stand in your way. Just be positive all the time and you will come through. Makket and Blepp, this is Tumarok, your colleague as of this instant."

"Thank you, sir." Tumar was sincere. She turned to the guards. "I'm glad to make your acquaintance," she said and smiled. The smile instantly transformed her austere face into radiant beauty, which immediately won the hearts of both men.

"Right, let's go and get you a room for the night. Makket, you stay on guard, and you, Blepp, get a plastic bag for the contents of the tray. We'll be back in about half an hour. Before I forget, remember to introduce Miss Tumarok to the nightshift and tell them not to allow unknown staff or medics into the room like you two innocents did."

They were back in an hour. Tumar had told the receptionist at the hotel that she would bring her luggage in the evening. They did some shopping on the way back, for Tumar had left everything she owned at Lur's place. Karna paid for everything, explaining that the money was from the Fighting Priests' coffers and would be deducted from her remuneration, since he would put her down as a trainee as of that same morning. He gave her a small advance for incidental spending, such as food.

Kyr let Tumar know she would be virtually useless for the next five or six weeks, so she was going back with Karna and would stay with him until her kitten was born. When Karna left, Tumar thanked him and hugged him spontaneously. Blepp had borrowed a covered laundry trolley, and he pushed Nogene, who was feigning unconsciousness but which did not deceive an old hand such as Karna, to the car.

After they left, Tumar sat with her father, holding his hand for half an hour before a nurse came in. Tumar gave her a penetrating look before Makket introduced her as Tumarok, the daughter of the patients, Joemer and Imatob. Tumar memorized the names; no one had thought to tell her the names of her parents, and she still had to find out what her last name was, but she wouldn't ask anyone except her parents, and then only in private.

When the nurse had fussed around the important patients

and had gone again, Tumar sat with her mother and took her hand. She lost track of time. Then she felt her mother's hand tighten. The grip was hard, but Tumar's was strong and to her the grip was just firm. Then Imatob opened her eyes and looked at her with astonishment.

"I...I...dreamed that you were here, my sweet Cookie." Her voice was just a whisper and Tumar felt the tears coming. "Is it really you? I'm so glad Dai found you. You have become a beautiful girl." The tears came, and Tumar rose and bent over the bed to hug her mother tenderly, for she didn't know what injuries had been inflicted on this still-beautiful, middle-aged woman. When her mother let go of her, Tumar first wiped the tears from her mother's face before she wiped her own. She felt happy for the first time in her harsh life.

"Do you know how your father is?"

"He is in this bed next to you, Mom. Karna arranged for both of you to be in the same room and guarded day and night, but he said he will have to move you two to another clinic for you are not safe here anymore. They say that Father's condition is stable, but he is still unconscious. You must rest now and not talk too much, but I will stay with you for a few days. Then I'm going for some training with the Fighting Priests, and when we can, Dai and I will go after the people who did this to you. When you feel better, you must tell me what happened."

One of the guards had called the medic. When he came in, Tumar moved to her father's side to hold his limp hand. She willed him to heal quickly so she could get to know him a little before she left.

57

Dai needed sleep desperately, and he was hungry, but he kept on pulling the grav-trolley up the smooth, steep incline. Koro was guiding him to a cave he had discovered in solid rock on top of a lonely hill that stood almost unnoticed and very uninviting, out of the way at one side of the canyon. It was almost as if the solid hill discouraged eyes from seeing it properly. Mouf snored lightly in deep sleep on the trolley. He had been burned in the right shoulder two days ago when he was too slow in taking cover. The bolt had just gone through the skin, and to Dai the wound didn't even look half as serious as the one inflicted on Murima. He had treated it, but Mouf seemed slow to recover from such a slight wound. He complained that it throbbed, his arm was numb, and his body felt so weak he could scarcely relieve himself.

He was an unnecessary burden, and Dai was considering leaving him where he would be safe and then visit him once a day to bring fresh food and water. He knew that any wound was painful for a few days, but he was puzzled that such a negligible wound incapacitated an otherwise tough and healthy Mouf to such an extent. It made him suspicious. The wound was definitely healing quite well when he changed the dressing last night. Mouf was supposed to be a tough character, and this weakness mystified Dai. If he was shamming, he was very convincing, and Dai gave him the benefit of the doubt—for the time being at least—but he wondered what was behind this sudden, inexplicable shirking.

The cat was lean and hard and moved gracefully and as alert as his wild cousins. They had been fighting the invaders which they believed to have been small tactical teams sent from Mars, Shaytan and Earth; running and moving for the past ten days with little chance to sleep, and Koro had done his share of scouting and killing. He had found out the hard way that a full belly impeded fast action, and it taught him to eat more than once a day when he could and not too much at one time. Dai had taught him, away from Mouf, whenever there was need for

313

it. Koro always followed his advice without query or question, for he knew it was honestly given.

One watches from afar, Koro informed him. *Not friend, not unfriendly, but thoughts blocked. Not danger to us but curious to see where we go.*

When you hunt, go see who it is. The range and acuteness of Koro's senses sometimes astonished Dai. He still missed Kyr, but he found that Koro was just as good, and better in some ways, and he wasn't as sarcastic because he didn't still see Dai as a bumbling kid, as Kyr did. He learned to love Koro just as much as he loved Kyr. They complemented each other in many ways, and Dai felt they were getting to be like extensions of each other.

The last sixty or so meters to the cave was bare rock and quite steep. Dai took a very careful look into the canyon, and he used his senses to scan the area as well before venturing out of the sparse cover onto the bare rock. Koro said he was going to hunt before dark and would check on the watcher; the entrance was near the top and concealed, but Dai wouldn't miss it if he went straight up from here. Koro faded away like a red shadow.

The entrance was L-shaped and the "cave" itself was a surprise. The high doorway, for doorway it was, was carved out and should have had a door, and perhaps did have a door once, Dai thought. This place was carved out of solid rock for people twice his size and height, and heat tools had been used to smooth the surface of the walls and floor. *I wouldn't be surprised if this place was used as an outpost or a secret hideaway in ages past. It is high up, and the view of the canyon is unobstructed and superb. This would be a good place to leave Mouf*, he thought with delight.

Dai played the strong light into every corner to check for snakes and other surprises, but he only saw dust and Koro's tracks. In one corner was a sophisticated carved-out fireplace complete with a chimney to draw the smoke out. Not surprisingly, next to it was an open doorway. There were no tracks going that way, so he decided to settle down and make supper before he explored.

There was enough firewood on the trolley to prepare supper. As he removed an armful, Mouf awoke and sat up quickly. There wasn't the usual groan of pain, and Dai didn't see any of the usual grimacing and twisting of features in the bright light of the torch. He must have forgotten to sham, Dai thought distastefully.

"I…uh…feel much better," Mouf grunted as if reading his thoughts.

I don't doubt you do. You must feel obliged to explain the sudden lack of the usual groans, Dai thought. *I haven't had as much sleep in ten days as you've had in one.*

"Where are we? This looks like a room."

"It *is* a room," Dai commented. "Koro found it around noon, but it took me a few hours to reach it. You can stay here until you are fully recovered. It should be safe enough if you keep a lookout during the day. I'll prepare supper first and then we can explore the rest of it. There's another doorway next to the fireplace behind you."

Mouf got up to help carry some firewood with one hand while Dai ignited the fire. He put the wood down away from the fire and returned for more, but his impatient attitude reflected his almost irresistible urge to explore. He eyed the torch Dai had hung onto his belt, and his attention kept going to the doorway, which was plainly visible in the light of the flames. Dai tried to sense what he was thinking, but the natural impenetrable block was there as usual, and no thoughts were divulged, as Koro had assured him after a few days.

"Uh, won't this glow be seen?" Mouf asked after a while. He was squatting next to Dai and looking at the fire and the simmering cooking pot, which contained the same fragrant-smelling stew Dai had prepared the night before.

"There's a massive outcropping a few steps from the entrance which conceals it pretty well. I'm not sure how the smoke is vented away, and it might be visible, but hopefully it won't lead anyone here. I think most of the intruders are gone. Those arrows scared the heck out of them. I just regret not being able to I recover the arrow heads for reuse."

"We can always make some heads from flint if you want to. Most of the pain is gone, and I'll do my part again from tomorrow. I'd like to explore this place after supper. Are you up to it?"

"I'd like to have a long, peaceful sleep for a change. I'm so tired I can't even think coherently anymore, but I agree we

315

should check this place out. It seems the prudent thing to do. Koro should return in a couple of hours, and then he can take the watch."

They ate hungrily as usual and finished every scrap of stew. Dai washed the pot and both dishes in a little water, since he didn't want to inconvenience Mouf. Dusk was falling when he went outside to throw the dirty water out.

The room wasn't cold, but he left the fire smoldering since there wasn't anything that could catch fire. The half dormant volcanoes kept the canyon and everything in it warm. The temperature only started to drop significantly about halfway up the canyon walls.

Dai played the light over the walls when they entered the next room. There were thick piles of dust in places along the walls, as if the few pieces of furniture that had stood there had crumbled to dust thousands of years ago. There was nothing noteworthy, so they entered the next room. In a row against one wall stood long, strange, rod-like weapons with knob-like ends that might have been guns but were too big and heavy-looking to be used by present-day humans. On shelves or recesses cut into the solid rock rested an assortment of dusty, smaller weapons, presumably hand weapons. Dai wondered how they operated, or more accurately, how they'd operated in ages long gone.

"I don't think any of those work anymore," Mouf whispered in awe, "but I'd like to take one of each to check them out."

"They are too big for us present-day humans. You can always come back to try your luck, but I think you will be disappointed. They look thousands of years old and so weird that you might point the lethal end at yourself and not know it until it's too late. I don't even see anything that remotely resembles a trigger, but one can always negotiate with researchers or museum authorities to buy them. There's another door. Let's see where it takes us."

Both forgot to breathe when Dai shone the light into the room. Recessed shelves contained figurines cut from crystal and precious stones, and they sparkled blindingly in the strong light. A gigantic crystal with a flat, smoothened top stood in the center of the room like a working desk. Dai stared in disbelief and awe. Did crystals naturally come this big in that lost, forgotten age when this planet was younger? he wondered.

Then he noticed a dusty, flimsy sheet of an unknown metal or metal alloy lying in the center of the flat space. Taking a deep breath, he moved closer and picked it up, then gently blew the dust from it. It was very light. He looked at it to see if anything was written on it. It could be valuable to the few scholars who were interested in the forgotten languages.

Dai gasped inaudibly when he found that he could read it. He recognized the old language he had been coached in, but this was an even older variation of that forgotten language. This could be from the same period as the treasure, because his mother had said she was able to read some inscriptions but not all.

"This is really something." Mouf's voice was awed, but there was a note in it that rang a warning bell in Dai's mind. He looked at Mouf, who was rubbing his left wrist. "What do you intend to do with it?"

Dai replied cautiously, "Perhaps we should report this find to the queen since this canyon may fall within her kingdom. You will be well rewarded, I should think. I'm taking this tablet that survived the passing of who knows how many centuries to see if I can decipher it. I have had some tuition in the forgotten languages. I'll put it back before we leave this place." No need to tell Mouf that he would be able to read it with a bit of concentration. "There's another door which means another room, so let's take a look at it." Dai's tiredness had shifted to the background. This was getting interesting.

The next and last chamber was filled with machinery that seemed, to Dai at least, to be communications equipment. This place was in a fairly well-preserved condition, and it seemed that the long-vanished race knew how to build equipment to last. He wondered if the mountains had interfered with signals to and from this equipment, which didn't seem to have used outside antennas—at least he didn't notice any when he approached, or perhaps the antennas had malfunctioned ages ago. If these machines could be restored to working order, it might revolutionize the current communication system.

"I wonder what these machines were used for." Mouf seemed to be excited, and Dai couldn't find fault with that. If the safety of the world wasn't at risk and he wasn't involved in it, he would have been excited, too.

Dai decided not to enlighten Mouf; he didn't think Mouf would believe him anyway. "Let's go back. I really need some sleep, but I want to try and read the inscription on this ancient tablet."

He couldn't read Mouf's facial expression, but it looked as if Mouf had stopped breathing for a moment. Dai was fighting fatigue again as he walked back rapidly with a silent Mouf behind him.

When they reached the "kitchen," as Dai thought of the front room, he put some wood on the fire because fire comforted him, and then sat down on the trolley, which he had pulled closer to the fire. He began to read slowly and silently.

58

Dai deciphered the tablet slowly so that he would be sure of the correct meaning of every word. It seemed to him that the ancient writer had put down his thoughts as they came into his mind, for they weren't in a coherent form or logical sequence. He read:

The airwaves are dead, and I don't think my equipment is at fault, for it is the very best money can buy. A few days after the ground shook and the planet reeled dizzily as if it was shifting orbit, my wife and son left in our flyer to check if any of our married children, relatives, and friends are still alive after this very frightening occurrence. They have not returned yet, and I fear the worst. I can only hope that they will still return despite my misgivings, but they are now too long overdue.

I elected to stay and look after our farm and our valuable collection of art and sculptures. Because everyone knows that cities are the main targets in every war, we came here to our country home when war was declared a month ago by the power-mad ruling priests.

I leave this note to explain my plight to anyone who may find this remote place. I don't think that I will survive very long and this civilization may also perish soon because the ground and perhaps the whole planet shakes severely at regular intervals. The heaving land is changing shape, but this sturdy dwelling was carved from solid rock and it will survive unless a volcano springs up near or underneath it. This previously lonely hillock in flat country is now a small foothill and is still gradually rising higher together with the cliffs of mountains being pushed out of the ground all around me.

It is getting colder as the land cools off without the incoming solar radiation from the sun. The sun, when I can see it through the black clouds, is smaller, and it rises and sets in the wrong place. The days are shorter. Even the gravity is heavier and it is difficult to walk without tiring rapidly. The river vanished and it looks as if the land there is sinking. Since the flyer is propelled by energy from the sun, I am very concerned about my wife and son. At least the craft doesn't require a runway.

My food and water supplies are depleted and I will have to go outside to hunt and see where the water went, but it is dangerous to venture too far, as I can see the carnivorous reptiles preying on each other and other warm-blooded animals. The fences disappeared weeks ago, and everything is being trampled. The dark, ominous clouds on the far horizon may be radioactive dust. I don't know what to do as the wind is blowing this way most of the time and the clouds are drawing nearer every short day. It is useless to run away, for there is nowhere else to go without swift transport. Mountains are rising almost overnight out of the grain fields.

If I do not survive, beneath this artificially created control crystal block is a small, concealed trapdoor that opens onto narrow stairs. Open the door by thinking it already done. The stairs lead to the main house and the real treasures we have so painstakingly accumulated for our family over many years. The camouflaged back door opens onto a narrow ledge, and the downward angle at the back is very steep in order to discourage criminals. If you have an honest heart, check if any of our sons and daughters have survived, and share this collection with them. It is valuable enough to let a hundred people live in luxury for half a century at the current prices. Tomorrow I will venture outside, for I have no other choice.

A list of unpronounceable names and addresses or locations followed, and the note ended with an equally mystifying signature and name. He wondered how this sad story had ended. If the man had come back, the tablet, or note, would have had an addendum.

Sorry, but it's a bit late to look for his family, Dai thought. Some people must have survived, for a derivation of this language was spoken up until a couple hundred years ago. But nowadays it was used by a select few of the very best scholars for studying old historic records and by the Fighters to pass secret or sensitive information over public, insecure communication units. Dai sighed and put the tablet down next to him on the trolley. He stood up and stretched his tired body.

"What does it say? Were you able to decipher those strange signs?"

There was an undertone of avarice in Mouf's voice, which

was not how Dai had come to know him. He decided to tell an outright lie, at least for now.

"I could guess the meaning of a word here and there. I studied an old language that I thought may be similar to this one. I think I'll take this tablet along and ask the linguists if they are able to read it."

"Well, please tell me what you understood." Mouf was almost dancing with anxiety, and Dai could understand his curiosity as he, too, would have been just as inquisitive had he been in Mouf's shoes.

"I'm guessing mostly and putting two and two together, understand? It seems that there was a war and the owner of this dwelling came here to hide. Maybe he brought the sculptures we saw with him. This country was flat and an awfully mighty bomb used near here changed the terrain. It awakened volcanoes, shaping the flat country into these mighty mountains and canyons. The process had only started when this tablet was left for us to find. I wish someone could read this thing, for I'm almost dying of curiosity, but I need to get some sleep at this point."

"Don't even think about turning around or reaching for your guns." It was Kuras's voice behind him. "I shall grant you both your wishes if you so much as twitch an ear, but first we'll get the real story out of you. It took you just too long to decide that you could only read a few words."

Dai was so tired he hadn't heard the woodsman's soft entrance. So this was the onlooker from afar, who clearly knew how to trail and stalk, which wasn't surprising. This wasn't a new situation for Dai, and he could retaliate quickly enough if necessary. Both men were within reaching distance, but he wanted information first. That was always the highest priority, and it could be vital. Those who think they have the upper hand are usually willing to explain their own cleverness. He could afford to wait while he put them at ease. Perhaps there was more to the situation than mere greediness.

"Can Mouf make us some tea while we talk? We only had supper and nothing to drink yet. I have a dry throat."

"First, take those guns you are so handy with out of your belt and hand them to Mouf, butts first." Dai did so with a hesitant show of reluctance.

321

"Raise your hands!"

Dai put his hands straight up into the air after grabbing the sleeves of his tunic under his bent fingers. They shouldn't be that observant, he hoped, otherwise he would have to kill them quickly without hesitation and without any information.

"Check him out, Mouf. He still has his knife and perhaps other hidden weapons." Mouf did, and he removed the hunting knife, but he neglected to pat Dai's elevated arms, which would have brought instant death to himself and Kuras. As it was, they still had a few minutes to enjoy the remainder of their lives.

"Why are you doing this?" Dai asked with an innocent voice. "I liked both of you, and I thought you were honest men." He really did like them, until Mouf became a shirker and Kuras snuck up on him. Now he fished for information.

"It's not a long story, Dai," Mouf replied. "We are tired of this hand-to-mouth existence. That gluttonous priest Hedra asked us if we knew about the treasure buried here by a mythical civilization. He told us that the priestess Justina and another man discovered it and were keeping it to themselves. We had already heard about it from a mountaineer who stayed overnight in our village about a year ago, but we thought he invented the story to get more ale, for he enjoyed free drinks. Anyway, Hedra promised to give us anything we wanted, even make us kings, if we could locate the treasure and lead him to it.

"When you came from her, we thought you could lead us to it, and we were right. Now that I have seen it, Hedra can go to hell, for that is where he belongs. The hog just wants to be filthy rich with someone else's sweat and without lifting a cowardly finger himself. I said too much slipped when we camped that night, but Kuras covered nicely for me."

I am ready to attack and distract this one nearest the entrance, Dai. Just let me know when you are ready.

Dai almost smiled. Mouf and Kuras had forgotten about the cat, or else they didn't know how loyal and lethal such cats were. Fortunately Mouf wasn't present when Dai had taught the nimble Koro to creep up on an enemy and rip his throat out.

I can kill both of them, but I want information first. I will tell you if I need you to screech or attack, for I don't want you injured. After tonight you will have to guard me when I sleep. Projecting his thoughts now came easier.

To Mouf and Kuras he said, "I'm disappointed in both of you. I really liked you both, and we could have been friends. I'm tired of carting a shamming Mouf around for days while he sleeps his addled head off. Do you mind if I lower my arms before they fall down and you decide that I'm attacking one of you?"

"Okay, you can lower your arms. Mouf, make us some tea as he asked, if you please. I've had something to eat, and I can do with something hot. Okay, Daiyus, start talking."

"Um, first tell me: did you take the guns to the village, Kuras, or don't you care about your people anymore?"

"Thanks to your brilliant idea, I did. And I gave the bearskin to Mouf's outsized wife. Satisfied?"

"No. Did you ask some of the men to guard, uh, the priestess Justina?" Dai was trying to waste some time so that he could get into a position to observe both of them a little easier. *Koro, do not stay directly behind Kuras.*

"Yes, I did. She once saved my life, and now that debt is paid."

"Thank you. Can I turn around? It feels too unnatural to talk to someone behind my back."

There was a moment's silence as if Kuras was weighing the thought. "Do it slowly, but step away from Mouf to the other side of the trolley while you're doing it. I'll shoot you in the hips if you make just one wrong move. We have heard how good the Fighting Priests are, and you implied that you are one of them. Now start talking if you want to live a while longer."

"The value of this treasure is vast—ask Mouf. So why not share it with me? Why do you want to hog it all?" Dai asked as he slowly stepped around the trolley. Mouf had piled almost all the wood on the fire, and the room was quite bright.

"You said you would give it to that high and mighty Surra!" Mouf almost yelled.

"Is that so?" Kuras asked in mock anger. "Talk!" He glared at Dai.

"Allow me one more question, please. Then I'll tell you what else the note said. How did you know that we found the treasure?"

Kuras laughed derisively. "Mouf, show him your wrist." When Mouf did, Dai knew why he had been rubbing it a while ago when it wasn't really necessary. A directional indicator/finder was strapped to his wrist. The moment it was switched on, Kuras knew he had to show up quickly.

"You two fooled me nicely," he complimented them to make them relax. It was the last compliment they would ever receive from anybody. "Did you two innocents even consider that when you disappear without a word, Hedra will send his hounds after you? I don't envy you your brief taste of a luxurious lifestyle, but I guess that's your problem."

He saw both stiffen, but he continued as if he was unconcerned.

"The tablet is evidence that this particular treasure is a private art collection from a forgotten era, perhaps a million or more years ago. This area was farmland then. The guy who wrote it knew he was going to die, but he didn't know his farm was going to change this much. That is really all the tablet discloses. This is not the treasure Hedra is after. See? I'm quite honest with you two backstabbers."

He saw both go red in the face, but now he was ready to draw the needler.

"Yes, the mountaineer you met and his mate stumbled across the *real* treasure, and Justina saw it twice. It's not far from here, and I think I will go and explore before going back. My understanding is that Hedra and his superiors could destroy the planet with what they will find in that vast cache."

Like the amateurs they were, Mouf and Kuras made the fatal mistake of taking their eyes off Dai by looking at each other, and that slight distraction was exactly what Dai had in mind. Maybe they were going to discuss the possibility of letting him live a while longer, but he wasn't interested in letting these two betrayers of trust enjoy that privilege any longer either.

Dai's sidestep to get out of the line of fire of Kuras' gun was very fast, but even as he moved, he flexed his left wrist and the slender gun jumped into his right hand. He shot Kuras first without aiming as he had practiced so many times that he had lost count. Then he just turned his wrist a little to fire a small explosive, poisonous needle into Mouf's heart.

The astonished expressions on their faces were familiar. He had seen it too many times to even think about it. He felt sad that such good men could so easily be corrupted by greed and the prospect of easy living. He sighed with regret. This was not an unusual story.

59

Dai felt let down. Mouf and Kuras could have been good friends and would have ended up extremely well off, but they chose greed over common sense. Oh well, it served no purpose to dwell on what could have been. He was used to being all by himself, with just an honest cat for company, but he felt the loss because they were competent and intelligent men.

I need to get some sleep, Koro. I'll drag their bodies out and heave them down the slope if they won't slide down.

I'll keep watch while you sleep. You can let me sleep on the trolley tomorrow. Will that be fine with you? I don't see much blood leaking out of them, Dai, but they died very quickly.

You're a treasure, Koro, and I love you as I love Kyr. Of course you can sleep on the trolley anytime you feel like it. The lazy Mouf won't ever have it all to himself again.

I'm glad I found you, Dai. The idle temple life was definitely not for me.

And I'm glad you thought me worthy of your companionship, Koro. Kyr looked after me when I was sent to Karna when I was two years old because she knew I was mentally handicapped when my memories were blocked to protect me from the wrath of an evil man. Tumar's mind was also damaged by evil people, and perhaps that is why Kyr wants to look after her to see that she comes to no harm. Her real choice of companions is Lur, but she likes Tumar. Sadly, she is getting old and slowing down, so that is another reason I'm glad you chose me, but I still love and miss her. After she gives birth to her kitten, she will live with Lur.

I miss Kyr, too, Koro thought to Dai. *She can be a real pain under the tail, but she asked me to spend some time away from the temple and learn from you and her before I got too plump and indolent. Since then she's taught me things I couldn't have dreamt of, and I do a lot of dreaming.*

She has lots of experience…and brains too, of course.

During the conversation, Dai tiredly dragged the bodies out one by one and let them roll down the steep slope. He made sure they disappeared into the struggling but encompassing vegetation at the bottom of the standalone, otherwise uninviting hill. He didn't want to attract attention to the hill, which had turned out to be a place full of unexpected surprises.

The smoke from the fire drifted away by way of an ingenious chimney. Dai dumped the tea into the fire, stacked everything neatly, and then slumped down on the blankets Mouf had loafed on. Soon after, he gratefully passed out.

He awoke reluctantly to drumming in his head. For a moment he thought that Kyr was a damned nuisance. Then he remembered where he was. He opened his eyes and saw a faint light around the doorway.

Koro told him, *Day is here, Dai, and I think it's time to get going. Scavengers dragged the bodies away during the night, but they were too big to chase away.*

That is a very good thing, Koro. I don't want anyone else to find this place, and I'm glad scavengers came to help us clean up.

Dai thought he should check the "main residence" while he had the chance, to see what needed to be guarded with so much care and, he was sure, expense. If he didn't, it would occupy his thoughts, and he couldn't afford to be distracted by such things. He took the last two pieces of dried meat and gave Koro one to chew on for breakfast while he was gone. He told the cat what he intended to do and that he would let him know if anything was not all right.

Dai tried to move the crystal block, which didn't look too heavy but apparently was. He tried to lift it, to no avail. The mechanism the tablet provided details about couldn't possibly still function after all this time, he thought. Disappointed, he gave up, stood back, and gazed directly at the offending crystal block. He wished that the door was already open for he didn't want to waste more time. Surprisingly, there was a shrieking groan, as if ancient, unused mechanisms were being overtaxed. The massive crystal block started to tilt slowly, accompanied by creaks and cracks of tortured old machinery. Dai grabbed the block to keep it from falling, for he didn't want it damaged, but it continued to tilt. He let go as he realized that the sculptured block was part of the trapdoor, and perhaps the controlling mechanism was embedded in the block of crystal to preserve it.

The creaking and groaning stopped when the side of the crystal block touched the floor. *A surprisingly enduring, ingenious piece of engineering*, he thought.

He switched his torch on and played the light over the upright trapdoor, which was plano-convex. The flat topside seemed part of the original rock floor, which was somehow welded to the block of crystal. They had a wonderful technology, and the mechanism still worked after all this time, he marveled as he shined the light down the stairs. *It might have been narrow for the original owners*, Dai thought, *and perhaps they had big feet and broad hips, but it's right for me with room to spare. They must have been humanoid at least. I wonder what they looked like.*

He descended slowly and carefully, scanning each centimeter of carved-out stone stair and wall for hidden surprises before he took the next step down. The stairs ended about seven or eight meters down in a high, broad passage that curved sharply to his left. If there were any traps, they didn't work after all this time, he thought. Logically there shouldn't be any, for any sane man wouldn't endanger his own family or legitimate visitors, but Dai had been taught to always proceed carefully and suspiciously in unfamiliar territory.

He ended up in an enormous room he guessed to be easily five meters high and ten by twenty meters wide. Perhaps it was a small reception room for them, but Dai thought it quite big. The floor was more or less clear of dust, and he guessed that the trapdoor and back door fit tightly and the filters still functioned well, since the air was neither stale nor musty.

He played the light over the floor first, since that was where he had to walk if he wanted to proceed. There were scattered heaps of dry matter that might have been perishable material ages ago. This must have been a lounge, he thought. Here and there were extra-large frameworks of what could be a metal alloy or imperishable plastic that looked like parts of huge chairs and tables. Then he flashed the light along the walls, starting on his right.

In the middle of the right-hand wall, a very large, almost-black, flat, square screen was embedded. It could be a viewer of broadcast programs, he thought, and it had withstood the ages intact—on the surface at least. There was nothing else of note in the room, but two open doorways led out of it. He walked over to the nearest after checking the floor. He didn't want to disturb anything or kick up a cloud of these powdery remains of…whatever it had been.

It was a bedroom. Chest-high, thick, sturdy, metal-alloy frames for two huge beds stood next to each other against one wall. The powdery remains of the material the mattresses were made of had sifted through the mesh onto the floor. Dai didn't enter the room, but he estimated that the frames were over four meters long and two across. He felt very small in comparison. There were wardrobes made of some kind of plastic or metal alloy, but he didn't even think of opening them. He was only interested in a quick, cursory inspection. He entered a doorway to the left and was greeted by a smooth plastic-like bath that could be used as a paddling pool by preteens.

The other doorway from the lounge led to a huge kitchen. Dai felt like a tiny tot lost among adult furniture. The cupboards were brownish-red and made of what Dai could only think of as a kind of plastic, and there was something that could be called a stove. Six still-functional chairs, the seats on a level with his heart, were pushed beneath a table he could walk upright under. Dai opened a large roller-drawer at the bottom of a cabinet and almost laughed. It was filled with well-preserved cutlery, and he thought the table knives could be used as short, two-handed broadswords if anyone still used those ancient weapons. The forks could be used to cultivate a garden. He didn't pick up any of the eating utensils, but closed the drawer. A glance at what might be a wash-up sink reminded him that he needed a bath. He wondered how water was obtained and where it came from in that bygone age. Three other open doorways, one in each wall, led from the kitchen.

The first doorway led to another, bigger bedroom, which he supposed might have been used by the children or guests; it had the remains of ten beds. An open door to his left led to another bathroom. He retreated and entered the second room that led from the kitchen.

It was a sort of storeroom with shelves of the same durable plastic or metal. Strange-looking guns for giants were neatly arranged on grooves near the doorway. He didn't touch them, but he really yearned to examine them. There were empty

329

plastic-type crates and empty recesses or shelves that could have contained the food mentioned in the note. On the far side, an oblong crystal was embedded in an oval of dark metal or rock. That should be the back door, Dai thought, but he didn't approach it.

He supposed that the remaining room would contain the alleged valuable treasure. He entered and played the light on the floor.

The room was at least twice the size of the lounge. Dai gasped in unexpected astonishment. Row upon row of smooth, deep recesses cut out of the solid rock along the walls were filled with miniature replicas of strange and familiar animals and statuettes of humans. In the torchlight they sparkled in all colors, from maroon to a clear brilliance, as if they were cut from various types of precious stones. There were also tiers of bigger sculptures and figures of humans, birds, and strange animals, standing or lying flat. Together they shone with such brilliance that it threatened to blind Dai. The far wall was lined with dark plastic or alloy chests—which might contain jewels or coins, he thought.

I'll come back one day and check everything in detail before I decide what to do with this breathtaking treasure. This really is a timeless treasure, and Mouf and Kuras definitely missed out on something so wonderful as to defy imagination, but I just can't feel sorry for those backstabbing snakes.

Dai was fascinated, and he entered the room almost against his will. He slowly walked down the rows, starting from the right and shining the light up and down from wall to floor at every step he took to see what there was or where he was going to put his suddenly clumsy-feeling feet. Halfway to the back, he was drawn to a very brilliant, dark-green flame. He stopped in front of the small emerald statuette, about twenty centimeters high, and stared in fascination. It was carved from an emerald as thick and almost as long as his forearm, he thought, or perhaps it was artificially created, like the crystals; but what astonished him was that the face was an exact replica of Tumar's. *These ancients must have been our ancestors, only much bigger than us*, he thought.

He just couldn't help it—he took the figure and put it in an inner pocket for safekeeping. He felt he was entitled to it, and it

330

was another gift for Tumar. He passed along the other shelves and rows and took a dark red one, which could be ruby, and three others, each a different color and all resembling Tumar. He didn't open any of the chests. That could wait for another time. He didn't care about wealth, but he wanted a few days to examine every artifact one by one before he made the location known to Surra or whomever he thought suitable to receive this fabulous collection of ancient masterpieces. He felt tempted to collect some for himself, but thought that should be left for a future, leisurely visit.

Dai returned to the upper rooms and closed the trapdoor by picturing it as he first saw it—closed. He glanced at his watch and saw that only about an hour had passed since he'd entered the "main residence." As he walked to the front room, he let Koro know he was on his way back.

He carefully wrapped the five precious figurines one by one into a spare, albeit somewhat smelly, shirt and then thrust the bundle into a separate pocket of the rucksack. He would make sure they came to no harm.

Then he packed the extra guns on the trolley, one of which was Tumar's—the present from the former king. Koro said he couldn't sense any human around, but Dai also carefully searched the surrounding area with his senses because he was still developing the new ability. Then he checked the canyon with a pair of powerful binoculars he had taken from a body about eight days ago.

The canyon was deserted, the same as the day before. He invited Koro to jump onto the trolley and take a nap before he took it down the slope. He trotted in the direction they had been going the previous day. People too discouraged from staying around or warded off were becoming mighty scarce, and perhaps that was why Mouf had feigned the injury. Perhaps he'd thought he might as well take an undeserved holiday at Dai's expense, or maybe he had reasoned that Dai would disclose the location of the relics if he was overly tired.

Dai had a general idea of where the much-sought-after legacy from the distant past could be found, but it wasn't just around the corner, as he had implied. The day before, through a gap made by a side canyon, he had recognized a peculiar mountaintop from the details his mother had impressed on his brain, but he wanted to be sure that the interlopers—in this canyon at least—had been induced to depart for safer pastures.

He found the main campsite of the invaders later that same afternoon. It was completely deserted, and from the impressions on the ground, he gathered that big transporters had been used to evacuate them. It indicated that influential and wealthy individuals or organizations were the moving power behind this secretive invasion. They must have a lot of clout, or maybe corrupt governments were involved as well.

Dai ran on until he found a stream a few kilometers farther on, where he replenished his water containers. Then he left the trolley grounded to hunt with Koro. He had to live off the land, for his meager supplies had been depleted some days ago. The late Mouf hadn't restrained himself when it came to food.

He returned from his hunt with a young antelope, which he let slide to the ground, then gathered tubers to make a nourishing stew and dry wood to make a bed of coals to dry the surplus meat overnight. There was plenty of firewood left, for the campers had brought modern camping stoves instead of relying on nature for cooking purposes, or maybe they hadn't had time for leisurely companionship around the fire.

Dai built the fire, then skinned the buck and cut the meat into thin strips, which he salted and hung on the fresh sticks he had cut for that purpose. He then placed them on forked sticks over the coals to slowly dry off. Part of the liver went to Koro, and the rest he cut up, seasoned, and threw into the cooking pot with wild onions and a few tubers. Mouf had shown him which ones were safe to eat and how to prepare them if they couldn't be eaten raw. Dai quickly built a separate, smaller fire for the pot.

Dai planned to move fast from now on because he needed to see whether the treasure was still undiscovered, and, if it was easy to gain entrance, he wanted to see just what the insidious legacy consisted of. Then he would try to create another rockfall to conceal the entrance for another few centuries. Like Lur, he sadly knew that their civilization definitely wasn't ready for it. Avarice and greed were all too rampant. Killing to achieve ends still came too easily and cheaply.

Then he would go back to so-called civilization and help rid the planet of Hedra and his fellow conspirators. Dai was sure that Hedra would by now be in charge—unofficially of course—of Bojon and the palace; Heltos and Sorcuk would be cunningly manipulated by a master. If Hedra encountered opposition, he would resort to his preferred methods: force and torture. Hedra seemed to enjoy the latter; it was his favorite method to overcome any show of resistance.

As he sat by the fire, Dai remembered how he had sensed something else in Surra's offer to accompany him, but he wasn't sure what to make of it. He remembered Gemur's quick resentment and hoped that Surra hadn't decided she no longer liked the father of her son. If he were in Gemur's shoes and really loved Surra the way the guy was supposed to, he would have found a way to contact and reassure her years ago.

He liked her well enough and could easily come to love her, but he didn't want to marry a throne that had no meaning for him. He wasn't interested in that kind of life.

I should rethink my attitude toward Surra before we meet again, he thought, *but there is plenty of time to think about it and figure it out*. Then he thought that the presence of Ekaasi, Nogalithe, and Murima the cook at the camp would soothe Gemur's jealousy—if it was jealousy, for Dai was sure that Surra and the former king had accepted his explanation for not wanting to have anything to do with the ruling of Bojon.

Then, unexpectedly, he thought of Tumar and how he missed her silent, confident, and uncomplaining presence. She would make a good companion for someone who could appreciate her quiet, confident nature. He took the tiger's tail out of the pocket in his rucksack on the trolley and felt the pliable softness he had kneaded it into. In Bojon, he thought, he would look for the right clasp or buckle for it. He put it away again with care.

The canyon was strangely silent and he felt alone. The larger animals and those that preyed on them had departed for quieter regions, free from human interference and uncalled-for harassment. Dai missed the two men he had been forced to kill, he missed Surra, and he missed Tumar most of all. Koro was trustworthy and the best of companions, but he couldn't tell or appreciate any silly human jokes.

Finally the food was ready, and he ate with relish, as only a hungry person can.

60

Twilight descended on the canyons as Dai finished his supper. He pushed the trolley closer to the smoldering bed of coals and went to sleep. Koro played the role of silent sentry, but Dai awoke at intervals to replenish the fire and to check whether the meat was dry enough to hang over the strings he had strung between the trolley's front and back railing. Koro drummed him awake just after midnight.

Something is approaching slowly. It is not well and very thirsty and hungry. The smell of the meat over the fire attracted it from far away. I cannot sense what it is, but the mind is not that of animal or normal humankind as I know them. I sense only an undefeatable will to survive because of an objective it has to reach.

Koro's senses had been sharpened to the point of perfection, and he learned surprisingly quickly for a citified cat, Dai thought. In fact, he had become Kyr's equal in that department in only ten days, which not even Kyr could equal. *He's a natural and he doesn't even know it.*

Koro's description sounded weird and made Dai curious and suspicious. It could be that weird creatures had survived in these remote, unexplored canyons. As a safety precaution, he took the gun Kuras had intended to use to kill him, for it was of large caliber and could be adjusted to rapid fire by flipping a lever and still had a full clip. He felt a moment's regret that it wasn't the old percussion type because the racket that old guns made served to scare wild creatures away. He thought he must obtain more ammunition for it, but it wasn't worth going back to check what was left of every malodorous cadaver.

He asked Koro to protect the trolley and the meat as he moved away from the revealing light of the fire. In one hand, he held a torch ready to be switched on at the required moment, and he probed the surrounding area with all his natural and developing mental senses.

He sensed and heard the stumbling creature coming from the direction he planned to take in the morning, but he was puzzled. The stumbling sounds were made by a two-legged humanoid, he thought. He couldn't sense anything that felt animal-like. All he could detect was a fierce determination to stay alive and on its feet. Then an intense thought leaked out of the tightly closed mind as it started to lose coherence: *Must survive…cannot give up…get to Lur.* The man seemed to lose what little consciousness and determination he had left at that instant, and Dai knew that the stranger had lost consciousness, but he also knew exactly where to find him.

Dai didn't even consider how he was able to catch the stranger's thoughts. He found himself running in that direction before he knew what he was doing. The mention of his mother's name spurred him to full speed. Who knew his mother by her real name except the noxious Hedra? He must know who the man was and why he was so determined to find his mother, for there couldn't be another Lur anywhere in these canyons.

He hurdled over the stream and found the man, dressed in strange, dusty clothes, lying on his stomach within fifty steps of the stream. *So near and yet so far from succor,* he thought as he turned the man over and felt his pulse. It was beating slowly. He lifted the man to a sitting position. Then he saw that the man's fingers on both hands were burned, as if he had touched red-hot wires some time ago. He wasn't very heavy and groaned deeply, as if he wanted to talk, when Dai picked him up. He might be injured, Dai thought, and he walked back through the stream to the fire as rapidly as he could with the stranger cradled in his arms.

Dai put him down on his back near the fire and covered him with the still warm blanket he had been using. He wished he'd brought a sleeping bag, but it never got cold in the canyons, according to the late Mouf. He stoked the fire and put some water in the kettle to boil. While he waited, he hung the pieces of heat-dried and cooked meat over the strings on the trolley.

Once that was done, he wet the square of rough cloth he used for drying himself and cleaned the man's face. He hoped the man wasn't too far gone to revive, and he was reluctant to pour water down a weak, unconscious man's throat. He felt the pulse again. It was very slow. He started to wipe the man's arms and neck with the wet cloth. If he weakens more, Dai thought, I'll have to take a chance and pour a little water down his throat and make him swallow it.

Then he slowly and carefully checked the man's body for broken bones, but everything felt solid. He put some ointment on the half-healed hands and fingers, but he didn't think it necessary to bandage them. The burns were a few days old and had started to heal. Dai suddenly wondered if this was a victim of a rare air crash, which might account for the burnt fingers. In that event, there might be more survivors in urgent need of attention.

Dai pinched the man's forearm skin, but it took a while to return to normal. *He's severely dehydrated and has lost a lot of weight. I wonder how long he's been without water and food,* Dai thought and marveled at the man's supernatural determination to carry on until he dropped. *I think I'll dunk him into the stream if his condition worsens or if he is still alive by morning. I admire the limitless courage this man has demonstrated. But all his courage and determination will avail him nothing if he means harm to my mother.*

It was an unwritten law that one must aid those in need out in the wilderness, where help is seldom available. Dai would have to make sure that every available container was filled with water when he went after survivors in the morning. He didn't even think of going back the way he had come. His mother was the nearest help, and she was about two hundred kilometers away. The stranger was far gone, and if he was still alive by the following night, he might stay alive long enough to make it worth the effort to get him to her.

While he was so near the legacy from the past, he might as well make an effort to see if it was still undisturbed. It wasn't far away, if his sense of direction was correct, but if this man was a survivor of a crash, he must go and see if there were others still alive. Any kind of crash with modern air-cars or aircraft was a very rare occurrence and usually had a reason, such as sabotage or sloppy maintenance. He wished the stranger could tell him whether it was worth going to investigate.

Dai poured a handful of strengthening herbs into the boiling kettle and let it boil for a few minutes before he took it off the fire. Ekaasi had taught him to always carry a small bag of the herbs and to replenish or add to it when he came across the rare herb. He rummaged in the late Mouf's rucksack for his beaker and then washed it before he poured some of the brew into it to cool. It might be a good idea to start early, before it was light, he thought.

On impulse, he kneeled on his right knee, lifted the unconscious man's upper body, and supported his back with his left knee. He kept the head almost vertically in the crook of his left elbow and held the steaming beaker under his nose with his right hand. He was just about to put the beaker down when the man groaned almost inaudibly and coughed faintly. His mouth dropped open, and Dai let his head tip back a bit before he poured a little of the brew into it, then closed the jaw with the hand of his supporting arm.

Surprisingly, the man swallowed the few drops and coughed again through his nose. The man's obstinate will to live was amazing. Dai offered the beaker to the closed lips again. The man's unconscious mind must have responded to the offer, or perhaps he thought he was dreaming. The mouth dropped open again, and Dai tipped another half mouthful into it. He closed it again with his fingers, and the man swallowed. In this way Dai let him finish half the beaker, then gently lowered him to the blanket. It would be fatal to let him drink too much the first time—for Dai could just about guess how long the stranger had been without any form of liquid—but it might be enough to save his life.

The stranger's pulse increased slightly, and Dai asked Koro to watch the man and call him if there was any change. Then he stretched out on the other blanket, but on the other side of the fire. He really had to catch up on his sleep, since he had been denied such luxury before the intruders departed this part of the canyon and because of Mouf's faked weakness.

He was drummed awake by Koro just before sunrise. The man seemed to be sleeping, and he checked his pulse again. It was stronger. Again Dai marveled at the stranger's indomitable will to keep living and moving despite the awful odds he must have encountered. He must have a stronger constitution than was evident from his emaciated appearance and an awfully good reason to drive himself past ordinary endurance.

Dai shook his head again, then took stock of the stranger's clothing in the faint light of early dawn. It was neatly made of some unusual material, and it could be some sort of uniform. There was a knife and a strange-looking handgun in an equally

337

strange holster buckled around the emaciated hips. Dai had never seen anything remotely resembling that type of gun, and he suppressed the urge to touch it, since it might be booby-trapped, like his own guns.

He took an empty bag and walked to the stream to search for edible tubers and wild onions along the banks. He would make a nourishing stew for breakfast while he waited for the stranger to wake up by himself. Otherwise he would try to let him drink more of the cold brew before he ventured farther up the canyon. He knew he couldn't risk leaving the man alone for even a short while, but thankfully Koro was there to assist and would call him if he was needed.

When the bag was full, he returned and found Koro sitting with his eyes locked on the stranger. Koro and Dai knew each other quite well by now, and Dai wondered what was going on. But he knew better than to interfere by asking stupid questions. He stoked the fire and put a pot with water, salt, and a few selected herbs on it. The vegetables and tubers were already washed, and he sliced a few into the pot—enough for two grown men and Koro. He sliced meat into the pot while he waited for Koro to tell him what was going on.

Koro spoke at last. *This human has a very strange mind, and I don't think there is another one quite like him. He tossed around, and I tried to send soothing thoughts into the brain as Kyr taught me. Then, strangely, his brain told me that it was okay and that the body and personality just needed time, sleep, and water before it could wake up. I almost jumped out of my skin. I arched my back and felt I should take off fast and run, but you said that one must die only once, at the end of his life, and not ten times every day, so I calmed down and stayed to talk to the human's brain. You can give him more of that herb water, and the body will drink it under the direction of the brain, but don't give him food until he wakes up because he won't be able to chew and would likely choke on it. It is too weak to cough, the brain said.*

Koro watched the stranger curiously while Dai gave him the herb water, following the same procedure as before. This time he allowed him almost a full beaker before he stopped. Half an hour later, he repeated the process with the same amount. The man's heartbeat was increasing, and Dai prepared another kettle of the stuff. He was anxious to get going and would have traveled without breakfast, as he and Mouf had done the previous ten days. A nourishing supper was all his body required to stay strong.

When the brew was ready, he removed it from the fire to cool while he dished up the stew for a rare breakfast treat for Koro and himself. After he had washed everything and filled every canteen and container with fresh water, he secured the brew and the remaining stew. Nothing would spill much unless he stopped or started abruptly. Then he arranged the blanket he had used on the trolley and gently lifted the stranger onto it. The other blanket he shook vigorously to remove the dust before he covered the man with it.

He made sure the fire was doused thoroughly before he asked Koro to jump up to sleep or keep in touch with the brain of the stranger, or both. He adjusted the floating height of the trolley to one meter and grasped the thill in reverse. Then, instead of pulling the trolley as usual, he pushed it because he wanted to watch the man so he wouldn't roll off the trolley by accident if he suddenly woke up or tossed about.

Dai walked for an hour to give his digestive functions a chance to complete their work. There was no clearly marked trail, so he followed the faint scuff marks made by the stranger on the hard ground, more or less in the middle of the canyon. Perhaps he could find out where the man came from. At first he found it a bit difficult to steer the trolley, but after he had secured the thill upright to the front rail, he spread his arms wide apart on the horizontal bars to steer it. After the first hour, he jogged for another hour before stopping to give the man a full beaker of the brew. The man's pulse was now almost normal, and Dai thought that Ekaasi definitely knew her stuff.

From then on he ran at his normal pace with the trolley before him. Then the canyon widened, and the terrain became bleak, dusty, and bare. Dai ran on the stranger's faint tracks, still roughly in the middle of the canyon, which he estimated to be more than two kilometers wide at this point. The sparse, thorny scrub vegetation hinted at shallow soil. In the far distance, the canyon made a gradual turn to the east. But perhaps it was just another of the numerous twists that were characteristic of these long canyons.

Dai had slowed to a walk when a narrow, sandy canyon joined abruptly from the west. In the undisturbed sand, he saw the tracks left by the stranger clearly for the first time. Dai was astonished. The tracks were uneven, indicating that the stranger already staggered badly when he'd passed this sandy point. His esteem for the man jumped sky high. Either the man had the courage and determination of a hundred men, or he had a mission so important he would kill himself to reach his objective. Even so, Dai thought, if he meant harm to his mother, the man's suffering would have been in vain. Either he would kill him, or his mother would. He did not doubt that she would or could, for he had shared her thoughts and knew she stayed in training. She, too, had killed when she had to, but she preferred to heal bodies and minds instead of destroying them.

On the other hand, if the man was a survivor of a crash and was the only one capable of moving, the chance that anyone else was still alive was clearly just wishful thinking. A look at the man's hands this morning told him that the burns were at least five or six days old. If that was anything to go by, he was wasting his time by going any farther along the tracks.

Dai looked at his watch and saw that he had run for more than two hours without giving the stranger the life-restoring liquid. He estimated he had covered about twenty-five kilometers, which was a bit slow, but he needn't hurry now. He had already decided he was wasting his time if he thought there were more survivors waiting to be rescued—unless, of course, they had a source of water nearby.

He gradually brought the trolley to a halt. It was hot, and he was sweating profusely. Koro was sprawled on his left side and snoring faintly. Dai drank some water and then administered more of the brew to the unconscious stranger. He wished the man would come to so he could find out if he should go on to rescue anyone else. As if responding to his wish, the stranger groaned deeply and opened his eyes.

Shock registered briefly in his eyes when he saw Dai, but then he relaxed. Dai saw fierce, dark-gray orbs regarding him without astonishment. The man must have learned to control his facial expressions, he thought, and the intense eyes expressed the man's fierce will to survive against all odds. Dai liked what he saw reflected in the eyes. The stranger tried to speak, but only croaks came out of the dry throat.

Dai offered the beaker, which was still about half full, and said, "I'm glad you came to, sir. I'll hold you up while you finish the rest of this beaker. But first a question. Just nod or shake your head slightly to answer. You seem to be the victim of an air crash. If so, are there any other survivors?"

Dai watched the stranger closely. He tried again to speak, then shook his head slowly with immense effort. Dai thanked him and let him have the rest of the beaker, which he drank slowly with Dai holding it at his lips. The stranger's eyes closed abruptly, and then he went to sleep, or perhaps he lost consciousness again. Dai put the beaker down and gently made him comfortable. The man didn't behave like a criminal or enemy except for the brief flicker of shock, which almost hadn't registered in his eyes, and Dai didn't sense enmity, only gratitude.

It was just past one o'clock. Although the joining canyon looked like just a giant sandy crack in the side of the wide canyon he had been following, it seemed to run in the direction he wanted to go. He turned west into it and started to jog again at a relaxed pace.

61

The smaller canyon was strangely silent as he jogged on, but he wasn't surprised because he hadn't seen animal tracks in the undisturbed sand since he had turned into it. Even the sounds of birds and insects were absent. Animals tended to stay where water was within easy reaching distance, and this sandy side canyon was really arid, which he hadn't expected; still, he was used to nature's vagaries. He ran through the parched country until late afternoon, when he came to the first cluster of trees he had seen since he'd turned into this canyon. He slowed down gradually and then stopped.

He had followed the most level part of the canyon floor, roughly in the middle, and was only about a hundred meters from the rocky walls on his left. The sheer granite walls of the canyon on both sides didn't promise the possibility of caves or hollows as far as his eyes could see. It was getting late.

Dai didn't think he would find a safe haven for the night, and this clump of almost-stunted trees offered dry wood for a fire and a promise of more than enough to take along. Fire would have to provide protection during the night, which meant little or no sleep for Dai. He really missed Mouf, who had been a good companion until he'd stupidly got himself slightly wounded—or perhaps that slight wound was prearranged. He didn't think he would trust another man soon.

Dai didn't sense anything out of the ordinary, but he wasn't sure, because he felt that something wasn't quite as it should be. Perhaps it was the absence of sentient life. He told Koro how he felt and asked him to check the area to the front for life, while he gathered wood and started a fire.

After stretching his muscles lazily but thoroughly, Koro jumped off and galloped away to exercise other muscles. Unlike most of his kind, he liked to run, and he bounded along exuberantly. At first, like Kyr, he only ran full out when it was necessary to stay alive, but when he found that he could outrun Dai, he really went for it with gusto. Unfortunately, Dai always caught up when Koro tired, which was always too soon to suit the cat; he believed no human should be able to catch up with him if he didn't want to be caught up with, not even the partner he had chosen, so he worked on improving his stamina with every opportunity.

While he galloped joyously, he scanned the area all around him with his eyes and other senses by moving his head from side to side. Like Dai, he didn't hear or sense anything, and that made him uneasy. It was unnatural, as Dai had implied, and he didn't want surprises for himself and the partner he had come to love.

After Dai had carefully lowered and grounded the trolley, he collected fallen branches as fast as he could. He stacked near the trolley quite a heap that could be loaded in a few minutes. Once he was satisfied he had more than enough firewood, he started a fire. Then he poured the last of the brew into the beaker and fed it to the stranger. Dai was worried. The man's pulse was strong, and by now he should have come to again. He might be tough, but only he knew how long he had been without food and liquids.

This man needs medical attention, he thought, *and not what little I can do for him. His body should be receiving nutrition and fluid replacement through an intravenous drip, for he is suffering from severe dehydration and might not survive for long. Nevertheless, I have to check that other canyon on the way back before I can make a speedy effort to get him to Lur and then to a clinic in Bojon. I don't think they will still be on the lookout for me, but I can always wear some sort of a disguise. I wonder if Karna included the aging cream I requested in the package he delivered to Nogalithe. Then again, he never forgets and always delivers what he promises.*

Dai put water into the kettle and set it to boil to make a fresh brew for his patient, and then slowly ate the cold stew he had saved for the stranger. When he was finished, he cleaned the pot, poured water in it, and put it on the fire. He felt like some bitter coffee for a change, but that could wait a while. He wondered what Koro was doing, but he didn't make contact with him because he might distract his attention at the wrong moment.

When Koro felt a slight trembling in the ground, his hard gallop changed to a wary trot. He held his head high and still moved it warily from side to side to check a wide area, but he was ready to break off and skedaddle with a moment's notice. He heard a strange, faint rumbling unlike anything he'd ever heard in his two years of life and almost stopped in alarm. The hair on his back rose involuntarily, and he felt an instinctive urge to arch his back, lift his tail up straight into the darkening sky, and run back as fast as his legs could carry him. But he had resolved to live as Dai and Kyr did and not to die mentally every day, so he trotted alertly, if hesitantly, using all his natural senses, as Kyr had taught him. He sensed or smelled nothing, and then he couldn't even hear himself trotting because the faint thunder had suddenly increased to an almighty roar. He could smell water and knew he was approaching the source of that sense-dulling din.

Koro sensed he must halt and did so immediately. He always looked where he was going, but the deafening thunder and his apprehension had distracted him. He was shocked when he realized he had stopped about a meter from a seemingly bottomless chasm. His eyes traveled to his feet. He saw that he stood on solid rock, but he refused to take another step forward to see how steep or deep this drop into eternity was. It was impossible to see downward anyway because the chasm was already shrouded in darkness, so instead he checked to see if there was any obvious way to get past this obstruction.

On one side the chasm ended against the sheer side of the canyon wall; on the other side, it might be scalable, but if one slipped, one would drop a long way down into a mighty mass of water that came from the north and fell down into the black, bottomless pit in front of him—or so it seemed to Koro. It made him dizzy just to think about it. He turned abruptly and fled. Dai could come and investigate it himself if he was interested. It was no place for a lonely cat all by himself. No wonder all the animals and birds shied away from this canyon.

On his way back, he looked for rodents, but even they avoided this place, he noticed. It was already dark when he trotted into the temporary camp. Dai had made fresh stew, and Koro ate a generous portion while he silently related what he had seen.

Dai said they would go see in the morning. He somehow had to get past this obstruction, for the place he was looking for should only be a few kilometers beyond the waterfall. He believed this was the waterfall his mother had shown him in his mind, but she must have seen it from a distance on the other side. He didn't realize he was so near his objective, since this was unfamiliar territory, and right now he just couldn't get enthusiastic about exploring these wild canyons much farther.

Dai had just finished his second cup of bitter coffee when the stranger groaned and rolled onto his right side, as if to expose his front to the fire. Koro said the human was going to wake up, as the brain had just told him that the personality was taking over again. Dai got up to push the trolley closer to the fire and then added a few sticks. He poured brew into the beaker and set it to one side to cool. Then he poured the last of the coffee into his own beaker and watched the stranger's face while he sipped the bitter brew. Dai often wondered why he liked the vile-tasting stuff, but he had developed a taste for it.

The stranger cleared his throat as if testing whether he still had a throat to clear. Then he took a deep, shuddering breath and opened his eyes slowly, as if afraid that his nose had betrayed him.

"Welcome back to the insane world of the living, sir," Dai said gently. "I was just beginning to despair when you decided to stir again."

The stranger tried to sit up, and Dai helped him to a comfortable position with his back against the trolley's back rail. The man cleared his throat again and tried to speak, but Dai held the beaker to his lips. He drank slowly, obviously controlling himself not to gulp, while he held Dai's hand with weak, trembling fingers.

The man had obviously gone without water before, and when he tried to push Dai's hand away after a few mouthfuls, Dai told him he could finish it all because he had drunk about three full beakers during the day. The man's face expressed astonishment, but he gratefully finished the beaker.

Dai put it to one side and said, "Now, sir, we'll let that settle for a while. Then I will give you more and a little food. I can see that you've starved and thirsted before, so I don't have to tell you to take it slow. You'll obviously want to know where you are and how I found you, and I'd like to know who you are and where you came from, but take your time to recover and let me do the talking for now."

He knew how to put men at ease, usually to make them relax just before killing them. Dai ladled some of the stew into a spare dish and put it next to the man. He added a spare fork, the only one he had.

"Try a taste of my away-from-home cooking whenever you feel brave enough to take the chance. The pot was prepared for you, so just help yourself. This kettle has about two beakers full of that strength-giving brew left." He poured a beaker full and put it and the kettle within the man's reach on the trolley. "My name is Daiyus, but you call me Dai right from the start. I have an honest admiration for courage in any individual, man or animal, and you have enough for at least a dozen.

"I found you at about four this morning, about fourteen hours ago. You collapsed near my camp, just about fifty steps from a shallow stream. The cat"—Dai pointed to Koro and saw the man's eyes widen a bit—"sensed you coming and woke me up. His name is Koro, and he was brave and reckless enough to team up with me about a month ago.

"I was coming this way, the way you came from, on an urgent mission that I must try to complete, so I brought you along with me. I thought that since you came from the same direction I intended to travel, I might as well check whether there were any other survivors. The nearest help is about three days away if one has the stamina or an urgent reason to hurry. Koro told me just now that a massive waterfall blocks this canyon. If I can find a way past it, I can complete my mission tomorrow or the day after, and then I will take you to where you will get better medical attention than my primitive ministrations. If I can't get past, I will have to take the roundabout route I came today, and that may add another day or two before I can get you to the nearest help.

"I'm sorry, but our safety and welfare is of lesser importance right now. The world is just about ready to plunge into an all-out war because of a few greedy, uncaring individuals or governments. They are willing to destroy our world based on a rumor of a dangerous legacy left by a long-forgotten, unknown civilization. The legacy may be buried in this same canyon a few kilometers past this waterfall, and as far as I know, they have been unable to locate it. I must check if it is still undiscovered or

346

whether another rockfall has exposed it again.

"Where you briefly woke up this afternoon, I came across your tracks, and you were already staggering badly, but you continued on for about another thirty kilometers before you finally collapsed from dehydration and exhaustion. I think you were too far gone to be able to crawl the fifty or so steps or hear or smell the water, but perhaps your subconscious mind did. I think it was your indomitable determination not to give up that brought you that far. The chances were about one in several trillion that I was in the right place at the right moment and that Koro was there to sense your approach. I would have only found you about three or four hours later, and by then it might have been too late."

The man cleared his throat and croaked through dried, cracked lips, "I want to thank you, young man, and you too, Koro. I thought you reminded me of someone I knew long ago and that I was hallucinating when you asked me about survivors. Ah, yes, I was alone, so don't worry about survivors or dead bodies. When I regain some strength, I will tell you an amazing story that you may find hard to believe. I don't remember much of what happened after the crash, but I remember only too well every single thing that happened before." He stopped and licked his parched lips.

"Please eat as much as you comfortably can and drink that herb concoction as often as you can, sir," Dai said. "I have enough of those herbs left to prepare another kettleful in the morning. Of course you know that sleep is now important. I can't wait to hear your story, sir, but only when you have rested. The moon may come up a bit earlier tomorrow morning, and perhaps the light will be bright enough to allow me to go and check out this mighty waterfall Koro was telling me about.

"You were not attacked or followed by a wild beast yesterday or last night. I didn't find tracks or any sign of a living animal, bird, or insect at all this afternoon. It's unbelievable, but I'm guessing we are safe for the night, and Koro will be our sentry. We have this handy arrangement that he sleeps all day while we travel, and I get to sleep all night when allowed, which unfortunately hasn't worked out too favorably for me lately."

Dai helped make him comfortable just before he passed out again. Dai put the food and the kettle down near the fire to keep it lukewarm but within reach of the stranger. Then he asked Koro to wake him up if anything did not seem right and, if the stranger woke up, to tell him to drink and eat, assuming he could still communicate with a cat when he was conscious.

62

Koro drummed him awake in the early hours of the morning when sleep was deepest and the night its coldest. Dai was awake in an instant and ready to grab the gun next to him. He heard an eerie moaning sound rise and fall, and the hairs on the nape of his neck stirred. Koro came and sat down tightly against him.

I am not afraid, Dai, but I feel more comfortable closer to you. What is that sound?

Dai put his arm across the cat's back and rubbed his pelt with affection. *I like you to sit so close to me, Koro, for that's what friendship is about. I do not know what causes that weird noise as I have never heard anything like it before. It sounds like a million lost souls.*

The fire was almost cold, and the coals underneath the ash were just a feeble glow. Dai blew some of the ash away and then added a handful of dry brush and blew on the coals again and again until they started to smoke. When they finally burst into flame, he added thicker sticks until he had a merry fire going. He considered making some tea or coffee before he investigated, for it might take a couple of hours.

He heard a cough from the trolley and a few grunts. The fire was bright enough to illuminate the figure struggling to rise. Dai was at his side immediately and helped him lean against the back rail again.

"Hell," the stranger grunted between clenched teeth, "I'm so weak I can't even blink my eyes if my life depended on it. You're an early riser, Dai, or did that weird moaning sound wake you up?" His voice was stronger, no longer a croak.

"No, I was sleeping like a log, sir. Koro woke me up when it got too eerie for a lone sentry to bear. I have never heard it before, and I think I had better go and investigate."

"No need to, Dai. It's caused by the wind, and that scary sound every night likely drove the birds and animals away an eternity ago. They won't return, even if this canyon were endowed with lush growth and an abundance of water. You said our way is blocked by a massive waterfall. When that much water cools down at night, it causes wind to form, and if there is an opening in a convenient place where the wind builds up, it is forced through the crack, which acts like a whistle. That unearthly moaning is the result. Would you make us some tea or coffee if you have it, please? If you don't feel like sleeping again, I'll tell you a little of my story. I am somewhat rested, and now I feel the urge to unburden my soul to another human being."

"First, sir, drink as much as you can of this concoction and eat something again. I should learn to carry a bigger quantity of these herbs with me, but I didn't expect to need them, and unfortunately they don't appear to grow in this particular area. I'll make some coffee just now." He ladled some of the stew into Koro's dish and some for himself. Then he put a spoon into the pot and told the man that the rest was his. He and Koro would eat meat tonight if they didn't come across edible tubers to add a little taste to the plain fare.

The stranger ate very little and paused every now and then to take a mouthful of the herb water to moisten his throat as he talked. He started by saying, "I forgot to introduce myself last night as I could not even think two coherent thoughts in sequence without passing out in between. My name is Ogath—"

Dai choked on his food and turned his face in the other direction while he coughed his lungs out. "I'm sorry," he said in a husky voice, "I must learn not to forget that I'm swallowing while I concentrate on listening." He knew it was a lame excuse, but Ogath was not a common name, and if by one chance in a quintillion he was Dai's father, everything else could go to blazes while Dai got him to his mother and to medical care.

Ogath had politely paused to allow Dai's spasm to subside before he slowly continued. "I am an Explorer, and I was the commander of an experimental scout ship, humorously named 'Where To?' by the inventor of the faster-than-light drive, a propulsion technology that enables spaceships to achieve superluminal travel. We had tested the drive for short distances a number of times, and our holds were always full of provisions and equipment, even spare parts in case something went wrong and we were out of reach of ordinary ships. I was told that the government shelved the new drive as too risky when we went missing, but now I'm convinced that the backbiting snake Hedra was just trying to cover up his crime at the time of our disappearance.

"Hedra, at the time, was head priest of the scientific department, and the Explorers were his responsibility. He dabbled in politics as well and didn't allow the inventor, whose name was Marog, on our training flights. He had him physically restrained for some obscure reason, but the lame excuse he used was that he didn't want to put the genius inventor at risk because he was irreplaceable. Then, when we were ordered to give the ship a real long-distance test at full speed, the genius went missing three or four days before the planned experimental flight.

"Anyway, we were given instructions to take off without the spare drive, which Hedra said must first be tested on another ship. According to Hedra, this was just another test before real exploration was organized. We would just have the drive on for one hour at full speed and see how far we could go in that time. We were foolish enough to fall for it like babies in the woods, because we hadn't tested the experimental drive for more than ten minutes.

"Now, twenty-one years after the event and only after he created this new dilemma for me, I realize that we should have questioned his illogical reasons because we had already calculated how many light-years we could travel at full speed in one day—or one hour, for that matter. One is always wiser after the fact, but being as trusting and naive as I was, I managed to get caught more than once with the same ploy. We should have risked being jailed for insubordination, but we didn't have the faintest suspicion that anything was amiss at the time, as we were eager and perhaps too overly enthusiastic to explore the unknown. We wanted to visit new planets and see the universe, since that is what we trained so long for. Little did we know that we would see too much of the universe in too short a time.

"Our holds were crammed with everything we thought we could need if we accidentally discovered a new planet or if something went wrong during the training flight. We didn't say good bye to our families because we expected to be back within a week, and we took off without ceremony, as we were ordered to do. We cruised on our normal drives for two days, for we had to get well away from any planets before we could engage the

FTL drive without blowing it. On the second day, much to our surprise, our scientist came out of hiding and told us not to report him for it was the only way to accompany us and experience his invention stretching its legs. That was why he'd slaved to perfect his idea; he also wanted to see the universe, and Hedra wasn't going to stop him.

"We aimed for the nearest constellation, and the navigator said he was activating our rear cameras as well, for that was the prudent thing to do, and it was his job to get us back. We all laughed, but afterward we blessed his foresight—or perhaps it was intuition, for that recording was the only thing that brought us back. Astro-navigation was still in its infancy, and star charts were not reliable.

"I told everyone to strap down and as usual, I counted dramatically from five to zero and pushed the FTL drive lever about a third of the way forward to get us going without too much acceleration. Then the unexpected happened. The ship took off under full power, and we all lost consciousness under the crush of uncountable gravities. We regained consciousness eight days later when the ship had reached its maximum acceleration and the crushing weight ceased. It took most of a day to recover our senses. I reversed the lever, but the speed didn't diminish. By then we knew that one of us hadn't survived, and we stowed him in one of the holds for burial when we could. Luckily it wasn't the inventor, but being middle-aged and not in the least fit, he took a day longer to revive.

"We realized something had gone awfully wrong, and when our navigator took a peek outside, he cried out in an amazed voice that it was totally black outside. Like sheep we all rushed to an observation port to see for ourselves."

Ogath paused to take a bite and chewed it thoroughly before he swallowed it with a mouthful of water. While Ogath chewed, Dai began to pack the few things he had used back on the trolley. They might as well start early because he wouldn't be able to go back to sleep anyway.

"Am I boring you with my story, Dai?"

"Not in the least, sir. I just have a feeling that we must start early. This is not a place to linger, as the nearest available water source I know of is about thirty-five kilometers away. I'll make some coffee later if you don't mind, but I'd like to hear your fascinating account to the end before we leave, for I might not get another chance soon to listen to your utterly captivating tale. Before we go, I also want to tell you a story, a very short one. But yours first, please. Then I'll take a look at Koro's waterfall, and if we can't get past it, I'll take you for medical attention as fast as I can. I can then use the easier way to come back to complete my mission."

"No, Dai, you mustn't abandon your mission this close to your goal, and to come back later may be too late. You'll find a way past, even if you have to go on alone. I have survived worse plights than this one, and I can rest here a day or two by myself. My body is weak, but my heart is strong. I'll survive. I see you have a long rope on the trolley. You can try to pull water up out of the fall. That is all I need right now, and I can—and have—survived on less than this dried meat if you stay away longer than you intend to. I insist that you finish what you came for."

"I can always come back, but you only have one life."

"Let's not argue about it, please. You said we are not important. Let's check the waterfall at first light and then decide. As I have found out many times in my life, there may not be another opportunity, so let's go for it first thing."

"Okay then, sir, and thank you. Please continue. You must leave out the details for now, just the main points, please. I'd like to hear everything you experienced, but we'll make time for that later, after you are well again. I promise."

"Agreed. I'll stick to the relevant points. We were lucky that the inventor had escaped Hedra's detention tactics and was hiding on that specific flight, for otherwise we may never have made it back. He opened plates and inspected the drive— suitably isolated of course, for the drive was nuclear driven. He declared that something had caused a short circuit and that vital components had fused together. We didn't carry spares because that type of fault wasn't anticipated. Innocents that we were, we thought that someone must have been very negligent while inspecting the drive. I'll skip the details, as you've asked.

"Marog, the inventor, said he would try to make new components and repair the connections. First he had to disconnect the drive, very carefully of course. He knew and remembered everything about the engine and went about it slowly and meticulously while he explained the process to me,

353

using me as a sounding board, I suppose. I helped him because there was nothing else to keep me occupied. The navigator reported that we were more than halfway to the next island galaxy and that he was carefully duplicating the recorded pictures of our exit from our galaxy. Otherwise, if the only set got damaged, we wouldn't know where to return to.

"We cruised at many times the speed of light for about a month and were beginning to despair, for we still couldn't get the drive to shut off. We were almost on the other side of the next island galaxy when we suddenly came to a halt. But it was done gently, and we weren't squashed against the bulkheads as we feared we would be. It felt as if everything and everyone was grabbed and held in place by an invisible force, as we learned later. The universe did a sort of somersault, and for the first time we could see the strange constellations clearly and normally, and not as streaks of light. Whatever or whoever had stopped us had disabled the recalcitrant drive as well.

"I'd love to tell you the full story later, Dai. It was a peacefully inclined race of manlike, or to be exact, humanoid lizards, called the Scrii, who captured us. They were at war with a ruthless, vicious race—scaly descendants of reptilian ancestors, who'd invaded their domain. The Scrii are, scientifically speaking, a million or more years ahead of us and sort of telepathic. After individually interrogating every one of us, they accepted our story that we were from another galaxy and that we were willing to help them fight off the invaders. They said they sort of admired our guts for crossing the great emptiness in a ship with such a primitive drive. Their mirth knew no bounds when we told them that the crossing was involuntary and not by our choice, that the drive went out of control. They helped us repair our 'quite primitive' drive during the periods when the enemy licked their wounds or regrouped, for vicious as they were, they could not match us earthlings for courage and battle ingenuity.

"It took about five years to completely rebuild the drive, for it was damaged beyond repair. In the process I studied it closely and eventually knew as much as the inventor himself, for I was determined never to be caught unprepared again. I was too naive to suspect sabotage, but now I know that the sneaky Hedra tinkered with the drive, even though I have no evidence to prove it in any court of law.

"In between repairs and constructing tools to make the required parts, we helped the Scrii defeat the invaders. Their leader gave me this weird-looking gun and the holster as a present before we left, because he knew I would not use it for selfish purposes. It is called a personal protector because no one other than me can touch it with impunity. It detects a fast-approaching object, such as a bullet or a bolt, at a distance and instantaneously generates a field of protection around me to deflect it. The gun is a kind of disintegrator, but it only works on living, animate things. Otherwise, in theory, it might cause an entire planet to dissolve into dust or nothingness.

"The Scrii helped us pinpoint the exact point of exit from our galaxy. Unfortunately, it was on the other side of this island galaxy, and it took us almost fifteen years to find our own solar system. If I survive long enough, I will tell you about the hair-raising adventures we experienced along the way when we visited planets to replenish our dwindling food supplies. Unfortunately, we lost the lovable, bumbling Marog, but he was the only casualty.

"The rest, five of us, eventually made it back, but when we landed, we were hushed away without any explanation. We were told that there was no record of a lost scout ship and that they were keeping us locked up to investigate our claim. They also tried to take this gun away from me as evidence, but it's a personal gun. It shocked the hell out of anyone who touched it, and I refused to take it off, saying it was an alien thing and I dared not touch it either. I demanded insistently and continuously to see Hedra for debriefing and to secure our release. I sensed that I should not mention any other names, for something didn't smell right. Now, belatedly, I know that we caused panic in certain quarters.

"After about two weeks, I was secretly brought to Hedra in a palace in a place called Bojon. My chronometer indicates that was eight days ago. At first he pretended he didn't remember me or the FTL ship, but after I jogged his 'poor' memory and asked him where my wife, Lur, was, he had a sudden, vague recollection and told me he had heard that she was nursing primitives somewhere here in one of the canyons. He promised he would make inquiries and have a flyer ready for me the next morning with a preprogrammed course, assuming he could find the correct coordinates. All I had to do was to engage the autopilot when I was at the required height and point to the high mountains.

"He promised to have my crew released, but now I doubt they are still alive. Like the simple, addle-brained, trusting fool I was, I thanked the smooth-talking, backstabbing jerk for his kindness and took off in the flyer. How he must have laughed! The one thought uppermost in my mind for the past twenty years had been to get back to Lur and the child I had never seen, and being so close must have befuddled my brain. As I engaged the auto, everything locked, and the flyer rapidly accelerated. As with the spaceship, the speed kept increasing when I pulled the lever back, and the autopilot also refused to be disengaged.

"That jogged my memory about the ship's behavior twenty-one years ago, and I remembered, belatedly, that Hedra, among other things, was a wizard with electronics. Then I also remembered that Lur had complained that Hedra was after her with his tongue hanging out, which I had laughed off as temporary because I knew she could handle it. In my trusting innocence, I had forgotten that that gargantuan excuse for a human being was an unforgiving and very dangerous enemy.

"Anyway, I still remembered where the control computer was located, and I kicked the panels in where I couldn't remove them with my knife. In the process I noticed that the antigrav unit was also sabotaged, at which point I knew for sure that I was meant to die. This gun was useless for disabling the computer, for, as I told you, it doesn't affect anything but living organisms. I finally exposed the control box, and then I just pulled the wires out. I didn't care about being shocked and burned because the flyer was heading out toward the upper reaches, where I would suffocate very quickly.

"I saw Bojon in the far distance in the rear-viewer camera just before it went dead. With the engine disabled, the flyer flipped over onto its back and fell nose first, almost straight down. I had almost no control. With the auto dead, I tried to guide the falling flyer back the way I had come with the manual controls, but the glide was that of a flat brick since the rudimentary wings were just added for show—though they did help a little. When the flyer hit a severe updraft, I managed to level it out somewhat and reduce speed. I still hoped it would glide all the way over and out of this canyon country, but after I barely managed to avoid a high peak, a downdraft forced me to crash-land the damned thing in the almost-level bed of an arid canyon. It bounced and scraped along for more than two kilometers before it cracked open against solid rock where the canyon made a slight turn.

"I was lucky to be alive, but I had no water or provisions, nor any container to carry water in if I found a stream. The murderous Hedra had thought of everything, for he had removed the emergency supplies and even the first-aid kit. I realized he had wangled the sabotage of the ship to look like negligence in the unlikely event that we made it back, but this time he thought I couldn't beat him. I was badly shaken up, but no bones were broken. I still had my compass strapped to my arm, so I started to walk south as soon as I realized I was meant to die. I found a tiny rill the evening of the second day, but then the canyon gradually became a desert, which was strange but not uncommon, where hot currents circulated freely. On the third day, I encountered a lost giant reptile, which I disintegrated when it charged. That's the drawback of this gun. You cannot hunt with it.

"I remember getting hungrier and thirstier as the days went by, but I don't recall much else. I suppose I was wandering in a total stupor for a long time before I collapsed."

63

Ogath drank some water and then tiredly remarked, "I am determined to survive so that I can roast that despicable lowlife of a scumbag slowly over a small fire to hear him scream and beg. He doesn't deserve a clean, painless death. I wonder how many potential rivals he has killed to become the leading priest of our country. I question his ability to head any organization, never mind a country."

Dai replied, "You'll have to get in line somewhere behind me, sir. Hedra must be aware that there's a host of individuals who'd like to get their hands on him, for he commands dozens of personal bodyguards. But be that as it may, you'll find this as hard to believe as I do, but by the merest fraction of a chance, perhaps one in a quadrillion, I was in the right place at the right time to find you. Very few people ever visit these wild, unexplored canyons. And can you calculate what the odds would be that your own son would be the one to find you?"

Ogath's mouth dropped open, and he didn't say a word or take his eyes off Dai. After a moment, tears began to flood his eyes, and he held out his arms. Dai gently hugged him, all too briefly.

"We'll get acquainted as we go along, Dad. It really feels strange to call a complete stranger 'Dad,' but I'll get used to it. My mother only told me about you when I met her for the first time about two weeks ago, but she can tell you the story herself. She said I have the same eyes as she remembers you having."

Ogath swallowed hard, but his voice was strong. "I thought I recognized Lur in your features but ascribed that to wishful thinking or perhaps a fever dream. I find it equally strange to call my savior, 'Son,' but I'm proud to say it. I see a faint discoloring in the east, so let's get ready to depart. My constitution is weakened, but I've been in this situation twice before, and I know I will survive. And now I have the best of reasons as an additional incentive. If you find that alleged legacy from the past accessible, I, too, would like to see it. I can read and understand all the known old languages, for that was part of my training to prepare for learning alien languages. I can even speak the Scrii's language, which is mostly just clicks and hisses to the human ear."

Dai felt a little guilty about the coffee, but decided he would make it soon enough. "Okay, Dad, we'll go and have a look at the falls. If we find a way past the obstruction and if we can get in, we'll take a brief look at the ancient legacy and then I'm taking you to Mother, and from there to a clinic where you can get proper treatment. Then I'll focus my undivided attention on Hedra. I don't think he's the mastermind behind this interplanetary plot we're trying to put a stop to. His thinking is more on a small-scale level. He would be too scared to go for something big like this legacy on his own, and he wouldn't be able to handle it. I think he's just a front, a dupe for a more powerful group or groups, but a wily and dangerous stooge. What will happen if you shoot him in the foot with the Scrii gun?"

"Judging by the grim tone in your voice, I wouldn't want to be in Hedra's shoes for all the power and riches in the universe. I pity the mangy, dirty old dog. Ah yes, I haven't tried that one, but I would think he might have time for a brief yell. It would be too merciful a death."

Dai made sure his newly found dad was comfortable before he stowed the remaining things he had used and doused the fire thoroughly, as usual. He checked the heavier gun to make sure he had a full magazine before he slung it over a shoulder, ready to grab and fire at a moment's notice, and he also hung a full canteen over a shoulder and around his neck. Then he put on the rough but strong harness he had made ten days before to leave his arms free. He strapped the handle of the trolley to his back.

Koro jumped onto the trolley, since the eerie sound still unnerved him. He'd rather cringe than run alongside Dai. Ogath noticed his uneasiness and sent him a thought to relax: *The sound will diminish and then fade away as the sun rises.*

That may be so, but it's still scary to someone who hears it for the first time, Koro replied. *Can I sit next to you? I will be more comfortable.*

"Yes, of course, Koro. We now are family, all of us, isn't it so? Come, I'll put my arm around you like Dai did."

Koro was quick to comply. He tried to relax but wasn't

entirely successful. Ogath's arm around him was reassuring, but he worried about the lack of energy and strength he felt in the hand and arm that held him.

The narrow canyon was still shrouded in darkness. Dai walked to permit the sun to catch up with him, but it was still too early. He was wary, although he felt sure the canyon was devoid of life. As he came closer to the waterfall, he, as Koro had, first felt the ground starting to tremble under his feet before he heard the thunder of the mighty waterfall. Now he began to understand Koro's reluctance to explore. He had visited waterfalls before, but never one as deafening as this, or where the ground shook as if an earthquake was in progress. This must be the grandmother of all waterfalls, he thought, for even the eerie moaning was drowned out by the thunder of thousands of tons of water crashing down.

Mindful of Koro's warning about the chasm, he switched on the powerful torch and played it out front to see where he should put each foot down. The ground was hard but relatively level and cleared, as if washed periodically by a gentle flooding of water—which must come from somewhere, Dai thought, but not from down canyon. Then he was on solid rock, and the muted yet thundering noise of inestimable tons of water crashing down a long distance somewhere below him was totally deafening; the noise was too overwhelming to hear oneself think. He wished daylight would hurry up so he could see properly.

Dai went back a little distance to where it was quiet enough to talk, even with the eerie wailing sound. As he stopped the trolley, Ogath said, "I've seen really big and high falls on half a dozen planets, but judging by the sound, this one must drop into the deepest abyss imaginable."

"While we wait for enough light to see, I'm going to make that coffee I promised you." Dai took wood from the trolley and proceeded to make a fire and coffee. As they sipped the scalding, bitter brew in silence, the light gradually grew brighter.

Eventually Dai saw the precipice he had stood on in the dark, but as he thought earlier, the waterfall couldn't be seen from canyon level, so it must be lower down. He could see the continuation of the canyon in the distance, but no river flowed down it.

He was intrigued, but finished his coffee before he said, "Dad, take your time to finish your coffee while I pull the trolley closer to where we can see what we have here. It might be an undiscovered natural wonder, and if it is, it can stay that way if I have a say in it."

Dai doused the small fire with the dregs from the kettle. The canyon here was denuded of vegetation, so there was no risk of fire. He nevertheless covered the remaining coals with a layer of sand. Then he took the thill and pulled the trolley after him toward the thunderous sound. The eerie wailing had gradually ceased while he made the coffee. As the sun rose, the light grew brighter and the air warmer.

When he again stood on the lip of the precipice, Dai felt like a god looking down on his creation from far above. Ignoring that lofty feeling, he maneuvered the trolley so his father could share the view. Koro crouched down and hid his face against Ogath's leg; he definitely wasn't interested in looking down dizzily into a big slash in the ground that nature had created in a moment of whimsical thoughtlessness.

Wordlessly, Dai and his father stared down into the massive, seemingly bottomless oval hole. Dai didn't even attempt to estimate the depth because he couldn't see where the half-kilometer-wide, massive wall of water ended up at the bottom. As far as he was concerned, the water poured into the bowels of the earth, creating a thick mist some distance down so that the bottom, if there was one, was lost to view from above. The massive flow of water had its origin somewhere to the north, and it raced down a chute about 400 meters wide, about 150 meters below the precipice. The falls was in a carved-out recess about a hundred meters to the right of the canyon, and the cliff on which they stood deflected most of the deafening sound the other way.

Beyond the hole, much lower than the falls, a wide valley started with the usual high walls characteristic of the canyons quite a distance on either side. Yes, Dai thought, this could be the canyon his mom ingrained in his mind. He saw a number of rocky hills, some high enough to be classified as small mountains. About five or six kilometers away, on the southern side of the valley, was a roughly conical peak that could be two kilometers high. He guessed the circumference of the massive

361

base to be more than twenty kilometers. On its southern side was an almost sheer cliff until about halfway up. Then it curved sharply the rest of the way to the top. That could be the one the climber fell from, he thought. The steep, mostly solid rock slope on this side could be where the cave and the cache were located. Dai saw that the valley was cluttered with small, rocky hillocks, enormous boulders, and stunted trees. No streams were visible.

Now they must find a way around this obstacle. He looked down the precipice at his feet. Farther down was a broad ledge that was so smooth and uniform it looked as though it could have been carved by humans out of the solid rock. His eyes followed it, first to the north. It started ruggedly more or less where the canyon wall was a hundred meters away, about a meter wide, as if it had been smashed off at that point, and less than a meter below the lip of the precipice. Then it widened abruptly to about nine meters, and it stayed more or less the same width as it gradually sloped down to the south. It really looked like a steep roadway, Dai thought; it could be a way past this obstacle.

The ledge roadway continued on its downward slope more than halfway around the gigantic hole in the solid rock. Four or five hundred meters lower down, it broadened abruptly and turned into a large, arched hole that definitely wasn't natural. Dai felt the hairs on his neck rise. The cliff around the hole was sheer all around, and he couldn't see even a single crack in the smooth surface around the hole. That hole, he thought, could be the cause of the eerie sound. Had he been alone and with nothing else to do, he might have been tempted to investigate, but now he felt he must shy away; it couldn't be a way past the waterfall.

He felt a light tapping against his leg. As he looked down, Ogath pointed north and beckoned him to bend down. When he did so, his father shouted in his ear, but he couldn't hear a word. He started to shake his head, but Koro said in his mind, *You dad says, "Let's go back a little way to where we can talk and hear each other."*

When Dai had moved the trolley to a quieter location, Ogath told him, "This hole may have been created by a volcanic eruption in a bygone era, and there may have been—and still

362

may be—a huge lake or river somewhere to the north. It looks as if convulsions in the Earth's crust cracked the north wall to divert the water in this direction. Through the centuries erosion caused the softer part of the rock to form the channel that acts like a chute. The seemingly bottomless hole is obviously the beginning of a raging underground river. I am just surmising, but if you know as much about geology as I do, you'll agree with me. Northward, a little way up, there will be a twisting slit that narrows at the top, which would create the eerie moaning we heard earlier. Perhaps a tree, if one is conveniently located, could be made to fall over the slit, or you could use this rope as a bridge. If you look closely at the break in the wall on the north side next to the chasm, you'll see there is a sort of shallow channel where water runs periodically. Go check it out and see if there is a way over."

"I didn't get as far as looking north because I was checking a ledge below us that looked like a manmade road," Dai said, "but something told me to stay away from it. I can't explain it."

"Then stay away from it. We have a natural sense that warns us when something may be detrimental to our health."

Dai grounded the trolley and asked Koro to stay and guard his father, since he might be away for quite a while. He walked toward the chasm, keeping close to the north wall. As he came to the chasm, he saw that the break in the wall was ragged, as if a shard had broken away ages ago, which might account for the broken ledge he believed to be an artificial roadway.

About a meter up, a shallow channel about three meters wide hugged the edge of the precipice to the north. It had been smoothed over many centuries by water draining from above. He grabbed a handhold and pulled himself up onto it. It was slippery in places, and he stayed close to the wall as he gingerly edged upward in a bent-over position to prevent him from slipping and sailing off into the awe-inspiring abyss on his left. It was an experience he'd rather let pass, he thought wryly.

The shallow channel twisted upward around corners, and he lost sight of the canyon after he passed the falls. The wall on the other side of the chute remained sheer and wasn't the way to return to the canyon if he found a way over the chute. As he edged upward, he looked down on the chute from time to time and saw it disappear into the crack, as his father had predicted.

Then the walls of the gap he was negotiating began to converge until he could almost jump across. He looked up and couldn't see the sky above. He fervently prayed that this was not the bridge he was looking for. It was impossible to climb three or four kilometers of sheer rock that leaned inward without the necessary equipment. Even then it would be wasted effort. He nevertheless continued along the channel as fast as he safely could. He estimated that he had come less than four kilometers after passing the falls when the walls abruptly parted company as if fed up with each other.

The channel he was negotiating flattened out onto a wide clearing, about two hundred and fifty meters at the broadest point. He welcomed this natural half-circle haven, which gently sloped upward for about two hundred meters. It was covered with sparse, dry grass, and a few scattered scrub trees struggled to survive in what must be very shallow soil. There was no sign of animal life. The small haven ended against a low, seemingly chopped-off ridge, an estimated forty to fifty meters high but only about eighty meters long as it ended near the edge of the chute, which left a precarious way to pass between the two. About eighty to a hundred meters from where he was, the ragged half circle became a flaked sheet of rock shelf more than a hundred meters wide, which sloped quite steeply down toward the channel and narrowed rapidly toward the ridge. Shards and flakes were scattered all the way to the ridge, which might cause the unwary to slip and slide down into the channel, but it was not impassible. The side against the canyon wall offered a narrow but almost-level footpath if it was cleared of debris.

He had been conscious of an increase in the sound of rushing water, and as he leaned over the precipice to look down into the slit, he saw that the water flow was closer, as if the bottom were rising. It was now only about a hundred meters down to the water level, and he could actually see the rippling in the fast-rushing stream as it hastened on its mad journey to where it fell into the bowels of the earth. The slit seemed to become shallower and somewhat wider toward the north.

With a sigh of relief, Dai stood upright. His back was aching from the strain of creeping upward, bent over like a question mark. He flexed and stretched his back muscles to relax them and then walked hurriedly toward the rock shelf. He didn't have all day, and he definitely didn't want to spend another night with that hair-raising lamentation filling his ears.

A few acres of almost naturally landscaped scenery greeted his sight on the other side of the chute, and it indicated the beginning of a valley, for it widened out rapidly, but the ridge was too close and obstructed his view. Clumps of winter-bared trees grew around huge boulders, but he noticed this only at a glance. The vegetation quickly petered out and ended in solid rock, which gradually sloped down to the five-hundred-meter-broad chute. But he wasn't interested in details right now because he was looking for a way over to the other side. The ridge should be easy to climb, though he didn't think it would be wise to bypass it at the edge of the chute with the trolley, but now he must get on top to see what lay ahead.

He walked carefully along the highest point against the high canyon wall, kicking and pausing to push out of the way debris that slid noisily down toward the slit. He was making a slip-safe path to follow with the trolley. Then he easily climbed the not-so-steep ridge.

The terrain on both sides of the deep chute gradually rose to another low ridge across the canyon about two kilometers away. From this distance it looked promising because he could see no break in it, but he wasn't sure. He followed the chute, which was carved out of solid rock, all the way with his eyes. It narrowed again toward the ridge, but what fascinated Dai was a tremendously thick and irresistible column of water spouting through a low-angled opening in what looked like solid rock a short distance this side of the far ridge. The angle was about thirty degrees, but the water traveled for more than a hundred meters before it fell into the deep slit, which gave it a running start downward. There must be a tremendous amount of water above the ridge to create that much pressure to force such an incredible amount of water constantly through a tunnel under that ridge, he thought with wonder, or otherwise a fairly big river must rush down from high up in the canyon.

This rocky ridge was more than twice the height of the short one lower down, he realized as he climbed the weathered side twenty minutes later. When he reached the top, he was figuratively kicked in the stomach. Breathlessly, he blinked his eyes, then looked again through the few trees in front of him.

365

Perhaps I should call this ridge a wall, he thought, for his eyes didn't deceive him. A deep lake dotted with rocky islands of all sizes stretched out before him. The high canyon rapidly widened to about two kilometers before it bent eastward a kilometer away. The solid ridge, adorned with a few stunted trees, seemed to be a natural barrier to contain the lake. The sides of the lake against the canyon walls and some of the islands were covered with high trees and lush vegetation. Small waves lapped against the sides.

He regretfully reminded himself that he wasn't here to admire the view or speculate about what he was seeing. This might be the bridge he was looking for, and he must check it out quickly, for the day was advancing rapidly. He climbed around boulders and other obstacles to find the spout, which was the key factor. Then he felt the same kind of faint tremor he had experienced in the early dawn when he'd approached the waterfall. The rhythm increased with every step he took, together with the sound of a splashing roar. He saw the spout and thought he could run across behind it without climbing the ridge, but he didn't think he was in such a desperate hurry to take chances. Directly across from the spout, Dai found a huge whirlpool a hundred meters across and too close to the ridge for peace of mind. In ages to come, he thought, this ridge would be weakened enough to give way. He was quite sure he wouldn't be around when that day came, for the ridge was solid rock except for above, where vegetation and trees had rooted.

Dai had seen enough, but he looked along the cliff to the west, starting at the chute to see if there was possibly a way down to reach the continuation of the canyon past the hole. The terrain there was rugged, and gigantic boulders almost blocked his view, but he thought he saw the mouth of a very narrow canyon—actually just a fissure, he thought—which might take them west and southward. There were no other promising exits except high above the lake to the north. He would have to explore the fissure first to see where it led, for there was no way down the other side of the chute back to the sandy canyon. He hurried back as fast as he dared.

64

Ogath was sleeping quietly. Koro said he was still exhausted and in a deep sleep; it was best not to disturb him unless an emergency developed. Dai agreed. After he had elevated the trolley to one meter, he loosely wound an end of the coiled rope twice over his father's body and knotted it so he wouldn't fall off if anything happened. He made sure the handle of the thill was still securely attached to the harness he had made, since he needed both hands free to negotiate the slippery channel. The harness was strong, but Dai always tried to think ahead; accidents usually happened without warning. Fortunately, the trolley would always stay level, even up or down the steepest incline, but it tended to slide backward to more or less level ground to find its preset height when it wasn't grounded or tethered to an anchor, and then it acted like a wheeled vehicle, picking up speed in the process, which was hard to control.

It was past midday when he wearily climbed the lake's barrier wall a second time. When he started to feel the vibration caused by the water being forced through the short tunnel, he untied the thill, reversed the trolley, and pushed it before him. He knew it was quite safe to cross by way of the ridge, or even below, behind the spout. Nevertheless, he wanted something to hang on to just in case his extra weight might cause a weakened area to cave in. He wasn't going to take a chance with his newly found dad's life. He felt like tiptoeing when the faint vibration began, but as expected, nothing happened except that the trembling increased slightly and then ceased completely as he passed the whirlpool. He thought he should wake his dad to look at this extraordinary creation—and how right he had been—but Koro admonished him not to be silly; his dad was exhausted and needed to rest as much as possible. If he was interested, he could come back when he was well again; otherwise Koro could share his mental images.

Thank you, Koro, but perhaps not your mind images. He is not used to seeing things from your angle, and it might confuse him. Look through my eyes and offer him this picture.

When he felt the cat's presence, he looked back to where he came from. The canyon narrowed rapidly down to where the walls almost touched, forming a narrow portal through which the wind played its nightly eerie lamentation. Dai's eyes traveled the route he had come, then over the barrier ridge, the lake, the gigantic whirlpool, and the awe-inspiring spout.

It looks different from up there at your eye level, Dai. I have never thought about it, but I see what you mean. I will give your dad this picture and your accompanying thoughts.

The high ridge flattened out to rising ground where it angled sharply to the north. Thirty meters after the turn northward, the ridge petered out to almost level ground. He noticed the presence of herbs, tubers, and other vegetables in the longish grass along the sandy banks of the lake. Although it was past the middle of winter, the plants were growing unchecked in the slightly warm, clammy soil, since no animals were courageous enough to brave the terrifying moaning at night to feed on them. Except for the splashing of the distant spout and the lapping of tiny waves against the shore, it was unnaturally quiet; even Koro's perception of normality was disturbed. Not even a single representative of the universally pestiferous flies came buzzing around to annoy them. Only the cool breeze perpetually blowing down the canyon was normal.

This was a rare opportunity to replenish their depleted supply of herbs and vegetables. Dai grounded the trolley higher up on dry ground, grabbed the empty bag, and collected vegetables and tubers that were familiar. Unknown vegetables, although delicious looking, he reluctantly left to grow in peace. He warily washed the chosen ones in the lake, keeping an eye out for opportunistic carnivorous lake dwellers that might have strayed into the area. When the bag was full, he collected the herbs he required. They had to air dry, so he used open pots to store them. He would spread them out on a groundsheet at night when he used the pots. He refilled every spare container, as well as the two canteens, with fresh water—something he never neglected.

After reattaching the thill to its harness, Dai hurriedly took off to get as much distance between them and the nightly entertainment before it started. He was quite willing to use one of the powerful torches after dark because it was unlikely that enemies were here in this secluded canyon. The ground rose rapidly for a distance, flattened out for a few hundred steps, and then gradually sloped down toward the southwesterly canyon wall.

Soon enough, he found the narrow fissure among the huge boulders and broken rock. For humans, it wasn't really a split, since it was at least eighty meters wide where it started. The floor was strewn with sharp segments that had periodically broken off the walls higher up. At first glance, fragile vegetation obstructed the way, but he just trod on them after pushing them down. The vegetation soon disappeared because it couldn't root where there was no sunlight. After the first turn, the fissure narrowed in places, and he realized the sun very seldom penetrated the perpetual dusk that reigned here in the tiny three- to four-kilometer-high crack in the solid canyon wall.

Dai squinted upward but could see the sky only as a thin, scarcely visible ragged line of sunlit blue far above. For the first time in his life, he felt small and insignificant. The walls seemed to squeeze inward, but he was disciplined and knew it was only his imagination. He should keep his eyes focused on where he was going, for the floor was far from level. He frequently encountered ancient rockfalls, and he squeezed past them where he could or climbed over them where they blocked the passage. About two meters higher than he could reach upward, the walls were smoothened, as if water had flowed in the fissure—briefly, as measured against the centuries that must have passed since then. It indicated that this was a way out unless the fissure was blocked by an insurmountable rockfall or cave-in. He could check by continuing on.

The fissure meandered so tortuously through solid rock that Dai lost all sense of direction, and only his wrist compass showed that at times he was going directly west. He ruthlessly suppressed the primitive urge to start running but continued to walk rapidly. After an indeterminable time, complete darkness descended abruptly.

Dai stopped with one foot raised. He might put it down into nothingness, which could end in eternity for him. He stepped backward and detached the thill to reach for the other rucksack where he kept Bolly's more powerful torch. When he found the torch, he switched it on but didn't play it directly onto the trolley. In the reflected light, Ogath still seemed peacefully asleep. Out of habit, Koro's eyes were tightly closed to keep a tab on Dai's thoughts.

Dai's first thought was that night came early in this fissure, but when he glanced at his watch he saw that it was just past three. Shining the light upward, he saw that they were inside a smoothed-out but seemingly natural water conduit. Somehow the ceiling, which was about thirty meters high, seemed too smooth and even in height. He checked the walls closely; they appeared ruggedly chipped out by a mechanical device, but smoothened somewhat by water or heat. The fissure was definitely natural, but this tunnel was made by machines, he thought. Shrugging his shoulders at this enigmatic puzzle, he reattached the thill to the harness so he could have both hands free for the heavy-caliber rifle he now held in his hands. It was probably unnecessary, but he preferred to be ready if some animal used this tunnel for a lair. He played the light on the floor, walls, and rounded ceiling in rotation as he proceeded warily. Time didn't matter, but the safety of his father did. He hoped he would get some sleep later on since he still hadn't caught up with lost sleep.

After a while the tunnel gradually sloped downward. If it wasn't for the thill digging into his back, he wouldn't have noticed. Now he was of two minds: should he continue for a while yet, or should he return the way he had come to look for another way down? He tried to let his senses probe ahead but encountered nothing. He should still be above the level of the canyon he was trying to reach.

He had just decided that he might as well carry on when Koro spoke in his mind. *Go on, Dai, but be ready. I sense an opening far ahead, but something crouches there, and it has been waiting for a long time. I'll try to find out what it is and why it waits there. It's no use to creep up on it, so I must try to probe its mind, if it has one.*

Dai thanked him and now only briefly played the light on the walls and ceiling. The light along the tunnel would reflect the eyes of any animal looking this way from a long way off. There would be enough time and distance to spray the tunnel with deadly energy bolts to destroy the fastest or biggest animal.

I cannot touch the mind, but I can sense it has been waiting for a very, very long time. It is old and is not hunting, for it is not hungry. You must be very careful, Dai, for I cannot sense if it is dangerous or what it really is.

I'm always careful, as you should know, Dai replied, *but thanks for the warning and your concern. I wish I had one of those hand bombs we destroyed when we found them on the invaders, but I detest the things. How is Dad doing?*

His pulse is beating faster, as if he is going to wake up. If he does I'll warn him to keep quiet and bring him "up to speed," if that is the correct thing to say.

Dai told him that it was but that he should focus his full attention on what lay ahead. He cocked the gun and shifted the level to rapid firing. A second clip was in his hand.

He didn't slow down because he was already walking slowly and warily. He wasn't trying to be stealthy—the light advertised his presence—but he was as alert and ready as could be. He didn't know how long he had been advancing because he dared not look at his watch, but he was feeling even more tired. He hoped he would get some sleep before morning.

The tunnel continued, but there was a large opening on the right side that gave access to a fairly large, roughly rounded chamber. Dai stopped in the doorway and took a slow, deep breath, trying to smell what he couldn't see. He shone the light over the floor, looking for tracks, but the floor was surprisingly free of dust. He slowly entered the chamber and quickly played the light all over it. The floor, walls, and ceiling were covered with a thick, transparent coating. Perhaps he imagined it, but the half-round, fist-sized knobs protruding from the walls and ceiling reminded him of sensors. Then he noticed a platform in a niche at the far end of the chamber about one meter above the floor, four meters square, and twice that in height. It might be a convenient place to sleep, he thought. He advanced upon it.

Don't step on it, Dai! Koro almost shouted in his mind. *That thing is waiting behind it!*

The platform was part of the wall, and it, too, was covered with the thick layer of transparent coating; nothing could hide behind it. Dai carefully shone the light on and around it, but he couldn't see anything suspicious. It wasn't a doorway and it didn't have the feeling of an ancient trap, but he suddenly had a strong urge to step onto the platform. This inexplicable urge out of the blue made him think twice. Why would he feel that way?

Ask your dad. He is awake and looking at the same thing.

Dai almost jumped, but he controlled his enthusiasm. He shone the light so he could see his dad but so the light would not blind Ogath.

Before he could ask, Ogath spoke. "Koro told me how we arrived here and showed me the pictures. I have come across many odd things in my wanderings, and this seems to be another artificial intelligence setup, which I didn't expect to come across here on Earth. It must be very, very old. I don't think it is meant to do us any harm. The urge to step onto the platform usually is an invitation to exchange information or to report. It's a sort of mind-exchange thing usually. I know how to handle it, so please lift me up onto it. You may keep a grip on my ankles or around me if you like."

Dai did as requested. He put his dad in the center of the square and then shifted his hands to a secure grip on both ankles, but his head and shoulders remained over the square. He therefore shared the strange experience, but if the platform so much as quivered or squeaked, he would yank his dad off in a flash. The strange communication started in an incomprehensible language and then shifted to picturesque images and impressions they could understand. Dai lost his distrust but didn't move onto the platform.

I sense that you are of the small people who came later and then departed very rapidly without communication. No maintenance or replacement parts are required for I have shut down everything including myself due to the inactivity. I am waiting for the master (incomprehensible name) *to come and check why the water stopped flowing and the power lines were cut. That was some time ago, but the secondary connection to sun energy is intact and powers this installation. I report as follows:*

When the water ceased to come, I isolated the turbines by sealing the entry and exit tunnels to preserve the turbines, as I am instructed to do. When the sensors tell me they need attention, I service them and then test them briefly. They are ready to run when the water flows again. I opened the service entrance a long time ago, but you came by way of the channel. I assume you are inspecting the channel for the water to start flowing again.

Due to some peculiarity, perhaps built into the platform, Dai shared Ogath's slow reply. His thoughts surfaced as if he were trying deep down to suppress what he was really thinking: *You have done what is expected. A break in the wall diverted the water elsewhere and will take a long time to repair. We have inspected the tunnel and found debris that must be removed. If the water starts flowing without warning, can you hold it inside until you sense that the power lines are repaired?*

That can be done by again closing the door through which you entered this control room and by closing the service door to the outside.

Good. I am injured and must get outside to seek medical attention before you may close the outside door. Tell us where the outside door is located. Can you comply?

I can comply. The tunnel is sealed on both sides of the turbine rooms to protect them from dust and accidental damage. The door to the smaller tunnel that leads to the outside door will open next to the communications platform when I have closed the protecting door I opened for you to enter. There are sensors all the way along the service tunnel, and I will close the outer door once you have passed it. An obstruction prevents the full closing. You must clear it before it can be closed tightly as required.

Will comply, Ogath replied and asked Dai to help him back onto the trolley.

A surprisingly thick door descended almost noiselessly on the outside of the opening they had entered through. That must be hellishly strong and tight to keep the incalculable pressure of the water outside, Dai thought.

Ogath gripped one of his arms, held the forefinger of the other hand to his lips, and then waved the hand before his serious face while he shook his head slowly.

Dai understood that he mustn't talk or think. He nodded his head and thought about picking his dad up and making him comfortable on the trolley and then removing an obstruction from a door.

They felt the pressure on their eardrums ease a little as another thick door next to them was raised with a slight hiss. Dai thought of expressing thanks, but Ogath sensed his attention and hit him lightly on the chest, again shaking his head as vigorously as he could. Dai made his dad comfortable, and then they departed. The door closed silently as soon as the trolley was clear. Koro stayed silent, and Dai thought only about how he would feel when he was out in the open again.

The tunnel was a uniform eight meters high and an ample four meters broad with a level floor. Dai felt like trotting but suppressed the desire. They would be in the open shortly, he hoped, and he kept that thought uppermost in his mind. He estimated they had come about three quarters of a kilometer when he saw the open doorway in the light of the torch. He stepped over a large rock into a dusty, natural cave and turned around to wrestle the rock out of the doorway. He couldn't see any sign of the door, but he quickly cleared the doorway of sand and debris with his hands. When he was finished, he stepped back and thought the door could be closed now. He didn't know how it worked, but a slab, looking the same as the natural rock, eased down to close the opening seamlessly. He wondered how, if he ever wanted to enter again, he would find the place and if he must ask for the door to be opened. Then he noticed a light-colored round rock embedded in the natural rock above the door. Perhaps one should knock a code on that natural-seeming square block and state his business, he thought impishly.

"Let's see if we can find the exit," his father said. "I think it's safe to think and talk now, but let's move away from the door. These artificial intelligence installations can be helpful but very dangerous if approached incorrectly. This particular one is quite primitive, as it was created for the purpose of controlling the flow of water and regulating the supply of power created by the turbines. The problem is that they can think to a degree, but they take every word or the thought that accompanies the word very literally and act accordingly. One must be very, very careful with the ones that can intercept and understand your thoughts.

"Fortunately, the Scrii knew about these surviving inventions of advanced, older civilizations and trained us. I'm more than grateful that I had the sense to listen to them, for that training saved my life more times than I can remember. There are many more vanished civilizations out there in our galaxy than one can imagine, and some of them left dangerous inventions behind that were not or perhaps could not be deactivated when those civilizations declined. I don't know why I told this one to contain any floods, but I think its reference to the generators and power lines made me say it. It's not impossible that one day a quake might close the gap and force the water this way, and I wonder if that door will be strong enough if the lake cannot find an outlet when the level rises high enough to build up tremendous pressure."

Dai could now see the vague outline of a dimly visible opening. As he slowed down to advance cautiously, he said, "Thanks for warning me in there, Dad. We have not yet reached the stage where we have developed dependable artificial intelligence, so we don't know anything about it. I'd like to learn from you, and perhaps one day, if I survive that long, I'd like to see a bit of what you have seen. But right now I'm hungry, and I know you are, too, based on how little you've been able to eat. At the lake I found a surprisingly big patch of the herb that imparts strength to one's body, and I will prepare a kettleful again. But first I want to see where we are."

Beyond the exit was a broad ledge that served as a balcony. Dai cautiously ventured out onto it, then pulled the handheld trolley out after him. From fairly high up, they looked down into the canyon valley Dai had observed in the early morning. It was now near sundown, but Dai saw that they were quite near the high peak where the cache was supposed to be buried.

"That conical peak, Dad"—he pointed to it, although it was the only one in sight—"is supposed to be the place where the cache was found. From here I don't know exactly where to find it, but I'll know when I'm close enough to see details clearly."

"If you have enough water left, Son, I suggest that we stay inside, a little way from the entrance, for the night. I can see that you are tired, and I think it will be quite safe here."

"As is my habit, Dad, I refilled every spare container and the two canteens at the lake. I still have enough wood to cook us a meal, which I'll do as soon as I see how we can get down to level ground."

To the left of the cave were the remains of a broad, stepped ledge, but it was ruined ages ago, perhaps when the ground shook to divert the water from the lake. On the right side, debris loosened from higher up had piled up to form a barely negotiable slope. Dai was tired, but he thought he would be able to get down that way, though it would be difficult with the trolley, even when he was rested. He wouldn't take the chance of letting the trolley slide down on its own with his dad tied to it, but a night's uninterrupted rest would make a lot of difference.

65

Dai piled the last of the wood onto the fire and made sure his dad was as comfortable as he could make him under the circumstances. He put a torch within reach of his father and took the powerful one he had been using in the fissure for himself, then made a hollow for his own hips on the floor. It was cool in the cave, so he wrapped the other blanket around him as he lay down. He asked Koro not to wake him up if the moaning sound started again, since he needed to sleep through the night without interruption to be at his best the next day. If the sound became too disturbing at this distance, he must hide his head against Ogath. Koro said he didn't sense anything alive as far as his senses could reach, but he would stay on watch anyway, for he didn't need much sleep.

Dai slept through the night, the first time in a fortnight, and woke up naturally at six o'clock. He was rested for a change and felt able to tackle the slope. His father was still sleeping. Dai sensed Koro outside on the "balcony." He took a canteen and two pieces of meat and gave the cat water in his dish and a piece of meat, drank water himself, and chewed on the dry, half-cooked meat while they sat and waited for full daylight.

When he could see properly, he studied the slopes on both sides of the balcony. He confirmed the previous night's observation that the gap on the left side couldn't be negotiated because the break was sheer, and there were no viable handholds above, below, or along the break. The slope beneath the balcony was too precarious. Whether he liked it or not, he needed to choose a route down the steep, debris-strewn slope on his right. There was a drop of about five meters from the balcony to the first solid-looking fragment, then a slide on loose debris for a few meters to the next solid fragment, and so on.

If he held on to the trolley at a few places, he could use its gravity-neutralizing propensity to negotiate the risky gaps to the next solid-looking point, but he would have to be careful. The last hundred meters or so he might have to rely on the trolley. He and Mouf had used the trolley a few times downhill to escape enemies or to gain distance rapidly without tiring themselves.

The problem was that the gravity-defying trolley tended to slide happily along on its preset height, picking up speed as if it had giant wheels and no brakes, until it bumped against an obstacle or was halted by other means. If he lost control of it down this steep slope, it would only be stopped by the distant conical peak—and quite abruptly, because it was downhill all the way past it. It wasn't the speed that killed you, it's the sudden stop. Perhaps the base of the peak would persuade the trolley to veer away. He dismissed the speculation as unnecessary idle thoughts.

Koro said he was going down by himself, since it would be easy on his own. He didn't feel like excitement today and perhaps he could catch a sleeping rock-rabbit basking in the early sun. He sensed life down there. So saying, he leaped down onto the fragment below and rapidly made progress downward.

Dai watched him a moment and then looked for an anchor to loop the rope around to slide down to the fragment under the balcony; it would have to be done slowly and softly so as not to dislodge the ledge with the sudden addition of his weight. He went back to the entrance and found a smooth protuberance that would have to do. Then he gently shook his dad awake and offered him the rest of the cold stew left over from the evening. He thought his dad looked much stronger than the previous day, which was encouraging.

As Ogath slowly ate and took generous swallows of the strengthening herb brew in between, Dai briefly outlined his plans for getting down to the canyon floor and his apprehension of an involuntary ride downward on the trolley if he slipped.

Ogath stopped chewing and said, "You have a long rope here. You should find a fairly heavy rock somewhere around in the cave. Tie one end of the rope around it and load it on the trolley to serve as an anchor. Tie the other end to the rails or the thill. If the trolley somehow slips from your control, I can push the rock overboard with my legs. The last hundred meters or so you can get onto the trolley, and we can cruise along as far as you want before heaving it over the side. I'm an old hand, remember? I also feel much stronger this morning, but I can't volunteer for hiking yet."

Dai slapped his forehead. "I'm supposed to be intelligent. Why didn't I think of it before?"

"You've had too many responsibilities forced onto you too abruptly at too young an age, Son, and it takes a brilliant genius to think of everything all the time. I have experience, and it is therefore easy for me to come up with a solution that has been used before. Now go find that rock, but it must be rounded and not too heavy or it will tear the rail off or break the rope if it snags on something."

"I previously used to push the thill in to brake, but that wasn't on steep slopes. It only slowed the trolley down a little until it reached level ground, or I jumped down when it had slowed down sufficiently." Dai was happy to see his dad eating more than the previous day. That was a good sign, and he was thankful that he'd found some more of the invaluable herbs. He took the strong torch and started along the left side to find a suitable rock.

He didn't find any big enough, but the rock he had removed from the entrance door was the best choice. Picking it up, he returned along the other side. About halfway back he found what looked like an ancient fireplace, for there was a small circle of rocks that must have been used as cooking stones or to contain the fire. The largest of these was a better choice and he replaced it with the one he had in his hands. Perhaps he did it to preserve the almost perfect circle, or perhaps he did it out of respect for the ancient cook of a forgotten era, who must have brought them in from outside, since they were obviously not from inside the cave. He would have liked to inspect the area, but he experienced a vague feeling of urgency and decided not to waste time doing something useless out of curiosity.

He knew how to loop a rope around a roughly round object, then tie it securely. After he did that, he put the rock on the trolley near the side, where it could be pushed off easily enough, but didn't attach the other end of the rope to the rail. He first had to use the loose end of the rope to get down the first step. His father had finished breakfast and directed Dai to secure everything loose on the trolley into a groundsheet. Mindful of the precious statuettes, Dai wrapped the rucksack with a blanket before he cut a piece of rope to tie everything to the trolley, including his dad.

After jacking the trolley to maximum height—about a meter and a half—he secured the handle to the harness and looped the loose end of the rope around the protuberance he had selected earlier. Then he looped the end of the rope around his right hand and let the rope slide through his left while he backed down the balcony. He scraped his elbows somewhat while passing the balcony, but after reaching the fragment, which shifted a little under his weight, he let go of the loose end of the rope so it could slide around its anchor above, and then he tied it to the main rail. He looked at his father, who smiled at him. There wasn't the faintest trace of fear or apprehension on his face, which reassured Dai to no end. It gave him confidence, and he swung the trolley slowly around so he could precede it during the awe-inspiring drop down the steep slope. He wondered how his father managed to cope with the emptiness under the trolley.

The trolley tended to try to push him out of the way, but the pressure of the thill against his back slowed it down. Still, it was wearing him out. Fortunately, the nature of the antigravity trolley was such that it didn't try to swing around him. Dai proceeded carefully and managed to reach the last foothold without any serious mishaps, but he was shaking with fatigue. Now it was nearly straight down. He might slide down, but once he got going there was no way to slow down and escape injury. He rested for a while and drank from the canteen his father passed to him when he detached the harness and swung the trolley alongside. He wondered if the trolley would now fall down steeply until it reached its preset height.

As if reading his thoughts, Ogath said, "You'll have to jump on now, Son, and fast. Remember that you're the anchor right now, but it's free the moment you let go. It's the nature of the gravity neutralizer not to fall down straight, but the trolley will rapidly drop down diagonally alongside this almost precipice, which acts as a sort of anchor or reference point. It is unfortunate that the slight downward angle won't let us glide directly to your goal, but we'll pass near enough. Have another drink or two before you pass the canteen back for me to drop over a shoulder, then push the thill upward and jump on in the same motion. Then cling on for dear life with both hands until we reach the bottom and level out."

Dai felt a bit recovered and did as instructed. The trolley abruptly fell away under him and he really had to cling for dear life until equilibrium was reached, but he maintained a strong grip with both hands. The trolley raced to the bottom along the very steep slope and gradually angled away from the wall as it followed the outward slope lower down. Dai would have enjoyed the speedy ride if he could swallow his stomach down to its proper place. Then they were racing over almost-level ground at a hair-raising speed, and Dai's stomach returned by itself to its normal position. After checking that there was no immediate danger of smashing into an obstacle, Dai looked at his dad to see how he was doing. He grinned back when he saw the impish smile on his dad's careworn face.

"We must do this more often, Dad. It would be thrilling if one were doing it for kicks. I am impressed because I didn't know the trolley was capable of this much speed." Deep inside he blessed the late Bolly for the trolley and his aunt Nogalithe for the foresight to make him take the bus.

"I wouldn't recommend that you try it in rough terrain unless you are forced to, Dai. Then you have to do a very quick mental calculation of where you would end up before you push off or, if you are lucky enough, you may end up in the infirmary, using crutches to learn to walk again."

Dai saw the huge conical peak loom up on his left more than a kilometer away. Another large hill was almost directly in front of them but a longer way off. The ground was sloping upward and their breakneck speed diminishing. He threw the "anchor" out after making sure it wouldn't snag on anything more solid than a bush.

The anchor bounced dangerously for a few heart-stopping moments before it began to drag in the grass. Dai then knew that a bigger anchor would have been more effective, though this was the biggest available at the time. Still, the trolley was slowing rapidly enough, and he pushed the thill in, for it acted as a break as well. As they came level with the conical peak, the trolley slowed enough for Dai to jump off with the thill in his hand The addition of his weight on the handle rapidly slowed the trolley.

When the trolley was stationary, Dai said he must find out what happened to Koro. Ogath, a sensitive himself and wise with experience, said he would sleep now that the risky part and excitement were over and that he must be woken up when they were ready to enter the place where the cache was. Dai closed his eyes and searched for Koro with his senses back along the way they had come. He found the cat a long way back, loping with his mouth half open and his tongue protruding a little.

I will come to you, Dai, but it will be night by then. There is a little water here and there, and I want to hunt and eat on the way. There is prey here, but too big for me. I must find something smaller, and that may perhaps not be before night. Don't worry about me; I will find you as always.

Dai was glad his companion was unscathed. He attached the harness to the thill and started off to find the legacy of the ancients. He hoped it was still undiscovered and the entrance closed, but, as he had experienced over the last fortnight, tremors and rockfalls were frequent. He trotted with a gun in his hands and his eyes now and then on the base of the conical peak. He was on the north side but now had a feeling that he should veer to his left and start looking from the eastern side. The peak was enormously wide at the base, and it would take two days at the very least to jog around it.

Dai stopped and sat down on a flat rock to think. He closed his eyes and tried to recall the image his mother had shown him. He hadn't given it much attention at the time because he had no intention of ever having a look at the alleged ancient treasure. Both times the climbers had approached the peak in the late afternoon from the other side, which must be from the south or southwest because the sun was to their left and slightly behind them. Then they had turned to their left along the base and started to ascend the peak with the sun obscured by the peak, so they must have been on the east or southeast slope. The first time they had reached the cave of the dying climber just before dusk, Dai was almost sure, and he tried to recall reference points.

Ah yes! The guys had climbed the sheerest side, which was adorned with cracks that provided convenient handholds. The steep slope underneath it led up to an enormous half mound that seemed welded to the cliff. It gave the impression that the missing part of the conical peak had crumbled and slid down to enlarge the base, forming the gigantic, rough half mound. Dai was sure that the cave was there and the cache less than a kilometer from it on the eastern or southeastern side and that there was a rill cascading down as a tiny waterfall from above to the right of the cave, which must be on this side and about halfway between the cave and the cache.

Dai took a mouthful of lukewarm water from the canteen, rose and stretched a few muscles, and then started to run. His watch indicated that it was half past ten, and he wanted to get going and find the place. He felt restless, and the cache didn't feel *that* important all of a sudden. Perhaps he was sick of the canyons, or perhaps he wanted to take his dad to his mother and expert help. He just wanted to check if the place was intact because he didn't want to go to all the trouble of trying to open it out of pure curiosity. He didn't have the time, and he wasn't *that* curious. The reference points were now fairly clear in his mind, and he would find the place—sooner rather than later, he hoped.

The base was surprisingly broad and high all around as far as he could see. It was a small mountain by itself, and there were many obstacles, mostly heaps of fallen rock, broken from the peak in the distant or not-so-distant past, that rolled down the steep slopes until they lost momentum. He avoided the obstacles by running well away from the base. From far off he saw the sun highlighting the tiny cascade, but he didn't increase his pace. Clear, cold, fresh water would be very welcome right now, he thought, so he would visit it first to refill the receptacles and canteens. His watch said it was almost noon.

Dai's heart almost stopped in dismay when he saw that a fresh rockfall from high above had exposed a wide opening where the cave with the treasure was supposed to be, or perhaps someone had blasted it open. He nevertheless ran past to obtain the fresh water. Water always was the most important, and the new opening, which perhaps didn't lead to the cache, could wait an hour longer to be investigated. It wouldn't make the slightest difference anyhow. If it exposed the treasure, how in heaven was he going to cause a rockslide to cover that huge, very obvious, and beckoning opening?

66

Dai returned a little more than a half hour later and started to climb the rubble-strewn way up to the opening, which he guessed was about three-quarters of a kilometer above the surface of the canyon. The climb was made more difficult by the trolley, which tended to be a drag, but he didn't even think of leaving it behind because Ogath wanted to see and evaluate the treasure. He'd acquired a lot of expertise during his wanderings, and anyway, finding the treasure was why they had tackled the difficult way to reach the millennia-old buried vault.

He could only hope that another violent tremor or shakeup didn't occur while they were here on the steep slope or trapped inside. What a stupid, irresponsible place to hide dangerous inventions—just below a high peak that was bound to crumble over time! Those guys must have liked to live dangerously, Dai thought, for why would anyone in their right mind even think of choosing such a location? Perhaps they didn't think in terms of millennia or care about future generations.

While he rested more than halfway up, he told Koro that the climb was difficult and the massive piles of rock debris made it even trickier. If he preferred to rest, he could wait for them at the tiny waterfall. Koro replied that he'd see when he got there.

Dai didn't rest long, for time wouldn't slow down. He overcame the obstacles one by one, towing the trolley behind him, with his dad still fast asleep on it. Eventually he arrived at the new opening and looked for the rare plant his mother had planted, but he didn't see it. Shrugging his shoulders, he looked through the meters-thick, wide opening, but his eyes weren't adjusted to the gloom inside. He slung the rifle over a shoulder and untied the trolley from the harness to get hold of a torch.

Once inside, he towed the trolley with his left hand through an amazingly thick wall. He estimated its thickness at about five or six meters. It puzzled him that a rockfall could rupture such a thick wall, but maybe the fall occurred very high up and was heavy enough to cause this much damage in a weakened spot. As he stepped past the entrance onto a level floor, he sensed immense space before him in the impenetrable gloom and quickly switched the torch on.

He played the light over the floor area first. There weren't any surprises awaiting him, so he shone the light around at hip level. He saw big machines of all descriptions parked seemingly equidistant across an immense hall. He shone the light upward. The ceiling was dome-shaped—for strength, he thought—and arched high overhead. Some sort of rather large round lightbulbs seemed to be floating halfway up.

The image his mother left in his mind was that of a broad passage lined with machines on the inner side, so this must be the main treasure vault, which she didn't have the good fortune to find. Now it was exposed by another whim of nature. He was suddenly glad that his dad had persuaded him not to abandon the opportunity to look at these wonders from the distant past, but he wondered how he, all by himself with no proper tools or explosives, could conceal the fairly large opening. He would laboriously have to stack a wall, but that would have to wait for later. He didn't really feel like spending another day doing it, but what must be done would have to be done. Now he must see what was inside.

Now, where and how can I turn the lights on? he thought. *I'd like to have them on so I can take a thorough look at this legacy from the ancients without going from one to the other and shining the torch on it.*

When the lights suddenly turned on, he jumped and his heart skipped a few beats. Then he realized that his wish was received by some intelligence that acted on his thoughts. He raised his shield quickly, as he had been taught, and gently shook his dad awake.

Ogath opened his eyes without moving. Then he tried to sit up. While Dai helped make him comfortable, he explained, "We are here in the place I told you about. It is gigantic. Another entrance was created, presumably due to a rockfall from very high above." He proceeded to tell Ogath about the lights and asked if he had ever encountered anything like that. He knew the question was needless but had to ask it as a sort of warning if his dad was not fully awake yet. He offered his canteen, and Ogath took a few sips.

Ogath glanced around the vault and, without looking at

Dai, said, "It may not be necessary, but guard your thoughts until we know more. Only allow thoughts concerning this room to surface. These machines are perfectly preserved, as if wrapped in a time-nullifying place, but I don't think that's it. Let's randomly examine a few, for it would take forever to check them all out."

Dai pushed the thill upward and pushed the trolley next to him with one hand. He didn't know why he did it that way, but it felt more companionable.

Ogath remarked, "I don't know what these machines are made of, but it's not steel or any known form of metal. They look ready for use, but I can only speculate about their intended purpose. There's some sort of motion sensor, for the lights are turned off as we pass through the various areas, presumably to conserve power. It is incredible that anything still works after all the eons that must have passed since this place was built. The architects knew something, all right.

"It is not impossible that these machines may be activated by thought, so for our continued health and mobility, try not to think of them starting or being used for whatever you believe they can be used for. Control your imagination and just think of them as stationary objects. Look, there's a light flashing slowly to our far right as if beckoning us. Let's go see what it is. I don't think it's wise to ignore it."

As Ogath spoke, the immense vault darkened and only dim lights toward the beckoning light illuminated a path to follow. They passed rows of big, heavy machines with telescoping attachments, squat machines with all kinds of attachments, and rounded, wheeled, tank-like machines with various attachments that could be guns as well as a host of all-purpose technological marvels. Dai could take an educated guess at the purpose of some because their equivalents existed in this age, but others were yet to be thought of and invented. Dai thought the only drawback was that all were designed for someone two or three times their size, and the controls were a little too big for comfort. His urge to finish this casual inspection of the treasure and be out of the confined, crowded place intensified, but deep down he knew he couldn't leave so soon, for there were things he must know and see before he could leave with a clear conscience. It was clear that this vault was controlled by an artificial-intelligence device similar to the one in the turbine control room, but this one would be considerably more sophisticated.

As they approached the flickering light, Dai proceeded ahead of the trolley, a subconscious, instinctive gesture of protection. The lights behind them switched off; it was obvious that their progress was being monitored. At last he stopped before a ring of dim, soothing green lights emanating from a shaded lamp attached to the end of a thin, long rod ten meters above a massive oblong machine. He noticed the smooth, polished rock surface of the wall behind it.

A voice spoke. No, it wasn't speech. It was a mental image directing him to sit down in the ring of light. The dome, as he thought of the vast hall, was now totally dark. Ogath asked to be moved from the trolley into the circle of light. Dai spread a blanket out on the ground and lowered his dad onto it before sitting down cross-legged next to him.

The unfamiliar picture-voice told them a strange, almost unbelievable story. Ogath and Dai lost track of time as the pictures and accompanying thoughts, which their brains interpreted as a voice, told them a tale of the ancient past.

This recording is left for those who may come later and have advanced to the stage where they can find and open this repository of our scientific achievements and knowledge. We urge you to seal this repository again if your civilization is not ready to use our accumulated knowledge for peaceful purposes. In the unlikely event that an act of nature caused enough stress, leading to the rupture of the rock, you will find canisters of sealant a few steps from here. Please have the courtesy to take one or two of them with you when you leave. Place them upright in the opening and twist the lever on top. We strongly suggest you seal any accidental openings, for some of these inventions are extremely dangerous and will destroy this world if not handled properly or without a proper understanding of the purpose of each invention. Be warned!

The controlling brain-simulation system utilized in this repository can provide any knowledge regarding our sciences and the purpose of any machine, as well as how to operate and control them. There are unfortunate inventions in the adjoining, sealed repository we advise and urge you to leave untouched. If you have to handle them for any reason, do it slowly and gently.

They are so sensitive that we dared not inscribe warnings directly onto them, and regrettably, they cannot be deactivated or destroyed. We dared not move them to another planet as the risk was too high that they might explode and destroy that planet and its atmosphere. They were placed against the innermost wall of the elongated, reinforced repository so that we could leave impervious inscriptions with dire warnings for accidental visitors to leave them there until such time a civilization evolves that can gently move them to a wandering comet or asteroid. They were invented for leverage, but let us tell the story so you will know that these are not idle warnings.

This planet once revolved closer to the sun. The climate all over the planet was hot and tropical, and there were no seasons. It was a paradise unappreciated by quarrelsome, covetous inhabitants who weren't short of anything, as far as material possessions were concerned. There were more or less constant skirmishes between cities, regardless of which country or countries the cities were located in.

In retrospect, we the inventors now know that it was a natural form of population control, but as with everything else, some individuals exploited the situation for personal power and gain. No one was ever content with what they had, and the East and West were always on the brink of war. No one was safe, and there was no peace anywhere.

A few individuals with the same values and convictions in the East and West gravitated together to pursue an end to the eternal conflict and endless, malicious destruction. Among us were many scientific geniuses from both sides who specialized in the various sciences, but what a lot of naive, well-meaning idiots we proved to be!

Our life expectancies were quite long, so we had ample time to develop and to learn, but alas, very few people were disciplined enough or learned to control their violent nature and greediness, which impeded progress, or so we thought. As a group we resolved to endeavor to bring peace to this prosperous world at any cost, for the constant conflict was unnecessary and useless as it left no time for spiritual development. Just about every individual thought he or she knew it all and that it was the others who were unintelligent and illogical. It was an intolerable situation for rational people, as our group, in our conceit, thought

388

we all were.

We isolated ourselves in the country away from cities and inquisitive minds to discuss ways and means to force the governments of both East and West to make peace and to control and educate their citizens so that we could create a harmonious environment where everyone had the time and opportunity for self-evaluation and advancement. That was the vision we had in our grand delusion of superiority. We didn't want to control the world, just coerce the two governments to cooperate and promote peace or even enforce it when necessary.

We tried various ways and means to achieve this, but were scoffed at and ridiculed each time. The last time we attempted a peaceful solution, our envoys were arrested and sentenced to long terms of imprisonment. We rescued them with ingenious precision and decided that we had exhausted the peaceful way and now had to create something so dire that they would finally take us seriously. We developed superbombs and weapons so powerful that the priests of the cities and the two continents had to listen and meet our demands. We never realized that we were inexperienced in politics or that we would have to test or demonstrate our superweapons, for we knew that they would work and assumed that the governing priests would appreciate that.

We invented and constructed some fascinating weapons but never realized that the priests would be too senseless to understand or give credence to our scientific jargon, which illustrated the havoc our bombs and other weapons could create if activated. They didn't have the slightest idea what we were talking about and demanded physical demonstrations to corroborate our claims. We naively told them that if they had the background to understand the written proof that our inventions were as powerful as claimed, they would realize that a demonstration would destroy our beautiful planet. They subsequently jeered and challenged us to use our weapons to change their minds about rejecting our illogical demands.

We were supposed to be geniuses, but in our ignorance we created a host of weapons we dared not test or demonstrate to show that we meant business. Beleaguered and defeated, we had to construct a safe place to store our dangerous inventions, for if our hidden laboratories were found, we knew there would be catastrophic consequences.

We carefully calculated the possible outcomes of moving the inventions by various means, but they were too ingeniously, yet thoughtlessly constructed. All of them were so sensitive that we couldn't tinker with them to deactivate or dismantle them, and they were, and will be for hundreds of centuries, capable of destroying this beautiful, flourishing planet. We dared not destroy or move them to another planet because the acceleration to achieve escape velocity, even with antigravity assistance, would create enough pressure to activate them. Perhaps after a million years or more, they might deteriorate enough to allow dismantling or moving them off the planet to explode them somewhere in space, but we won't live anywhere near that long.

While we cursed our lack of insight, we calculated that solid rock that would not likely crack or have the tendency to deteriorate would be the safest place to store the sensitive inventions. Away from prying eyes, we created this repository, a site deep in the rock, above ground level at the base of this distinctive peak. We imprinted the dire warnings on imperishable material, which we welded to the wall at intervals, and then we cautiously encased all the devices in shockproof material before we brought them here to install in their designated spaces. They are insulated against earth tremors and won't be affected that way. They are quite safe unless someone removes and handles them without care.

Unfortunately, our enthusiasm and misguided effort to bring peace to this war-torn planet invited all sorts of torment from the quarrelsome population and especially the political priests. One of the most brilliant Eastern scientist's family members were imprisoned in an effort to locate him, and through him, us. The abduction and call for his surrender was advertised in the media at regular intervals. Although he didn't show his grief, he used his expertise to assemble another bomb, which he assured us wouldn't do more damage than wipe a small city off the map. He had taken our mistakes into consideration and wanted it as a demonstrable example to extricate his family from the clutches of the vicious priests who were in power at the time.

In the meantime, we constructed another machine with a

gadget that would vaporize rock and could be used as a death ray. We thought that this time we would do something right and get to the politicians, even if we had to dig them out from underground or follow them into space.

We helped the Eastern scientist to secretly transport his small bomb to the capital city of the East and then returned on his insistence. He was going to blackmail the complacent priests and didn't want to endanger us. He assured us that everything would be all right, and we believed him. A few weeks later there was a tremendous explosion that rocked the entire planet. We were fortunate to survive because we live in the country, and our dwellings and laboratory were located in solid rock, which remained intact. We were thankful that we at least had the foresight to adequately protect our reckless inventions.

It is of no use to spend our time in recrimination because we don't know what really happened other than that there was now a huge crater where the main city of the East used to be. To our consternation, we also now have a planetoid as a satellite, which revolves around our planet at regular intervals and rotates around its own axis in the same amount of time. We don't know where it came from, but the same side of the planetoid always faces the Earth. It is in synchronous rotation with our planet and so close that it creates strong tides in the ocean.

Various other changes have taken place over a number of years, but we believe that the explosion triggered a sequence of events that forever changed the planet and life as we knew it. As the sun dwindled, we despaired, because gravity increased and the planet slowly reversed rotation and eventually revolved around the sun in the same direction, rotating faster than before. The days were therefore shorter. The axis had shifted, and the planet now tilted at an angle. The enormous crater, which was in the east, ended up in the celestial north, which was icing over rapidly. It is gradually getting colder, and we manufactured heavy garments to keep us reasonably warm. We believe the planet will eventually stop moving away from the sun, but we know that we will not live long in the vicious gravity and the colder climate, as we are too old to adapt. We therefore use gravity belts, which were designed for certain types of weightless sporting events. We hope that some of the younger children will adapt and survive. We now experience changing climates like the fourth planet as we revolve around the sun in the new orbit.

On our reconnaissance flights around the planet, we see new continents that have risen out of the sea, and the old continents have broken up and are in the process of moving away from each other or sinking to find equilibrium, for the planet wobbles slightly. There are now gigantic pits of molten rock spitting fire into the sky all over the globe, and we can only hope that our misguided inventions will not accidentally be set off.

We have resolved to gather and create repositories of our achievements before we die. There are two repositories: this one and another in new mountains near the huge crater. We can only hope that our efforts are not in vain and that the planet will survive and our repositories along with it, as a guide and perhaps a warning to future generations.

You were scanned and found responsible and intelligent enough to verify if the weapons next door are still safely in their places and the long room sealed. It is respectfully requested that you do so and report before you leave.

You will find a few small devices with the deposit of sealing canisters that will enable you to open and close the designated entrance, identifiable by a discolored area, from the outside. You are both invited to return and learn about what you are interested in as I am instructed to pass our knowledge and experience on so that your civilization may benefit and not make the same mistakes. You are requested to do so as you appear to be peacefully inclined.

Ogath asked, *What is the purpose of reporting? Don't you have sensors in that area?* Dai had had the same question but waited for his dad to ask the question in the correct way. *What can an immobile AI do anyway?* he thought. To his surprise the brain responded.

I am an artificially created brain tasked with guarding the repository. I am not mobile. The sensors I had in the vault played rays over all the machines to accelerate their decay without activating them. My inventors thought that may be the only way to undo their insidious creations. My connections to the sensors were damaged when a violent tremor shook the peak many centuries ago. I respectfully entreat you to investigate and repair damage to the outer wall if necessary. My other functions are to interpret brainwaves of visitors to verify their intentions and pass on information if they are deemed worthy. I can also eliminate evil-minded visitors if required.

We will comply. Where is the entrance? Again it was Ogath who responded.

The young man will need your assistance in translating the old language. When you return, I will direct you to the medical facility. We have technology that will help facilitate your rapid recovery after your ordeal. Young man, do you have any objections if I call you Dai? You must allow your dad treatment, and while he is recovering, I will instruct you in the old language and transfer other knowledge you will need. For the moment, this is how you activate the medical machines.

No, and I thank you, Dai said, ignoring the look his father gave him. He felt a strange sensation in his brain as the image of how to switch the automatic scanner on and other relevant information was implanted in his memory. Dai marveled at the sudden revelation and how easily it was transferred.

67

Ogath asked Dai to help him back onto the trolley since he was still very weak. They passed a large number of neatly stacked canisters. Those technically adroit ancients didn't do anything by half measures, Dai thought. There were enough canisters here for an army, and he wondered how big of an opening one could cover. He also wondered if the canisters still worked after all these years, but if the AI brain was anything to go by, they most certainly would. This ancient civilization apparently had a lot of scientific knowledge, and if he ever had the chance, he would return to learn all he could.

He measured the size of one of the canisters and tried to lift it, but it was too heavy. The trolley wasn't big enough, and even if it was, he wouldn't endanger his dad. The weight of a canister might crush the rails of the trolley. He decided that if they needed a canister, he would come back and roll one to where it was required, for they were round like a drum. He put two of the small gadgets, each about the size of a shoe, onto the trolley. One should never take anything for granted, he thought. Perhaps I should test them to see if they are still in working order, but that would have to wait until later.

They passed through the door, but the lights didn't automatically turn on in the wide, circular passage, which was lined with sizeable gadgets on one side. The earthquake that caused the connections to be broken must have been pretty serious, he thought. He played the bright light of the torch over the walls and ceiling, which was about twenty meters high and rounded for strength. The vault was about twelve meters wide.

When he shone the light on the ceiling, Dai saw a deep, jagged crack that appeared to be up to thirty centimeters wide in places. It extended from wall to wall, but the floor was untouched, or so it seemed at first glance. Dai didn't investigate further, for he wasn't here for that purpose, but he would report it. Perhaps there was a way he could repair it and the broken connections before he left. He moved to the nearest odd-looking object, which was about a meter high and wide and two meters long. It looked as if it was slapped into a roughly oblong shape by giant hands.

He adjusted the height of the trolley so Ogath could read the inscription behind it as he kept the light steady on it. "I can see that it is a much older version of the old language I was taught, and I would be able to read it if I had enough time to decipher everything. Can you understand it, Dad?"

"Yes. I will translate, but it will take some time as my skills are a bit rusty when it comes to this particular old language. We can read an inscription here and there, for we can always return when I'm strong enough to stand on my feet, but let's take the time to check a few and see if there are any similarities. We may never have the chance again, even though it is our intention to return one day. I have learned to make use of opportunities as and when they present themselves."

"Okay, Dad. If there is a medical facility, there may be some sort of a kitchen as well. Maybe I can prepare supper for us. What does this inscription say?"

Ogath translated haltingly, "'It must be stressed that this invention is very dangerous. If activated, it will convert the life-giving oxygen in the atmosphere into its individual components. As a deterrent, it is useless as it will kill everyone on the planet. Beware! It is very sensitive and must be handled and moved slowly with the utmost care. A slight bump may activate it. Do not remove it from its stand!' That's all it says, which is short and sweet. Let's move on to that oblong one, third from here to our right." Ogath had the other torch in his hand.

Ogath could read the second warning a bit more easily. "It has the same warning message but this one burns if activated and will burn until no oxygen is left on the planet to sustain life of any kind.

"Can you imagine inventing something even a five-year-old would know can't be used other than to destroy the very thing you want to save? No wonder they were constantly bashing each other's heads in. There are only nine inventions, but if I interpret the brain correctly, each one has the capability of destroying the planet. Let's check one or two more. The device that looks like a dumpy aerial bomb, for instance."

As Dai pulled the trolley in that direction, he said, "I agree with your remark about the ancient ones, Dad. They excavated this vault underneath the highest pinnacle of rock they could find. They should have realized that rockfalls will occur if a high peak, even of solid rock, is shaken often enough and that rock gradually deteriorates over time. It almost looks as if they really wanted the Earth destroyed once they were safely dead. Perhaps they relied on the rays and could foresee that an act of nature would destroy their effort. It's a miracle that one of these was not accidentally activated when the vault was bashed open, but hopefully they are not quite so sensitive after all these centuries."

As they moved from one invention to the next, Dai inspected the walls for more cracks or perhaps old or potential openings. He would have liked to see the opening that his mother and "the boys," as she referred to them, had repaired. It also might need reinforcement from inside. He stopped at another interesting-looking aerodynamic invention. It was rounded, about two meters thick and four meters long, with a sharp point at one end and small stabilizing fins at the other end. It was lying in a cradle on its side. He thought it would be very awkward and difficult to handle and would drop like a rock.

Ogath read aloud, "'This is a planet buster. We don't know why we invented such a completely useless thing. Our mistaken belief was that it would convince our ruling priests that we meant business. Comply or deal with the consequences! Naturally, they just laughed and invited us to demonstrate the superweapon. We really were a bunch of unthinking lunatics, a gathering of gifted children who invented dangerous, useless toys to see if they could do it. This device can be transported, but the contents will explode with the mightiest bang imaginable if dropped on its nose or if it is cut open. All that a remote observer will see is a miniature sun for a day or two. Leave it where it is for eternity, for that is how long the outer cover will last if not cut open or tampered with.'"

"Wow! They must have competed with each other for the most dangerous, unusable invention," Dai said. "Why don't I leave you at the machine that looks like a grav-car with a hollow nose and look for any breaches. We can't spend the entire night here reading about their well-meant, brilliant but dumb deterrents." Dai looked at his watch for the first time and whistled in surprise. "Dad, it's already seven o'clock! We spent more time listening to that recording than we realized. I told Koro that he can wait for us a little distance away at a rill because the way up is dangerous. I must get hold of him to tell him that we will be up here for some time."

"It's okay, Son. At least we can sleep here in safety without constant vigil. Carry on with what you have to do so that we can report. I must rest as soon as we have spoken to the AI. Like most AIs, it seems to be somewhat telepathic, but this one's range appears to cover the entire vault. It could be dangerous, and I wouldn't want to be an unwelcome intruder."

Dai quickly inspected the rest of the elongated vault. At the very end he found the repaired breach. It was night outside, so he couldn't see if any cracks existed. It looked rough and flimsy, so he went back and rolled a canister to where he thought it was needed. He positioned it in a gap, instinctively checked that the spout contraption was pointed toward the wall, and twisted the lever on top of it the only way it would go. Now he would see if it still worked after an incalculable length of time—maybe a million years or more.

He moved away rapidly as the substance started to flow and then began to blow forward as if pressure was suddenly applied from inside the canister. The sticky substance quickly enveloped the canister and completely covered the area. Then, while he watched as closely as he deemed safe to satisfy his curiosity, the substance hardened quickly and perfectly matched the color of the rock.

Now this is an invention I'll be interested in, he thought as he rejoined his dad. "This machine was designed to fly with someone sitting inside to guide it," Ogath said. "It was their last invention, and it has a sort of death ray that comes out of that pipe-like spout in front. It will kill any living thing in its path and can be adjusted to vaporize rock. They decided to shelve it with the rest of the devices when the planet shifted orbit. Now let's eat something before we report."

There was enough food left for his dad, but the herbal brew was finished. Dai chewed on a few raw tubers and a piece of meat while he towed the trolley back at a leisurely pace, and he didn't even think of asking the brain if any of the museum pieces (as he thought of them) could be used to cook a meal on.

He entered the green circle alone and reported their

findings. Then he asked if he was required to try to repair the connections. The brain said that would require instruction but could be done at a later date. The task required the use of the right equipment and might take a considerable amount of time. Right now he must follow the lights, help his parent into the medical unit, and then return for instruction while he slept.

Dai followed a dimly lit path next to the wall. Ogath said he doubted the medical unit would still function, but anything was worth trying once. Hedra had much to answer for. Dai vowed that he would follow the douche bag into the next galaxy if necessary, but pay he would.

They arrived before a closed door and a pale-green half circle was visible when the lights suddenly switched off. As Dai stepped into the half circle, the familiar voice said, *Leave the trolley here. The next room is a reception area. I recommend you leave your clothes and weapons there. In the next adjacent, small room you will both be decontaminated by rays that may affect your weapons. Your skin may dry, but ignore the powder as you will not be harmed in any way. Dai, assist your parent if he is too weak to stand. Then help him into the healing unit, take a shower, get dressed again, and return here. Ogath, I will take over and you will sleep for a few hours while your body is being rejuvenated to a functional level. Proceed.*

This time Ogath thanked the AI, the first time he could remember doing so anywhere during his epic journey. This one felt different from all the others he had encountered. Dai helped his dad into the reception area, helped him undress, and proceeded to the so-called decontamination room, where a number of colorful rays played over them for a few seconds. Both were astonished by the amount of skin that turned into powder, but they didn't feel any ill effects.

When the rays ceased, a door on the opposite side of the small room slid open. Dai helped his powder-covered dad into the next room, which was divided into cubicles. He lifted Ogath onto a table with a suspended cover above it. The table was big enough to accommodate a giant of five meters. The AI's mental voice instructed Dai to take a shower back in the reception area. Everything was automated so there was nothing else he needed to do. The door of the cubicle hissed closed behind him.

68

Dai told the AI that he was first going to roll canisters to the opening through which they entered so that they would be ready to activate when they left.

The brain replied, *I have extracted your terms of measurement from your thoughts. If the entrance point is wider than three meters, you must put them in the middle as measured from the sides and as measured from the inside to the outside, with the spouts pointed to the sides. The foam from two canisters will seal an area four meters in circumference, but it is better if you use three or four canisters. Is that the approximate size of the breach?*

Dai confirmed that the estimate was more or less correct. He rolled four canisters one by one into the breach and positioned them as directed. Then, thoroughly tired, he rolled himself into a blanket and went to sleep right in the circle of dim green light. The light dimmed before he dropped off into a deep sleep. The long-slumbering, inactive artificial-intelligence system implanted knowledge of a quite different science, which it divined the sleeping entity might need to survive until it returned. Its designers had given it the ability to scan and evaluate the state of evolution of any entity that entered the vault and either destroy it or lure it into the circle of rays. Part of its design was the discretion to discern and decide what knowledge to divulge or bestow on an entity that had reached a certain level of responsibility regardless of its civilized state. But it unwittingly stimulated a few dormant and unsuspected abilities in Dai's brain because its structure was somewhat different from the brains of the Old Ones.

Dai woke up very early. He felt refreshed and wondered how it was possible, since the surface was hard and the blanket didn't soften it any. His watch indicated that it was just after four o'clock, and he wondered how to spend the time until it was light enough to see what he was doing. Perhaps he could prepare food again if the means were available.

You have the knowledge. I imparted the information while

you slept, as you indicated the need for preparing a meal for your parent and expressed the wish to clean yourself. I will light the nearby alcove for you. There is an ablution facility available in the same area.

I thank you, Dai replied. *I didn't know or realize such facilities were available.*

I am impersonal and expression of appreciation is not required, but your courtesy shows a higher level of civilization than I perceived. Follow the lights to the alcove when you are ready. Unfortunately, you are much smaller than the Old Ones, but the facilities are in working order since I have some control over them. Your parent is recovering well and he will be completely healed by tonight. You can pass the day by checking some relics, as you call them. I can explain the function of each and you can just think any questions because I can now talk to you anywhere in the vault.

Dai automatically expressed his thanks, but the brain didn't comment again. He folded his blanket neatly and stowed it before he towed the trolley after him to the alcove carved out of the wall. The ablution area was dust free and had a door for privacy. The kitchen, or whatever it was called, was also clear of dust, and in it was a bench and five stools. For a giant more than twice his size, they would have been low stools, he thought. He pulled one of the stools into the "bathroom" to get around better.

He contacted Koro and the cat said he would wait by the small waterfall because the hunting was good and there was a small, safe place where he'd stayed overnight and could stay during the day and another night if necessary. The way up was very difficult to scale at a few places because he had tried during the night without much success.

As was the case in the "Lone Hill House," as Dai called Koro's discovery, the stove was just below eye level. He pulled a bench close to the stove and prepared the ingredients for the meal on the bench. Then he climbed onto the bench and lifted the pots to a plate on the stove. With the knowledge implanted in his brain, it was easy to use, but he had to watch everything closely because it was an unfamiliar experience.

He refilled his canteens at what looked like a sink, featuring automatic spigots that switched off when he removed the canteen. He wondered where the water came from, for it was fresh and tasted pretty good.

When he was finished, he made sure everything was neat, then returned to the green circle and expressed his thanks again since it was an ingrained habit. He had left the trolley in the kitchen, but he carried a canteen with him because he didn't want to return there for a drink of water every time he felt thirsty.

Despite your reduced stature as compared to that of the Old Ones, which I deduce is caused by the heavier gravity, you really are a fascinating creature, Dai, and it is regrettable that your culture is still a violent one, but there is hope yet. I perceived that you are engaged in uninvited conflict to safeguard the world and my location, which is appreciated. I will remember your personality and your name. I sensed that you have taken keys for the entrance which now is sensitized for use by you and your parent. Yes, that is an unadvertised precaution, and both of you may return with peacefully inclined companions of your choosing.

At the opposite end of the vault, you will see a short stairway leading slightly downward, about two meters, and the entrance used to be almost black. I suggest you test both keys: one to open and the other to close it again. The key is a signal to me to open or close the outside entrance. I suggest you familiarize yourself with the location of the entrance from outside for it may be blocked by rockfalls, which the Old Ones didn't foresee, for they didn't think in terms of thousands of centuries.

The mental voice, or perhaps it was just an impression on his brain, was impersonal, despite the attempted friendliness. His father was right. One must be very cautious when dealing with these aloof, insensitive inventions. They were very dangerous, for more information was concealed than was obvious at first impression, and he kept his thoughts shielded as best he could.

Dai found the stairs and the sort-of alcove, but although he could hear the creaks as ancient machinery strained to lift the door, nothing happened. Then the sounds ceased, and Brain (he liked the sound of that name better than AI) told him, *Would you go outside and check, Dai? Something, probably a heavy rockfall, is preventing the door from shifting, and I cannot overstrain the motors by forcing them. It should be the same color as inside, but I cannot be sure after the elapse of such a tremendous amount of time.*

Dai checked the doorway. It was almost black with a sort of reddish tinge, while the walls were a smudged orange-brown. The blending of colors looked very natural. Dai counted his steps as he followed the wall to the break; he couldn't rely on the color alone on the outside. He counted 157 steps to the break. Then he thought at Brain that he was going outside to check.

Dai was very careful when he tried to climb up the side, but he couldn't get a grip on the almost vertical rock face, and the way around was obstructed by large boulders that were also impossible to climb. It was just too dangerous, and to go down to the floor of the canyon was a waste of time, for he wouldn't know where to look for the entrance from half a kilometer down. He went back inside. As he approached the green circle, he broadcast his thoughts to Brain.

Is there any type of gravity car that I can use to go around to the entrance? I can't think of any other way to check how it is blocked or how to clear it. We are six or seven hundred meters above the canyon surface, and it will be impossible to see or do anything from down there. In his mind he formed a picture of the outside and the difficulties he was facing.

There are several types, but I do not think they are suitable for one man, and a short one at that, to clear obstacles. I can only recommend the last invention of the Old Ones. I will teach you how to operate and fly it and what it can do.

Dai sat down in the green light and the detailed knowledge was transferred. He just had to be very careful with the huge levers and other controls. He knew he would have to start slowly, as if he were flying a very sensitive aircraft, but he could do it. It wasn't that much different from a present-day grav-car or aircraft. When Dai had thought it over, Brain opened the connecting door.

Dai inspected the ray machine, as Brain named it, very carefully in the light of the strong torch. Then he climbed into the overly large seat and inspected the layout to familiarize himself with the position of every pushbutton, control lever, knob, and flip switch. Dai took his time, and when he was satisfied that he wouldn't make involuntary mistakes, he flipped a switch and started the machine. Thankfully there were no foot pedals, otherwise he would have been in a precarious situation, given the size of his seat. He slowly lifted the machine and was surprised how responsive it was and how sensitive the controls were. He'd have to be very careful until he was out of the vault, he thought, and until he had a better feel for it. Perhaps he should make a safety belt with the rope from the trolley.

As he passed slowly through the meters-thick connecting door, he heard strange creaks and groans from overhead. The hair on Dai's head stood up straight, but he was too absorbed in familiarizing himself with controlling the machine to hurry up. He couldn't afford to rush and could feel his body tense slightly, but he was safely past and almost level with the green circle when there was a sharp crack from above and behind. The connecting door didn't fall down with the expected earsplitting thud, but instead it rumbled down slowly as if still under partial control.

As Dai wondered what happened, Brain's voice said, *I suppose something like that was bound to happen sometime. The mechanism was damaged when the vault shook during the quake that disconnected the dangerous vault from my control. There was no way to warn you of the danger until you returned.*

I, too, am learning from you and your parent. I now know that I must apologize for not warning you of the danger and possibility of the mechanism failing. I do not have what you call the experience or implanted knowledge of such things.

It is okay, Brain. I'm just happy that the barrier didn't collapse on top of me. It came down slowly enough for me to accelerate the ray machine and escape. I'm going to land here so I can make some sort of safety belt to keep me strapped in if something goes wrong outside. He visualized what he was going to do so that Brain could understand his thoughts.

I follow your reasoning, Dai, and I'm learning. The Old Ones made provisions for the possibility of failure due to acts of nature when they erected the barrier doors. That much I know. The power I use is absorbed by the rock from the sun, and I have the means to store a considerable amount, and it is always kept at full capacity to accommodate future needs.

We know how to tap the power from the sun directly and how to store it, but it seems that we still have more to learn, Dai replied.

While the thought-picture exchange was going on, Dai grounded the car and fetched the rope, which he was reluctant to cut.

To his surprise, he found rings on both sides of the giant seat. Apparently the Old Ones had taken safety into account, but the harness or belt had disappeared centuries ago or had never been attached. Dai was grateful, and he double-looped the rope through the rings and tied the remainder at the opposite end to be out of the way. He fastened the remaining loose end over his lap when he was half-seated, half-standing, leaning against the seat while making sure he was still able to reach all the controls. He started and slowly maneuvered the ray machine through the opening without knocking the canisters over.

69

Dai had prepared for a sudden drop in height when he passed through the opening and was surprised it didn't happen. The machine flew serenely on as if a level floor were beneath it. He knew he must let it absorb power directly from the sun to recharge all the various components, for the sun was its main source of power. Like Brain, it also drew power from surrounding rock, as it could be used to tunnel to a specific target. So far, so good, Dai thought as he slowly pushed the speed lever forward. The ray machine accelerated sluggishly. It was just as well, Dai thought. After all these centuries, its power must be depleted. Hopefully it also drew power from the dangerous elements in the other gadgets.

The machine wasn't equipped with collision-evaders or anything to avoid accidents, so Dai wanted to get thoroughly acquainted with it before he flew close enough to anything or used the weapon to clear debris from the vault's entrance. Perhaps there was a reason for the omission, or perhaps the inventors just didn't think it necessary. Dai banked the death-dealing craft, as he thought of it, to fly away from the waterfall. He would invite Koro on board when he returned.

Dai didn't touch the speed lever again, but the craft accelerated as he flew up the canyon. Presumably the speed increased as it recharged. Very soon the controls became very sensitive, and he had to pull the speed lever back drastically. He suspected that the ray machine would easily outmaneuver present-day military craft. He had handled quite a few, and their performance didn't come anywhere near this craft.

As he turned the craft, he asked Koro if he wanted to accompany him back to the lake. In addition, their supplies were low and this craft had ample storage space, so he might as well gather food while he waited for his father to finish his treatment. He had decided he would keep the machine, as it might be safer if guarded by the Fighters, and perhaps it could be used to defeat the enemy.

Since he had tested its maneuverability, when he picked

Koro up, he kept the craft steady because the cat was not yet adapted to flying. Koro sat close to him with as much of his body under the rope as he could manage without discomfort. Dai flew over the waterfall and followed the path he had taken on foot, for there was no other way he knew of. Everything was still the same. He took the opportunity to fly a few kilometers over the long lake, but soon returned to gather greens and tubers, for time, too, was flying.

He returned to the vault the same way. It looked vastly different from up in the air, and he really had to guess where the constructed outer door was supposed to be. There was a pile of rubble around the break that stretched for kilometers on either side, and even the top, which must have been smooth once, was piled high with debris. Countless rockfalls must have occurred over time. No wonder the way up was so difficult. It was a wonder, and also a pity, that the whole vault wasn't buried under many tons of rubble. Another hundred centuries might get the job done, Dai thought, but right now it was a different matter altogether.

Dai let the craft hover a few meters beyond the break, but on a lower level, and started to vaporize the rock in the direction of where the outer door was located. By the gods, he marveled, this weapon is extremely powerful. Where it was pointed, meters of rock turned to dust in seconds, and he constantly had to move the craft forward. It was really easy, but he had to remember that tons of rubble waited above for an opportunity to shift downward. He tried not to think about whether it was worth all this trouble, for other falls and shifts would most certainly occur in the future.

Where necessary he moved the craft up to vaporize the rubble on top of the vault above the curve to prevent the rubble from sliding down. He could only hope that it was not too obvious, for it might signal the vault's location to attentive searchers. Karna would have had the satellites' orbits changed by now, so he wasn't concerned about being observed from up there. After a while he passed a discoloration in the rock, but he continued to clear the rubble for about two hundred meters more before he turned the weapon off.

Then he returned to the natural-looking discolored rock, which was now about two meters above the pile of accumulated rubble. He pressed the only button on one of the door keys. As a section of the rock shifted outward and upward, he pressed the other key, and the door stopped its upward shift and closed again. There was no indication of a concealed entrance left other than the discoloring. He returned to the breach and flew inside.

Koro had quietly gone to sleep while Dai was clearing the accumulated rubble to one side of the vault, but now he suddenly woke up. Dai was astounded that he could follow Brain's conversation with Koro with no effort at all, and so was Koro.

I inadvertently stimulated certain centers in your brain, Dai, which awakened some unusual abilities that I am unable to explain. Ogath also responded very fast to treatment and now complains of hunger. He is waiting in the place you call the kitchen. I suggest you prepare a meal, and while you are busy, we can talk, for I sense what your brain perceives while you are with me.

When Dai joined him, Ogath looked well and said he felt great. Dai explained, for Brain's benefit as well, that he considered his mission completed and would take the flying weapon-craft, if he was allowed to, because the "dangerous" vault was now permanently isolated until forcefully opened either by accident or intentionally. Brain thought it over for a second and then conceded that it was all right to take the craft away, as the machines in the main vault were meant for peaceful everyday use.

Ogath remembered the description of it he had read and agreed that as a weapon in responsible hands, it would be difficult to beat. Dai used a piece of the rope to attach the trolley to the craft, but it was late, and they decided to stay over and leave early in the morning. Although Koro might establish a link with Lur, it would be difficult to find her place in darkness.

The following morning, Ogath walked to the breach to activate the canisters as Dai slowly eased the craft with the attached trolley through. Once out, he turned the craft around in a tight circle so his father could board on the other side. Koro again lay close to Dai so that the makeshift seatbelt could cover him as well. For the Old Ones, it would have been a one-man vehicle, but there was enough space for two present-day humans and a huge cat.

They watched as the canisters were overwhelmed by the rapidly expanding brownish liquid spouting out as if under constant pressure. The substance quickly spread into every niche and crack to completely seal the opening and took on the color of the dark-brown rock while it quickly dried. Dai knew that it was already nearly as hard as the rock itself and would be in about an hour. The Old Ones knew what they were doing, all right, he thought. The greedy ones of this age would give their front teeth and murder their mothers to learn these sciences.

He slowly turned the craft away and gradually increased speed, since he didn't want to lose the trolley with their equipment and waste more valuable time. He was glad his father didn't look so haggard and half-dead anymore. His step was spry and his face was lit with an eager smile of anticipation. Dai thought how he had a lot to thank the Old Ones and Brain for, because his own brain felt suspiciously clear and his senses were more alert than ever before. He decided to keep a close tab on himself until he had discussed things with his mother and Ekaasi. The Permerian would independently evaluate these unexpectedly awakened dormant powers and guide him as to their proper use.

The craft had fully powered up the day before and was therefore fast. They turned into "Lur's Canyon" within the hour, just as the morning sky brightened. Dai asked Koro to warn his mother that they were near and to not shoot when they saw the strange craft. He flew on at a reduced speed until he recognized the area around the cave.

Lur came skipping down the steep path as lithely as a woman half her age, and Dai had to ground the craft quickly because Ogath loosened the rope safety belt and jumped out. He seemed to be running before he hit the ground.

Dai wisely lifted the craft, made a circle around them, and hovered up to the old cave, where he grounded the craft and powered off. Surra walked into view as she came to find out why Lur had left them so suddenly. Dai wondered how he knew this without trying to read her thoughts. He must talk to Ekaasi before he made an ignorant mistake he might regret.

He gave Surra a mock curtsy and said with a smile, "Good morning, Your Majesty. You are up nice and early."

Surra gave him a fierce hug, but not for long, and Dai

knew why. Gemur might be watching. "I missed you, you rascal. I'm glad you're back. Who's the stranger your mother is hugging so long and fiercely?"

"You're not going to believe this, but I found my father we believed lost, wandering in the canyons looking for us. I am very lucky, you know. First I found you, then my mother, and now my father. I must have done something right in my life to deserve such good fortune. Next, I'm planning to go after Heltos, Sorcuk, and Hedra."

"This time I'm coming with you. By the way, where's Mouf?"

"He got himself killed, together with his friend Kuras." A sudden thought occurred to him. "Did any other villagers arrive here after we left?"

"No, but Laecur is still here. He refused to leave us defenseless. Why do you ask?"

"I was promised that a few villagers would come to guard you while I was away, but it's not important at this point. I think we should all relocate tomorrow, including my mother and Laecur."

Just then, Lur grabbed and hugged him equally as fiercely. She was crying silently, and he somehow knew how she felt. She couldn't speak because she was filled with joy and overcome by gratitude. Dai returned her embrace because he somehow shared her feelings and didn't want to ruin the moment, but it was important that he get her to act right away.

"We will talk before I go, Mom. You are not safe here, as Mouf and some of the villagers sold out to Hedra and company. Don't trust any of them except Laecur, and take him along if he wants to go. It is important that you leave by tomorrow at the latest, if not sooner. Dad can fly you out in the bus, and you can home in on Aunt Nogalithe or Skrot. I must leave here as soon as possible because I must talk to Ekaasi urgently. You can probably feel that something strange has happened to me, and I believe you can help, but Ekaasi may be more experienced in such matters."

Dai ignored Surra's inquiring glance because his involuntary roaming senses had encountered an approaching party, and it wasn't friendly. Somehow, without conscious thought, his observation and decision to discourage the raiding

409

party was transferred to his mother, father, and Koro. Surra felt bewildered and left out when Lur took her arm and guided her back to the hideout, but Dai knew his mother would offer some sort of logical explanation.

Koro knew the drill. He galloped down the path and would fade out of sight the moment he sensed the enemy's nearness to keep Dai informed of their progress and intentions. He would allow them to pass and then attack from behind when asked to do so. Dai required his father as backup, and Ogath, without knowing how or why he did it, since he was used to being out in front, fell a few steps behind as they silently stole down the path. Dai was grateful that his father was an old hand in the game of surprise and being quiet.

When they reached the main trail, Dai turned onto it until he arrived at a small clearing a few steps farther on. He sensed that the party was still a few hundred meters away. Koro let them know that there were eleven in the party and only the two in front had evil minds. The rest were reluctantly there under orders. Dai quietly invited his dad to take a seat somewhere and be an observer. Then he moved to the middle of the wide trail and took a wide-legged stance with his arms folded, waiting with his head bowed as if in contemplation, but his eyes were alert.

70

The first man was a slovenly villager. Dai immediately recognized the leader as Huram, a poltroon kicked out of the Fighting Priests for being too much of a coward about eight or nine years ago, even before Dai had started training. There had been a big stink because Huram was well connected politically. He was a type Dai just couldn't tolerate.

The villager ignored Dai and tried to pass, but Dai extended a hand and shoved him back into the so-called leader. Both went down, but the troops didn't react as they would have if they had any respect for their leader.

As expected, Huram jumped up and reacted angrily. "I know you! I'm going to have your oysters for obstructing me in carrying out my orders! Those miserable Fighters have gone too far this time."

"You'll have diddly-squat," Dai calmly told him. "I know you are here to abduct an innocent priestess for the pleasure of your master. So how are you going to explain that in a court of law, you phony?"

Huram went red in the face. Before he could think of an appropriate retort, the villager charged Dai. Dai sidestepped swiftly and hit him with the side of his hand just below the skull behind the neck. There was the sickening crunch of bones. Huram went white in the face as the villager took another three steps before he fell down on his face. Fortunately for Huram, he didn't raise his gun, for he would have died instantaneously.

Dai tried a little reason before taking drastic measures. "Why don't you march back to Hedra and tell him the priestess's place was deserted when you got there? It might save your life, at least for now."

"Don't threaten me, Daiyus. What I do has nothing to do with you. You are interfering with official business. I order you to get out of my way, or I'll have to use my weapon. You don't stand a chance," Huram blustered.

Dai replied in a cold, measured voice, "To you, I'm Dart the avenger, and I've already made it my business. It's my mother you came to abduct for your master's pleasure. If you have any god to pray to, start now or turn around and report whatever you like. You will not get past me." He saw Huram's face turn ashen with bewilderment and trepidation.

Perhaps Huram's fear of Hedra was greater than his ingrained cowardice; Dai felt him gathering a kind of desperate courage—or maybe it was panic. Huram suddenly lifted the rifle with a shout and pointed it at Dai. The needler seemed to jump into Dai's left hand, and Huram died with a needle in his head.

Dai noticed that the men had not even tried to ready their guns. One stepped forward and introduced himself by name. He said, "We were ordered to accompany that cowardly piece of excrement, sir. If you will permit it, we will withdraw and return. We will take the bodies with us, although we would rather not." He stood proudly at attention.

Dai rather liked the disciplined soldier and the courage he displayed by not asking for clemency and leaving the decision to Dai. He put his hand out to the man, who shook it.

"I know you are not here by choice," Dai said. "Leave them here, and the scavengers will clean up by tonight. Tell your commander that these two were separated from you during the march, and you don't know what happened to them. I'll leave the details to you. Also say you found that the location where the priestess was supposed to be abandoned. I have a few supplies. Do you need any?"

"No, sir, we don't need any, but thank you. We have our hard rations, and we might go back and kill an antelope at a watering hole a few kilometers back."

Dai put his hand out again. The soldier shook it with a smile, then told his companions that they had a long way to go and the sooner they got a move on, the better.

Dai turned to his father, who nodded his approval. As soon as the soldiers were out of sight around the first bend, Ogath took his strange gun out of its holster and said, "You already have two very handy weapons, but I'm going to give you this one as well, for you will need its unique properties to outsmart our enemies. When we reach the camp I'll show you how it may be transferred to another person who is deemed worthy of it. Watch what it does."

He pointed it at Huram's body and pulled the trigger.

412

There was a brief hum-hiss and then Huram's body disintegrated and evaporated in a flash. The same happened to the villager's body. Only their guns remained as evidence that they had been there.

Koro came out of the bushes like a silent red-brown shadow.

"As you've seen, Son, this is the perfect weapon for murder. That is why only a person with absolute integrity and no criminal tendencies is entrusted with such a weapon. It will be yours in a week or two. The holster can be thought and shaped into a shoulder holster."

While they walked back, Dai thoughtfully remarked, "Dad, as you have already experienced, there are sudden, powerful wind-shear conditions in these canyons. I left the remotes for the bus's lock and nullifier with Mom. I suggest you engage the nullifier and take the bus up directly to where you are free from severe drafts. Mom can contact Aunt Lithe or the old lady cat called Skrot to guide you in. I urgently need to talk to my Permerian friend Ekaasi, for she can help me control these sporadic flashes of sure knowledge that Brain accidentally stimulated. I'm just going to introduce you to the gang I'm responsible for, and then I'm off."

Dai left his rucksack on the ray machine and towed the trolley up toward Lur's hideout, for they would need it to load the bus. He told his dad about the former king's heart condition and that he must be handled diplomatically. The boy, Krekur, or his father, Gemur, could pull the trolley.

Ogath assured him that he need not worry; he knew how to sum up and handle strangers, including royalty.

Koro was unsure whether he should go with Dai or stay to guide Lur and Ogath. Somehow Dai shared the cat's indecision and told him that he would appreciate it if he stayed to guide his parents to the camp with the assistance of the lady Skrot. Koro reluctantly agreed to stay there and guard while the humans loaded the bus.

Dai introduced his father and then gathered the rest of his personal things. He quietly told Laecur that Mouf and Kuras were no longer in the picture, but didn't share the details. Laecur shrugged his shoulders and said he had nothing to return to in the village and that if Dai and the priestess didn't mind, he would

413

join his childhood friend, Murima, at the camp. He could hunt and act as a lookout.

Dai relayed the information about Koro and Laecur to Lur. Then, sensing Surra's intention to accompany him, he quietly left when she was not around.

Not caring that the small machine might register on someone's sky-scanning equipment, Dai took the craft up high above the mountains and pushed the speed lever forward. He was surprised at the speed it attained in a few seconds. *Man, this machine is really something*, Dai thought happily. Once over the mountains, he dived down to ground level and changed direction toward the camp.

The surprise in Skrot's mind was evident when he contacted her to pinpoint the camp's location. The journey had taken less than fifteen minutes, which pleased Dai. He landed the small craft inside the clearing and moved it under the overhang. Nogalithe, Ekaasi, and the cook welcomed him with broad smiles; they clearly were genuinely pleased to see him. Murima, true to his profession, left to prepare coffee. Dai took a few minutes to talk to Skrot and ask about her general well-being, which she appreciated. She could walk around without pain and was back to her old self, but with a few reservations. She liked it here away from the hustle and bustle of the city.

Dai almost didn't recognize Nogalithe. Her face was rounder, and she was almost a replica of his mother. While he had coffee and the women had tea, he told them of his problem and how it started two or three days ago. Lithe and Ekaasi looked at each other, and Dai could almost, but not quite, follow the rapid exchange of thoughts by the two priestesses.

Then Ekaasi spoke. "We feel genuine compassion for you, Dai, but this actually increases your chances of survival by about two hundred percent. This artificial stimulation should not have happened, but seeing that it did, we will help you all we can. What is done cannot be undone, but this plays havoc with the prophecy. An unknown factor has been introduced by the capricious gods, and who knows what can happen now. You have had certain centers of your brain stimulated that normally take years to develop. We will have to do something drastic, as time is running out. Will you trust us to deeply hypnotize you and bring you into a trance state so that we can transfer our knowledge to you?

"We will also implant the knowledge that allows you to restrict and control what we can only call 'automatic scanning' or 'recognition of innermost thoughts.' Otherwise it can be very embarrassing, or even downright dangerous at times if one cannot control his or her tongue. We are glad, because these abilities will give you a definite advantage over our enemies. But at the same time, we are sad because it will be a burden you will have to bear the rest of your life. It will not be easy.

"To spell it out for you very carefully, Dai, you have the natural ability to peer at a person's innermost thoughts and emotions. You also have the ability to influence and persuade a person or groups to do whatever you want. But be warned. There is a terrible price to pay if you misuse your gift for selfish purposes. It will project back to you and destroy you, body and soul, within a very short period. Keep this dire warning in mind, always. At times it may be irresistible, but bear in mind that once used for personal gain, you won't be able to resist the lure of evil.

"With that said, we will also have to teach you how to shield your mind so you cannot be controlled to force you to misuse those abilities. Then we will have to make you suffer until you can withstand the onslaught of both Lithe's and my mind together. I'm sorry, Dai, but unfortunately it is necessary for your psychological health and safety. The suffering will develop your mind and make you strong. Now I have to ask, are you willing? The world may survive, but you may join the evil forces if not properly trained. What do you say?"

Dai nodded. He knew Ekaasi very well and sensed she hadn't told him all of it. His natural inclination to seek help had been correct. He had no wish to control anyone or to be a puppet on a string for anybody else. He said, "I came to you two and not to my mother because I had a feeling that I could be dealing with something so powerful and dangerous that it might get out of hand if not handled correctly. Will you two promise me one thing? If you ever find out that I'm under the control of a more powerful mind, or discover that I'm using these abilities for self-gain, please neutralize me."

They knew he was serious and solemnly promised that they would try their best, but they were sure it wouldn't be necessary. Ekaasi said they must start his training immediately, but they should move to a nearby location within earshot of the camp where they would be away from inquisitive eyes. They had to have absolute privacy with no disturbances of any kind. Dai said he would ask Skrot and Koro, when he arrived at the camp, to discourage anyone from getting close.

Ekaasi showed him the place she had in mind. It was a dense growth less than four hundred meters from the camp, away from grazing patches and the trail to the camp, but still against the ridge that formed the overhang. A small stream ran through it.

Dai fetched an axe and cleared a path to the ridge, then pulled the cut-offs into openings to make the dense, thorny growth inaccessible to anything except snakes and rodents. He cleared a wide half circle against the rock, which fortunately still had something of an overhang, albeit not enough to form a decent shelter. At Ekaasi's request, he stacked dry firewood, for Lithe would need to keep a fire going all the time to brew restorative concoctions. Dai gathered enough to keep a cooking fire going for a week. By that time Bolly's bus had arrived, and it was time for supper.

Dai asked the former king if he personally knew any medic at a clinic, preferably not in Bojon, who could be trusted implicitly to treat him. He asked him to use the caller in the bus to speak to the medic and instructed his mother to use as much of Tumar's money as she deemed necessary to see to the king's needs, in addition to buying supplies and anything else that was needed. He asked Lur to take care of things because he was going to be otherwise engaged. His father would take care of the bus, and Lur and Lithe should discard their robes for civilian clothes. They must keep in mind that every stranger in Bojon would be watched like a hawk, he said, and it might be better to shop and use a clinic somewhere else. He told his father that Lithe would explain the properties of the bus and that he must make use of those properties to safeguard the bus and its passengers.

71

Dai's brain felt too big for his skull. It wasn't exactly a headache, but his head throbbed with a vengeance. He fought on regardless. Both Ekaasi and Lithe's faces were white, and they, too, fought to control Dai. The very air around them throbbed with the intensity of the battle.

Koro couldn't take it anymore. He took to his heels and galloped away from the camp. A friend can only take so much. He had been told not to interfere to try to help his friend, but he couldn't understand why so much mental punishment was being inflicted on Dai. This had been going on for eight days, and even he could feel Dai's exhaustion. Every time Dai collapsed, a haggard Lithe would brew some concoction on the fire, make him drink it while she and Ekaasi did the same, and then the punishment would start all over again. Humans!

This time Dai stubbornly held onto his shield even when Nogalithe collapsed. Ekaasi touched him on the shoulder and told him to relax while she attended to Lithe's welfare. Dai staggered to his feet and walked around to ease his cramped muscles. He had slept very little during the past week, but he felt grateful to Ekaasi and Nogalithe for their unselfish devotion to get his brain into shape to withstand almost any onslaught.

Lur had felt the cessation of conflict and mentally asked an exhausted Ekaasi if she could come and assist. She was more than welcome, Ekaasi told her, for she was on the verge of collapse herself. But Lur had other news as well.

When she joined them, she told Dai, "I didn't want to disturb your training, for even Karna thought it a priority. Over the last ten days or so, there have been some strange occurrences, including the disappearance of a number of identified key figures on Earth, Mars and Shaytan. There is no concrete evidence to prove anything one way or another. Karna thinks the masterminds behind all this are now on Earth and turning their attention to Bojon. There are rumors and indications that something big is going to happen very soon. It may be vital to check on the palace at the first opportunity. Your father and I can help as well."

While Lur helped her sister drink her own concoction, Dai looked at Ekaasi. "Well, old friend, what do you think?"

"You are worn out, Dai, but ready, I think. We must all get a good night's sleep, and you can deal with the palace invasion in the morning. Have Koro accompany you. We will stay in constant contact with him and mentally assist you if and when necessary."

Dai went up to her, put his arms around her torso, and gave her a tight hug with his cheek against her soft pelt. "Thank you, my friend. I have a feeling that you and Lithe saved me. I owe you both more than I can repay in this lifetime."

She patted him on the shoulder. "The Permerians owe you a debt of gratitude for what you are about to do. Now go for a walk and relax a while before supper and a night's sleep."

Lur took his hand and walked with him in the general direction of the camp. Dai felt the fatigue of the past few days' mental battles—first against Lithe, then against Ekaasi, and then against both—overwhelm him, but there was something he had to do. He mentally sent a request to his father to join them. He now had a powerful mind, but it didn't please him. Ekaasi was right. It was definitely a burden to watch one's thoughts and desires all the time.

Ogath joined them a little way from the camp. Dai quietly led them away from inquisitive eyes to a scattering of rocks and asked them to be seated. He told them of the discovery made by Koro, then took their hands while he transferred mental images of the location and what he'd seen inside.

"I will give you the tablet, and on the off chance that I'm not around when Tumar returns, will you give her the statuettes, Mom? They are a gift, as they are almost perfect replicas of her. I'd like to keep something of the treasure for myself, but the rest is yours. You can decide what you want to do with it. My idea was to give Surra the contents of the house's upper story to use as decoration for the bare throne room in the Bojon palace."

"We'll decide together when this is all over," Ogath said when Dai paused. Then he told Lur he wanted to transfer the Scrii gun to Dai and that it would take a while. She left them alone and returned to the camp.

Ogath explained to Dai how to operate the gun, how to

418

reshape the holster by mental and manual shaping into any form required, and then the process of transferring the gun to someone else. After the gun was transferred to Dai, he tiredly reshaped the hip holster into an underarm holster because of the need to hide it from casual inspection. He thanked his father and halfheartedly joked that he felt like a one-man invasion force. As they walked slowly back to the camp, Dai asked his father to wake him before dawn and then drop him and Koro off in the woods near the palace.

"I am fully recovered, and I would like to go with you, Son, but I also realize that I will just be in the way. That is why I decided to transfer the gun to you for additional protection. I still have the urge to hang Hedra upside down over a small fire and pull his toenails out one by one. Maybe I will still get a chance if he manages to slither away. I know it's just daydreaming, but it's nice to imagine him begging and squirming like the worm he is."

"I understand, Dad. I will see what I can do to accommodate your wish. He's not the type who will ever regret his evil ways, though."

In the early dawn of the next morning, Dai approached the northwest corner of the palace. He asked Koro to stay well back and check the vicinity for enemies or unwelcome visitors while he entered the correct sequence to open the entrance. His newly developed senses, so unexpectedly awakened by Brain, screamed a warning of terrible danger. He fully expected a tremendous blast and therefore stood well to one side while he let the door swing slowly and partly open, held in check with the short, slender pole he had cut for that purpose. He was greeted by a strong snake odor. He opened his tunic and drew the Scrii gun, for the odor wasn't that of any earthly snake.

Dai recognized the smell though, and it made him furious to think that anyone could be irresponsible enough to smuggle the deadly flying dragonsnakes of the fifth planet, Shaytan, to Earth. Even zoos were not permitted to import the species because they would multiply like rodents, which would make Earth a very unsafe place to be. The dragonsnakes preferred remote jungles, but would find the warmer climate of Earth ideal for rapid propagation and would quickly adapt, especially in the remote and hot canyons. If a pair escaped, they would be impossible to hunt down and exterminate, for they would lay eggs all over the continent, and sooner or later, some of the snakes would find their way to other continents.

Knowing the reaction of cats to snakes, he warned Koro to stay away, then pushed the barrel of the Scrii gun through the opening and pulled the trigger. His dad's instinct had been correct; he needed the gun. If any were near, they would be vaporized so that he could enter. He told Koro what he suspected and to warn Ekaasi while he made sure the vestibule, the most likely place dragonsnakes would roost, was clear before he let Koro accompany him.

Dai once again opened the door just wide enough to get an arm through, pointed the gun first left, then right, then up, and then toward the tunnel, each time pulling the trigger. There was no antidote for a dragonsnake's venom, and even if there were, it would be useless because the victim's body was almost immediately paralyzed, and death followed within seconds since breathing was impossible.

He opened the door, jumped through, and closed the door in one fluid motion. Then he switched on the torch in his left hand. He relied on his enhanced senses to warn him if any living thing approached, and he inspected the little antechamber thoroughly for eggs that might have escaped the Scrii gun's beam, since this place would be ideal for a den. He didn't find any, but his instinct warned him of danger approaching. He turned to face the tunnel and raised the gun.

A two-and-a-half-meter-long dragonsnake came charging toward him on four legs, its blinded, slitted eyes fixed on the light and the fangs in its wide open mouth dripping venom. Dai was grateful that its wingspan was too wide to allow flight in the narrow tunnel, but even on the ground it was fast. He pulled the trigger just in time. It was quite unnerving to watch the deadly reptile disintegrate just about a meter from his face. He waited a few minutes before he pressed the sequence to open the door for Koro, who hissed angrily when he jumped into the chamber.

Don't let the smell upset you, Koro, Dai told him. *I know of one I killed, but there may be more. I have to proceed slowly to check every crack for snake eggs, but follow some distance behind me and watch for enemies from behind. Don't charge past me to help, for then I might kill you as well. Control your fighting instincts, please, for Dad's gun does not distinguish*

*between friend and foe. I'm going to build a partial shield to be
ready for anyone who might want to control me. You must act
very disinterested in me. Give the impression that you followed
me in by accident and that only the snake smell interests you.
Start right now and keep it up until we are out of the tunnel. That
way you can ask Ekaasi for help if I find myself in a situation
where I'm controlled by someone else. If you sense someone
else in my mind and I act stiff-like, raise the alarm. Otherwise
please follow me and report, if you can do so without being
detected.*

*It will be difficult, Dai, but I will try my best, as I'm here to
look after you. I'll try to warn you if I sense a snake thing ahead.*

Thanks, pal.

Dai formed a shield around his mind but, because it still
required concentration on his part, just loosely so he could
tighten it instantly if necessary. As they followed the tunnel, he
kept the gun pointed in front of him and the light playing along
the sides and floor as far as it would go until the next twist in the
meandering tunnel. Logically, the snakes, if more than one had
been introduced to guard the tunnel, would make the chamber
their den, so he hoped they were all dead, but he couldn't stay
alive on assumptions. He let his senses probe cautiously ahead,
ready to cut the probe the moment he sensed the presence of
another human mind.

Dai didn't dare switch the torch off when he passed the
marker. Surra had said that light should only be visible inside the
chambers when the peepholes were opened. The last part of the
tunnel was straight, so he let the light shine briefly along it, for it
would reflect snake eyes. He saw nothing, so he assumed he
had killed any snakes that might have been in the small
chamber, but he nevertheless kept the gun ready in his hand.
He didn't probe the chambers, nor did he open the peepholes as
he passed them. The door to the king's chamber had been
forced open and was now boarded over. Dai's senses probed
the room briefly but found no life. He proceeded to the throne-
room door.

The trap was as he'd left it some weeks before. He
dismantled the trap and pocketed the nerve bomb. So, he
thought, they only looked in the king's room for a secret door,
found it, and activated the nerve bomb. Then they introduced

421

one or more dragonsnakes and boarded it over with perhaps a small door to feed the dragons.

Dai cautiously probed the throne room and felt instantaneous alarm. An irresistible force clamped his mind into a viselike grip. He wasn't overwhelmed and didn't fight back for he wanted to enter the throne room, ostensibly under control, with the gun in his hand. Someone who could, out of fear, infest a tunnel with such delightful pets could not be trusted even with a gun pointed at her. He was sure it was a female mind, but couldn't explain, even to himself, why he knew it was a female with such tremendous power. An ordinary, untrained mind would have been totally lost.

He felt Koro's alarm, but somehow sent him the assurance that he was in control of his senses. He was to wait and follow when all eyes and attention were focused on Dai.

The female tried to probe his mind, but Ekaasi and Lithe had shown him how to deceive without arousing suspicion. He projected an ordinary, servile, obedient mind on a mission without disclosing particular details. He felt the contempt of someone so sure of herself that she didn't even consider deception. She ordered him to come to her. Koro had moved up against his legs and bumped him to make sure that his friend really could take care of himself. Dai rubbed his back and felt him relax. In a whisper he asked Koro to softly close the door when it was safe to do so, and then he opened the door.

A strange female, vaguely resembling Sorcuk but older, was sitting regally on the throne, complete with crown and scepter. What amused Dai was that the hard throne was now bedecked with soft, luxurious cushions. A meter or two away, and somewhat in front of the throne, was a muscular man feasting his eyes on Dai over the barrel of a very-large-caliber gun. Dai was sure it was an automatic repeater since the guy was obviously a bodyguard. He noticed Hedra and an assortment of individuals sitting on not-so-comfortable benches just below the stairs.

He was aware of everything, but his eyes were on the woman because she expected him to be completely under her control. He contemplated smiling at her but resisted the temptation. He must appear as she fully expected him to be: hers, to do with as she pleased. He let the gun hang down at his side. The woman was very sure, even overconfident, of her mental powers because she exerted pressure on his brain, but he resisted the compulsion to go down on his knees and crawl to her. He walked right up to the guard, who tried to take the gun from him.

Dai had to exert fierce control over his facial muscles not to laugh at the fierce yell the guard uttered as he grabbed the gun and then twisted in agony until his muscles relaxed in unconsciousness. Dai only felt a mild tingling. The woman jumped up in alarm. Dai saw that she used to be quite muscular, but the muscles were turning into flab. She must still be quite strong, he thought, and her strength must not be underestimated.

She commanded, "Let go of the gun, boy, or I'll have you shot."

Dai just looked at her as if he was deaf and dumb. His friends had trained him in all aspects of control over the last week.

"Answer me!" the woman yelled furiously.

Dai felt her control on his mind slip, but he didn't put his cards on the table. He just said in a monotone, "I can't."

The woman was taken by surprise. It showed in her eyes, but she said, "Why not? Answer me!"

"It was given to me by an alien," he lied without blinking an eye and still in a monotone as if under her control. "I found him in a canyon, dying of thirst. I don't know how he got hold of one of our flyers, but the flyer was sabotaged, and he crashed in a dry canyon. That was about ten days ago." Out of the corner of his eye, he saw Hedra's face go white. Then smug satisfaction replaced the shocked expression, but Dai was going to change that.

"He didn't die, though. I was looking for my friend, Princess Sorcuk, who can help him recover further. She told me of this tunnel and how to get here. Where is she and what are you doing on her throne?"

He saw Hedra's face go ashen again. The man seemed to sag like a melting butterball, but his eyes revealed that he was already scheming. He didn't appreciate that his nemesis had caught up with him in the form of Dart.

423

72

The woman's eyes hardened. "You are not permitted questions, boy! But to answer this one: she and her boyfriend, Heltos, are fornicating in hell. Both thought they could blackmail and threaten to punish us if we didn't do what they wanted. By the way, how did you get past my pets, and what did you do to them?"

Dai decided to lie. Not only did he want to inflict unbearable physical pain on Hedra, but he also wanted to subject him to extreme mental torment if possible. So he asked innocently, "What pets? The door to the tunnel was open, and I didn't see any pets. There was only a strong smell of snakes, which is why you see the gun in my hand. It jumped into my hand, and now it won't unlock my fingers. I guess there are still snakes around here somewhere."

The woman's face went white as a sheet, and Dai felt her vise on his mind slip somewhat. She fell back on the cushioned throne, while Dai saw and heard Hedra fall off the bench. He suppressed a smile.

The woman groaned and held her head between her hands. "This lovely planet is doomed, and it's all your fault, Hedra. You assured me they couldn't get out. You neglected to feed them properly while stuffing your own overly fat face! Get up and do something right for a change, you miserable slob, or you're past tense!" The woman's voice was shrill with panic. "The dragons have no natural enemies on Earth, and we'll have to abandon our plans to take over this beautiful planet. No one will be safe, thanks to you, you despicable lowlife!"

Hedra struggled to his feet. Those around him hurriedly vacated their places while holding up their noses in disgust.

Hedra pointed an accusing finger at Dai. "I know him, and he's lying. He's a trainee with the Fighting Priests, and he was prying around in the canyons, trying to locate the treasure of the ancients. His name is Daiyus, and he has built up quite a reputation, although it's mostly hearsay. I think he killed your dragons and is lying to get me into trouble." But his voice was shrill and unconvincing.

Very sure of herself, the woman viciously told him, "No one under my control can lie to me, you slob." To Dai she said, "If that's the case, you have been scouring the canyons in vain. We know the exact location. After all, we bribed and seduced the chief priest of Earth's satellite surveillance team. He gave us the photos and coordinates showing the priestess and her three companions entering a small opening and later closing it. Two of our new super-antigrav ships from Mars landed last night and opened the vault. Apparently, the previous opening was not completely sealed. With their sophisticated equipment they were able to find the exact location and gain entry without using explosives. They are loading the treasure onto both ships at this very moment. One will go to our spaceports on Mars and the other to Shaytan. After today, we won't need this palace."

Dai went numb and ice cold. *I didn't completely seal the entrance to the vault from the outside*, he thought. Dai sat down in the still-unconscious guard's chair. In shock, he let go of his shield, and the woman also sat down quickly. She was as white as Dai, who stammered, "This may sound strange coming from me, Hedra, but I honestly and truthfully wish the thieves the best of luck. I fervently hope they are successful, because if they as much as let one of those dire inventions fall over, we needn't worry about escaped dragonsnakes."

"You're an accomplished liar, Daiyus!" Hedra said. "You were taught to lie convincingly. I don't believe a word of it. Try again!"

But he gave the impression that he was trying to persuade himself. He was visibly quaking in his shoes. Dai managed a wan grin. "You sound very sure of yourself," he said, which elicited a few derisive laughs. Dai held the alien gun aloft. "Try this for lying, Hedra. I'm the one who is called Dart. Don't you recognize Ogath's alien gun? He's alive and well, you know! He and my mother, Lur, are going to roast your rounded backside over a small fire while I watch—" But Dai had to stop. An unpleasant smell filled the throne room, and Hedra started to shake like a leaf in a strong wind. He wailed like a lost soul in the netherworld.

"Get out, you miserable stinking dog!" the woman on the throne yelled to Hedra. "GET OUT, NOW!" She had completely

425

forgotten about controlling Dai.

Hedra waddled hastily to the door, and everyone got energetically out of his way with a grimace of distaste. Perhaps he realized his days were numbered, but he didn't see Dai draw the needler with his left hand and flip the lever with his thumb for single shot. He had almost reached the door when the needle-like hollow projectile exploded in an ample buttock. Despite his considerable weight, he jumped a meter into the air and let out a bellow of surprise and pain before crashing the double door open. No one had seen Dai draw the needler, and no one had time to laugh as he pulled the trigger of the alien gun and each of their bodies disintegrated in a flash.

Dai felt the clamp on his senses again, but he calmly pointed the gun at the woman, saying, "Sorry" before he pulled the trigger, and then he did the same with her unconscious bodyguard. If there was still an Earth left by tonight, let the enemy take a wild guess as to the whereabouts of these unscrupulous characters.

Enough turmoil had been inflicted on Dai that Koro entered the throne room. He had quietly closed the secret door behind him. Dai asked him to ask his father to come and collect them as soon as possible. There wasn't time to return through the meandering tunnel, and he urgently had to speak to Karna. After a few seconds, Koro said Ogath would be at the corner of the west and north walls in half an hour.

Dai left the throne room through the double door, with Koro right on his heels. The palace was strangely silent, and the guards usually stationed at the door were absent. They found Hedra around the third corner down the corridor. The layers of flab had slowed down the spread of the poison, and he must have lived a good three minutes after crashing through the throne-room doors.

Dai didn't spare him a glance, for he only had one thing in mind. He must tell Karna to let those spaceships leave Earth without interference. And he must recall all operatives from the other planets because those ships would have extremely dangerous inventions on board that might still explode if they entered the atmosphere too fast or experienced an extremely rough landing.

He could only pray that the radiation Brain mentioned had

426

lessened the sensitivity of the elements to such an extent that they would survive the initial escape acceleration of the ships. Fortunately, the heavier gravity of Earth had forced the inhabitants of Mars and Shaytan to invent more sensitive gravity neutralizers, and the reports he had read about the new superships were encouraging. He wished them every success.

Koro told him he had asked Kyr to let Karna know he should expect an urgent call from Dai. He had put the guns away when he found the palace deserted, and now he sprinted toward the gate. Individuals stopped and stared open-mouthed at the young man running as hard as he could while being chased by a temple cat —or so they interpreted it. Even the two guards at the gate quickly closed the door of their guardhouse, for they had a healthy respect for those huge cats.

Dai was thankful that they let him pass unhindered, for he would have shown no mercy. He was in no mood to be delayed, for the safety of Earth was at stake. Those ships must feel safe to take off in their own sweet time. He wished he could tell them that. As soon as he was out of the gate, he turned right and ran along the south wall, then turned north along the west side.

Ogath deactivated the nullifier as Dai neared the north wall. Dai stormed into the bus and reached for the comm-unit, but he took the time to thank his dad for being so prompt. He activated the scrambler before he entered the memorized number. Karna answered immediately.

So Karna would realize the urgency, Dai said in normal language, "The treasure is being loaded on two spaceships as we speak. The thieves should not be disturbed or interfered with, or we might not be around for much longer. I can only pray that they believe they have all the time in the world, for if they mishandle even a single gadget, they will more than likely destroy our planet. I'm scared out of my wits and not trying to give orders, but please evacuate our colleagues from the other planets because a ship will go to each if they survive takeoff."

Karna knew Dai well enough to realize he was dead serious and not out of control. He curtly said, "Call me in an hour with a full report," then put the comm-unit down. Dai did the same and found that he was trembling.

He looked at his father, who handed him one of Bolly's expensive liquor bottles. "The women told me you might need this. I already took two big mouthfuls when you started your quick report to Karna, so I won't take off immediately. Take a few sips and tell me what happened in the palace. It will help you calm down."

Dai did. He briefly told of Hedra's ignominious behavior and death. "I would have left him alive, Dad, for that would've been a more fitting punishment. He would have lived in constant fear of running into one of us. He was fortunate to die a quick death since I couldn't let him live with the knowledge of what he saw in the throne room. Their ultimate goal is to take control of our planet, but I think those weapons will be idle threats, just as they were when they were invented. You can't destroy the very thing you want, just as those unthinking ancients couldn't, but I sincerely hope they are successful in removing those dire inventions from our Earth, I really do."

Dai was quite light-headed by the time the hour was up, but he gave a full report of everything that had transpired since Karna collected Tumar, right up to the present moment, only leaving out Koro's discovery.

After he was finished, Karna told him that he'd requested the military and space authorities to not challenge any ships leaving Earth's atmosphere, and he gave as the reason a top-secret operation not to be disclosed until completed. Then he told Dai that if the Earth still existed the following day, to use any means and methods necessary to clean up all the crime in Bojon and reinstate its rightful heirs. Then he must await further instructions, depending on the outcome of the return of the supergrav ships to their home planets.

Dai thanked him and said he would report as soon as the ships departed—successfully, of course. He suddenly remembered that the woman had mentioned they had bribed the chief of the satellite surveillance team, so he apologized and added the additional piece of information to his report before he signed off.

73

Dai was cold sober by the time they arrived back at the camp. Ogath said the best way to spy on the ships was from high above, perhaps at the top of the canyon or thereabouts. It would be cold, but they could dress warmly and take the bus instead of the ray machine, since the bus could be heated to keep them from freezing, and with the nullifier on, it would only be detected by very special instruments.

Dai thought it over. It would definitely be more comfortable, since the tops of the mountains were all sheathed in ice and snow, but on the other hand, it wouldn't be for long. If the robbers were only raiding the gadget vault, they should be nearly finished by now, even if they had the sense to insulate the inventions against damage and shock before handling them. Brain had told him that he had the means to protect the main vault from raiders. Logically they would want to finish as soon as possible and therefore couldn't afford any delays for fear of being detected.

On the other hand, perhaps the chief of satellite surveillance had informed them that the satellites were temporarily rerouted, and that might be why they took the chance to raid the vault. No, he would forgo comfort, take the cold but insulated ray machine, and go alone. Koro could rest for a few hours. Dai told his father about his decision and the reasoning behind it. It was a way to close the vault forever if it was empty. He didn't think anyone would attack the spaceships, but the ray machine would discourage anyone from being too inquisitive.

Koro said he would use the opportunity to improve his hunting skills, since the lady Skrot was also tired of Murima's cooking and would welcome something freshly killed.

Dai dressed warmly, packed a gun and night-vision equipment, and took some provisions, as well as a full canteen, although melted ice would do as well. He departed with what was left of the expensive liquor to keep him company if night rolled around while he was still there. It was past noon, and he flew high up because he knew the craft could not be detected by present-day instruments. He saw the distinctive peak in the distance and made a wide detour to approach it from the north, as it was common knowledge that countries and kingdoms in that direction had no interest in the canyons.

When he was near, he slowed down to a virtual crawl, flying low over the nearest mountain, and stopped a few meters from the edge. It was bitterly cold as he got out and crawled up to where he could look down. He was a bit behind the peak, so he moved the craft a few hundred meters to the left, behind a huge outcrop of ice-covered rock formation. He walked bent over to the edge and peeped over cautiously. The ships were directly below but a few kilometers away. He went back to the craft and took the binoculars he had brought along.

Taking care that there could be no reflection from the lenses, he focused on the vault. As the picture became clear, he felt like applauding the raiders. They were using a motorized antigravity sledge-like loading vehicle to carry one gadget at a time to a ship. The machine was securely clamped, and there was no chance of accidental slipping. The gadget he saw on the vehicle before it slowly entered a ship's loading bay was thickly wrapped in what looked like antishock material. They were very careful not to accidentally damage anything. He wondered if they had anyone who could decipher the old language, but he couldn't take the chance of reaching out with a thought tendril to find out. There would definitely be more than one sensitive down there.

Dai couldn't help feeling anxious. He was tense. His stomach felt queasy, and his muscles just couldn't relax. His brain refused to let go of the idea that anything that could go wrong might go wrong at any moment. He certainly wasn't used to miracles, and at any moment he expected to see a flash and then a tremendous explosion that would rip his body apart. He fervently wished he was somewhere else, but the rational part of his brain told him his imagination was running wild, and he must get it under control.

Dai lowered the strong binoculars and checked himself. He felt shaky, even though his hands were pretty steady. He should do some exercises, but the ice was slippery, and he might slide over the edge. He returned to the craft and forced himself to calm down by doing the correct breathing exercises. Alcohol would have helped, but it would be dangerous to indulge in this freezing air. Dai fiercely persisted until he was in complete control of himself before he returned to watch. Excluding the area around the vault, he let his senses search as far as possible, but he found no indication of human presence.

The vault was four kilometers down and two away. His night-vision equipment wouldn't reach that far, and he hoped the raiders would finish before sundown. He was sure they would not want to risk drawing unnecessary attention to themselves by using floodlights. It was already close to four o'clock. He wondered how many gadgets they had loaded. He closed his eyes and recalled the mental picture of the vault and counted. He came to the figure of just eight, four to a ship. The ninth, and last, was this relatively safe invention he was flying around in.

When he opened his eyes, he saw the carrier come out of the vault again with what was obviously the last load, for the loading crew came out of the vault aboard two other vehicles, one of which went to the ship that had received the previous load. The rest entered the ship after the carrier. After a few minutes, the cargo doors on both ships closed.

Dai went back to the ray machine and edged it closer to where he could watch the ships. It was somewhat cozier in the closed craft, since the freezing wind was cut off; it was a relief, for he was cold despite the warm clothes.

He waited tensely while he supposed that the ships' crews made sure the "precious" cargo was secure, or so he nervously hoped. He closed his eyes and formed an image of Karna in his mind while he willed his body to relax. He was as astonished as Karna when he made "contact." He mentally apologized for the intrusion and said he took a chance because the ships were getting ready to depart, and he was so nervous he couldn't think straight. Karna thanked him, then advised that if they were still alive by the time he got back to the camp, to ask one of the priestesses to teach him how to mentally make contact with another human without interfering at an inopportune moment. Then he cut Dai off, or so it felt to Dai when contact was severed. Karna must be under tremendous pressure to identify and locate the mastermind or masterminds behind this ludicrous conspiracy, Dai thought.

Dai was really surprised that he'd successfully contacted Karna. This opened up opportunities he previously could only dream of, but he reminded himself that he was here for a purpose and must concentrate on the job. He saw that nearly ten minutes had gone by, but the ships were still on the ground. His heart skipped a beat as he noticed the reason for the delay. A man had placed a large object, which could only be a bomb with a timer, in the breach and was returning to the nearest ship. He prayed that they had taken all the inventions; otherwise Earth was doomed. He wondered if it was worth trying to use the ray craft's weapon, switched to tunneling, to vaporize the bomb, as he'd done with the debris. He would surely try as soon as they lifted off, for that bomb looked way too big to be trusted so close to the breach.

The ships slowly lifted off in tandem. Dai wished them a safe journey. He activated his craft as soon as the ships were above the mountains and angling away from each other, moving upward in separate directions.

Dai descended nose down at an accelerated speed through the air while he prepared the craft for tunneling. He chose an angle away from the main vault and activated the tunneling beam from a distance because he didn't know how much time he had. The craft slowed down drastically when the beam met resistance, but Dai was prepared for it. He pushed the hover lever to stop the craft, for he had aimed directly at the bomb.

There was a brief flash and he involuntarily closed his eyes and braced himself, but nothing happened. He partly opened one eye and saw that the breach was clear.

He slowly flew inside and grounded. Then he donned the night-sight equipment. It wasn't dark outside yet, but the sight worked well enough in the gloom for him to inspect the entire vault. The numbness he'd felt in his body earlier ceased as he saw that only the dire warnings were left in the otherwise bare vault.

The ships must be nearly out of the atmosphere by now, and he felt that the worst was over, but it was still too early to bless the greedy thieves. He started to undermine the solid ceiling to close and seal the empty vault forever.

Apparently the unscrupulous masterminds had studied the satellite images and assumed that this vault was all there was. They didn't realize what was next door and that Brain even existed, but in a way they were fortunate, since it would have dealt with them harshly if they had forced their way in there.

The irony of the situation was not lost on Dai. *They removed the insidious inheritance and left the real treasure behind. The healing powers embedded in the artificial intelligence system is the true treasure that survived the test of time. It's our Time Treasure*, Dai thought and smiled.

Epilogue

With the assistance of his mother and Lithe, Dai had mastered the technique of mentally conversing with another human being. He now could, with a little effort, ascertain the thoughts of most humans and animals.

While he was being taught, he and Koro had enlisted the local temple cats to help identify all those who had associated with Heltos and Hedra. Dai questioned them one by one privately, mostly without their conscious knowledge. Those he felt were deceived and manipulated into service they ignored, but those who were up to their ears in the plot quietly disappeared without a trace. He obtained quite a lot of information, which he passed on to Karna or which he would follow up on after Bojon was cleared, as ordered. Tumar was often on his mind, but he was too busy to inquire about her welfare and progress. Karna had mentioned that both her parents were safe and had fully recovered from their ordeal, but hadn't offered any further information on Joemer, Imatob or Tumar.

When spring was not far off, he was ready to move on. Surra had helped where she could, and she showed her appreciation in the way any hot-blooded young man would appreciate. She and her son, together with a much healthier Hespus, had moved back into the palace, and she asked Dai to stay until her wedding. He regretfully declined, pleading a busy schedule with too many unfinished tasks ahead.

A very relieved Ekaasi had accepted a ride on Bolly's bus back home to Krisa, strapped on Bolly's bunk, when Ogath, Lur, and Lithe left after the dangerous inheritance was safely gone. The lady Skrot was invited along, and she accepted.

Dai had divided the treasure Koro had discovered, the camping equipment, horses and most of Tumar's loot between Murima and Laecur. The statuettes and Tumar's purloined riches he left with his parents for safekeeping. He still had the ray machine, but it was now fitted with proper seats and safety features, installed under the supervision of returned Fighting Priests. The craft should come in handy later. According to intelligence gathered during the mission, a very secretive and elusive individual was the true mastermind behind the theft of the treasure.

Dai was saying a very private farewell to Surra when a strange, eerie sensation was experienced all over the planet. They rushed outside as soon as decently possible to unobtrusively join the crowd on the palace roof. The night sky was strangely lit by what could only be described as a small sun in the direction of where the fifth planet should have been. Dai went ice cold. The strange feeling of unease persisted. Dai felt the apprehension around him, but just then Karna asked if he could talk. Dai said a mental "yes" and Karna continued.

According to the astronomers, Mars is also burning. They say it happened a few minutes after they became aware that Shaytan had exploded, and it is, of course, a complete mystery to them. We'll keep it that way. There will be a warning broadcast every hour that people must stay indoors as much as possible, as meteor storms can be expected within three or four days. It appears that Earth is now the only inhabitable planet in this solar system. Get back here as soon as you can. Ask the cats to warn everyone. Kyr is giving birth at the moment and can't do it. He was gone abruptly.

While Dai told Surra what Karna had just told him, he mentally broadcast a warning to the local cats to pass the message on all over the planet. Gemur arrived out of breath, and Dai went over to Hespus and Krekur to inform them of what happened and to say good-bye. Then he told Koro they were leaving and to meet him at their transport.